South East

ou should
ich you
amped
olication

PROGRAMME MUSIC

PROGRAMME MUSIC

*A brief survey
from the sixteenth century
to the present day*

LESLIE ORREY

DAVIS·POYNTER
LONDON

First published in 1975 by
Davis-Poynter Limited, 20 Garrick Street
London WC2E 9BJ

Copyright © 1975 by Leslie Orrey

All rights reserved. No part of this publication may be reproduced, stored in a retrieval system, or transmitted, in any form or by any means, electronic, mechanical, photocopying, recording or otherwise without the prior permission of the publishers.

ISBN 0 7067 0171 2

Printed in Great Britain
at the
University Printing House, Cambridge
(Euan Phillips, University Printer)

851125

To Elsa

CONTENTS

Preface 9

PART I
PROGRAMME MUSIC IN THE CLASSICAL AGE 13
1 *An Introduction* 15
2 *Programme Music to the end of the Eighteenth Century* 29
3 *Nature Pieces and Battle Symphonies* 45

PART II
PROGRAMME MUSIC AND ROMANTICISM 59
4 *Tone Poem and Programme-Symphony from Weber to Spohr* 61
5 *Liszt and the Symphonic Poem* 77
6 *Programme Music and the Keyboard* 86
7 *Late Romantic Programme Music (I)* 101
8 *Late Romantic Programme Music (II)* 128

PART III
PROGRAMME MUSIC DURING THE LAST HUNDRED YEARS 139
9 *The Transition from Romantic to Modern* 141
10 *French Programme Music from 1870* 159
11 *Programme Music in America* 170
12 *Conclusion* 184
Appendix 193
Bibliography 211
Index 216

PREFACE

The first important survey of the subject was by Frederick Niecks: *Programme Music in the last Four Centuries; A Contribution to the history of Musical Expression* (London, 1906). Niecks, born in Düsseldorf in 1845, was trained as a violinist, and came to England, or rather to Scotland, in 1868, as a member of A. C. MacKenzie's quartet. He spent the rest of his life in this country, becoming a naturalized citizen in 1880. His appointment to the Chair of Music in Edinburgh was a landmark in the history of that university; his system of music instruction there, and especially the annual series of historical concerts given by him, were in advance of his time, at least as far as British universities were concerned. On his retirement in 1914 he was succeeded by another notable scholar, Donald Tovey. He died in 1924.

His study was detailed and all-embracing, and still remains the most complete account up to the end of the nineteenth century. Beginning his work, he says, in a spirit of impartial enquiry, he found himself acting almost as devil's advocate in favour of some compositions which ordinarily would have passed for no more than 'expressive' music.

The subject had previously been treated in English in a succinct article by Frederick Corder in the third volume of the first edition of Grove's Dictionary (1890). Though this betrayed something of the writer's prejudice *against* the form, the bias was as nothing compared to that displayed in later editions of the dictionary, where not only was Niecks's work ignored but his book not even mentioned in the inadequate bibliography. A very early nineteenth-century discussion was by A. B. Marx, *Über Malerei in der Tonkunst* (1828). This was polemical rather than historical, but Marx did refer to one or two earlier writers such as Engel and Reichardt, and he made the point that all the great composers had used tone-painting in their more serious compositions.

The most important German contribution appeared a few years after Niecks. This was Otto Klauwell: *Geschichte der Programmusik* (1910). This, though less comprehensive than Niecks's work, supplements it here and there, especially in some of the German and Austrian byways. Though there is no French work dealing exclusively with programme music an important book, issued about the same time as Niecks's volume, is Lionel de la Laurencie's *Le Goût Musical en France* (1905), which contains much of relevance. A selection of other specialist writings will be found in the bibliography.

To study programme music is to embark on an integrated course involving literature, painting, history, geography, folklore; we have to pay some attention to aesthetics and philosophy, and are inevitably drawn into a consideration of music as a component of the social and artistic life of the times. Take the example of Maeterlinck's *Pelléas et Mélisande*, first performed in 1892, which was responsible not only for Debussy's opera (1902), but for instrumental music by Fauré (1898), Schoenberg (1902-03), William Wallace (1903) and Sibelius (1905)—works composed in four widely separated cities, Paris, Vienna, London and Helsinki. The artistic movements in the first two—impressionism-cum-symbolism in Paris, the Secession in Vienna—are familiar, but the similar movement in Finland is an unknown quantity for most people. In England the strong musical ties with Germany did not rule out a French influence, which at the turn of the century was stronger than we sometimes think. Fauré's *Pelléas* music was written for a London performance; and strange as it may seem, there is often a Gallic tang in Elgar's music, while Vaughan Williams was guilty of some distinctly impressionistic music in, for instance, *Silent Noon* and *On Wenlock Edge*.

Other instances of 'group activity' that come to mind are the display of nationalistic or ideological fervour in Czechoslovakia, the United States and the Soviet Union, or the rash of battle sonatas and symphonies in the 1790s in Paris, London and Vienna. It is odd, too, to find two French composers in the period after the Franco-Prussian War turning to an eighteenth-century *Sturm und Drang* poet, Bürger, and perhaps even odder to find a rather strange play, *Penthesilea*, by another German, Heinrich von Kleist (1777-1811), exerting a strong attraction not only on the fellow Germans Karl Goldmark and Felix Draeseke, but on the Austrian Hugo Wolf, the Swiss Othmar Schoek (an opera), the Frenchmen Alfred Bruneau

PREFACE

and Marc Delmas, the Pole Karol Szymanowski and the American-born Kelterborn.

It remains to say a few words about the organization of the book. With few exceptions (notably David's *Le Désert* and Berlioz's *Roméo et Juliette*) I have confined the discussion to purely instrumental music, and have excluded oratorio and theatre music. This decision, dictated partly by reasons of space, has led to some anomalies; thus Britten's *Sea Interludes* from *Peter Grimes* are not mentioned, while the interludes from Bloch's *Macbeth* are. The argument here, for what it is worth, is that *Peter Grimes* is an entity, freely available in the theatre or on disc, in a way that *Macbeth* is not. I have further limited the discussion to music where we have good evidence from the composer himself as to his intentions, whether by way of a descriptive title, a programme (by the composer or sanctioned by him), or by other supporting documents. Thus Tchaikowsky's Fourth Symphony, which has a programme, is included, but Schubert's Unfinished, where a programme is at best a supposition, is not.

As with all writing on the history of music the presentation of the material posed problems. Music is no respecter of geographical boundaries, but flows across national frontiers in a beneficent artistic free trade. In the case of programme music these problems turned out be be fairly simple. Beginning in the countries, principally Italy and Germany, where instrumental music was first nurtured, by the nineteenth century the lead had been taken by France. From there it spread to the emerging nationalist schools before the ascendancy returned to Germany at the end of the nineteenth century. A similar pattern can be seen in the music of the past one hundred years, the main influences being French impressionism and a second wave of nationalism. This, broadly speaking, is the scheme I have adopted.

I am grateful to Dr Watkins Shaw, Librarian of the Parry Library, Royal College of Music, London, for permission to inspect the orchestral parts of Knecht's Grand Symphonie. I am also indebted to the British Library and the Library of the University of London, without whose help and co-operation in providing access to music, books and gramophone records my task would have been well-nigh impossible.

LESLIE ORREY

PART I

Programme Music in the Classical Age

CHAPTER 1

An Introduction

The validity of programme music is no longer in question. However dubious its claims may have seemed to professional aestheticians, and however ragged and ill-defined its boundaries, composers and audiences over the years have accepted its premises with only few reservations. It is now generally acknowledged that under suitable conditions instrumental music can be descriptive, can tell a story, or at least help to render the details more vivid; and that it can throw an illuminating light on the sister arts of painting and literature. The principle is called in question only when the composer has overreached himself and the musical results are not commensurate with his stated or implied intentions.

It may well be argued that all music that holds an emotional significance for the listener is programmatic. Niecks in his preface gives as his opinion that 'whenever the composer ceases to write purely formal music, he passes from the domain of absolute music into that of programme music', and continues by saying that programme music as he understands it is so comprehensive that a history of it goes far towards being a 'History of Musical Expression'—and leaves us to draw the conclusion that 'purely formal music' (which he defines as 'music with none but aesthetical qualities') is devoid of musical expression. But to fling the net so wide is to make the subject almost unmanageable, and limitations of space, if no other considerations, have imposed a concept and treatment somewhat narrower than Niecks allowed himself.

Nevertheless, although the controversy between 'absolute' and 'programme' music has almost entirely lost its power to excite, it is not without interest to examine some of what has been written on the subject, if only to illustrate changing fashions in artistic theory. The outlook on music as expressed by the eighteenth-century philosophers differed in many respects from the opinions voiced by the champions of romanticism in the nineteenth century, and the complex relationship between painting, music and literature in the Paris of Debussy's time was far removed from the attitude of such a composer as Bach. In our own day Deryck Cooke in *The Language of Music* has not only propounded at length the thesis that music is fundamentally an art that expresses emotion, that it is 'about' something (as all languages are), and that it is not merely a manipulation of sounds as it were *in vacuo*, but has gone further and outlined a basic 'vocabulary' of musical units which, he claims, composers over a period of about 600 years have used consistently, with something like a 'one to one' correlation between these musical units and the emotions expressed.

The opposite contention, that music is *not* a language, is maintained with clarity and elegance by an American, Sidney Lanier, who none the less nailed his colours to the programmatic mast. Lanier was a poet, a literary critic, and a musician; he lectured on literature at Johns Hopkins University, Baltimore, and for a time played the flute in the Baltimore symphony orchestra. He also composed some programme music for solo flute, for example *Field-larks and Blackbirds*, and *Swamp Robin*, in 1873, thus anticipating by more than half a century Messiaen's preoccupation with bird song. In an essay, 'From Bacon to Beethoven', published in a volume entitled *Music and Poetry* (New York, 1909) he writes:

> Perhaps the most effective step a man can take in ridding himself of the clouds which darken most speculations upon these matters is to abandon immediately the idea that music is a species of language—which is not true—and to substitute for that the converse idea that language is a species of music [incidentally, in his own poetry he tried to exemplify this].[1] A language is a set of tones segregated from the great mass of musical sounds, and endowed, by agreement, with fixed meanings. The Anglo-Saxons have, for example, practically agreed that if the sound *man* is uttered, the intellects of all Anglo-Saxon hearers will act in a certain direction, and always in that direction, for that sound. But in the case of music no

---

[1] He saw verse as primarily musical, seeking to incorporate in his ballads and lyrics the sound patterns of music. In a poem called *The Symphony* (1875) he 'employs a rich, complex versification to give an onomatopoeic expression to the different instruments in an orchestra, and personifies each of them to discuss social questions of the time, particularly the inhumanities of trade and industrialism, and to set forth a philosophy of aesthetics, ending "Music is Love in search of a word" '. (Quoted from the section on Lanier in *The Oxford Companion to American Literature*.)

such convention has been made. The only method of affixing a definite meaning to a musical composition is to associate with the component tones of it either conventional words, intelligible gestures or familiar events and places. When a succession of tones is played, the intellect of the hearer may move; but the Movements are always determined by influences wholly extraneous to the purely musical tones — such as association with words, with events or with any matters which place definite intellectual forms (that is, ideas) before the mind.

He argues that:

The most common and familiar musical instrument happens to be at the same time what may be called an intellectual instrument — ie, the organ of speech. The tones of the human voice, which are as wholly devoid of intellectual signification in themselves as if they were enounced from a violin or flute, are usually produced along with certain vowel and consonant combinations which go to make up words and which consequently have conventional meanings.

This is a very rationalistic analysis. By 'idea' he is clearly meaning a verbal concept; like many writers, he apparently rules out any question of a 'musical concept' that might be susceptible to a logic of its own — ie, that would 'cause our intellects to move in a certain direction'. But if musical sounds, in themselves, are denied the power to persuade the human intellect to move, they are granted some influence in the emotional field. Intellect and emotion can be partners, as in programme music, and in song:

Certainly if programme music is absurd, all songs are nonsense. The principle of being of every song is that intellectual impressions can be advantageously combined with musical impressions in addressing the spirit of man. It is precisely this principle that underlies programme music.

Lanier's remarks may be compared with the following observations from Louis Laloy's *Debussy*:

La musique est l'art symboliste par excellence, puisqu'elle ne représente les mouvements, les formes et les couleurs que par le moyen de sons, c'est-à-dire de sensations auxquelles on peut n'attacher aucune signification conventionelle, et qui, n'ayant pas de rapport direct aux objets, suggèrent tout sans rien monter!

Again, it is clear that the '*signification*' of which Laloy writes is a verbal one, an intellectual 'meaning'; he no doubt would not have denied the possibility that music might be invested with a different kind of 'meaning', even if he had been reduced to the shift of defining the 'meaning' as the music itself.

An extensive body of philosophizing concerning the nature of music, and art in general, is due to the pamphleteering enthusiasm of the eighteenth century. Some of the most important names are the Encyclopedists Diderot, d'Alembert and Rousseau, the Abbé Dubos, Batteux and Lacépède. The Scottish writer who made one of the most useful contributions was James Beattie, and a compendious German work was Sulzer's *Allgemeine Theorie der schönen Künste*, which appeared in 1771-74; the musical articles were by the composer J. A. P. Schulz.[2] The importance of these writers in our present discussion is minimized first of all by the fact that their attentions were almost wholly focussed on opera. The self-subsistent instrumental music—the symphonies of Haydn, the concertos of Mozart, even the abundant keyboard music written in France from 1770 onwards—that we now recognize as the outstanding musical achievement of the eighteenth century was all but completely ignored. Second, they were hamstrung in their thinking by a slavish reverence for the theories of Aristotle and by an unswerving allegiance to the theory of art as an imitation of nature (all art, including music; not just painting). Almost the only writer to voice misgivings over the current theory was Beattie, in his essay *On Poetry and Music, as they affect the Mind* (published in 1776, but written some fourteen years earlier). His conclusions concerning music as an imitative art are summed up in the following:

> Shall I apply these, and the preceding reasonings, to the Musical Art also, which I have elsewhere called, and which is generally understood to be, Imitative? Shall I say, that some melodies please, because they imitate nature, and that others, which do not imitate nature, are therefore unpleasing?—that an air expressive of devotion, for example, is agreeable, because it presents us with an imitation of those sounds by which devotion does naturally express itself?

This, he cautiously remarks, he regards as at least dubious. In doubting that music is wholly an 'imitative' art he says he means no disrespect to Aristotle, or to music:

---

[2] Extracts from some of these can be found in Oliver Strunk's *Source Readings in Music History* (New York, 1950). See also Ernest Newman's *Gluck and the Opera*, first published in 1895, and A. H. Oliver, *The Encyclopedists as Critics of Music* (New York, 1949).

I allow it to be a fine art, and to have great influence on the human soul . . . [But] when I am asked, what part of nature is imitated in any good picture or poem, I find I can give a definite answer; whereas, when I am asked, what part of nature is imitated in Handel's *Water Music*, for instance, or in Corelli's *Eighth Concerto*, I find I can give no definite answer—though no doubt I might say some plausible things; or perhaps, after much refinement, be able to show, that music may, by one shift or another, be made an imitative art, provided you allow me to give any meaning I please to the word *imitative*.

His attitude, and indeed the attitude in general of the eighteenth-century philosophers towards the range of subjects open to music, is illustrated by the following:

The end of all genuine music is, to introduce into the human mind certain affections, or susceptibilities of affection. Now all the affections, over which music has any power, are of the agreeable kind. And therefore, in this art, no imitations of natural sound or motion but such as tend to inspire agreeable affections, ought ever to find a place. The song of certain birds, the murmuring of a stream, the shouts of multitudes, the tumult of a storm, the roar of thunder, or a chime of bells, are sounds connected with agreeable or sublime affections, and reconcilable with both melody and with harmony; and may therefore be imitated, when the context has occasion for them: but the crowing of cocks, the barking of dogs, the mewing of cats, the grunting of swine, the gabbling of geese, the cackling of a hen, the braying of an ass, the creaking of a saw, or the rumbling of a cart-wheel, would render the best music ridiculous. The movement of a dance may be imitated, or the stately pace of an embattled legion; but the hobble of a trotting horse would be intolerable.

To us nowadays such doctrinaire pronouncements on what is and what is not fitted for musical commentary seem impossibly and unnecessarily narrow, and indeed its strict application would have led to the exclusion of innumerable passages in Couperin, Gluck, Handel, Haydn, Rameau, Vivaldi and others of Dr Beattie's contemporaries. But this preoccupation with the aesthetic qualities of music and the attempt to draw fine distinctions between the acceptable and the unacceptable continued to occupy the minds of writers on music even throughout the nineteenth century. It is disconcerting, to say the least, to find Niecks writing the following (he is discussing Liszt's piano music):

Not infrequently we are constrained to admire the earnest

endeavour, where the result is unsatisfactory; but hardly less frequently our artistic sense is outraged by extravagant futility or appalling ugliness . . . the ugly, I think, has a greater space given to it in Liszt's than in any other composer's creations.

Such opinions seem to point to a lack of sympathy with and understanding of Liszt's intentions in his programmatic piano music.

The arguments claiming all the arts as imitations of nature which crop up with monotonous regularity in all the eighteenth-century writers have, as an almost inevitable corollary, the thesis that good art must be natural—ie, simple. This is used as a stick to beat composers for overloading their music with complexity. Thus Dr Brown, in a typically prolix and confused *Dissertation on the Rise, Union and Power, the Progressions, Separations and Corruptions, of Poetry and Music* (London, 1763), finds fault with songs in which there is 'too much musical Division upon single Syllables, to the Neglect of the Sense and Meaning of the Song', and finds:

> Choirs sometimes calculated more for the Display of the Composer's Art, in the Construction of *Fugues* and *Canons*, than for a natural Expression of the subject . . . The farther musical Sounds depart from *Simplicity*, the farther they depart from *Nature*: So, the Consequence is clear, that a *Simple melody* (though an imperfect Imitation) may be *pathetic*; while a *complex* and *artificial* melody (by departing from Nature beyond a certain degree) wiil entirely *lose* its *affecting Power*.

In such sentiments as these the author displays that utter blank towards the fundamentals of the art of music which has so often characterized English men of letters.

One of the best of the eighteenth-century treatises is *La Poétique de la Musique*, by Le Comte de Lacépède (Paris, 1785). Lacépède was more than a mere scribbler; he had in fact sufficient practical knowledge of music to write a couple of operas, and some of his observations, especially on the use of instruments, are of more than passing interest. For him music is a language, but 'un langage plus touchant, plus énergique que le langage ordinaire'—a language capable of more expression thàn ordinary language, since it offers much more variety. He goes on to specify thus:

> Pour peindre d'une manière plus fidèle, la promptitude avec lacquelle se succèdent nos mouvemens, nos passions, nos agitations intérieures, et pour en représenter le désordre, on ne s'est-pas contenté, comme dans le langage ordinaire, d'aller d'une portion quelconque de l'échelle musicale, à une portion

très-voisine, mais suivant qu'on l'a cru nécessaire, on a franchi de très grands intervalles, et passé avec rapidité des tons les plus graves, aux tons les plus élevés. On a recueilli avec soin, les cris que la passion arrache, ceux de la douleur, ceux de la joie, tous les tons enfin, que la nature a destinés à accompagner, et par consequent a caractériser les effets que la musique veut peindre. On n'a rejeté que les bruits, quoiqu'on puisse quelquefois les employer, au moins avec certain précautions.

This, and especially the acceptance in certain circumstances of *'les bruits'*, noises, shows a good deal more insight into the true nature of music than we find in most of the writers. But shortly after this, in the inevitable 'imitation of nature' discussion, he reveals himself as hamstrung as the rest by the conventional thinking of his time, getting round it only by the Tweedledum-like exploitation of the word 'imitation' that Beattie had objected to:

Tout ce que peut être entendu, la musique le peint en le faisant entendre, en produisant exactement le nombre, l'ordre et la nature de sons qui composent l'objet qu'elle veut montrer. C'est ainsi, par example, qu'elle imite le murmure de l'eau qui coule, le chant des oiseaux, le fracas du tonnerre.

But this passage will not stand up to examination. The noise of thunder can be 'imitated' more or less exactly; but the capturing of the exact number, the order, and the nature of birdsong is a much more elusive undertaking. It is, moreover, debatable whether the result would be worth the effort. The realism of Beethoven's cuckoo, quail and nightingale has proved a stumbling-block to many who are enchanted by the 'unreal' billing and cooing of the ringdoves in Handel's *Acis and Galatea*. As for the sound of running water, music in 'imitating' this does not come within a hundred miles of reproducing this 'sound of nature'—though in his delicious 'water' songs Schubert almost persuades us to the contrary. Our appreciation of the water images in Liszt's *Au bord d'une source*, Ravel's *Jeux d'eau* or the opening bars of Smetana's *Vltava* depends on a complex interplay of ideas in which verbal correspondences ('running' passages, 'rippling' arpeggios, equating with 'running' streams and the 'ripples' on the water's surface) are as important as any tonal similarities.

While all these writers devote much space to the more obvious aspects of imitation there is even more discussion on the ability of music to express or 'imitate' states of mind. To quote Beattie again:

It must be acknowledged, that there is some relation at least, or analogy, if not similitude, between certain musical sounds, and mental affections. Soft music may be considered as analogous to gentle emotions; and loud music, if the tones are sweet and not too rapid, to sublime ones; and a quick succession of noisy notes, like those we hear from a drum, seem to have some relation to hurry and impetuosity of passion.

This so-called 'doctrine of the affections', though in the first instance addressed to the opera and the cantata, is not without its bearing on the discussion of programme music, and we find for instance that some of the more ambitions nineteenth-century examples are much more concerned with the 'psychological' exploration of character or the expression of abstractions such as aspiration or religious ecstasy than with a straightforward pictorialism.

It is the great merit of Cooke's *Language of Music* that he has assembled a large quantity of music examples drawn from a wide range of music that seem unequivocally linked to subjective feelings such as joy, sorrow, serenity, and the like. A similar tabulation of musical resources was attempted by some eighteenth-century writers. 'The wealth of baroque affections' says Bukofzer[3] 'was stereotyped in an infinite number of "figures" or *loci topici* which "represented or depicted" the affections in music'; and Làng remarks[4] 'While these (musical) figures seem naive and are cloaked in a formidable scientific garb, there can be no question that the theoreticians merely tried to express in the current rational-scientific manner what was widely practised by the musical composers.' In fact the extent to which composers were influenced by such apparently theoretical considerations has been debated; nevertheless the fact that such tabulation was, necessarily, undertaken by musicians, rather than by the musical amateurs Batteux, Chabanon, Beattie and Brown, is an argument for examining them seriously.

It is, however, not only melodic figures—what we should now call motifs—that can be applied to express the 'affects' (the most obvious ones being joy and grief); the different qualities of sound associated with the various instruments come in as well. Here is de Lacépède on the subject:

Le musicien en emploiera les diverses espèces, suivant la nature des affections qu'il voudra peindre. Il n'a pas besoin que nous lui indiquions les flûtes pour les choses douces, tendres, tristes,

---

[3] *Music in the Baroque Era*, page 388.
[4] *Music in Western Civilization*, page 442.

religieuses; les hautbois pour les pastorales, pour les morceaux pathétiques, brillans, animés; les clarinettes pour les peintures touchantes, pathétiques, religieuses, militaires, &c; les cors, les bassons, pour les effets majestueux, nobles, touchans, terribles; les trompettes pour les choses éclatantes, martiales, pompeuses; les *tromboni*[5] pour les tableaux lugubres, sinistres, effrayans.

Many of these are obvious, and have been given in great detail by Berlioz in his *Traité de l'Instrumentation* (1844); but it is interesting to note that not all eighteenth-century writers agreed with the various classifications. This is due sometimes to the changing character of the instrument itself. Mersenne in his *Harmonie Universelle* of 1636 says concerning the oboe:

> Elle est propre pour les grandes assemblées, comme pour Balets . . . pour les Nopces, pour Les Festes des villages, et pour autre rejouissances publiques, à raison du grand bruit qu'ils font . . . car, ils ont le son le plus fort et le plus violent de tous les instruments si l'on excepte la trompette.

By the middle of the next century the oboe is noted by Ancelet[6] to have 'la qualité du son tendre et cependant partial'; while by the 1770s Burney could thus rhapsodize over the playing of the Bezozzi brothers, in Turin:

> It is difficult to describe their style of playing. Their compositions when printed, give but an imperfect idea of it. So much expression! such delicacy! such a perfect acquiescence and agreement together, that many of the passages seem heart-felt sighs, breathed through the same reed.[7]

The last clause of Burney's final sentence is highly significant — *all are notes of meaning*. Discussing Lully's orchestration Henry Prunières[8] says:

> Bien qu'il n'y eût pas de règles fixes, chaque famille d'instruments avait un emploie particulier. Les flûtes convenaient aux effets nocturnes et élégiaques, aux tendres plaintes et aux ritournelles annonçant l'arrivée des dieux amoureux. Le hautbois accompagnait les chants et les danses

---

[5] The French did not have a word for 'trombone', and simply borrowed the Italian word. A contemporary Italian-French dictionary defined 'trombone' as a 'sort of long trumpet'

[6] In *Observations sur la musique, les musiciens et les instruments* (Amsterdam, 1757); quoted in Georges Cucuel, *Études sur un Orchestre au XVIIIe siècle* (Paris, 1913).

[7] Charles Burney, *The Present State of Music in France and Italy* (London, 1773).

[8] In his *Lully* (Paris, 1927) pages 112-113.

rustiques. Les trompettes exécutaient les *bruits de guerre* et les marches triomphales. Enfin, les violons faisaient entendre les douces symphonies qui berçaient le sommeil des héros et les traits rapides des *tempêtes* et des *songes funestes*.

It is clear from these quotations—and dozens more could be adduced, from Brossard's interesting *Dictionnaire de la Musique* of 1703 to Guinguiné's *Notice sur la vie et les ouvrages de Piccinni* of 1800—that the notion that instrumental colour had some extra-musical or programmatic intent was widespread throughout the eighteenth century, and that the seemingly 'romantic' interpretation of Berlioz's treatise was in evidence long before his day. A final extract from another French work is particularly interesting. In 1837 Georges Kastner brought out a book on orchestration which is a clear forerunner of Berlioz—*Cours d'instrumentation considerée sous les rapports poétiques et philosophiques de l'art*. In it he writes of the cello in these terms:

> Le Violoncello offre un caractère religieux bien prononcé; mais il a un son pénétrant et pour ainsi dire nerveux qui le rend aussi propre à exprimer la crainte, le découragement, le douleur, la volupté, le désir et généralement toute les passions extrêmes.

Some of his characterizations of other instruments are the following:

> La flûte exprime le contentment et la paix de l'âme, le désir et la tendresse; la clarinette est l'instrument de l'amour et des sentiments tendres [a considerable change from its earlier, warlike character, suitable for leading armies]. Le cor est l'instrument le plus romantique; le trombone . . . son timbre vibrant et grandiose nous transporte dans les regions d'un monde extérieur.

Lastly, the eighteenth century's passion for classification extended to keys, each of which was deemed to possess its own individual characteristics. Rameau in his *Traité de l'Harmonie* of 1722, and elsewhere, discussed the significance of keys. Some years earlier, in fact before the eighteenth century was born, the French composer Marc-Antoine Charpentier had given a table of keys with their attributes.[9] His list is as follows:

---

[9] They were in a little volume, *Les Régles de la Composition*, written c. 1692 for his royal pupil Philippe d'Orléans, Duc de Chartres, and later Regent. See Claude Crussard, *Marc-Antoine Charpentier* (Paris, 1945) page 37.

C maj   Gay et guerrier
D mi.   Grave et dévot
E mi.   Effemmé, amoureux et plaintif
E flat maj.   Cruel et dur
F maj.   Furieux et emporté
G. maj.   Doucement joyeux
A mi.   Tendre et plaintif
B flat maj.   Magnifique et joyeux
B maj.   Dur et plaintif

C mi.   Obscur et triste
D maj.   Joyeux et très guerrier
E maj.   Querelleur et criard
E flat mi.   Horrible, affreux
F mi.   Obscur et plaintif
G mi.   Sévère et magnifique
A maj.   Joyeux et champêtre
B flat mi.   Obscur et terrible
B mi.   Solitaire et mélancholique

This list does not agree in every particular with Rameau's classification, nor is it in accord with what we can deduce from Mozart's practice. The exquisite *Terzettino* from *Così fan tutte* sung by Fiordiligi, Dorabella and Don Alfonso (No. 10, page 74 in Eulenburg's miniature score), in E major, is far from being 'querelleur et criard'. Beethoven, like Mozart, had one or two keys such as C minor and F minor which he used for certain moods; but F major, the key of the 'Pastoral' Symphony, he certainly did not find 'Furieux et emporté' but rather tranquil. The same gentle mood is to be found in the music of J. S. Bach, writing much nearer in time to Charpentier, in his amiable *Pastorale* in F major for organ.

As we move into the nineteenth century we are at once aware of a notable shift in emphasis. The composer himself is now articulate, and eminently capable of expounding and defending his own artistic viewpoint. But in reading him we must bear in mind that he is speaking for himself, and himself alone; he is not propounding universal systems of aesthetics. Nor is he necessarily formulating a theory that will hold good for all his own creations. His function is that of creator, not philosopher; so we must not be surprised or dismayed if we find inconsistencies in his statements, or practices that contradict his own professed creeds. And, since there has been a persistent idea that absolute, or 'pure' music, is of a higher order than descriptive music, we must be prepared for composers, when asked the 'meaning' of their music to prevaricate, to practise self-deception, to avoid at all costs the straight answer, 'this is a cuckoo', 'this is a donkey braying'.

A well-known passage by Mendelssohn is much quoted by those who fear the taint of 'descriptive' music, as indicative of Mendelssohn's considered thoughts on the matter. It comes from a letter of 15 October, 1842, in answer to a correspondent who had enquired as to the meaning of some of his 'Songs without Words'. He says:

> People often complain that music is so ambiguous, that what they are to think about it always seems so doubtful, whereas everyone understands words; with me it is exactly the reverse; not merely with regard to entire sentences, but also to individual words; these, too, seem to me so ambiguous, so vague, so unintelligible when compared with genuine music, which fills the soul with a thousand things better than words. What any music I love expresses to me, is not thoughts too *indefinite* to put into words, but on the contrary, too *definite* . . . If you ask me what *my* idea was, I say—just the song as it stands.

He goes on to make the observation that if he had had in mind a definite word or words, he would have been reluctant to disclose them, becaue 'the words of one person assume a totally different meaning in the mind of another person'. This may be true enough of the words he chooses as examples—resignation, melancholy, the praise of God, even a hunting song. He goes on, however, to say that 'the music of the song alone can awaken the same ideas and the same feeling in one mind as in another'; this, however, begs the whole question: for it is surely just as debatable whether that can happen, as that the same words can produce identical reactions in different hearers.

But that is not the heart of the matter. The 'Songs without Words' are hardly programme music. At most they are mood pictures, as such no further from absolute music than a Chopin nocturne or many a sonata movement, and certainly by no means as programmatic as Schumann's little piano pieces. He did, however, write a quantity of genuine programme music (most of it, incidentally, some years before the letter quoted above) in which we are asked to identify concepts far more concrete than the vague 'resignation' or 'praise of God' of his letter. It would have been more valuable to have had his pronouncements on *A Midsummer Night's Dream Overture* or the *Italian* symphony.

In the twentieth century the most controversial and in many ways the oddest writing on the subject of programme music comes from the distinguished German musicologist, Arnold Schering (1877-1941). He made his name early in the century with some important books on music history—a history of the concerto, 1905; of the oratorio, 1911, and he also did valuable work in editing older composers' music for the series *Denkmäler deutscher Tonkunst*. Then in the 1930s he turned his attention to Beethoven, and in a series of articles and books he made some extraordinary claims concerning a number of sonatas, symphonies and chamber music works. His findings were summed up in two compendious books, *Beethoven in neuer Deutung* (1934) ('A new interpretation of Beethoven') and *Beethoven und die Dichtung* (1936) ('Beethoven and Poetry').

His contention is, that a number of Beethoven's master works are not only engendered by extra-musical stimuli (with which most people would probably agree), but that they are directly and closely related to certain specific literary works or passages from plays and poems. He claims that no fewer than thirty-eight of Beethoven's most important works, including the Seventh symphony, the Razoumovsky string quartets, the *Appassionata* and *Waldstein* sonatas, the *Kreutzer* violin sonata and the piano trio in B flat, are all derived from definite portions of works by Shakespeare, Schiller, Goethe, Homer and others—which would make Beethoven the champion '*Programmusiker*' of all time.

How seriously should we take all this? The short answer would be, not at all, were it not put forward by a man of Schering's reputation and ability. He marshals his material with Teutonic thoroughness, making great play with Beethoven's own known utterances and the observations and opinions of contemporaries and later commentators.

Beethoven spoke of having '*Bilder*' (pictures) in his mind when composing; he talked of himself as a '*Dichter*' (poet) rather than a '*Komponist*'; in answer to a query as to the 'meaning' of the piano sonata in D minor Op. 31.3 he refers the enquirer, Schindler, to Shakespeare's *Tempest*; he is known to have read a great deal, especially Goethe and Shakespeare, and his letters contain many allusions to these works. His friends all spoke of his odd manner of composing, his notebooks crammed with words as well as notes; his admirers, whether writers like E. T. A. Hoffmann or A. B. Marx or composers like Schumann and Wagner all agreed that Beethoven in his music was struggling to express extra-musical ideas.

These seem flimsy arguments, if indeed they are arguments at all. Beethoven's own words do not add up to a confession. They may suggest he was a bad character, but we cannot, on the strength of what he has said, convict him of offences against Shakespeare, Goethe, Homer or Schiller. As for the commentators, in his lifetime and after, the position seems to be this. Beethoven's music, often difficult of comprehension, gives all the appearance of being concerned with extra-musical matters, in other words it has a 'meaning'. For the commentators, practitioners in words (Schering was one too), this 'meaning' implies words and verbal concepts; it should therefore be possible to put this 'meaning' into words, and Schering quotes a number of examples, by A. B. Marx, Rochlitz, Oulibichef, Lenz, Schumann, Wagner and Grove, of such verbal interpretations. But unless we have the composer's explicit statement that he had such and such a visual or verbal notion in his mind when composing such and such a work, we have no right to regard such verbal interpretations as anything more than fumbling analogies, which at their best may help both listeners and performers to a better understanding of the music, and at their worst betray the commentator's blank incomprehension in the face of a work which transcends his own imaginative grasp.

CHAPTER 2

Programme Music to the End of the Eighteenth Century

Though the embryo of programme music can be detected in the vocal music of the fifteenth century or earlier it was not until the secular madrigal of the sixteenth century that musical illustration became a noticeable aspect of a composer's style. Our attention is drawn in particular to the last few years of the sixteenth century, at the time when not only was music in the process of transition from the '*Prima Prattica*' of polyphony to the '*Seconda Prattica*' of the monodic aria and the early opera, but when instrumental music, with which we are solely concerned, began to blossom as an art form in its own right. The increasing popularity of the lute and more especially the plucked keyboard instruments (the names harpsichord, clavicembalo, virginals (in England) and clavecin (in France) apply to instruments all with the same principle of tone production) created a demand for instrumental music and thus encouraged the development of a self-sufficient instrumental style. The demand was met in a variety of ways—by dance tunes, by sets of variations, by transcriptions of vocal pieces, and by the writing of little *genre* or 'character' pieces. Only the last two have any direct bearing on the history of programme music.

Transcriptions interest us because, as opposed to the emptiness engendered by the facile writing in some of the sets of variations, they represent a conscious attempt on the composer's part to harness instrumental technique to artistic ends. The endeavour not only to find means of equating the sustained vocal line with the transient sound of a plucked instrument, but also to capture the emotions expressed in a madrigal, led to music of high quality. As with later transcriptions (for example, Liszt's piano transcriptions of Beethoven's symphonies and Schubert's songs), the experience gained led to a widening of the instrument's expressive resources. The *genre* pieces, with titles such as Giles Farnaby's 'Tower Hill' or his 'Dream', are often quite delightful, but they are often only on the fringe of true programme music. Among the exceptions is a Fantasia by John Munday—a 'meteorological' piece, depicting 'Faire Wether', 'Lightning', 'Thunder', 'Calme Wether' and 'A cleare Day'. The stormy portions are dealt with in quite a realistic way, using the same techniques to be found in later 'storm' music by Vivaldi, Rossini and Beethoven—little jagged rhythmic motifs for lightning, rushing scales in the left hand for thunder.[1]

Another piece that deserves more attention, especially in view of its numerous successors, is 'Mr Byrd's Battel'. Very little seems to be known as to the origins of this. It appeared in another manuscript collection, *My Ladye Nevell's Booke*, compiled about 1591[2], so that it must obviously have been written about 1590 or earlier; but so far nobody has suggested reasons why the somewhat austere Byrd should have indulged in such a *jeu d'esprit*.

Battle pieces, vocal or instrumental, were quite popular at the time. Examples exist by Andrea Gabrieli, Annibale Padovana, Hermann Werrecore and others. The most famous and widely disseminated was that by Clément Jannequin, *La Guerre*, for voices, supposed to refer to the Battle of Marignan (1515), and first published in 1529, in which the sounds of battle are imitated. It is quite possible, indeed very likely, that some of these pieces were known to Byrd. His 'Battel' is really a Suite, in fifteen numbers: 1. *The Earle of Oxford's Marche* or *The Marche before the Battell*; 2. *The Souldiers' sommons;* 3. *The Marche of Footemen;* 4. *The Marche of Horsmen*; 5. *The trumpetts*; 6. *The Irish Marche*; 7. *The bagpipe and the drone*; 8. *The flute and the droome*; 9. *The Marche to the fight* (this is in two sections, the first headed 'Tantara tantara', the second 'The battels be joined'); 10. *The Retraite*; 11. *The burying of the dead*; 12. *The Galliarde for the victorie*; 13. *The*

---

[1] These pieces were among the 300 transcribed for the virginals at some time in the early seventeenth century by Francis Tregian which appear in the large manuscript now known as *The Fitzwilliam Virginal Book*. It was first published in modern notation in 1899, edited by J. A. Fuller Maitland and W. Barclay Squire; a modern reprint of this is available, in two volumes, published by Dover Publications, Inc. (New York, 1963).

[2] This was first published, edited by Hilda Andrews, in 1926. Byrd's composition will also be found in Vol. XVIII of *Byrd's Collected Works*, edited by E. H. Fellowes (1950).

morris; 14. *The souldiers' dance*; 15. *The souldiers' delight* (a variation of the preceding number). The musical content, it must be confessed, is not of high quality; the most interesting piece is No. 8, *The flute and the droome*—a gipsy-like melody of almost Central European character over an *ostinato* bass.

Though Byrd's contemporaries and immediate successors such as John Bull (c. 1568-1628) and Thomas Tomkins (1572-1626) continued to write virginal music only a few pieces, for instance Bull's *Battaille*[3] or Tomkins's *The Sad Pavan; for these distracted times*[4] (dated 14 February, a few days after the execution of Charles I), have much relevance to our discussion, and in the seventeenth century the cultivation of programme keyboard music passed to the continent, and particularly to France, where the great dynasty of clavecin composers began with Jacques Champion de Chambonnières (1602-72).

I shall return to a consideration of these composers later in the chapter. In the meantime a new factor of the utmost importance must be considered.

In the early seventeenth century the musical monopoly of the Church had been challenged by a rival, the Opera; to Church and State (for in a sense that was what the Opera represented) was now added a third estate, the People, in other words, the public concert. This, becoming increasingly powerful until today it almost dominates our musical thinking, rapidly became secularized and mainly instrumental, and composers consequently found themselves increasingly involved in the problems of abstract musical form unaided by words.

The initiation of the instrumental, secular concert is generally attributed to an Englishman, John Banister, who inaugurated a series of concerts in London in 1672. This was rapidly followed by similar ventures on the continent, for example Buxtehude's '*Abendmusik*' at Lübeck in 1673 and Kuhnau's '*Collegium Musicum*' at Leipzig in 1688.

Programmes it is true were not limited to the instrumental and the secular; thus the '*Concerts Spirituels*' of Paris (1725), which found imitators in other centres in Germany, included oratorios and sacred cantatas. But they were all concerts to which the public was invited,

---

[3] BM Add. MSS 23623; printed in Vol. XIX of *Musica Britannica*.
[4] Printed in Vol. V of *Musica Britannica*.

in contrast to the private music-making of all kinds, from the fairly humble middle-class household, which could muster a few players gathered round a keyboard, to the more ambitious nobleman with his own chapel organization under the command of a *Maestro di Cappella*. All this led to a tremendous growth of secular, mainly instrumental music—including programme music.

Now it is notable that, among the composers working along the Bologna-Milan-Vienna-Mannheim-Paris axis, those who had most to do with the growth of the abstract musical forms made the least contribution to programme music. Thus Corelli, who laid the foundations of modern string style and the trio sonata, left only one movement that could be construed as programmatic; among Vivaldi's 400 concerti the *Quattro Stagioni* Op. 8 and some of the works in his Op. 10 stand out as exceptions; the great bulk of the instrumental work of G. B. Sammartini, J. C. Bach and Mozart is of purely abstract design. A number of Haydn's symphonies have nicknames, for which in most cases he was not responsible; but for every one such there are a dozen symphonies, string quartets or sonatas in which Haydn's sole concern is with the musical building materials of motifs, themes, harmony, cadences and modulation.

Since most of these composers also wrote vocal music, which sometimes, as in Haydn's *Creation*, is graphically descriptive, the temptation to interpret analogous passages in purely instrumental works in a comparable way is almost irresistible, and indeed programme music would have been impossible had not opera and oratorio given a lead. The 'Frost' scene in Purcell's *King Arthur* (anticipated by Monteverdi and others of the Italian school), the tempests and pastorals in the operas of Lully and Rameau, the resourceful descriptive writing in for example Handel's *Israel in Egypt*, paved the way for the purely instrumental movements in Kuhnau, Vivaldi and, later, Beethoven and Berlioz. Such time-honoured devices as the falling melodic semitones coupled with chromatic harmony to suggest grief, suffering or death, trumpet fanfares for military scenes, the 'winding of the horn' that is associated with the chase—all these can hardly fail to evoke similar emotions or thoughts when they appear in purely instrumental contexts.

Purists have sometimes objected to this. With regard to Bach's choral preludes for organ, for example, they have maintained that some commentators have pushed the programmatic interpretation too far. Harvey Grace in his book *The Organ Works of Bach* says (p.107) 'There is sometimes a tendency to read into the music more than is actually there' — a reference no doubt to Albert Schweitzer's imposing study of the composer's works,[5] in which he found an impressive array of motifs representing grief, joy, flight, etc. But it is undeniable that in the choral preludes there are many passages which stem from the words of the hymns with which the tunes are associated, and indeed Grace himself has noted a number of instances of pictorialism such as the ten entries of the subject in the prelude *Dies sind die heil'gen zehn Gebot* ('these are the holy ten commandments') or the airy little figure in *Wo soll ich fliehen hin?* (Whither shall I fly?). All the evidence points to at least some awareness of the need to practise '*Tonmalerei*'.[6] Nor was Bach alone in this; he was merely following on and improving the work of his German and Italian predecessors Tunder, Boehm, Buxtehude, Froberger, Pachelbel and Frescobaldi.

Programme music was cultivated not only by the keyboard composers but by the violinists. Two composers influential in the early development of violin technique were Carlo Farina (fl. end of the sixteenth century, and working at the Court of Dresden from 1625 to about 1630) and Marco Uccellini (fl. first half of the seventeenth century). In the former's *Capriccio stravagante*, published in 1627 at Dresden, we find examples of hens cackling and dogs barking (cf Vivaldi's *Seasons*, discussed below), while Uccellini in 1669 published as his Op. 8 a set of *Sinfonie boscareccie*, for violins and figured bass, which anticipate the 'sylvan glade' of Vivaldi's work just mentioned, with its choir of singing birds. A more important figure is Heinrich Johann Franz von Biber (1644-1704), who in about 1671 wrote a set of fifteen *Mysterien für Violin und Klavier nàch kupferstichen biblisches Historien*. This is a very early, though not quite the earliest example (there is a previous instance by Froberger) of a work based on pictures — the 'copperplate engravings'

---

[5] *J. S. Bach* (2 vols.), first published in German in 1903 (at about the time Niecks was preparing his *Programme Music*), and in an English translation by Ernest Newman in 1911.

[6] Niecks goes so far as to say 'Was not J. S. Bach a clandestine cultivator of programme music?', and mentions in support of this some of the instrumental portions of the *St Matthew Passion* and the *Christmas Oratorio*, but, curiously, does not mention the choral preludes at all.

of the title.[7] They were intended for the fifteen 'sacred mysteries' of the Rosenkranzfeiern or Festival of the Rosary, celebrated in October.[8] The fifteen pictures take us through the story of Christ from the Archangel Gabriel's Visitation to Mary to her Ascension into Heaven and Coronation, but only in No. 12, 'Christ's Ascension', does the music make any real attempt to be descriptive. The finest is No. 6, 'Christ's Agony on the Mount of Olives and Judas's Betrayal', treated quasi-operatically and full of dramatic intensity.

They belong to that category of instrumental music, on the borderland of programme music, for liturgical use, which includes Corelli's Church Sonatas, Mozart's 'Epistle' sonatas and Haydn's *Seven Last Words* for string quartet. They also, on the secular side, point towards the important programme works of the first years of the next century by Couperin and Vivaldi, to be discussed later, and on the sacred side to Kuhnau's Bible Sonatas.

Johann Kuhnau (1660-1722), who from 1684 until his death was J. S. Bach's immediate predecessor at St Thomas's, Leipzig, published his six Bible Sonatas (*Biblische Historien nebst Auslegung in sechs Sonaten auf dem Clavier zu spielen*) in 1700, with a Preface which draws attention to previous programmatic sonatas, by Froberger and others.[9] The six sonatas are: 1. The combat between David and Goliath; 2. David curing Saul by means of music; 3. Jacob's marriage; 4. Hezekiah sick unto death and recovered of his sickness; 5. The Saviour of Israel, Gideon; 6. Jacob's death and burial. Each sonata is preceded by a summary of the story the music is meant to convey, and additional 'clues' are provided, scattered amongst the printed music exactly as Vivaldi was to do in his orchestral work, *The Seasons*. The first sonata for example attempts to portray (a) the

---

[7] The music is printed, with the engravings, and with the violin part as Biber wrote it, with the violin part tuned differently for the various numbers—ie, in '*scordatura*'—in DTÖ Jg. 12, 1905. It is also available in an arrangement by Robert Reitz (Universal Edition, 1915).

[8] For some very interesting details of this festival see the article 'Rosary' in the *Catholic Encyclopedia*.

[9] Reprinted in *DdT*, Vol. IV (1901) and, with the preface in English, by Broude Bros, New York. Peters also print all six. No. 4 is in Vol. 2 of the *Historical Anthology of Music*, and in Vol. 2 of *Early German Keyboard Music* edited by Howard Ferguson (Oxford University Press). Niecks prints some extracts from the Preface; and see also the description of the sonatas in J. S. Shedlock, *The Piano Sonata* (1895; reprinted 1964).

boasting of Goliath; (b) the terror of the Israelites, and their prayers to God; (c) David's courage; (d) the contest between David and Goliath; (e) the flight of the Philistines; (g) the praise of David; and (h) general joy of the Israelites. The second one, 'David curing Saul by means of Music', is in three parts, intended by the composer to represent (a) Saul's melancholy and madness; (b) David's harp-playing; and (c) the King's mind restored to peace. Such themes go well in musical guise, and Kuhnau here has written something that is not merely naively pictorial but curiously moving. The fourth sonata, *Der todtkranke und wider gesunde Hiskias*, is also in three sections; the first two, *Il Lamento di Hiskia* and *La di lui confidenza in Iddio* ('Hezekiah's lament, and Renewed confidence in himself'), are choral preludes on the familiar tune used frequently by Bach, 'Herzlich tut mich verlangen'.

William Newman in his *The Sonata in the Baroque Era* writing on these sonatas comments 'The more detailed effects, eg the scale passage depicting the flight of the stone from David's sling and the collapse of Goliath) now seem incredibly naive'; Niecks is somewhat more understanding, as indeed are Otto Klauwell, who describes Kuhnau as the first 'true composer of programme music in the modern sense,[10] and Spitta, who in his definitive study of Bach speaks quite highly of Kuhnau's music.[11] The naïveté of Kuhnau's pictorialism is on a par with the rending of the Temple veil in Bach's *St Matthew Passion*, or the hailstones in Handel's *Israel in Egypt*. Is it the medium harpsichord rather than orchestra, that suggests naiveté? But they were very likely thought of in terms of the organ. Kuhnau was an organist; and, like most organists, given to extemporization. His Biblical sonatas lie in the tradition of such improvisatory playing. Mattheson, Handel's friend and the author of several journalistic books that reveal something of the day-to-day musical life of his time, writes that 'Froberger could depict whole histories on the clavier, giving a representation of the persons present and taking part in it, with all their natural characteristics'; and he had in his possession a Suite by Froberger 'in which the passage across the Rhine of the Count von Thurn, and the danger he was exposed to from the river, is most clearly set before our eyes in twenty-six little

---

[10] Otto Klauwell, *Geschichte der Programm-Musik* (1910).
[11] *Life of Bach* (English translation) Vol. I, p. 238.

pieces'.[12] Johann Jakob Froberger (1616-67), who spent some time in Italy where he studied with Frescobaldi from about 1637-41, was Court organist at Vienna until 1657; he is reputed to have visited England in 1662 when (according to Mattheson) he arrived in London robbed and destitute, happy to accept a position as organ blower at Westminster Abbey. His music,[13] of great interest and importance in the history of the suite, hardly strikes us today as having the descriptive power attributed to it by Mattheson, though the 'Lament on the death of his Royal Majesty Ferdinand IV'; printed in HAM is a moving eloquent piece of writing.

Kuhnau, who enjoyed a considerable reputation in his own day (Handel was not above borrowing material from him), had a direct influence on at least one, admittedly very minor, composition of his great successor at St Thomas's. In 1704, when J. S. Bach was living at Arnstadt, his elder brother Johann Jakob left Saxony to take up service as an oboist under Charles XII of Sweden. The freakish composition Bach wrote at this time, entitled *Capriccio sopra la lontananza del suo fratello dilettissimo*, points clearly to Kuhnau as a model. There are five sections, each with a superscription in Italian. The first movement shows his friends attempting to dissuade him from his journey, while the second presents musical pictures of the possible disasters awaiting him by the wayside. The third is a slow movement, depicting the lamentation of his friends (this is built on a chromatic *ostinato* bass, similar to the familiar one in Purcell's *Dido and Aeneas*). His friends then take leave of him, and the last two movements are *Aria di Postiglione*, and a fugue based on the postillion's air.

A composer, younger than Kuhnau, with a much greater influence on Bach was the Venetian Antonio Vivaldi (c. 1680-1743). There is no reason to suppose that they ever met, but Bach's lively interest in Vivaldi's music is proved by the fact that he transcribed so many of the Italian composer's works, and that he demonstrably modelled his solo concertos on the principles exploited by Vivaldi, if not indeed established by him. The latter's acquaintance with Bach's music was probably nil, for although Vivaldi, like so many Venetian composers

---

[12] Quoted in Spitta, *op. cit.*, from Mattheson's *Der Vollkommene Capellmeister*.
[13] Three volumes in *DTÖ*. See also *Historical Anthology of Music*, Nos. 216 and 217, and Carl Parrish and John F. Ohl, *Masterpieces of Music before 1750* (Faber, 1953), No. 35.

of his time, had contacts with some of the South German states and Austria (he died in Vienna), Bach's circle was essentially different, and his music and his reputation were valued chiefly farther north, in Saxony and Prussia.

The few compositions published during Vivaldi's lifetime included a set of four *concerti* for orchestra which may be accounted the most ambitious essays in purely instrumental programme music that had yet been attempted. They were entitled *Le Quattro Stagioni ovvero Il Cimento dell' armonia e dell' invenzione* ('The Four Seasons, or the Trial of harmony and invention'). They were published as Op. 8, not in Venice but as far away as Amsterdam and Paris in about 1730, with a dedicatory preface to Count Wenceslao di Marzin (or Morzin) — a branch of the family that a few years later gave employment to Haydn.

Each of the four *concerti* is prefaced by a sonnet (the verses possibly by Vivaldi himself), and there are letters in the score[14] to indicate which line or lines of the sonnet the music refers to. There are other captions in the music which show even more clearly what Vivaldi had in mind. In the first movement of 'Spring' the "Canto d'ucelli' (bird songs) — trills on the solo violin — are so marked; in the second movement the harsh repeated notes on the viola are intended to depict 'Il cane che grida' (a dog barking); in the last concerto, 'Winter', repeated notes represent chattering teeth, and so on. In 'Summer' there is, as might be expected, some storm music — rushing demi-semiquaver scales for lightning, *tremolandi* passages for thunder. Nor is the work without its humour, as when in 'Autumn' the peasants having drunk too much wine under the hot sun become first quarrelsome and then drowsy. As with so much Vivaldi the effect is marred by the facile sequential passages, but on the other hand the themes themselves have a simplicity and directness that suggest folk music, appropriate to the rusticity of the whole. If, as seems probable, the work was played by Count Marzin's orchestra (Vivaldi's preface names him as *Maestro di Cappella* to the Count), this is rusticity once removed — the artificial play at shepherds and shepherdesses of the Court of Versailles and its imitators.

It is not too fanciful to see the influence of this work on another interesting piece of descriptive writing published a few years later, at

---

[14] See Eulenburg's Miniature Scores nos. 1220/3.

Augsburg in 1748. This was a *Kalendar*, a suite of twelve miniature *concerti* or suites, composed by Gregorius Josef Werner (1695-1766) of Eisenstadt.[15] A Preface outlines the programme of each month. With the exception of January each month has five movements, one of which is a minuet in two sections headed respectively 'day' and 'night', the lengths of each section depending on the season. Thus March and September, the equinoctial months, have day and night equal, twelve bars each, but in mid-winter December day has eight bars only, night sixteen. In January frostiness is denoted by shivering triplet semiquavers, and the date is spelled out by a fugue subject:

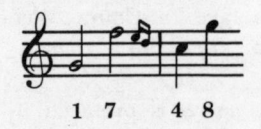

1   7   4   8

The fourth movement of April is headed '*tempo variable*', and, employing a pun on the double meaning of the Italian word '*tempo*' (time and weather), there is a riot of changes of time signature, 4/8, 12/8, 2/4, 3/8 and so on. In the fifth movement, headed 'Das Froschgeschrei', the music imitates frogs croaking. Each month is given its appropriate zodiacal sign; June being under the sign of Cancer ('Sonne in Krebs') this is illustrated in the second movement by a 'crab' canon. The third movement describes an earthquake, with rapid repeated notes and agitated arpeggios. In July we experience a summer storm, with *tremolandi*, repeated notes and rapid scales to depict rain. The second movement of October, 'Der Fassbinder' ('the Cooper'), is quite descriptive of casks of wine being rolled; there is a creaking mill-wheel in 'Il Molino' (November), and in the third movement of December ('Der Schlaf oder ein Nachtstück' — 'Sleep, or a Nocturne') there are some quite convincing snores. The whole is utterly charming and delightful.

There are numerous other works with programmatic titles such as the six symphonies by Mysliweczek (1737-81) depicting the six months January to June or Pichl's (1741-1805) nine symphonies, 'The Nine Muses', and there is a quantity of 'hunting' pieces (Jagdstücke) by Leopold Mozart, Stamitz, Gossec, Wranitsky and others.[16] It

---

[15] Reprinted in *Das Erbe deutsche Musik*, Bd. 31 (1956).
[16] See Otto Klauwell, *op. cit*.

would be misplaced labour to seek for much descriptive writing in many of these works. Any figure in 6/8 time which is vaguely reminiscent of the huntsman's horn is sufficient cause for a symphony to be labelled 'La Chasse'. Similarly, it is only necessary to write a gentle ambling, rocking movement in compound time, with something of the Siciliano rhythm or with the melody on the oboe, for our thoughts to turn towards the idyllic life of shepherds or, more specifically, the Christmas scene at Bethlehem. Corelli's 'Christmas' Concerto (No. 8) and the pastoral symphonies in Bach's *Christmas Oratorio* and Handel's *Messiah* hover on the brink of programme music, and in essence go back to Lully. They have their roots in the fanciful bucolic posturings of the French Court at Versailles and Fontainebleau; the artificiality of this in the seventeenth century, given a new twist in the eighteenth by Rousseau's 'back to nature' doctrine, was still capable of artistic fertilization in the nineteenth century when Verlaine, Debussy and others re-discovered the *'Fêtes champêtres'* of the eighteenth century painters Watteau and Boucher.

But visual stimulation through a picture was on the whole alien to the eighteenth century composer. The impulse came either from a direct fact of nature (storms, streamlets, bird song, times and seasons) or from literature. When Haydn joined the *entourage* of Count Esterházy in 1761 he made his *début* with three symphonies—*Le Matin*, *Le Midi* and *Le Soir*. Of these the middle one is incomparably the finest, but the other two catch our attention by reason of their programmes. The last movement of *Le Soir*, for instance, is subtitled 'La Tempesta'. This may have been written in emulation of Vivaldi's *La Tempesta di Mare*, Op. 10; he would almost certainly have known some of Vivaldi's music. But in any case there was a clear link between the two composers in the person of Werner, who was *Maestro di Cappella* for Count Esterházy when Haydn entered the Count's employ after his short period of about two years with Count Morzin.

Haydn's tempest is but a storm in a teacup, a gentle roaring compared even with Vivaldi. The likelihood is that at this period in his career Haydn was more interested in the problems of abstract musical design than in illustration, and in fact his most pictorial music is to be found in his mature works, when he no longer felt the need to demonstrate his command over the technicalities of symphonic construction.

The early biographers of Haydn, Griesinger (*Biographische Notizien über Haydn*) and more particularly Carpani (*Le Haydine ovvero Lettere sulla vita e le opere del celebre maestro Giuseppe Haydn*) quote statements, allegedly from the composer himself, which if true shed a strange light on the composer's methods of workmanship. Carpani, for instance, cites a symphony which describes the experiences of a young man, not well off, who travelled to America to seek his fortune. The outward journey is unadventurous, but landing in the New World they meet strange and savage sounds. The outcome, however, is favourable, but on the return voyage the ship meets with a violent storm, to the distress of the passengers. But all is well, and the journey is accomplished safely amid the rejoicings of his friends. Griesinger quotes another symphony as representing God speaking to a hardened sinner, but to no avail. Unfortunately these symphonies, and others mentioned by Carpani, are not precisely identified.

If all this were true, if Haydn had confided this in all seriousness to Carpani, it would considerably change our ideas as to the psychology of composition and render Schering's theories (discussed in Chapter I) more plausible. But despite the fact that Niecks seems to take it seriously (see page 76 ff.) and despite the brilliant instrumental introduction to *The Creation* which suggests that Haydn might have been able to create such elaborate programme symphonies had he wished, it is hard to swallow. Carpani's biography appeared in 1812, that is to say at precisely the time when Beethoven's contemporaries were puzzling over possible programmes in *his* symphonies. Either Carpani made the whole thing up or, as H. E. Jacob supposes (in *Joseph Haydn: His Art, Times and Glory*, London, 1950), Carpani was having his leg well and truly pulled.

Whatever reservations we may have had as to Vivaldi's tone painting or Kuhnau's David and Goliath, when we come to examine the miniatures of the French clavecin school we are quite disarmed. They are characterized by restraint, by understatement. They have the reticence typical of one aspect of French art; there is no flamboyance; 'la Stravaganza' (the title of Vivaldi's Op. 4) is foreign to their thought, which is conditioned by '*le bon goût*'.

The founder of the dynasty was Jacques Champion de Chambonnières (1602-72); he was clavecinist to Louis XIV, and his pupils included Louis Couperin (c. 1626-61), Nicholas le Bègue

(1630-1702) and Jean Henri d'Anglebert (1635-91). He also taught yet another Couperin, Charles (1638-79), the father of the most famous of all the Couperins, François (1668-1733), known as 'Couperin le Grand'. Their music is often only marginally programmatic, and their dance movements (of which there are many) make no pretence at being anything else. But they did cast back to the practice of the lutenists headed by Denis Gaultier (c. 1603-72) — whose *Rhétorique des Dieux* deserves mention — in giving fanciful titles to their pieces.[17] And while such titles by no means guarantee a 'programme', they are pointers to some extra-musical inspiration and thus edge towards programme music *per se*. The same is true of the *'tombeau'* — 'a gentle miniature composed in memory of noble persons' (*Music in the Baroque Era*, p. 168) — a *genre* which Bukofzer attributes to Gaultier. And like the English virginalists, they gained experience in handling the resources of their instruments by practising the art of transcription, in this case airs and dances from Lully's operas, first of all for the lute (by Mouton, a pupil of Gaultier) and for clavecin (by d'Anglebert, of whom Bukofzer says: 'he transferred the sonorities of the Lullian orchestra to the clavecin — a striking early parallel to the orchestral expansion of piano technique by Liszt'). All this paved the way for the more overtly programmatic compositions of Couperin le Grand.

Couperin's twenty-seven suites or *'Ordres'* were issued in four books between 1713 and 1730.[18] In an important preface to the first book he sets out his intentions in giving these pieces their titles. He writes:

> J'ay toujours eu un objet en composant toutes ces pièces . . . Les titres répondent aux idées que j'ay eues . . . Cependant comme il y a en a qui semblant me flater, il est bon d'avertir que les pièces qui les portent sont des espèces de portraits . . . et que la plupart de ces titres avantageux sont plûtot donnés aux aimables originaux que j'ay voulu representer, qu'aux copies que j'en ay tirées.[19]

---

[17] Bukofzer in *Music of the Baroque Era* suggests that 'these intimate titles had been taken over from the English virginalists'.
[18] Reprinted in the nineteenth century edited by Brahms, and in the present century in volumes 2 to 4 of the *Lyrebird* Edition of Couperin's Complete Works.
[19] A rather fuller extract is given, in translation, in Niecks, p. 32.
In his interesting book *La Musique en France au xviiie siècle* Pierre Daval, who quotes this passage, notes the 'systematic usage of titles either characteristic or picturesque' as an innovation, which his predecessors had used but rarely; and he sees it as a manifestation of the urge towards expression ('le volente d'expression'), which was already a trait of French music, in contradistinction to the 'decorative' Italian music.

The titles fall into three groups. First, proper names, of his family or his friends—*La Couperin* (his wife); *La Princesse Marie*; *La Forqueray* (a celebrated gamba player). Sometimes the identification is concealed under a more general name such as *Soeur Monique, La Babet*, or even a *soubriquet* such as *L'Auguste, La Seduisante*. A second group suggests inspiration from the painters of the period, for example *Les Vergers fleuris, Les Moissonneurs, Les Bergeries*. There is a third group that Daval describes as 'veritable descriptive frescoes'—*Les petites ages; Les Fastes de la grande Ménestrandise; Les Folies françaises*. At this distance in time and not enjoying the intimacy of Couperin and his circle there is much, inevitably, that we miss in these portraits—delicate line drawings, etched with economy and touched in with an engaging piquancy of colour; we can perhaps respond more readily to the picturesque quality of the more frankly realistic *Les petits Moulins à vent, Le Tic-Toc-Choc, Le Moucheron*, or *Les Tricoteuses*.

These frankly pictorial *vignettes* were less to the taste of the other great French composer of the period, Jean Philippe Rameau (1683-1764), but there are a few pieces to be found in his second book of clavecin pieces (1724) and the later collections of 1728 and 1741 (the first book, dating from 1706—ie, before Couperin's first *Ordre*—contains no titles). As with Couperin one suspects that some of the points are lost on us today, but in *Le Tambourin, Le Rappel des Oiseaux* and *La Poule* the intention is obvious.

As Court composer Couperin's activities extended far beyond the range of clavecin music.[20] He wrote music for the church's liturgy, for the organ and for orchestra; among the latter are a few transcriptions of clavecin works with titles such as *La Pucelle, La Visionnaire*, and two suites that push the programme principle very much farther. They are *Le Parnasse ou L'Apothéose de Corelli* and *L'Apothéose de Lulli*.

The first of these, dating from 1724, in seven parts, is a delicate tribute to Corelli as the founder-father of violin playing. The sections are: 1. Corelli, at the foot of Mount Parnassus, asks the muses to receive him among them; 2. Corelli, charmed by his reception, expresses his joy; 3. He drinks at the Fountain of Hippocrene (this is the 'Fountain of the Horse' on Mount Helicon in Boetia, sacred to the

---

[20] For a full discussion of his work in general see Wilfrid Mellers, *François Couperin and the French Classical Tradition* (London, 1950).

muses); 4. Enthusiasm of Corelli caused by the waters; 5. Corelli falls asleep; his companions play slumber music very softly; 6. The muses awaken him, and place him beside Apollo; 7. The thanks of Corelli. The Lully Apotheosis (1725) is longer and somewhat more detailed — fourteen numbers in all, but some of them quite short: 1. Lully in the Elysian fields concerting with the lyrical shades or spirits; 2. Air for the same; 3. The flight of Mercury to the Elysian fields to announce the descent of Apollo; 4. Descent of Apollo, who comes to offer Lully his violin and his place on Parnassus; 5. Subterranean noises by Lully's contemporaries; 6. Complaints of the same (flutes and violins, very subdued); 7. The carrying off of Lully to Parnassus; 8. Reception given to Lully by Corelli and the Italian muses; 9. Thanks of Lully to Apollo; 10. Apollo persuades Lully and Corelli that the union of Italian and French taste ought to make music perfect; 11. Lully and Corelli play in consort, Lully playing the principal part and Corelli accompanying; 12. Here the roles are reversed; 13. The Peace of Parnassus made on the proposal of the French muses, subject to the condition that when their language was spoken there, the words 'sonade' and 'cantade' should be said, instead of 'sonata' and 'cantata', on the analogy of 'ballade' and 'serenade'; 14. Saillie or conclusion.[21]

The music (which is available on gramophone records) is delightfully imaginative, full of whimsical touches of humour. Both suites were particularly relevant to their times, for this was the period of the controversy over the rival claims of the French and Italian taste. In design they owe much to the decorative ballets and theatre pieces glorifying the Sun King and his successor, Louis XV; the ballets had just such 'entrées' as Couperin envisaged, and one could imagine both works figuring as *ballets du cour*.

Classical mythology which was such a inexhaustible source for French opera and ballet was also the source of a number of important orchestral works later in the century. One such was the *Aventures de Télémaque* by Ignazio Raimondi (1735-1813), published in Amsterdam in 1777. Based on the French writer Fénelon's *Télémaque* of 1699, this was a long symphonic work lasting about one hour, beginning with a storm at sea and ending with a shipwreck. This is conventional enough, but Raimondi shows himself a little more enterprising in attempting to identify his

---

[21] For a more detailed discussion especially of the music see Mellers *op. cit.*

characters through instrumental tone. Thus Calypso is entrusted to the flute, Eucharis to the oboe, Telemachus to the solo violin and Mentor to the solo cello. The same subject was also similarly treated by Franz Anton Rosetti (1759-92) in his *Charakteristische Tongemälde Telemach und Calypso*, using the bassoon, oboe, flute and cello as solo instruments in association with the characters Mentor, Calypso, Telemachus and Eucharis.

The interesting article in the Leipzig *Allgemeine Musik-Zeitung* of 1799 credits Rosetti as being the first to write *'malenden Simphonien'*, but it looks rather as though he was a link between Raimondi and the earlier Francesco Geminiani (1667-1762), who in about 1760 had written *The Enchanted Forest*, in which, says Burney, 'he endeavoured by mere sound to represent to the imagination of the audience all the events in the episode of the thirteenth book of Tasso's Jerusalem'; and the Austrian Karl Ditters von Dittersdorf (1739-99), whose twelve Ovid *Metamorphoses* are the most ambitious programme works before Beethoven. Written in about 1783, they were first performed in Vienna in 1786, the first six in the Augarten and the remainder a few days later in the theatre. The titles of the twelve are: 1. *Les quatre âges du monde;* 2. *La chute de Phaèton;* 3. *Actéon changé en Cerf;* 4. *Androméde sauvé par Persée;* 5. *Phiné avec ses amis changés en rochers;* 6. *Les paysans changés en grenouilles;* 7. *Jason qui enlève la toison d'or;* 8. *Siège de Mégare;* 9. *Hercule changé en Dieu;* 10. *Orphée et Eurydice;* 11. *Midas élu pour Juge entre Pan et Apollo;* 12. *Ajax et Ulisse qui se disputent les armes d'Achille*. Of these only nine seem to be extant, numbers eight, ten and eleven apparently lost.[22] As with Vivaldi's *Seasons* the various movements are headed with quotations, in this instance from Ovid, as clues to the intended significance of the music, which strikes a happy medium between the more obvious and exterior type of tone-painting (as for example in the third metamorphosis when Acteon is torn to pieces by his own dogs) and the subtler characterization to be found in the music depicting the four ages of the world — gold, silver, bronze and iron.

---

[22] Niecks mistakenly supposed that all of the last six had vanished. The first six were reprinted in 1899 (the centenary of the composer's death), and numbers seven, nine and twelve were issued, in piano duet form, in 1890 — see *Dittersdorfiana* by Carl Krebs (1900). Another interesting Dittersdorf work which has been reprinted in modern times is *Il Combattimento dell'umani Passioni* (pride, humility, gentleness, contentedness, madness, constancy, vivacity).

CHAPTER 3

Nature Pieces and Battle Symphonies

Some of the works discussed in the last chapter seemed to anticipate the mood of the nineteenth century, when programme music was given an enormous fillip by Romanticism. With the links between music and the sister arts of painting and literature becoming ever closer the pressure on music to become more explicit and meaningful was intense. The mere manipulation of musical figures was no longer sufficient; the figures themselves had to be characteristic, descriptive or allusive, the manipulation significant. If a composer did write 'absolute' music it was apt to be misunderstood, and even the best commentators found it necessary to 'interpret' such music. It goes without saying that the misunderstanding extended to older music. In an eighteenth-century symphony the 'themes' (melodies or melodic fragments) and the 'non-themes' (the orchestral *tuttis*) are both essential to the musical structure. But it was possible to attach 'meanings' to the 'themes' but not to the 'non-themes'; so the 'meaningless' *tuttis* began to be seen as superfluous, as excrescences—the 'rattling of dishes between the courses'. It is perhaps one merit of the battle pieces to be discussed later that they suggested one way of attaching 'meaning' to apparently 'empty' passages like scales, arpeggios and broken chords. The tendency to seek non-musical 'meanings' in absolute music endured all through the nineteenth century and has lasted to our own times.

A factor of great importance was the changed attitude towards the means of sound production. New techniques in orchestration combined with refinements of instrumental manufacture opened out new vistas for the composer. It was a two-way traffic, new musical concepts demanding new attitudes towards music's raw material, sound, and new instrumental techniques and sounds themselves stimulating composers to fresh adventures. The wider range of colours available in the orchestra and on that other new instrument, the piano, can be likened to discoveries in the visual arts such as the invention of oil painting and the deployment of perspective. Older music, like the paintings of the old masters, was clear, in focus; there was no *chiaroscuro*, no haze, no distance to 'lend enchantment to the view'. This is broadly true of music up to the time of Beethoven, who in this as in so many respects is a watershed between the old and the new. The Ninth symphony, for example, begins in a haze; but the great tune bursts through the mist like a massive mountain peak—solid, almost tangible, and sharply outlined. In Bach's music, on the other hand, it is hard to say which themes, if any, in his polyphony are subordinate, in fact the question is almost irrelevant. The harpsichord's clear and even tone put each 'theme' in the foreground, in the clear light of day. By contrast the vast new range of nineteenth-century instrumental colour and dynamics meant that there was an almost infinite gradation of emphasis, in foreground, middle distance and background, with an associated range of possible 'meanings' at all levels from the most obvious to the most recondite. No wonder commentators have been tempted to read into music almost subliminal powers of association in the minds of listeners.

The most important and far-reaching programmatic work of the early nineteenth century was certainly Beethoven's symphony, No. 6, composed in 1808—important not only as a work of art in its own right, but for the fact that it was by Beethoven, who thereby gave the programme symphony the seal of respectability. It is the culmination of a long line of precedents.[1] The pastoral tradition can be followed in Italy from Virgil's *Eclogues* (an 'eclogue' is 'a short poem, especially pastoral dialogue'), through Boccaccio, Giovanni Battista Guarini's *Il Pastor Fido* and the Italian pastoral drama, whence it makes its way into opera (Monteverdi's *Orfeo*, Lully's *Acis et Galathée*), masque and ballet. But it was early taken over by instrumental music, and Sandberger cites a purely instrumental *Sonata pastorale* for two violins, viola, trombone and lute, written by Fr. Fiamengo in 1637, which he sees as the origin of the Christmas shepherd-symphony. Pastorals begin to appear in *concerti grossi* towards the end of the seventeenth century; one by Giovanni Lorenzo, of Lucca (1698) is named by Sandberger. Giuseppe Torelli (c. middle of seventeenth century—c. 1708) has a *Pastorale per il*

---

[1] See the two essays on Beethoven's *Pastoral* symphony, 'Zu den geschichtlichen Voraussetzung' and 'Mehr Ausdruck der Empfindung als Malerei' in Adolf Sandberger's *Augewählte Aufsätze* . . . Vol. 2 (Munich, 1924).

santissimo Natale in his Op. 8 published in 1709, which thus precedes the better known Corelli's 'Christmas' concerto of 1712. Another 6/8 movement in a *concerto grosso* by Manfredini has been suggested by Schering[2] as the pattern for Handel's 'Pastoral Symphony' in his *Messiah*.

However that may be, the rocking, 6/8 or 12/8 movement over a stationary bass can be found in movements by Lully, Campra, Bach, Gluck, Gossec, through Beethoven to Berlioz and later. There are keyboard examples by Bernardo Pasquini (1637-1710), Domenico Scarlatti (1685-1757), Girolamo Frescobaldi, Couperin le Grand, Louis Daquin (1694-1772), Johann Georg Walther (1684-1748), Johann Pachelbel (1635-1706) and Johann Caspar Kerll (1627-93).[3] Two of the movements of Beethoven's *Pastoral* symphony follow this compound time tradition—the slow movement ('Scene by the brook')—and the last movement—' a 'shepherd's hymn of gratitude and thankfulness', in 6/8 time, with a characteristic arpeggio theme which ambles along in a gently rustic manner.

Another interesting work which Beethoven may have known is a quintet by Luigi Boccherini (1743-1805), Op. XIII.6 (1771) in which there is 'Une scène champêtre, où le chant des oiseaux se marie au son villageoise'.[4] There is a lark, a quail and a cuckoo. The cuckoo, of course, is a 'natural'; it is one of the few birds whose call can be translated directly into a recognisable western scale. The characteristic dotted rhythm of the quail's song had been employed a year or two before by Beethoven, in a song, *Der Wachtelschlag*, in which the quail's rhythm was linked to:

♩. ♪ ♩   ♩.♪ ♩

'Furchte Gott', 'lobe Gott', 'danke Gott', 'bitte Gott', 'traue Gott'.

It is hard to say whether Beethoven had these words even subconsciously in mind when he wrote the movement, but they do express his own simple faith and, by implication, that of the peasants in the countryside.

The storm, which rages realistically in Beethoven and more

---

[2] In his *Geschichte des Oratorium* (Leipzig, 1911).
[3] Pasquini's *Pastorale* is reprinted in Torchi, *L'Arte musicale in Italia* Vol. III; Daquin's *Livre de Noël*, in which pastoral and Christmas themes are linked, is in Guilmant's *Archives des Maîtres de l'Orgue*; Kerll's *Capriccio der Steyrische Hirt* is in *DTB* Jg. II/2 (1901).
[4] Quoted from Picquet, *Notice sur la vie et les oeuvres de Luigi Boccherini* (1851). A modern edition of the quintet is published by Schott, edited Volbach.

poetically in Berlioz's *Symphonie fantastique*, has a long ancestry in opera. As we have seen, storms were progressively invading instrumental music, but eighteenth-century ones were rather tame affairs compared with Beethoven's torrential rain and Jovian thunderclaps. They were so popular that attempts were made to adapt them to the keyboard, but the piano by itself did not offer the scope that the full orchestra did, especially when the latter was augmented by the timpani. These had been in use, though sporadically, in the opera at least since the time of Lully, in the first instance it seems largely for their military associations. They gained ground in the symphony orchestra rather slowly; the impressive roll at the beginning of Haydn's Symphony No. 103, in E flat, was still at that time (1795) exceptional. The roll was not, I think, a feature of Mozart's symphonic writing, though he used it operatically, in *Don Giovanni* and elsewhere. Beethoven used it freely in all his works.

If the piano seemed restricted[5] there was, however, another keyboard instrument which offered possibilities, and that was the organ. Its early use in oratorios can often only be inferred, since the organ parts were not written out in full. But we know it was used illustratively in Handel's oratorios, and it certainly played its part in depicting the earthquake in the *St Matthew Passion*. It may be doubted whether Bach ever permitted himself to unleash the full fury of the organ during extemporizations to imitate thunder and lightning, but the gifted though erratic Abt Vogler (1749-1814), Weber's teacher, had no compunction in doing so. His restless career took him all over Europe including Vienna (where he met Beethoven). His organ extemporizations included *The Fall of the Walls of Jericho*; an attempt at representing in sound a picture by Rubens, *The Last Judgement*; and—very popular—thunderstorms. One that is described in Sandberger is *Spazierfahrt auf dem Rhein Mit dazwischen-kommenden Donnerwetter* ('a journey down the Rhine interrupted by a thunderstorm') which seems to anticipate Beethoven's peasants' merrymaking and their interruption by a storm. *The Fall of the Walls of Jericho* and the Rhine journey with its thunderstorms were both in a programme Vogler gave in the Mariakirche in Berlin on 29 November, 1800, and a contemporary reference in the Leipzig *Allgemeine Musik-Zeitung* describes how the effect of thunder was produced by playing several adjacent pedal

---

[5] The late eighteenth-early nineteenth-century piano, that is; later it became a useful vehicle for the effects Liszt demanded.

notes at the same time, while the tumbling walls of Jericho were simulated by putting both arms on the manuals, with full organ —note-clusters with a vengeance, long before Henry Cowell!

Another of Vogler's pupils was Justin Heinrich Knecht (1752-1817). Of his many compositions two are pertinent to our discussions One, for organ, entitled *Die durch ein Donnerwetter unterbrochene Hirtenvonne* ('Shepherds' rejoicings interrupted by a thunderstorm'), was published in 1794 with not only a detailed scenario of the work but a preface giving instructions as to how the various effects could be produced on the organ. The other, which was also published (in orchestral parts, not in score), is especially interesting for its anticipation, in intent if not in effect, of Beethoven's *Pastoral* symphony.[6] It is a symphony, in five movements, with title and headings of each movement in French, as follows:

> Le Portrait musical de la Nature ou Grande Symphonie à deux Violons, Alte et Basse, avec deux Flûtes traversières, deux Hautbois, Fagotts, Cors, Trompettes et Timbals *ad libitum*. La quelle va exprime par le moyen des sons:
> 1. Une belle Contrée ou le Soleil luit, les doux Zephires voltigent, les Russeaux traversent le vallon, les oiseaux gazouillant, un torrent tomb du haut en murmurent, le berger siffle, les moutons lautent et la bergère fait entendre sa douce voix.
> 2. Le ciel commence à devenir soudain et sombre, tout le voisinage a de la peine de respirer et s'effraye, les nuages noirs montent, les vents se mettent a faire un bruit, le tonnerre gronde de loin et l'orage approche à pas lents.
> 3. L'Orage accompagné des vents murmurans et des pluies battans gronde avec toute la force, les sommets des arbres font un murmure et le torrent roule ses eaux avec un bruit épouvantable.
> 4. L'Orage s'appaise peu à peu, les nuages se dissipent et le ciel devient clair.
> 5. La Nature transportée de la joie éléve sa voix vers le ciel et rend au créateur le plus vives grâces par des chants doux et agréables.

This last movement has a subtitle, 'L'Inno con variazioni'; it will be recalled that Beethoven's fifth movement is likewise entitled 'The Shepherds' Hymn—Thanksgiving after the storm'. The work,

[6] There are copies of the parts in the library of the Royal College of Music.

dedicated to Vogler, was published in 1784, and is thus a very early example of the *genre* programme-symphony; unfortunately Knecht's musical invention is hardly a match for his ambition.

Over and over again in Beethoven's *Pastoral* symphony we see the composer seizing on established practices and improving on them. The instrumental depiction of running water, which finds such wonderful expression in the second movement ('Scene by the brook'), was an idea of long standing. Choral music provides some fine examples. Beethoven may or may not have known Handel's *Acis and Galatea*, with its gently meandering stream in the final movement, but he certainly knew Haydn's brilliant 'Rollend in schaümenden Wellen' ('rolling in foaming billows', No. 6 of *The Creation*). Singers are most familiar with this aural illusion in Schubert's songs, which show a marvellously varied approach to the problem. But Schubert was a younger man, and the *Pastoral* symphony was written some years before Schubert's first extant song, and many years before examples such as those in *Die schöne Müllerin* (1823). It was left to Beethoven to demonstrate how this descriptive writing could become the bones and sinew of a large-scale purely instrumental movement. The last movement, too, shows Beethoven setting his own individual seal on material drawn from the common stock. Any theme derived from the notes of the common chord that jogs along in an easy rhythm has by long association become suggestive of rural, open air scenes. They recall the open notes of the huntsman's horn or the Alphorn. German commentators have coined the useful tag *Natur Laut*, or nature theme, for this. The main theme of the last movement belongs to this type, as do a number of themes from other works including the last movement of the violin concerto (1806).

Though the piano on its own might be too weak for the fury of the tempest it was a different matter when it joined with the orchestra in a concerto. In about 1798 Daniel Steibelt (1765-1823) was responsible for a piano concerto, the last movement of which was 'L'Orage précédé d'un Rondeau'. An alternative title which appears in some editions, and which is an even more illuminating commentary on the taste of the times, is 'pastorale: Rondo in which is introduced an imitation of a Storm'. It was immensely popular in its day and for long after; the British Library possesses printed copies of the 'Storm' movement dating from about 1805 to as late as 1909. The Rondo theme, it will be seen, bears a strong family likeness to many Beethoven 'nature' themes:

The storm begins with a threatening rumble on B (the dominant of the main key) after the first return of the rondo theme, and a few bars later bursts out in full fury in C major, 'Piano Forte with full orchestra' and lasts for some fifty bars (Niecks calls it 'happily of short duration') of *Allegro moderato*, C time. Over a left hand *tremolando* the right hand plays forceful descending arpeggios in octaves, in a texture that is not unfamiliar in Beethoven (eg, in the D minor piano sonata, Op. 31.2 (1802). Despite Niecks's strictures the work is not without merit.

The pictorial concerto was continued by the Irishman John Field (1782-1837), whose fifth piano concerto in C major is subtitled 'L'Incendie par l'orage' — a most interesting work, with some virtuoso handling of the piano *à la* Chopin. The storm this time is in the first movement, and Field has supplied a reinforcing second piano part for this because, as he says, 'un seul pianoforte seroit trop faible pour exprimer l'orage'. This second piano part mainly doubles the passage work in the principal solo part, in unison, octaves or thirds, but every so often it adds to the rumble of the storm by playing low down in the piano's range, with the sustaining pedal directed to be held down throughout the bar.

The orchestration deserves a glance. The work is scored for the usual strings (but with violas *divisi*), one flute, two clarinets, two bassoons, two horns, two clarini (trumpets), one bass trombone and two timpani. The trombone has nothing very distinctive to do; its place in the symphony orchestra was still a little uncertain at the time when this was written (1818 or thereabouts). The timpani on the other hand are used with enterprise, and in one passage with an almost Berliozian care over detail:

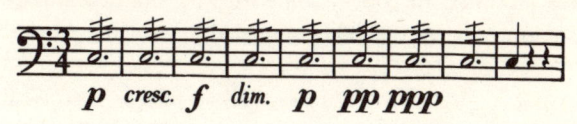

After the storm Field introduces a little instrument, unusual for the period—a bell; while at the height of the storm he calls for a tremendous stroke on the gong, *fff*. This must be one of the earliest, if not actually the first, instance of a gong being employed in the symphony orchestra, though no doubt there are some examples in the literature of the opera. Neither the work nor its composer, by the way, is mentioned in Niecks.

Beethoven's other ambitious pictorial symphony, *Wellingtons Sieg oder die Schlacht bei Vittoria* (1813) was also, like the *Pastoral* symphony, a culminating point in a movement that had lasted for about thirty years. It was the most famous, or notorious, of a large number of such descriptive works, some of which are discussed below.

This kind of 'descriptive fantasia' for which there was a great vogue in the 1790s continued its hold over at least some sections of the populace until well into the nineteenth century, and indeed the monster performances that are not infrequently staged in London's Albert Hall even today of Tchaikowsky's *1812 Overture* show that the attraction is still there. In the mid-nineteenth century that good musician and arch-showman, Louis Jullien, knew the box-office value of such works. J. W. Davison in his *From Mendelssohn to Wagner* gives a detailed and entertaining account of the quadrille, *The Fall of Sebastopol* 'which was the great feature in this season's (ie, 1854) Jullien concerts'. The *'analyse synoptique'* or programme note[7] quoted by Davison (page 201) runs as follows:

The first figure, commencing *pp* with drums and trumpets heard in the distance, represents the advance of the English, French and Turks. The second exemplified the bivouac of the French in the trenches, the ophicleide introducing 'Partant pour la Syrie', severally varied by two flutes, a piccolo, a flageolet and four cornets. The third figure contained a Piedmontese 'Monferina' interwoven with a march. No. 4 was a reconnaissance in the Valley of Baidar, with a movement of cavalry, followed by a dialogue of the Chiefs (on two cornets)—the cavalry gradually disappearing in the distance. In the fifth and last figure, the Malakoff and Redan were stormed, and the music was intended to convey some idea of 'the deafening noise of exploding mines, the roar of cannons, the whistling of the bullets,

---

[7] The analytical programme note had been initiated a few years before by John Ella.

NATURE PIECES AND BATTLE SYMPHONIES

the hurtling of the shells, the rattling of the drums, the shrill sound of the trumpets, the ships blown into the air, the cries of the fugitives and the shouts of the victors'. To relieve all this noise an episode, in the shape of a recitative on the ophicleide, represented the dying of a Zouave, while the Russian retreat was described in a fugue with respect to which we read in the *Musical World*, 'The effect of the Principal Theme, given out by the brass instruments with "augmentation", as the Contrapuntists call it, after an elaborately worked out pedal point of theme and episode near the end, is very powerful'. A climax to the whole was *Partant pour la Syrie* and *God Save the Queen*.

A number of these 'descriptive fantasias' or battle pieces, especially by Daniel Steibelt and Jan Ladislav Dussek (1761-1812) are listed in Niecks.[8] One from 1783 is described by Burney:[9] 'A more successful attempt at musical painting was made in the spring of 1783, in London, with *instruments*, by M. Kloffer, a German musician, who undertook to imitate by sounds, in a kind of *musical pantomime*, every circumstance belonging to an army, even to a *council of war*.' This was surpassed, in Burney's estimation, 'by the *bataglia* of Sigr. Raimondi' which, he says, has been applauded for the ingenuity of its effects, and for its merits as a composition.

But the work that far exceeded these two in popularity was *The Battle of Prague*, by Franz Kotzwara (born? d.1791), a Czech composer who came to England some time in the 1780s and who died in London. Written in about 1788 it commemorates the Battle of Prague, fought on 6 May, 1757, when the Austrians (the Imperialists) were defeated by the Prussians. Written for pianoforte or harpsichord (the harpsichord in the title is a concession to a dying instrument; not everyone had the increasingly popular pianoforte in his home), bass and drum, its scheme is as follows:

> An opening Slow March, sixteen bars, F major, C time
> Largo — Word of Command, four bars (a bugle call)
> First signal cannon (octave C, in the bass)
> The Bugle Call for the Cavalry (C major, seven and a quarter bars of C time — a fanfare on the chord of C)
> Answer to the first Signal Cannon (octave F, bottom F)
> The Trumpet Call (fanfare, F major; interrupted by)

---

[8] For a more comprehensive and detailed treatment see Elsa Bienefeld, 'Über ein bestimmtes Problem der programmusik (Darstellung von Schlachten)', in *ZIM* Jg. VIII Heft 5 (1907).

[9] *History of Music*, edited Frank Mercer, Volume two page 213.

Cannon (a slur of four notes upwards to low F, *ff*)
The Attack: Prussian, Imperialists.

This is the longest and most descriptive section. It begins *allegro*, F major, C time, with an Alberti bass in the left hand, chords and running semiquavers in the right. Cannon interrupts. Then comes a *tremolando* chord, RH, while LH plays arpeggios crossing over the right, to represent 'flying bullets'. This continues for some time while the music moves to C major, where the roles of the two hands are reversed. There is a fanfare, C major, 'Trumpets and Kettledrums'. We now move to G minor for an Attack with Swords, Horses galloping (LH Alberti bass, triplet quavers). The Light Dragoons then advance, in B flat — Trumpets and Cannon — followed by a Heavy Cannonade in C minor; then, over a rumbling pedal G, 'Cannons and drums in general'. 'Running fire', follows — scale passages in alternate hands leading to a climax. A fanfare in F major, similar to the first, with cannon, is the 'Trumpet of recall'. The cries of the wounded are heard (F minor); then comes the Trumpet of Victory and *God Save the King*. After a Turkish March the works ends with a Finale, *allegro*, in F major and 2/4 time.

A popular theme was *Admiral Duncan's Naval Victory of 11 October, 1797*; both Dussek and Steibelt contributed examples on this subject of what Niecks called 'this unholy class of programme music'. Steibelt's was printed by the London firm of Longman and Broderip and also (in 1800) by Imbault of Paris. He called it *Britannia: an Allegorical Overture*, and dedicated it to 'his most Gracious Majesty the KING OF GREAT BRITAIN ec., ec. '. It begins with an *Adagio maestoso* in E flat — 'The stillness of the Night . . .', 'The Waves of the sea . . .' (a sort of nocturne, not unpoetically done). When the fleet sails (*Allegretto*, C major, 6/8) the music expresses 'The roaring of the sea . . . Joy on sight of the enemy . . . Signal to engage'. The heart of the piece, the battle proper, is in G major, *Allegro moderato*, later quickened to *Allegro assai* for 'cannon . . . Discharge of small Arms . . . Falling of the mast . . . The cries of the wounded'. After *Rule, Britannia* the fleet returns victorious, with a repeat of the earlier *Allegretto*. The piece ends, after recalling the opening *Adagio*, with *God Save the King*.

In its exploitation of a wide range of dynamics from *ff* to *pp* and the employment of *crescendi* and *diminuendi* this is authentic piano music. The idea and its execution may charitably be described as naïve. Dussek's companion piece, '*The Naval Battle and Total*

NATURE PIECES AND BATTLE SYMPHONIES

Defeat of the Grand Dutch Fleet by Admiral Duncan on the 11th October 1797. A characteristic Sonata for the Piano Forte composed and dedicated to Viscount Duncan by J. L. Dussek', treats the same subject in a very similar manner but with somewhat more musical resource. There is a wider range of harmony, with more chromaticism; pedal points and climaxes are managed well, and the whole piece has a romantic flavour suggestive of early Beethoven.

We may profitably glance at one or two others of this very numerous class of compositions. *The Siege of Valenciennes* (c. 1793) begins with 'March of the British Forces — Duke of York summons the Garrison to surrender — French governor answers'. We then have 'Britons strike home' (this appears in several including Steibelt's battle). The Siege itself is very dramatic: 'Batteries open — Heavy cannonade — Attack with swords — Fire of small arms — Mine sprung (this is depicted by a rapid ascending scale)' — and so on, thirteen pages in all. The Duke of York enters Valenciennes to the strains of *See the conquering Hero comes*. A sonata 'In commemoration of the glorious 1st of August 1798' entitled *Nelson and the Navy* by Joseph Dale begins with four bars of *La Marseillais* (sic); its most striking feature is a passage labelled 'L'Orient blown up' illustrated by a rapid scale passage in both hands ascending through four octaves. Another interesting work, though not a battle piece, is by N. Sampieri, and published in 1799 — 'A novel, sublime, and celestial, piece of music, called night'. Its five parts, embellished with five plates, are headed: Evening, Midnight, Aurora, Daylight, The Rising of the Sun. The first, *Andante sostenuto* in E flat, is almost impressionistic. 'Midnight' is full of tremolos, 'to be played with pedal as soft as possible' (the damper pedal is presumably meant) to suggest 'The Horror of the Night'. 'Aurora' begins with 'Notes of various Birds', and thrush, blackbird and goldfinch are mentioned.

These and others by minor composers such as T. H. Butler and Theodore Bridault were all published in London, where Kotzwara, Steibelt and Dussek were living; but the continent did not lag behind. In Paris, for example, were published a *Grande Sinfonia La Bataille de Martinutie à la Gloire de S.A. Msgr. le Prince de Saxe Cobourg*, by F. C. Neubauer (1794); *La Grande Bataille d'Austerlitz*, by Louis Jadin, for orchestra; *La Bataille de Gemappe*, by Devienne (1796; Steibelt had one on the same subject). In Vienna there were works by Wanhal (*Die Schlacht bei Wurzburg 3 September 1796 — Ein Militärisch heroisches Musikstück für Clavier*

(1799) and *Seeschlacht bei Abukir*), Kauer (*Sonata militaire la Prise d'Oczakow*), and others.

However trite and childish these may appear, the profusion of battle-pieces composed in the unsettled years following the French Revolution suggests that they may have fulfilled some emotional need. Our twentieth century outlets are the cinema and television, whereby mankind experiences excitement, danger, distress and pain, vicariously and visually, together with music and 'effects' that are the twentieth century's equivalent to Admiral Duncan's cannonades. And the 'cries of the wounded' that figure in so many of the battle pieces are no more, and no less, lacking in taste than the depiction of such piteous scenes as were shown for example in the BBC's epic, *War and Peace*. But we should err, I think, if we attempted to credit these composers with any intentions of rousing the consciences of peoples and nations to the horrors of war or to any sense of disgust with themselves. If there were any catharsis, or purification through pity, it was subconscious and quite unintentional. It is equally futile to look for social commentary in Beethoven's *Battle of Vittoria*; if instrumental music has any moral comment to make (which is debatable) it is to the absolute music of the symphony or the string quartet that we must turn.

The suggestion that Beethoven should write a battle symphony seems to have come from his friend Maelzel (1772-1838), who besides inventing the metronome is important in the history of mechanical musical instruments. These were already in existence in the eighteenth century (both Haydn and Mozart had written for musical clocks), and in 1792 Maelzel had produced one that could reproduce flutes, trumpets, drums, cymbals, triangle and strings struck by hammers. He continued to work on improvements and in 1804 he built what he called a 'Panharmonicon' which could reproduce the music of an entire orchestra.[10] In 1813 he suggested to Beethoven that he should write a work for his Panharmonicon to commemorate Wellington's victory over the French under Jerome Bonaparte, at Vittoria on 21 June, 1813. He also seems to have outlined to Beethoven some of the details such as the use of *God Save the King* and *Malbrouk s'en va-t-en Guerre* to symbolize the English and

---

[10] See *Harvard Dictionary of Music*, Art. 'Mechanical instruments'. Nettl, however, in the *Beethoven Encyclopedia* defines it as 'a mechanical orchestra consisting of trumpet, clarinet, viola and cello'.

French respectively. He had rosy plans of taking both the composer and his Panharmonicon to London, but that project came to naught. After scoring the work for Maelzel's instrument Beethoven made a version for full orchestra, in which form it had several performances in Vienna in December 1813 and January 1814. The score, dedicated to the Prince Regent of England, was sent to London during April or May, 1814, and its first performance in this country took place on 10 February, 1815 under Sir George Smart.

The work is in two parts, the Battle, and a 'Sieges-Symphonie' which is a song of triumph, ending with variations on our national anthem. The battle begins with the two sides drawn up facing each other, the English represented by *Rule, Britannia* and the French by *Malbrouk*, scored for wind only, but later on the full orchestra. The French 'challenge' (trumpet fanfare) is answered by the English, and the battle begins. The score, liberally peppered with 'cannons', lacks the copious commentary of Dussek or Steibelt, but the intentions are much the same. The defeat of the French is whimsically implied by a version of *Malbrouk* in F sharp minor, dying away to *pianissimo*, before the triumphant last movement bursts in in D major.

Though it is impossible to take the work seriously (Grove in his classic study *Beethoven and his Nine Symphonies* does not bestow it so much as a glance) it is more than a mere curiosity, and it may have had more significance in Beethoven's development than has been realized. It was his last symphony but one (the seventh and eighth had been completed in 1812); thereafter he wrote no more absolute orchestral music. The only subsequent orchestral works were the Ninth symphony (itself programmatic, whether or not we agree with Schering's interpretations of the first three movements) and the two overtures, *Namensfeier* Op. 115 (1814) and *Die Weihe des Hauses* Op. 124 (1822), neither of which is entirely absolute music. Then, too, there are certain traits such as the profusion of shakes on long, sustained notes and the quasi-fugal treatment of *God Save the King* in the second part of the work that point to the style of his third period. A close study of the work might yield valuable clues to aid our understanding of his thought during the last fifteen years of his life.

PART II

Programme Music and Romanticism

CHAPTER 4

Tone Poem and Programme Symphony from Weber to Spohr

Before we look at the nineteenth-century programme symphony we must pick up one or two threads that are important in the discussion. The first composer to catch our attention is Carl Maria von Weber (1786–1826), with two works that are unquestionably programmatic in the strictest sense of the term. They are the *Aufforderung zum Tanze* (the Invitation to the Dance) for piano, and the *Concertstück* for piano and orchestra.

Though Weber had been drawn into Vogler's circle, first when he visited Vienna in 1803 at the impressionable age of seventeen, when he spent some hours each day studying with him,[1] and later at Darmstadt, in 1810, he never subscribed wholeheartedly to Vogler's programmatic ideas. It is true that his purely instrumental compositions, which include symphonies, concertos and chamber music, reveal him as uneasy without verbal inspiration, yet on the other hand he has confessed, in a letter to his friend Lichtenstein and elsewhere, that he was opposed to the 'descriptive fantasia' type of composition as practised by Dussek and Steibelt. Nevertheless there are passages in his patriotic songs *Leyer und Schwert* (1814) where the roar of cannon and the smoke of battle are, if one wishes, as much in evidence as the inner restlessness and anxiety which Weber desired to evoke, and portions of the operas, particularly the 'Wolf's Glen' scene in *Der Freischütz*, are as specific and descriptive as one could wish. But that was later, in 1821; and there is some evidence to suggest that composers become more programmatically minded as they grow older.

The *Aufforderung zum Tanze*, published in 1821, had been written earlier, in 1819, and even this is only the date of the final draft, for we know that some of the material goes back many years. It was

---

[1] See John Warrack, *Carl Maria von Weber* (London, 1968), p. 49.

dedicated to his wife, the singer Caroline Brandt, whom he had married in 1817, and it was she who furnished the details of the scenario. On the face of it it is a string of waltzes, framed between an interlude and a postlude, in the loose, episodic form favoured by Johann Strauss, and which Chopin copied. But Weber himself gave the following explanation:

> The scene is a ballroom. A young man approaches his intended partner; his invitation to dance, at first meeting with a coy, evasive answer, is pressed more ardently. She accepts, and they engage in some light conversation while they await the commencement of the waltz. After the dance he returns her to her seat and takes his farewell.

The work, redolent of old-world charm and gallantry, is now probably less familiar in its original form than in the orchestral arrangement by Berlioz, who used it as part of a ballet in *Der Freischütz* when that work was revived at the Paris Opéra in 1841; or as the music to another ballet, *Le Spectre de la Rose*.

The *Concertstück* hides its programme under a noncommittal title. Weber again gave the details when in 1821 he played the newly completed work to his wife and his young friend, Julius Benedict. Here is the programme as Benedict related it:

> The lady sits in her tower; she gazes sadly into the distance. Her knight has been for years in the Holy Land; will she ever see him again? Battles have been fought; but no news of him who is so dear to her. In vain have been all her prayers. A fearful vision rises to her mind — her knight is lying on the battlefield deserted and alone: his heart's blood is ebbing fast away. Could she but be by his side! — could she but die with him! She falls exhausted and senseless. But hark! What is that distant sound? What glimmers in the sunlight from the wood? What are those forms approaching? Knights and squires with the cross of the Crusades, banners waving, acclamations of the people, and there! it is he! She sinks into his arms. Love is triumphant. Happiness without end. The very woods and waves sing the song of love; a thousand voices proclaim its victory.[2]

The work is contemporary with *Der Freischütz*, being finished on the very morning of the *première* in Berlin, but its origins go back to 1815. In that year Weber wrote to his friend Rochlitz that he was at work on a concerto, and his words are worth quoting:

---

[2] See Julius Benedict, *Carl Maria von Weber* (London, 1881), p. 66.

I have an F minor piano concerto planned. But as concertos in the minor without definite, evocative ideas seldom work with the public, I have instinctively inserted into the whole thing a kind of story whose thread will connect and define its character—moreover, one so detailed and at the same [time?] dramatic that I found myself obliged to give it the following headings: Allegro, Parting. Adagio, Lament. Finale, Profoundest misery, consolation, reunion, jubilation.[3]

This is a sort of expansion of the scheme adumbrated by Beethoven in his 'Lebewohl' Sonata Op. 81a written in 1809, its movements headed *Les Adieux; l'Absence; Le Retour*. There is even some similarity of material, certainly in mood. (The definitive form of the *Concertstück*, in four connecting sections, *Larghetto*, *Allegro*, *Tempo di Marcia* and *Presto*, modifies the early draft considerably.) Weber's simple and touching little story is admirably reflected in the sweet melancholy of the opening, the proud march symbolizing knight-errantry, and the mild hysteria of the final reunion.

When *Der Freischütz* was first performed one of the younger members of the audience was Felix Mendelssohn-Bartholdy, then aged twelve.[4] Weber was already one of his idols, and the new opera with all its wealth of fresh orchestral colour held him spellbound. The experience was shortly to bear fruit in Mendelssohn's first orchestral masterpiece, the *Midsummer Night's Dream* overture. The urge to compose such a work, already stirring in his mind through the intensive Shakespeare studies he was pursuing, was further stimulated by the knowledge that Weber had been commissioned to write for London an opera, *Oberon*, based ultimately on Shakespeare's play. *Oberon* was begun early in 1825, when Weber was living in Dresden. He went to Berlin, where Mendelssohn was still living, to conduct the first performance of *Euryanthe* in that city (23 December, 1825). He naturally visited the Mendelssohns, where he played numbers from his still unfinished *Oberon*.[5] One of these was perhaps the Mermaid's song, 'O' tis pleasant to float on the sea'; at any rate a little four-bar phrase from

---

[3] Quoted from Warrack, *Op. cit.*, p. 236.
[4] Benedict, *op. cit*, p. 67. H. E. Jacob in *Felix Mendelssohn and his Times* (p. 14) has a pleasant anecdote of how young Felix, too shy to ride with Weber in the carriage his father had sent to bring him home from the Berlin opera, had instead raced home to open the carriage door for him.
[5] Schima Kaufman, *Mendelssohn, 'a second Elijah'* (New York, 1934) p. 99.

this, in barcarolle rhythm ('And the last faint light of the sun hath fled'), assumes considerable importance in the overture, and looks and sounds like a conscious tribute to Weber. The overture was completed after Weber's death, and received a resplendent first performance at Stettin on 20 February, 1827 under Carl Loewe.[6]

But the significance of the work is much more deep-seated than a deliberate homage to Weber would suggest. There is first of all the astonishing command of the orchestra, unprecedented in a boy of seventeen.[7] As yet there was no treatise on orchestration, but this mattered little for, like all great orchestrators, Mendelssohn used his ears and his imagination, with results that continue to enthral us. From the first four strange chords on the woodwind[8] to the serene coda there is scarcely a bar to criticize; the control and assurance are superlative. Even more amazing is the conception of the work, for it is the first example we have of a whole play being translated into instrumental music. Other overtures, for example Beethoven's to Goethe's *Egmont*, had sought to transmute the spirit of the play, but here we see practically the complete *dramatis personae*—the lovers, Duke Theseus and Queen Hippolyta, Bottom and his 'translation' (with realistic brayings), together with his comrades: and above all Titania, Oberon, Puck and his fairy host. The opening warns us that this is a land of enchantment, and the spell is reinforced by the eerie chord which interrupts the fairies' music at bar thirty-nine. The thistledown lightness of fairy music had been hinted at in Weber's *Oberon*, but this etherealized, unsubstantial weightlessness of the spirit world was Mendelssohn's own.

A Midsummer Night's Dream is the most detailed, one might say the most factual, of his programme overtures. His next, an interpretation of Goethe's poem *Meerestille und Glückliche Fahrt* (1828), is much less tangible. It would be wrong to call this study of the calm, immobile, threatening sea (threatening on account of its immobility; in the days of sailing ships a sailor's livelihood depended on the wind) the beginnings of Impressionism in music, for Schubert in setting the first part of Goethe's poem in 1815 had depicted the same utter stillness in his song *Meeres Stille*. But it was the first of the orchestral 'seascapes'—the equivalent in music of the marine pictures

---

[6] At the same concert Mendelssohn played Weber's *Concertstück*.
[7] It was originally written for piano duet, to be played by himself and his sister Fanny.
[8] His teacher Adolf Bernard Marx is reputed to have said, of these chords, 'A new music begins here'.

TONE POEM AND PROGRAMME-SYMPHONY

by his English contemporaries Turner and Bonington. A more vivid one, and one more distinctly programmatic, was to emerge during the next year, when he journeyed to Britain and made that memorable visit to Staffa in the footsteps of Dr Johnson. The impression as he stood in the awesome Fingal's Cave, overwhelmed by the grandeur of the scene, was no doubt fused in his mind with the memory of the stormy three-day crossing from Hamburg to London a short while before, when he had been prostrated with sea-sickness, and like Wagner later he was able to sublimate his experiences into a magnificent music-graph of the changing moods of the sea.[9]

Not long after *Fingal's Cave* received its first performance in London Mendelssohn was busy on another tone-poem (for despite the conventional title, 'overture', that is what these pieces really are). This was *Melusina*, written at Düsseldorf, where he had gone in May 1833 to direct the Lower Rhine Festival.[10] The inspiration for this, as he relates in a letter to his sister dated 7 April, 1834, was Conradin Kreutzer's opera *Melusine*, which he heard in Berlin in 1833. The libretto, by the Austrian poet and dramatist Franz Grillparzer, is a variant of the Undine-Russalka legend, which tells of 'the beautiful Melusine who is under a spell and must become a nixie every seventh day. She has made her husband swear not to attempt to discover the reason for her disappearance on this seventh day. Under the proddings of his kinsfolk, the knight breaks his vow, whereupon his wife must take leave of husband and children and live forever as a water-nymph'.[11] In the slightly different version in Brewer's *Reader's Handbook* Melusine becomes a serpent every Saturday, and her fate is 'to roam about the world as a ghost till the day of doom'.

This overture, it will be seen, combines the two themes that had animated his previous overtures, namely, the supernatural and water;[12] it was a combination to come to full fruition a few years later

---

[9] Though the impact was immediate, and immediately productive, the *Hebrides* overture seems to have given him more trouble than usual. The letter home giving the main B minor theme of the overture was dated 7 August, 1829. The overture in its first form was not completed until his Italian visit in 1830; a letter to his father from Rome dated 20 December, 1830 says 'The "Hebrides" is completed at last, and a strange production it is'. It was not performed until 14 May, 1832 when it was given, with some revisions, at a Philharmonic Society concert and was received rather coolly. The work is discussed in a most interesting article by Gerald Abraham in *The Monthly Musical Record*, September, 1948.

[10] The Dusseldorf visits were of great interest and importance; see below p. 66.

[11] Quoted from Jacob, *Op. cit.*, p. 309.

[12] The operatic project, on Geibel's *Loreley*, which he was seriously considering in 1847, the year of his death, also contained the two themes.

in Wagner's *Fliegende Holländer* and, yet more magnificently, in *The Ring*, and indeed the undulating figure Mendelssohn created for the billowing stream occurs, transposed from F to E flat, in the prelude to *Rheingold*. But this overture does not vie with *Fingal's Cave* in descriptive power. It is more of a mood picture, a portrait of the lovely Melusina, painted against a backcloth of her element, and as such characteristic of his contact with Düsseldorf. For this was the period when he was most active as a draughtsman, taking lessons in drawing and painting from Johann Wilhelm Schirmer, who actually painted a water-colour inspired by one of Mendelssohn's piano compositions, *The Rivulet* (water again), and discussing painting and other artistic matters with Friedrich Wilhelm Schadow, the head of the Düsseldorf academy who was building the artistic reputation of that city.[13]

Though the overtures remain Mendelssohn's chief contribution to programme music his symphonies require a word or two of notice. They are programmatic only in the sense that Beethoven's *Eroica* is, in that they are the embodiments of general moods rather than attempts to be precisely pictorial. The third symphony, the *Scotch*, grew out of his visit to Scotland in 1829, and more particularly to Holyrood Palace, where he found himself moved by the tragic history of Mary, Queen of Scots and oppressed by the foreboding of the castle, then in ruins. He was more successful in catching something of this brooding melancholy than in suggesting the wildness of the Highland scene or the skirl of the bagpipes, and we have only to compare this with the rugged Abruzzi mountains and brigands in Berlioz's *Harold in Italy* to see how the well-bred Mendelssohn shied away from the primitive and unbridled.[14] It is

---

[13] There are some fascinating glimpses of Mendelssohn's activities in Düsseldorf in Elise Polko's *Reminiscences of Mendelssohn* (London, 1869, translated by Lady Wallace). This was the era of the 'tableau vivant', an entertainment to which Mendelssohn lent his support by arranging some of Beethoven's sonata movements for orchestra, which were then combined with 'tableaux vivants, arranged in rare perfection, and with the aid of beautiful female faces, and male heads full of character', to produce the most brilliant effects. The same procedure was tried with Handel's oratorios, for instance *Israel in Egypt*. 'The most renowned artists painted the decorations; the surging sea and the noblest forms of Bible history met the eye in bright and living beauty.'

[14] He found himself little in sympathy with Berlioz either as a person or a composer; he thought him undisciplined and *farouche*. The two first met in 1830 in Rome, where Berlioz was staying as a *Prix de Rome* winner.

TONE POEM AND PROGRAMME-SYMPHONY

true that there is an *fff* climax in the first movement that is almost abandoned, but the trouble is, the material both here and in the frenzied finale is too polished, too decorous, to do justice to the composer's conception.

The *Scotch* symphony, though begun in 1829, lay unfinished until 1842, when it was first performed under Mendelssohn's direction in Berlin. In Italy in 1830 he found he could not get in the right mood for continuing it, but on the other hand the blue skies, the sunshine and the clear light exerted their wonted effect on the northerner, and his fourth symphony was written fairly quickly. And again, how different this *Italian* symphony is from *Harold in Italy*, which was beginning to germinate in Berlioz's mind at about the same time! Where Berlioz is subjective and romantic, Mendelssohn is objective, almost classical. There no programme as such, but the first movement might have borrowed a motto from Beethoven, 'cheerful impressions on arriving in Italy'. The slow movement conceivably had its origins in some religious procession seen in Naples or elsewhere; the exhilarating *Saltarello* of the last movement suggests a Roman Carnival such as Berlioz introduced into his *Benvenuto Cellini* and subsequently extracted and adapted to form his *Carnaval Romain* overture.

The same year, 1830, also saw the completion of Mendelssohn's fifth symphony, the *Reformation*. It was conceived under the stimulus of the tercentenary of the 'Augsburg Confession', drawn up by Melancthon and presented by him and Martin Luther at Augsburg in 1530 to the Emperor Charles V, thereby establishing Protestantism in Germany. Mendelssohn, Jewish by race but baptized a Christian, was a Protestant. In 1829 Protestantism was very much on his mind, for on 11 March had taken place the epoch-making performance of Bach's *St Matthew Passion* in Berlin under Mendelssohn's direction. A symphony in honour of the founder of German protestantism was already gestating, along with the *Scotch* symphony, while he was in Scotland in the late summer of that year. The score was completed by the end of May 1830 (before his Italian journey), for a copy was sent to Fanny from Weimar, where Mendelssohn was staying with Goethe. He was in Paris in the early part of 1832, and the *Reformation* symphony was rehearsed by the Conservatoire orchestra, under Habeneck, but laid aside. It subsequently received some performances in England and Germany, but never made the impression or enjoyed the popularity of his other two mature symphonies. The composer himself seemed to lose interest in it, and it was not published until after his death.

1830 was an *annus mirabilis* in the history of music, for besides the works just mentioned it saw the completion of another programme-symphony which has had a far-reaching effect on the whole of music. This was the *Symphonie fantastique* of Hector Berlioz (1803-69). Writing to his friend Humbert Ferrand on 16 April, 1830 he says he has just put the finishing touches to the score, and hopes to arrange a performance, if he can get the parts copied in time, on 30 May, 'avec un orchestre de deux cent vingt musiciens'. In fact the first performance did not take place until 5 December 1830, under Habeneck, and with an orchestra considerably smaller than he had hoped for.

A glance through the titles of Berlioz's compositions reveals not a single important work that, on the face of it, can be classed as 'absolute' music. There are no self-standing sonatas or symphonies: instead we have overtures which lean on literature (*Rob Roy, Waverley, Le Roi Lear*) and symphonic structures such as *Harold en Italie* and *Roméo et Juliette* which are apparently indebted to literature in a greater or lesser degree. Of all his works the *Symphonie fantastique* has been the subject of most controversy and misunderstanding. The circumstances surrounding the composition and presentation of the work are complicated. It is beyond question that its inception was bound up with his infatuation for the Irish actress Harriet Smithson, who in the autumn of 1827 had been appearing in Paris with an English company presenting Shakespeare; his marriage to her, which turned out disastrously, took place six years later, in 1833, three years after the symphony was finished and performed. The first crisis in the affair came in 1827/28, with Berlioz in a semi-crazed state over Harriet, who was at that time scoring a considerable success, and who must have seemed almost unattainable to the young, penniless music student. He dreamed up a grand scheme to attract her attention, a concert of his own works, which would be such a success that she would be forced to notice him, to recognize him as an artist like she was. The concert duly took place, in May 1828; Harriet knew nothing of it.

Meanwhile Berlioz had been subjected to another profound, and profoundly artistic, experience—Goethe's *Faust*, in Gérhard de Nerval's translation: he at once set about the composition of his *Huit Scènes de Faust*, which later became *La Damnation de Faust*. But he

TONE POEM AND PROGRAMME-SYMPHONY

also writes, in his memoirs, that he worked at the *Symphonie fantastique* under the influence of Goethe. His first idea apparently was to write a *Faust* ballet, intended for the Opéra, and Ernest Newman, in a footnote to his edition of Berlioz's *Memoirs*, says 'It is highly probable that the *Ronde du Sabbat* originally figured' in this ballet.

By this time Harriet Smithson was back in London, her career as an actress on the decline. She returned to Paris in 1830, but no longer the star she had been in 1827. Berlioz, far from remaining unflinchingly constant to his 'goddess', had become involved in an equally passionate affair with a pianist, Marie Moke, herself hardly a model of constancy; so that the exact state of Berlioz's mind when he wrote to Ferrand, in February 1830: 'J'étais sur le point de commencer ma grande symphonie (Épisode de la vie d'un artiste), où le développement de mon infernale passion doit être peint', and in his next letter (16 April) when he outlined the synopsis, is not too easy to gauge.

The scheme he sent to Ferrand is as follows:

Épisode de la vie d'un artiste (grande symphonie fantastique en cinq parties).
Premier Morceau: double, composé d'un court *adagio*, suivi immédiatement d'un *allegro* développé (vague des passions; rêveries sans but; passion délirante avec tous ses accès de tendresses, jalousie, fureur, craintes, etc., etc.).
Deuxième Morceau: Scène aux champs (*adagio*, pensées d'amour et espérances troublées par de noirs pressentiments).
Troisième Morceau: Un bal (musique brillante et entraînante).
Quatrième Morceau: Marche au supplice (musique farouche, pompeuse).
Cinquième Morceau: Songe d'une nuit du Sabbat.

These headings are amplified in the paragraphs that follow. Too long to quote here in entirety,[15] they contain the essence of the long programme note which Berlioz at first insisted should be printed each time the work was played:

Le plan du drame instrumental, privé du secours de la parole, a besoin d'être exposé d'avance. Le programme suivant doit donc être considéré comme le text parlé d'un Opéra, servant à amener des Morceaux de musique, dont il motive le caractère et l'expression.

---

[15] The translation is given in Niecks, page 251 ff.

He later modified this view, stating that it was not necessary unless the symphony were being played in the same concert as its sequel, *Lélio, ou le Retour à la vie.* Instead it would be sufficient to give the headings of each movement — Rêveries, Passions; Un Bal; Scène aux Champs; Marche au Supplice; Songe d'une Nuit du Sabbat.

Berlioz's detailed scenario proved a stumbling block to many people, the notion behind the last two movements being especially repugnant. The supposition is that the artist, despairing of ever possessing his beloved, attempts to poison himself with opium; but the dose, instead of killing him, simply induces horrific visions. He sees himself condemned to death, marched to the scaffold, and executed. A horrible dance of death, a witches' sabbath, with which is intertwined a theme from the plainsong Requiem Mass, the *Dies Irae*, rounds off the symphony.

Such a programme is always good box-office, as Berlioz well knew. It was more than that, however. The macabre was an essential ingredient of the romanticism of the time, permeating the work of such painters as Gericault, Thomas Martin and Delacroix.[16] Victor Hugo's poems include a *Ronde du Sabbat*, which Berlioz may well have read; the more horrible aspects of the supernatural were exploited in Poe's stories and in Mary Shelley's *Frankenstein* and, on the stage, by Meyerbeer's *Robert le Diable* (1831). As to the use of opium, Thomas de Quincey's *Confessions of an English Opium Eater*, first published in 1822, had appeared in a free translation by Alfred de Musset in 1828, and there can be little doubt that opium, in the form of laudanum, was used as LSD has been more recently, to produce an intensification of experience.[17] Berlioz, as a medical student and the son of a doctor, would be familiar with its effects, even if he never used it himself. He certainly intended to, or said he did. Hearing of Marie Moke's infidelity he set out from Rome, in novelettish fashion, determined to wreak vengeance. Resolved to return to Paris 'to kill two guilty women and an innocent man', after which he must kill himself, he procured himself, as a disguise, a lady's-maid's costume (which he lost), a pair of double-barrelled pistols, and two little bottles containing laudanum and strychnine.

---

[16] Delacroix shared with Ingres a liking for and understanding of music — but the music of Mozart rather than of Berlioz. See the article by G. Jean-Aubrey in *La Revue Musicale*, April 1927.

[17] See Alethea Hayter, *Opium and the Romantic Imagination* (London, 1968).

Thus Berlioz acted out his own 'fantastic symphony'—but after the composition was completed.

The symphony is prized today less by reason of its programme than for its purely musical qualities, which are such that the programme is almost superfluous, as Berlioz himself came to see. The mastery appears most obvious in the handling of the orchestra. Though written only three years after Beethoven's death the sound spectrum is quite new, and we are already in a completely different world. It is, however, much more than an orchestral *tour de force*. Berlioz, at least in the *Symphonie fantastique*, shows himself cast in the mould of the great symphonists, confidently in control of the grand design and the details that constitute it.

The circumstances surrounding the composition of Berlioz's second programme-symphony, *Harold in Italy*, are well known. In 1834 Paganini approached Berlioz with the suggestion that the latter should write a viola concerto for him. Why a viola concerto? Well, for one thing such a work did not exist; and second, Paganini had just acquired a new Stradivarius viola, and needed something to play on it. Berlioz was in no position to refuse such a commission, though he had misgivings. He worked rapidly, the composition was finished in May, and had its *première* on 23 November, 1834. But Paganini did not give the first performance. The solo part was too reticent, he felt; and his place was taken by a classmate of Berlioz, Chrétien Urhan.

The composition came easily because the material had already been simmering in Berlioz's mind, awaiting only the opportunity to work at it systematically and put it in order. His wanderings in the wild Abruzzi region of Central Italy had made a vivid impression on his imagination, ever receptive to influences of whatever kind; he had noted folk melodies played and sung by the inhabitants of that region, with whom he felt *en rapport*.[18] And like the *Symphonie fantastique* it was partly autobiographical. The *idée fixe* in the earlier work referred to the artist's lover—whether Harriet Smithson or Marie Moke or some idealized and unattainable divinity is immaterial. Here it clearly stands for Berlioz himself—calm, reflective, able to look back with an indulgent eye on youth's follies. The symphony was written during a short-lived period of domestic

---

[18] See Jacques Barzun, *Berlioz and the Romantic Century* (London, 1951, two vols.) Vol. I pp. 210, 252ff.

happiness, for he was now married to Harriet (they were wed on 3 October, 1833) and a son was on the way (born 14 August, 1834).

When the commission first came his way Berlioz had thought in terms of an illustration of the last days of Queen Mary Stuart, whose tragic life was much in the minds of artists at the time.[19] It is not clear when the idea of linking the work with Byron's *Childe Harold* occurred to Berlioz, but the Mary Stuart plan was abandoned early in 1834. Writing to Ferrand on 19 March, 1834 he says:

> Je suis à terminer la Symphonie, avec alto principal, que m'a demandée Paganini. Je comptais ne le faire qu'en *deux* parties; mais il m'en est venu une *troisième*, puis une *quatrième*.

Like Wagner's *Ring* it was growing almost of its own volition. In May of the same year he writes again:

> J'ai achevé les *trois premières parties* de ma nouvelle symphonie; je vais me mettre à terminer le quatrième. Je crois que ce sera bien et surtout d'un pittoresque fort curieux . . . Il y a une *Marche de pèlerins chantant la prière du soir,* qui, je l'espère, aura, au mois de décembre, une réputation.[20]

The four movements are headed: 1. Harold in the mountains: scenes of melancholy, happiness and joy; 2. Pilgrims' march, singing the evening prayer; 3. Serenade of an Abruzzi mountaineer to his mistress; 4. Orgy of Brigands. With regard to the last Barzun has some sensible things to say, suggesting that we are today misled by the words 'orgy' and 'brigands'. The Abruzzi was a sort of Italian 'wild West', where the peasants lived by their wits, far removed from the bourgeois middle-class morality of convention which stifled Berlioz in Paris. The 'brigands' of the Abruzzi have their counterparts in the pirates and smugglers of Mérimée's *Carmen*, which appeared in 1845. The work is in no sense a concerto, for it has nothing of the antithetical structure such a form demands. Nor is it simply a 'topographical' study, like the *Pastoral* symphony, but rather a sort of classical 'landscape with figures', for the human protagonists — brigands or pilgrims or Harold himself — are essential to the balance of the picture.

---

[19] Cf. Donizetti's opera *Maria Stuarda* (October, 1834). The *Gazette musicale* of Paris for 26 January, 1834, announcing the commission of the work by Paganini, said it was to be 'a dramatic fantasy for orchestra, chorus and solo viola, with the title, *Les Derniers Instans de Marie Stuart*'.
[20] Hector Berlioz, *Lettres intimes* (Paris, 1882).

TONE POEM AND PROGRAMME-SYMPHONY

The third and last of his programme-symphonies, *Roméo et Juliette*, was first performed at the Conservatoire, Paris, on 24 November, 1839, but its origins go back to 1828, when Berlioz was under the combined spell of Shakespeare and Harriet Smithson.[21] We owe this work also to Paganini, if only indirectly. The fee promised for *Harold in Italy*, 20,000 francs, was slow in materializing, and arrived unexpectedly in 1838. Berlioz, finding himself for once not too pressed for money, determined 'to write a masterpiece, on a grand new plan, a splendid work, full of passion and imagination, and worthy to be dedicated to the illustrious artist to whom I owe so much'.[22]

Romeo and Juliet has aroused as much controversy as any of Berlioz's compositions. Niecks described it as a 'monstrous jumble of incongruities'; Barzun, on the other hand, argues cogently and I think correctly that some of the later misgivings over the work arose from a too rigid sense of what was or was not suitable, imposed by the conditions under which orchestral concerts came to be given. The twentieth century has witnessed another change of heart in this respect, and we are now much readier to accept mixed *genres* of all kinds. Nevertheless, the forces required and the scale and proportions of the work are obstacles in the way of frequent performances.

By writing what he called a 'dramatic symphony' (he was insistent on this title; it was not a cantata, much less an opera) for orchestra, chorus and soloists, Berlioz was following in Beethoven's footsteps. It begins with an orchestral introduction, *Allegro fugato*, representing the quarrel between the Montagues and the Capulets. At the climax (p. 12 of Eulenburg's miniature score), the Prince intervenes (three tenor trombones and ophicleide, unison and octave—'*Fièrement, un peu retenu, avec le caractère du récitatif*'). Three 'prologues' follow. The first (p. 23), sung by a small choir in an unaccompanied recitative, with interjections by the harp and, later, by the full orchestra, outlines the position as regards the two opposing households and Romeo's love for Juliet. The second (p. 33), entitled 'Strophes', extols this pure love and Shakespeare's genius in giving it voice. The third, tenor solo, marked 'Scherzetto' (p. 41), tells of Queen Mab in her tiny chariot; the orchestral accompaniment

---

[21] See Barzun, *op. cit.*, Vol. I, p. 228. Juliet was one of Harriet's roles.
[22] Berlioz, *Memoirs*, p. 230.

anticipates the magical *Queen Mab* scherzo, to come later in the work. In Part II we find Romeo alone, giving voice to his sadness, in a long and very typical melody which later is combined with an *Allegro* theme (p. 91) representing the grand festival at the Capulets. Part III is a love scene in the garden of the Capulets (p. 126) — a long movement containing some of Berlioz's tenderest music. Part IV is the gossamer *Queen Mab* scherzo, followed immediately by Juliet's funeral *cortège* (p. 234). The Tomb scene follows (p. 248), wherein Juliet awakes in a transport of joy, which soon yields to despair, to her suicide and her dying breath. The Finale (p. 277) depicts the crowd at the cemetery, a last fight between the two families, and Father Laurence's sermon of reconciliation (the chorus plays an important role in this last scene).

It is curious how often a new development springs up apparently spontaneously and simultaneously under very different circumstances and in widely separated areas. Berlioz's *Symphonie fantastique* had hardly seen the light of day before another programme work, comparable in range and ambition if not in execution, was being planned in Germany. This was *Die Weihe der Töne* ('the consecration of sound'), described as a 'Charakteristisches Tongemälde in Form einer Sinfonie nach ein Gedicht von Carl Pfeiffer'. The composer was Louis Spohr (1784-1859). Written in 1832, it was his fourth symphony; he had also written operas (*Faust*, 1816, and *Jessonda*, 1823) and, in 1825, some incidental music to *Macbeth*. Two points instantly attract our attention — the word '*Tongemälde*' ('tone-picture') in the title, and the note to the score to the effect that for a complete understanding of the work a knowledge of the poem is needed, so that this (fairly lengthy, eighty lines) should either be printed and distributed to the audience, or should be read aloud before the work is performed.

Spohr, incidentally, must almost certainly have arrived at the form of his composition independent of Berlioz. Though the *Symphonie fantastique* was performed in 1830 it was virtually unknown in Germany until Schumann's important and discerning article in *Die neue Zeitschrift für Musik* in 1835.[23] As far as Spohr was concerned

---

[23] For an English version of this see Robert Schumann, *Music and Musicians* (London, 1888), Vol. I, p. 228.

he was inaugurating a new form. His first idea, as he tells us in his autobiography, had been to set the words as a cantata, but he found they did not lend themselves to such treatment. Conceived on an ample scale, the work extends to 178 pages of full score. The orchestra used is large, and includes trombones and some extra percussion (triangle, bass drum and military drum), but no harps, which were slow in being accepted in the German symphony orchestra.[24] The headings of the four movements are as follows:

> First movement: a. *Largo* — the unbroken ('starres') silence of nature before the creation of sound; b. *Allegro* — active life; sounds of nature; the uproar of the elements.
> Second movement: Cradle song; dance; serenade.
> Third movement: Martial music; departure for the battle; the feelings of those left behind; the return of the victors; prayer of thanksgiving.
> Fourth movement: Funeral music; comfort in tears.

After the short introduction in F minor, 3/4 time, nature awakens, in F major and in 9/8 time, with a main theme of an undulating, 'water' type. Bird calls are very noticeable, with a cuckoo (on the horn), a quail (oboe), a nightingale and others. There are growls of wild beasts, and a fine climax (*fff*), suggesting the 'Aufruhr der Elemente'. The second movement, *Andantino*, B flat, begins in 3/8, which alternates with a dance in 2/8, and a 9/16 section; all three rhythms are later combined. The third movement, *Tempo di Marcia*, makes no serious attempt at a realistic battle scene but is rather a grand military parade, with a brash march theme in the style of Italian opera; it opens with a trumpet fanfare followed by a triangle solo (an anticipation of Liszt's E flat piano concerto). A quieter, middle section in G minor-G major represents the feelings of those left behind. The return of the victors is signalized by the repetition of the first D major march; this leads to a final section, *Andante maestoso*, in which is introduced an 'Ambrosianischer Lobgesang' — a chorale, scored for flutes, clarinets and horns, round which the remainder of the orchestra weave counterpoints. The last movement, *Larghetto*, in F minor, also uses a chorale, 'Begrabt den Leib'. The movement opens with a timpani roll, and the first few bars are scored for wind and timpani only. After the chorale there is

---

[24] Rather oddly, perhaps, in Spohr's case, as his wife was a harpist.

a final *Allegretto,* and the music fades away, *poco a poco ritard al fine, pp,* with the last word on the timps.

Though Spohr lacked Berlioz's originality and was what Tovey used to call an 'Interesting Historical Figure' rather than a genius, the work is undeniably effective. It is moreover true programme music in that it sticks closely to its poetic scenario. Though the work as a whole might not stand revival except for its interesting position in the development of the programme-symphony, the rather wistful second movement, scored for a reduced orchestra (no piccolo or trombones, but with a solo cello), has something of the flavour of Mahler, and would make an attractive piece on its own.

As with a number of nineteenth-century composers Spohr did his best work as a comparatively young man, and his later compositions have less to interest us. In 1839 he attempted an 'Historical Symphony in the style and taste of four different periods'—the period of Bach and Handel, 1720; Haydn and Mozart, 1780 (an *Adagio*); Beethoven, 1810 (a *Scherzo*); Finale, the modern period, 1840. This was perhaps the first of such pastiches, which include Tchaikowsky's *Mozartiana,* Ravel's *Menuet antique,* Stravinsky's *Pulcinella* and Prokofiev's *Classical Symphony,* besides many examples in the realm of 'light music'. It was an offshoot of the heightened interest in the exploration of older music, of which Mendelssohn's 1829 performance of Bach's *St Matthew Passion* was the symbol.[25] But Spohr could not see that the kind of writing in his 'Historical' symphony was compilation rather than composition, and in any case the truly modern music of 1839 had already passed him by.

---

[25] Spohr also directed a number of performances in Kassel in the 1830s.

CHAPTER 5

Liszt and the Symphonic Poem

'The term *'Symphonische Dichtung'* or Symphonic Poem was coined by Ferencz Liszt (1811-86) to describe the orchestral works he wrote in the 1850s while he was in charge of music at the Ducal Court at Weimar. He did not invent the form, but rather built on foundations laid by Spohr (we have seen Spohr's use of a similar term, *'Tongemälde'*, for his symphony *Die Weihe der Töne*), Berlioz, Mendelssohn and Beethoven. It should be noted that although these symphonic poems are programme music to the extent that they are not absolute or 'pure' music, but are always the musical equivalent of some extraneous idea, yet they are only rarely descriptive. Like most nineteenth-century creators (Berlioz was perhaps an exception) Liszt was a moralist. As with Wagner, his most ambitious works were designed, not to amuse or entertain, but to elevate; after bathing in this musical Jordan (the Rhine in Wagner's case), one would emerge refreshed, reinvigorated. That such a consummation is far from being universally experienced after exposure to Liszt's music does not invalidate his intention, but means that either we have misunderstood him or that his musical gifts did not match his aspirations. Or both.

Liszt's active connexions with Weimar lasted from 1844 to 1858. He had at his disposal an opera house, small it is true, and an orchestra, also small, certainly by today's standards.[1] During the first three or four years he acted only in a 'visiting professor' capacity, but from about 1848 he was settled there with a vast programme of work on hand — writing, composing and directing, but very little playing. The first symphonic poem, *Ce qu'on entend sur la montagne,* was written in the following year and first performed in 1850. It is based on a poem by Victor Hugo, from his 1831 collection entitled *Feuilles*

---

[1] Or rather, yesterday's. Today's orchestras tend to be smaller than those of fifty or even thirty years ago.

d'automne, which Liszt prints at the head of his score, as Spohr had done earlier. It consists of nine stanzas of unequal length, eighty-two lines in all, and is couched in richly evocative language well calculated to appeal to Liszt's ardent idealism. Its suggestion of

> . . . un bruit large, immense, confus,
> Plus vague que le vent dans les arbres touffus
> Plein d'accords éclatants, de suaves murmures

—of 'une musique ineffable et profonde', and its mention of 'l'hymne éternel couvrait tout le globe inondé', were open invitations to the composer to match this poetry with musical sounds. We are indeed near to Impressionism, especially in the very opening bars with the roll on the bass drum, two bars unaccompanied, followed by mysterious murmurs in the strings, *con sordini*, pierced after a few bars by chords on horns and woodwind. Later the poem distinguishes two contrary voices—on the one hand, the sublime voice of nature, on the other, the agonized cries of the human race. The conflict between the two is expressed climactically in the eighth stanza:

> Frères! de ces deux voix étranges, inouies,
> Sans cesse renaissant, sans cesse évanouies,
> Qu'écoute l'Éternel durant l'éternité,
> L'une disait: NATURE! et l'autre: HUMANITÉ!

In the final stanza the poet muses on the problem of why the Creator, who alone reads in his own book, has combined eternally, in one fatal marriage, nature's songs and humanity's cries.

As in Spohr's *Die Weihe der Töne* the whole of the poem is reflected in Liszt's treatment. The themes used include a typical Lisztian rhetorical gesture to symbolize nature—or rather, more realistically and specifically, the flash of sunlight on the peaks; and a Wagner-like chromatic progression to signalize man's striving and questioning. Another important 'nature theme' is the scale passage, descending and ascending, first heard (p. 10 of the miniature score) on the oboe. The work is over-long, but has much of interest.

The two concepts, nature and mankind, permeate this work as they do so much of the art of the mid-nineteenth century. But we are no longer in the placid countryside of still waters, flocks and pastures. The landscape of Beethoven's *Pastoral* symphony, which was the rather gentle scenery immediately surrounding Vienna as we see it in the sketches of Schubert's friend, Moritz von Schwind, or in the oil paintings of the popular Viennese artist Waldmüller, has now been replaced by the grandiose and the sublime, by wild, mountain scenery which inspired awe and terror. The mountain tops were the abode of gods. Zeus ruled from Mount Olympus, Moses brought the tablets of the law down from Mount Sinai, the souls of dead warriors were transported, in Nordic mythology, to Wotan's Valhalla far above mortal reach. Man's aspirations to divinity, his striving towards his higher self, found an outer expression in the scaling of mountain peaks, in the overcoming of difficulties and the triumphing over hardship and danger; mountaineering became almost a sacrament. The Swiss Alps, with their folk hero William Tell, became a focus of such ideas. Artists such as Anton Koch (1769-1839) and Carl Friedrich (1774-1840)[2] sketched and painted mountain scenes of rugged grandeur, and in music Liszt's *Bergsymphonie* (an alternative name to *Ce qu'on entend sur la montagne*) was followed by his pupil Bronsart's (1830-1913) symphony with chorus, *In der Alpen*, Raff's *In der Alpen*, Novák's *In the Tatras* and Strauss's *Alpine* symphony.

Liszt climbed mountains metaphorically rather than physically, but much of his music symbolized this typically romantic striving after the unattainable. As a young man his objective was the perfection of a pianistic technique far beyond the bounds of what had been thought possible,[3] and this notion, of man's search for the ultimate in truth, beauty and goodness, is a feature of several of the orchestral works from the Weimar period. It can be seen clearly in Orpheus, first performed in 1854 on the occasion of the production of Gluck's *Orpheus* under Liszt's direction. The preface (in French; Peter Cornelius, who was working with Liszt at the time, translated it into German) which he attached to the score, is important. He tells us that, during rehearsals, two ideas came into his mind. He recalled an Etruscan vase he had seen in the Louvre, depicting Orpheus surrounded by wild beasts listening to his music; and he also imagined the shade of Orpheus hovering over Greece, the

---

[2] Not to mention Philippe de Loutherbourg (1740-1812), whose *L'Avalanche*, contemporary with Schiller's *Wilhelm Tell*, forestalled by a generation the typical Swiss mountain picture.

[3] It is notable that his early piano compositions have no programmatic leanings whatever. The first hint of such ideas begin to appear after about 1830 — that is to say, after his first mental crisis, and as a result of his readings undertaken with his first love, Carolyne de Saint-Cricq, his contacts with *littérateurs* such as Lammenais and Lamartine and, a little later, his intimacy with the Comtesse d'Agoult.

land of legend and myth. The wild beasts no doubt stood for man's grosser nature for he goes on to say:

> L'Humanité, aujourd'hui comme jadis et toujours, conserve en son sein ses instincts de ferocité, de brutalité, et de sensualité, que la mission de l'art est d'amollir, d'adoucir, d'ennobler

and later he remarks on

> le caractère sereinement civilisateur des chants qui rayonnent de toute oeuvre d'art; leur sonorité noblement voluptueuse à l'âme, leur ondulation douce comme des brises de l'Elysée, leur élevement graduel comme des vapeurs d'incense, leur Ether diaphane et azure enveloppent le monde et l'univers entier comme dans une atmosphère, comme dans un transparent vêtement d'ineffable et mystérieuse Harmonie.

This 'transparent garment of ineffable and mysterious harmony' is certainly the poetic and beautiful concluding bars, the English horn bewailing the final loss of Eurydice, who seems to vanish in the shrouding mist. The work, which is quite short, is reticent rather than flamboyant, with hardly a climax in it, but with much melody of an appealing kind, on horns, oboe, English horn and solo violin, with Orpheus's lyre (harp) giving almost constant support.

Two other symphonic poems were written as overtures to plays. In 1849 the centenary of Goethe's birth was celebrated with a performance of his *Torquato Tasso*, originally written in 1790, and in the following year Herder's drama *Prometheus Unbound* was revived. In both instances the subject is heroism — the hero as Artist, set apart from his fellow men by reason of his special gifts, misunderstood by his contemporaries but acclaimed by posterity; and the hero as Liberator, defying the Titans and, again, leading mankind towards its higher destiny.[4] These are noble and worthy ideals, but their translation into musical sounds without the aid of words is attended by difficulties. The line between moving eloquence and bombast is fine.

Both works have the customary preface by Liszt[5] outlining his intentions. Concerning *Tasso* he observes that he has been influenced not only by Goethe but by Byron, whose *Lament of Tasso* had appeared in 1817. Tasso lived and suffered, he says, in Ferrara (the

---

[4] Cf. Thomas Carlyle's *Heroes and Hero Worship*, dating, like Longfellow's vulgarization of the theme in *Excelsior*, from 1841.

[5] Or by Princess Carolyne von Sayn-Wittgenstein.

sufferings included some mental disorder of the manic-depressive type, which led to him being imprisoned for a time after a murderous attack on a servant), had his revenge in Rome, and lives on in Venice in folksongs.

> To bring him to life in music we recall first his great shadow as he wanders today in Venice's lagoons [the reference here is to a song sung by a gondolier to verses from *Gerusalemme liberata*, which is incorporated in Liszt's work]; then we see his proud and noble, sad figure, amidst Ferrara's festivities, where his masterworks were created. Then we follow him to Rome, where his genius was acclaimed, and where his martyrdom is celebrated.

The long preface to *Prometheus* speaks of 'audacity, suffering, endurance, and salvation: daring aspirations towards the highest destinies which the human mind can reach[6] . . . expiatory pains giving up our vital organs to an incessant gnawing'—and so on.[7] This is the basic programme of the work, a deep suffering triumphing through persistent defiance, represented by a brilliant motif, sharply rhythmical, and quite Wagnerian; another motif is somewhat prophetic of Siegfried.[8]

The most familiar of the symphonic poems is *Les Préludes*, about which there is more misinformation than usual. It is now well established that the work has little connexion with Lamartine's 'Méditation', *Les Préludes*; we no doubt owe the ascription, and the usual programme that goes with it, to the egregious Princess von Sayn-Wittgenstein. The facts are as follows. In 1844 Liszt met a minor French poet, Joseph Autran, and set one of his poems for mixed chorus. Three more poems were set the following year. The four choruses, which have never been published, were performed in 1848(?), under the title *Les Quatre Élémens*, and supplied with an overture which was none other than *Les Préludes*. But it was still

---

[6] How persistently this theme of aspiration runs throughout the nineteenth century, and into our own! One thinks of Shaw's *Back to Methusaleh* (1921)—'as far as thought can reach'—and Tennyson's *Locksley Hall* (1842).

[7] See Niecks, *op. cit.*, p. 301.

[8] Humphrey Searle discussing the orchestral works in Alan Walker, *Franz Liszt: the Man and his Music* (London, 1970) devotes only a few lines to *Prometheus*; Sacheverell Sitwell, in the only other sizeable biography in English, dismisses it out of hand. Arthur Hahn in his book, *Liszt's Symphonische Dichtungen* gives a fairly detailed analysis of this (as of the other orchestral works), relating themes to specific passages in Herder's drama.

called *The Four Elements* even when a new version of the score was prepared in 1850 by Raff.[9] Finally, a new score was prepared by Liszt and performed on 23 February 1854, and only now does the familiar title appear.[10] We therefore, it seems, have a piece of programme music, but with the programme grafted on to a work whose original *raison d'être* was quite different. But whether we expunge the later interpretation from our minds (and after all the programme as we have it today had Liszt's blessing, and he never repudiated it), it remains a satisfying work. It has the great merit of compression, being tautly constructed out of themes that are succinct and epigrammatic, and related to each other through the 'metamorphosis' process which became a significant contribution to musical form.

Another symphonic poem with a chequered history is *Mazeppa*, first performed in its orchestral form on 16 April, 1854. This time the Princess is not to blame. The subject of Mazeppa was developed in a poem by Byron, published in 1819, and subsequently by Victor Hugo in *Les Orientales* (1829). Hugo's poem of twenty-three stanzas is printed in the miniature score, with a German translation by Cornelius. It tells how Mazeppa, caught red-handed in a love intrigue, is strapped naked to a wild horse, and describes with vivid imagery the dreadful three-day ride to the Ukraine. The horse collapses; Mazeppa, half dead, is recognized by a crowd of Ukrainians who release him. The last few stanzas point the moral that courage and fortitude can withstand the most dreadful sufferings. The musical basis of the piece goes back to one of the twelve *Grandes Études* of 1838, and even to the studies of 1826 (before Hugo's poem was written), in which form it had no title. It was then published separately, still as a piano piece and with a dedication to Hugo, in 1840, entitled *Mazeppa*, and re-published as No. 4 of the *Études d'exécution transcendante* of 1851. As with *Les Préludes* the programme came after the music was written.

One of the symphonic poems was inspired by painting rather than literature. This was *Hunnenschlacht*, first performed on 29 December, 1857. The picture was a mural by Wilhelm von Kaulbach

---

[9] Concerning Raff and the scoring of Liszt's works see below, p. 129.

[10] See Walker, *op. cit.*, p. 288 ff. Searle says, 'The Symphonic Poem is not the philosophical meditation commonly believed, but a description of Mediterranean atmosphere'. He quotes themes and motifs from some of the four choruses, but does not make it abundantly clear how descriptive the original overture was.

in the newly built Art Gallery in Berlin, portraying the battle, in 451 AD, between Attila and the Christians under Theodoric, before the gates of Rome. The battle, so legend has it, was so fierce that the fighting was continued by the spirits of the dead warriors, and in Kaulbach's picture these can be seen in the heavens above the battlefield, the conflict now idealized as a struggle between evil and good, the forces of the latter ranged behind a shining Cross. So Liszt's poem is in two parts, the first, a real and exciting battle waged with all the strength of the full orchestra, and the second, a meditation on the ideal battle, the Christian faith symbolized by the melody *Crux fidelis*.

Liszt's most extensive works for orchestra are the two *Faust* and *Dante* symphonies. Each work was long in gestation. He first began sketching *Faust* in the early 1840s (the period of the inception of so many of his works), but it was laid aside for about ten years. A first version for small orchestra,[11] was completed in 1854, and the first performance was given at Weimar in 1857. He described it as a symphony in *'Drei Charakterbilder'*—three character 'pictures', Faust, Gretchen and Mephistopheles. In the first movement various facets of Faust's character are depicted. The first theme, a note-row founded on the ambiguous chord of the augmented triad, denotes the world-weary Faust, aged, his wisdom turning to bitterness, an adventurer who has lost his bearings and for whom life and religion no longer have meaning. Other sides of his character—as lover, man of action, as thinker—have their own motifs, which, as in Wagner, often seem to be inter-related or derived from a common '*ur*'-source. The idyllic second movement shows Liszt treating the innocent Gretchen with rare sympathy and insight. Faust's love for her is as yet pure and unsullied, untouched by the canker of evil. The material of the last movement is derived from the first movement. Mephistopheles has no themes of his own; he is not only the personification of evil, but he is the darker side of our own

---

[11] Searle (in Walker, *op. cit.*, p. 305) says 'it was scored for small orchestra, without trumpets, trombones or percussion'; but the Weimar orchestra even in 1851 contained these instruments (*op. cit.*, p. 281), so it is strange to find Searle asserting that 'the original size of the orchestra would explain why he first wrote the *Faust* symphony for an orchestra without trumpets and trombones'. Searle's chapter gives other changes that took place between the 1854 score and the present day version, but does not make clear what changes there were when the work was first performed in 1857.

nature, so his themes are distortions and mockeries of Faust's motifs. But the distortion does not apply to Gretchen, and in the end Faust's salvation and the final subjugation of evil are due to her purity. The original orchestral ending was later replaced, or rather supplemented, by a coda, a choral setting of the finale from the second part of *Faust*.[12]

In this work it is the psychological, inner life that has occupied Liszt. There are no externals, and we look in vain for a 'Ride to the Abyss' or even a spinning wheel. There is rather more pictorialism in the *Dante* symphony. This was inspired by Dante's *La Divina Commedia*, and, like the *Faust* symphony, began to stir in Liszt's mind long before its completion in 1856.[13] He had originally conceived the work in three parts, to correspond with Dante's own plan, but in the event he abandoned the attempt at translating Paradise into music, and the symphony was completed in two sections, Hell and Purgatory. The work is scored for a large orchestra, two flutes and piccolo, two oboes and cor anglais, two clarinets and bass clarinet, four horns, two trumpets, three trombones, tuba, percussion, harps, strings and women's choir (in Part II), and the first performance took place, not in Weimar but in Dresden.[14]

The sinners whom, perhaps understandably, Liszt concentrated on were Paolo and Francesca, condemned to be buffeted for ever by the hot winds of their illicit passion. The first movement begins with a short introduction (*Lento*) expressive of the well-known words 'Abandon hope all ye who enter here', and the theme associated with this phrase reappears with terrifying force in the ensuing *Allegro frenetico*. The descent into Hell and the whirlwind are graphically portrayed, and there is a tenderer section, not dissimilar to Margaret's music in *Faust*, allotted to Francesca. The *Purgatorio*

---

[12] For further details see Walker, *op. cit.*, and Hahn, *op. cit*. The latter gives a detailed analysis, linking various motifs and passages to extracts from Goethe's drama.
[13] Serious work seems to have begun in 1847. In about 1848 Liszt was in touch with a painter, Buonaventura Genelli, with the idea of collaborating with him in a 'diorama' on the subject, but nothing came of it. The diorama had been invented by Daguerre in about 1822. The linking of the musical with the visual was further pursued by Liszt, in a proposal to Kaulbach for a whole series of pictures, for which Liszt intended to write illustrative music, but for one reason or another nothing came of his suggestion. Mendelssohn's experiments at Düsseldorf have already been mentioned in Chapter 4.
[14] The Dresden orchestra, larger and finer than that at Weimar, was highly praised by both Berlioz and Wagner.

section begins in D major, in a *religioso* style reminiscent of Franck. A fugal section (*Lamentoso*), no doubt suggestive of the penitence of the two lovers, leads to an apotheosis in C major and a big climax in E flat. The movement, and the work, ends in the 'seraphic' key of B major with the women's choir singing the *Magnificat*.

CHAPTER 6

Programme Music and The Keyboard

With the piano becoming the universal household instrument there was an increasing demand for music to be played on it. The need was for pieces, not too long, not too difficult technically, not too demanding musically, to counterbalance the sonatas and sets of variations which were more for the expert. Composers rose to the occasion; the supply was almost limitless.

There had already been a move towards this class of piano piece in the *Bagatelles* of Beethoven and Schubert's *Moments musicaux*. These were only on the fringe of programme music. The piano pieces of John Field went a little further, for the title 'Nocturne' gives a verbal clue to the mood of the music. The term '*Characterstück*' ('characteristic piece') begins to appear, and the credit for more precisely specifying the composer's intentions in such mood pictures seems to belong to Robert Schumann (1810-56) — as distinct, that is, from the descriptive 'battle pieces' by Dussek and others already discussed.

A good portion, perhaps half, of Schumann's piano music is either downright programme music or on the verge. Even such a work as the *Nachtstücke* Op. 23 turns out to be more than just 'Nocturnes' in Chopin's use of the word. All the following are programmatic to some extent: *Papillons* Op. 2 (composed 1829 and 1831, published 1832); six *Intermezzi* Op. 4 (originally *Pièces fantastiques*, 1832); *Carnaval*, Op. 9 (1835); *Fantasiestücke* Op. 12 (1837); *Davidsbündlertänze* Op. 6, (1837); *Kinderscenen*, Op. 15 (1838); *Novelletten*, Op. 15 (1838); *Kreisleriana*, Op. 16 (1838); *Nachtstücke*, Op. 23 (1839). After a few years he returned to the genre with *Waldscenen* Op. 82 (1849); *Album für die Jugend* Op. 68 (1848); and three sets of piano duets, *Bilder aus Östen* Op. 66 (1848), *Ballscenen* Op. 109 (1851) and *Kinderball* Op. 130 (1853).

The inspiration for *Papillons* came from his favourite author, Jean

Paul Richter (1763-1825). Marcel Brion in his perceptive *Schumann and the Romantic Age* (p. 132) says:

> Schumann had just read the *Flegeljahre* again . . . 'Coming to the last pages, he found himself in the baroque palace of Zablocki in the middle of a strange Polish fête, curiously reminiscent of Faust's *Walpurgisnacht*'. Here, too, all is suggestion, allusion and symbol—the girl disguised as Hope, the giant Boot, borrowed from Goethe, which walks of itself, the oracular Wig . . . The story of Vult and Walt comes to its fulfilment, that is to a degree of initiation which gives to every fact and facet of life an esoteric meaning, making it a sign of profound significance. And Schumann could read the signs and knew their meanings. With that, it is easy to imagine how irritated he must have been when fatuous critics congratulated him on having so realistically evoked a flight of butterflies.

The chapter referred to, and which in Schumann's own copy had passages marked which referred to *Papillons*, is entitled '*Larventanz*'—ie, a masked ball. In German *Larve* has several meanings—a mask, a (pretty) face, a grub or pupa; it can also mean bogey, evil spirit. This was exactly the kind of double or quadruple meaning to appeal to Schumann; and of course a pupa will change into a butterfly. The masked ball, says Brion (p. 133) was for the romantics always the symbol of illusion and aspiration. The mask itself was a sort of prison, but it was also a magic instrument, a talisman, changing the wearer into the character of his disguise. And another theme dear to the Romantics was the 'double' or *Doppelgänger*, which 'recurs repeatedly in *Papillons* with curious insistence'.

The passages marked by Schumann, and the numbers of *Papillons* to which they refer, are the following:

> 1. As he came out of the little room, he asked God that he might happily find it again; he felt like a hero, thirsting for fame, who goes forth to his first battle . . .
> 2. Characteristically taking a wrong turn he first entered the punch-room, which he took for the dance-hall . . . Wina was not to be seen, nor any sign of Vult . . . At last, wishing to examine the anterooms, he reached the real resounding, burning hall full of excited figures . . . an aurora borealis sky full of crossing, zigzag figures . . .
> 3. What most attracted him and his astonishment·was a giant boot that was sliding around, dressed in itself . . .

4. Hope quickly turned herself round, an unmasked shepherdess and a simple nun with a half-mask and a scented bunch of auriculas . .

5. Now he stood for a second alone by the tranquil maiden, and the half rose and lily of her face looked out from the half-mask as from the flower sheath of drooping bud.

Like foreign spirits from two far cosmic nights they looked at each other behind dark masks, like the stars in a solar eclipse, and each soul saw the other from a great distance.

6. As a youth touches the hand of a great and celebrated writer: so — like a butterfly's wing, like auricule-pollen — he lightly touched Wina's back and withdrew as far as possible in order to look at her life-breathing face. If there is a harvest-dance that is the harvest, if there is a catherine-wheel of loving rapture: Walt the coachman had both . . .

7. He threw his mask away and a curious hot desert-aridity or dry fever broke through his gestures and words. If you have ever felt love for your brother, he began with dry voice and took the wreath off and undid the female costume — if the fulfilment of one of his dearest wishes is anything to you, and if it is not indifferent to your joys whether he has the least of the greatest, in short if you will listen to one of his most earnest entreaties:

8. To that I can only answer you: Joyfully. 'Then be quick' replied Vult without thinking.

9. Your waltzes up to now — don't be annoyed — have traversed the room as good mimic imitations, partly horizontal — of the coachman, partly perpendicular — of the miner.

10. As Walt entered, it seemed to him that everyone noticed his exchange of disguise; some women noticed that Hope now had fair hair behind the flowers instead of as before, and Walt's step was shorter and more feminine, as became Hope. But he soon forgot himself and the hall and everything else as the coachman Vult without ado placed Wina at the head of the 'English dance' and now to her astonishment sketched out a dance with her and, like some painters, at the same time painted with the foot — only with bigger strokes.

Towards the very end of the dance, in the hurried hand-reachings, the crossings, the runnings up and down, Vult allowed ever more confused sounds to escape him — only the breath of speech — only stray butterflies blown to sea from a far-off island. To Wina it sounded like a curious lark's-song on a summer night.

The passages,[1] it will be seen, are strange indeed. They refer only to the first ten numbers, which seems to confirm the suggestion that the last two, the *Polonaise* (a suitable dance if the ball was taking place in a Polish mansion) and the *Finale*, which includes the *Grossvatertanz* (also of possible Polish origin), were added later.[2]

The notion of using a ball as a framework for an extended compositon is pursued in *Carnaval*.[3] But Schumann is now more wary of openly avowing the programmatic content. The full title is, *Carnaval. Scènes mignonnes composées pour le Pianoforte sur quatre notes*.[4] Schumann sent a copy to Moscheles in 1837, and in the accompanying letter he writes: 'To figure out the Masked Ball will be child's play to you; and I need hardly assure you that the putting together of the pieces and the superscriptions came about *after* the composition'. This is true enough, insofar as the ultimate origin of the work was some variations on Schubert's *Sehnsuchtswalz*. He also wrote:

> The *Carnaval* came into existence incidentally, and is built for the most part on the notes A,S,C,H, the name of a small Bohemian village where I had a lady friend, but which, strange to say, are also the only musical letters in my name. The superscriptions I placed over them afterwards. For is not music itself always enough and sufficiently expressive? Estrella is a name such as is placed under portraits to fix the picture better in one's memory; Reconnaissance, a scene of recognition; Aveu, an avowal of love; Promenade, a walk such as one takes at a German ball with one's partner.[5]

But though the idea of a masked ball may stem from the *Flegeljahre*, the portraits are now drawn from his immediate circle—Chopin, Chiarina (Clara Wieck), Estrella (Ernestine von Fricken, the young lady from Asch with whom Schumann had an affair which he got out of with some difficulty and a bad grace), and himself in his masked

---

[1] Quoted from Gerald Abraham, *Schumann: A Symposium* (London, 1952) pp. 37, 38. This information was probably not available to Niecks: see Wolfgang Gertler, *Robert Schumann in seinen frühen Klavierwerken* (Wolfenbüttel, 1931).

[2] The *Polonaise* is actually a modification of passages from the *Polonaise* for four hands Op. III (1828), first published in 1933.

[3] Some details of the genesis of this, again unknown to Niecks, are given in the *Symposium*, p. 40 ff.

[4] The French titling was an affectation that appears in a few other compositions of this period.

[5] Quoted from Niecks, *Robert Schumann* (London, 1925), pp. 175, 176.

ball disguises, Florestan and Eusebius. There are also characters such as Pierrot, Arlequin and Colombine drawn from that other repository of masked figures, the Italian *Commedia dell'arte*. And too we are reminded that he saw himself and his paper as a spearhead against the prevailing indifference towards the highest aims of art; the last movement is a war march of the Davidsbund, a league of the believers, past and present, in the true faith against the Philistines of art. The whole work, novel in conception (the thumbnail character sketches in Couperin's *Ordres*, though delightful, can hardly compete) and brilliant in execution, consolidated Schumann's reputation as a composer and musical thinker of great originality.

The title of *Fantasiestücke* is borrowed from E. T. A. Hoffmann's *Fantasiestücke in Callots Manier* (1814). There are eight pieces, with titles. Of the fifth, *In der Nacht* Schumann wrote to Clara (21 April, 1838):

> After I had finished it I found to my joy the story of Hero and Leander in it. When I play 'Die Nacht' I cannot forget the picture—first, how he plunges into the sea—she calls—he answers—through the waves he safely reaches land—then the *cantilena* where they embrace—when he must away again, he cannot bring himself to part—then night once more shrouds everything in darkness.[6]

Hoffmann is also the source of *Kreisleriana*, in that the title refers to Hoffmann's Kapellmeister Kreisler; but Schumann seems to have kept his own counsel over the exact significance of these eight pieces. Concerning the *Nachtstücke* (the title again borrowed from Hoffmann) he writes to Clara (7 April, 1839), 'During this composition I kept seeing funerals, coffins, unhappy, desperate people'; and in the following January he put forward these suggestions for titles: 1. Funeral procession; 2. Strange company; 3. Nocturnal carousal; 4. Round with solo voices. He had at one time considered calling the collection *Funeral Fantasy*.

Of the *Novelletten* he writes to Clara (6 February, 1838) of 'jests, Egmont stories, family scenes with fathers, a wedding', and he makes a pun on Clara Novello's name—'Novelletten rather than Wiecketten, because your name is Clara, and Wiecketten would not

---

[6] Niecks, *Schumann*, p. 182. See also *Early Letters of Robert Schumann* (London, 1888), p. 274.

sound so well.'[7] No. 3 had appeared as a supplement to the *Neue Zeitschrift für Musik* in May 1838 with a motto from *Macbeth*, 'When shall we three meet again, In thunder, lightning or in rain?'. It is possible that there is a further Hoffmann connexion here, the title perhaps derived from Hoffmann's *Nouvelles musicales*.[8] As to the *Davidsbündlertänze*, he writes to Clara (5 January, 1838), 'There are many bridal thoughts in the dances, which were suggested by the most delicious excitement I can remember. I will explain them all to you one day.' Later in the same letter he described the whole as a '*Polterabend*', which Muret-Saunders defines as 'a wedding eve with loud rejoicings and noises in front of the bridal home'.

The *Kinderscenen* are revealing and interesting. Offering them to Haertel in March 1838 he remarked that he had first thought of them as a beginning to the *Novelletten*. He also, in a letter to Clara (17 March, 1838), says they derived from a remark of hers, that he sometimes seemed to her as a child. This no doubt pleased him immensely, for childhood was a condition holding special significance for the romantics. Brion writes:

> We find this complete universe, this unutterable felicity, from which adults are excluded, in Runge's allegorical pictures and still more in Schumann's *Kinderscenen*, which it would be wrong to take as anecdotic of the everyday life of children . . . Those who see in them only touching miniatures have missed their deep significance, sublime and mysterious.

Schumann's letter to Heinrich Dorn (5 September, 1839) complains of Rellstab's misunderstanding in this matter; but he also says:

> I do not deny that, while composing, some children's heads were hovering round me (for instance, Ottilie Voigt), but of course the superscriptions came into existence afterwards and are, indeed, nothing more than delicate directions for the rendering and understanding of the music.

This is a familiar excuse we have met before and shall meet again.

The *Kinderscenen* have had a far too numerous progeny; every

---

[7] Niecks, *Schumann*, p. 201.
[8] And could the odd 'Egmont stories' refer to a translation of Hoffmann's *Contes fantastiques* by Henry Egmont, which appeared in 1836?

twentieth-century pianistic fledgling has been brought up on 'A rainy day' or 'The wind in the trees'. But there have also been some distinguished successors, by Heller, Henselt, MacDowell, Smetana, Tchaikowsky, Debussy and Fauré. Schumann's own successor was his *Album für die Jugend*, written in 1848 with his own children in mind.

If these are of comparatively slight interest *Waldscenen*, Op. 82, are of capital importance to the student of both Schumann and programme music. The nine short pieces of this collection all have titles; in addition Schumann's original intention had been to attach mottoes, of which only one, to *Verrufene Stelle* ('accursed place')—some verses by Hebbel—was left. The finest of the nine pieces, *Vogel als Prophet*, had a line from Eichendorff's *Zwielicht* (set as a solo song by Schumann in 1840), 'Hute dich! sei wach und munter' ('beware! keep on the alert')—which hardly clarifies the title. The Prophet Bird clearly flies in, delivers its message of solemn import and flies away again; but what is its message? No matter; it remains one of the most perfectly evocative pieces of impressionism Schumann ever wrote.

Schumann's piano music has been dealt with at some length because of its importance. His contribution to programme music was concerned for the most part with mankind, with human relationships, often in an autobiographical sense. It dealt with persons, not things. Like his best criticism, and like his songs, it was subjective. These for example hardly ever exploit the graphic realism of Schubert, but explore a subjective response to the world around us. For the *Naturbild*, the landscape, we must turn to Liszt.

Interestingly enough Liszt's first compositions were non-programmatic. He wrote twelve studies for piano in 1826 (a projected forty-eight in all the keys remained unfinished). They were published in 1827 (his first publication). Later they were revised, expanded, with increased emphasis on pianistic difficulties, and published in 1839 as *24 Grandes Études* (though in fact still only twelve). A third revision was undertaken in 1851, the difficulties still further intensified. They were published in 1852 as *Études d'exécution transcendante*, and only in this edition were any descriptive titles given to any of them. No. 3, for example, was called *Paysage*, No. 8 *Wilde Jagd*, No. 12, *Chasse-neige*. The fourth, *Mazeppa*, has already been discussed in the previous chapter.

PROGRAMME MUSIC AND THE KEYBOARD

Somewhere along the line, then, Liszt changed from a composer of 'absolute' music to a 'programme' composer. Some of the responsibility for this has been attributed to Princess von Sayn-Wittgenstein, whom Liszt first met in 1847. She had a hand in the literary programmes of at least some of his symphonic poems and, for good or ill, exerted a considerable general influence on his life and thought. But his compositions had been tainted by extra-musical notions long before he met the Princess, and can perhaps be traced to his intimacy with an earlier Carolyne, Carolyne de Saint-Cricq, a pupil with whom he fell in love and with whom he read the newest romantic literature. This was in the winter of 1827-28. Literary studies were intensified during the next few years under the wings of the Abbé Lammenais, Lamartine and others. There was, too, the impact of Berlioz and the *Symphonie fantastique*, which Liszt arranged for piano in 1833; of Weber; of Paganini; of Schubert (the song arrangements, some of which are relevant to *Au Bord d'une Source* for instance, date from 1838-39); of Beethoven, whose *Pastoral* symphony he arranged for piano in c. 1837; and of Schumann, whose first programmatic works were in existence as early as 1829 (and played by Liszt).

The appearance of works with titles in the early 1830s should not, then, surprise us. After *Apparitions* (1834) and *Harmonies poétiques et religieuses* (1834) (the title was borrowed from a collection of Lamartine's poetry published in 1830) came the first important 'travelogue' in piano literature, the *Album d'un Voyageur* (1835-36, but not published until 1842).[9] It stemmed from Liszt's travels through Switzerland and Italy in the company of Countess d'Agoult. His liaison with her began in 1834 and they went to live in Geneva in 1835; their journeys in Italy began in 1837 after a brief return to Paris.

---

[9] An earlier 'travelogue' was the set of *Mélodies orientales* of Félicien David (1829-30). David (1810-76), whose symphonic ode *Le Désert* was destined to cause such a remarkable stir when it was introduced to Paris in 1844, was thus in the vanguard of the Orientalism made fashionable in the art world by Delacroix.

It is also interesting to note that when Liszt went to Paris in 1826 he studied composition with the Czech composer Anton Reicha (1770-1836). Reicha is known primarily as a theorist, but he was also the composer of some *Scènes italiennes* which date from as early as c. 1799. The leanings of nineteenth century Czech composers such as Smetana and Dvořák towards the 'characteristic' piano piece is thus noticeable even earlier than such works as the *Eclogues* (1810) of Tomašek.

Album d'un Voyageur, some of which were revised[10] and included in the First *Année de Pèlerinage: Suisse* (published 1855), consists of three books entitled respectively *Impressions et poésies; Fleurs mélodiques des Alpes; Paraphrases.* The programme pieces, contained in the first book, are *Lyon* (inspired by the unemployment and distress the travellers had witnessed there); *Le Lac de Wallenstadt; Au Bord d'une Source; Les Cloches de G . . .* (Geneva); *Vallée d'Obermann* (*Obermann*, a novel by Étienne de Senancour, which appealed to Liszt and to later generations of French writers by reason of its melancholy introspection); *La Chapelle de Guillaume Tell*;[11] *Psaume*. The nine pieces of the first book of *Années de Pèlerinage* omit *Lyon* and *Psaume* but add four others — *Pastorale*; *Orage*; *Eglogue* and *Le Mal du Pays*. Most of these are nature pieces, at their best when, as in *Au Bord d'une Source*,[12] they are left at that level with no attendant philosophizing, for even the quotation from Schiller which heads it is no more than a pointer to the mood. Deriving no doubt from his Schubert transcriptions, its gentle trickle is no less obviously the starting point of Smetana's *Vltava*. But the Swiss mountain scenery with its lakes, meadows, storms and pastoral life is behind them all.

The fruits of the Italian visit were the seven pieces that constitute the second year of *Années de Pèlerinage: Italie*, first published in 1858 but composed, or at least drafted, about 1838 or 1839. If Switzerland was a nature symbol, an idyllic land wherein man dwelt in harmony with his surroundings, drawing his livelihood by honest toil and deriving solace from the unsullied beauty on every side, Italy was a civilization symbol. It was the navel of Europe, the womb from whence modern civilization sprang. The Hero now was not Nature, but Man — the Creator; and Liszt sought to enshrine, in music, his thoughts concerning great poetry (Dante, *Divina Commedia*; Petrarch, *Sonetts*), great painting (Raphael, *Il Sposalizio*) and great sculpture (Michelangelo, *Il Pensieroso*). It is characteristic of the period that the texture of the last named, 'The Thinker', is harmonic rather than contrapuntal.

---

[10] The revisions were often quite extensive, but I know of no study which examines them in detail.

[11] Rossini's *Guillaume Tell* was first performed in Paris on 3 August 1829. Liszt was in Paris at the time; he must have attended a performance.

[12] 'One of the most perfect "water-pieces" ever written says Louis Kentner, in Walker *op. cit.*

The third *Année*, not published until 1883 but completed by 1877, is different again. Three of the pieces, *Aux Cyprès de la Villa d'Este* 1 and 2 and *Les Jeux d'eaux à la Villa d'Este*, can obviously be identified with the time he spent in Cardinal Hohenlohe's villa at Tivoli, some few miles from Rome, which he first visited in 1864. The gardens there are now overgrown, but the fountains, if not in the pristine condition of Cardinal d'Este's time, are still impressive and exciting. Liszt hardly needed the stimulus of the Cardinal's villa to turn his thoughts towards religion, for that had been a thread running through his entire life, but there is no doubt that in his latter years his 'pèlerinage' became more and more a religious pilgrimage, with the Villa d'Este as a sort of sanctuary. So in addition to the impressionistic pieces inspired by the atmosphere of the place (*Les Jeux d'eaux* must be singled out as a remarkable anticipation of the similarly named works by Debussy and Ravel) we have to mention the first, *Angelus! Prière aux anges gardiens*, dedicated to his granddaughter Daniela. Other important piano works which combine religion and impressionism are the two Legends of 1863, *St François d'Assis. Le Prédication aux oiseaux* and *St François de Paule marchant sur les flots*, and indeed something of this can be glimpsed as early as the first version of *Harmonies poétiques et religieuses*. Like so many works these were revised and added to later, and a particularly interesting addition in the definitive 1853 publication is the one entitled *Funérailles, Octobre 1849* — a funeral march inspired by the death of Chopin in that very month, and by the Hungarian revolution of 1848-49.

It would be difficult to overrate the importance of Liszt in the development, not only of programme music, but of music in general. His approach was in many respects opposed to classical procedures; or if not opposed, he was less rigidly bound by them than any of his contemporaries. He experimented freely and fearlessly. While it is very likely that much extemporization by Vogler, Beethoven and Schumann may have seemed too revolutionary to write down, Liszt had no such inhibitions. But then he was modern, *avant garde*, in his whole approach to composition. He worked in sound; his piano writing exploited the colour of the instrument in ways previously unthought of, much as Weber, Mendelssohn and Berlioz were widening the orchestral palette. The sound was used for pictorial purposes, to depict the rolling waves of the sea in 'St Francis walking on the waves', to suggest the tolling bell in *Funérailles*, or the sunlight glinting through the foliage of the forest trees in *Waldesrauschen*. His music is a series of sonorous images, portraying states of nature or revealing states of mind. The classical treatment of melody and harmony was not neglected, but was subservient to this. He used harmony in a new way, ie, not so much as a support for or originator of melody, but in its own right as a generator of emotional states, as a sort of musical incense. In this respect he was both of his time (contemporary criticism is constantly referring to the 'power' of harmony and, in particular, of modulation), and a prophet, pointing the way to Wagner and beyond.

Liszt's attitude towards religion has occasioned much discussion. Many have found his professed religious ecstacy impossible to reconcile with his unconventional love life and his uninhibited way of conducting himself in public. A glance through his list of compositions reveals a large number, apart from the vocal works, that are religion-inspired, that is to say, have some kind of religious 'programme'. Let us assume that they were sincere expressions of his faith, for we have no reason to suppose the opposite, and examine them in the context of the times. In Protestant, puritan England, for example, which on the whole rejected Liszt's music, the Oxford Movement under the leadership of Keble, Pusey and Newman (later Cardinal Newman) was advocating a revived conception of the Church as 'more than a merely human institution', but as an institution more concerned, and seen to be more concerned, with the mysteries of revealed religion, the Godhead and man's relation to his Creator. This movement was born in the 1830s, which is precisely the period when Liszt wrote the first of his mystical pieces. Newman subsequently became a member of the Roman Catholic Church, a conversion which can be paralleled in artists and writers in Germany; earlier there had been the Nazarenes, a sect founded in Vienna in 1809, and associated with the German artists Friedrich Overbeck (1789-1869), Franz Pforr (1788-1812) and, somewhat later, Peter Cornelius (1783-1867), the uncle of the composer Peter Cornelius who worked with Liszt at Weimar. If Liszt's religious outlook, like his music, was personal, it can certainly be seen as related to a much wider religious movement — a circle of resistance (ineffectual, as it turned out) against the increasing materialism of the times.

Schumann and Liszt between them, then, seem to epitomize the piano programme music of the nineteenth century. They drew on literature, both ancient and contemporary; on painting, nature and human nature; their musical resource, especially that of Liszt, prepares us for the later harmonic adventures of Debussy and Ravel. It was Liszt's ambition, as he himself said, 'to hurl a lance as far as possible into the boundless realm of the future';[13] some of his religious music seems to herald the stained glass ecstacies of Franck, Reger, Karg-Elert and, above all, Messiaen, while his harmonic daring lights the path to Wagner, Schoenberg and beyond.

Most of the piano literature of the nineteenth century is but a pale reflection of the work of these two in their very different spheres, though some—eg, that of Grieg—still has power to charm. Edvard Grieg (1843-1907), though a minor composer if one considers his absolute contribution to music, was in fact a good deal more important than he now appears. During his lifetime he compelled admiration from Liszt, Schumann and Tchaikowsky and, though unacknowledged, from Debussy.[14] He was in the van of the Nationalist movement which, especially in Czechoslovakia and Russia (not to say Finland) has been rich in programme music. But despite the fact that so many of the piano pieces in the ten volumes of *Lyric Pieces* have titles Grieg's music lies only on the fringe of programme music; like too many composers he is apt to assume that a poetic or allusive title is sufficient (b).

> Niecks, writing whilst Grieg was still alive, allowed his fancy to roam unbridled. 'He must' he writes 'be a dullard indeed who is not impressed, for instance, by the sea life depicted in the first movement of Op. 8, the Sonata in F major for pianoforte and violin. In short Grieg's concerto, sonatas and pieces make us hear, see and feel land and sea, woods and heaths, flats and mountain-tops, fresh breezes, thick fogs, rocking waves, rushing water, flapping sails, merry dances, melancholy musings, wild rollicking, stories of heroes and goblins, and much more.'

Schumann's immediate circle included Mendelssohn, Niels W. Gade (1817-90) and William Sterndale Bennett (1816-75). Mendelssohn contributed little to the *genre* apart from the pleasant *Fantasia* in E major, Op. 16.3, 'The Rivulet', composed in Wales in 1829; there is much charming music in the *Songs without Words* and

---

[13] Walker *op. cit.* p. 350. One is reminded too of Tennyson's *Locksley Hall* (1842)—'For I dipt into the future, far as human eye could see'.

[14] See Henry T. Finck, *Edvard Grieg* (London and New York, 1906) and Gerald Abraham, *Grieg: A Symposium* (London, 1948).

the *Christmas Pieces*, but they are too imprecise to be considered as programme music. Gade, important in the music history of his native Denmark, wrote some overtures (*Ossian, Hamlet, Michelangelo*) that have not outlived him, and there are a few piano pieces such as the *Aquarellen* which are mood pictures rather than true programme music. Bennett made a distinct contribution, with *Three Musical Sketches* Op. 10 — 'The Lake', The 'Millstream' and 'The Fountain'. They were written about 1835 — that is, before his visit to Leipzig and his friendship with Schumann, and therefore before he had any knowledge of Liszt's nature pieces in the *Années de Pèlerinage*. The second, according to the composer himself, was suggested by the millstream at Grantchester, near Cambridge.[15] Schumann wrote enthusiastically of these. A more ambitious and unusual work for piano was written much later. This was a four-movement sonata entitled *The Maid of Orleans*, composed during 1869-73 and published as Op. 46. Each movement has, as a motto, a line or two from Schiller's play:

1. *In the Fields:*   In innocence I led my sheep
   down the mountain's silent deep.
2. *In the Field:*   The clanging trumpets sound, the
   chargers rear,
   And the loud war-cry thunders in my ear.
3. *In Prison:*   Hear me, O God, in mine extremity,
   In fervent supplication up to thee
   Up to Thy Heaven above I send my soul.
4. *The End:*   Brief is the sorrow, endless is the joy.

His biographer is silent as to what prompted such an unusual work.

Two other contemporaries of Schumann must be mentioned, though they are greatly out of fashion now. Stephen Heller (1814-88), born at Pest, studied in Vienna with Anton Halm. Like Schumann, he drew his inspiration from literature (Niecks related that the composer told him his compositions were the outcome of his readings and experiences). His several collections of studies contain a number which are obviously indebted to Schumann (*Une curieuse Histoire*, from his *Album dédié à la Jeunesse*, Op. 138 or *Nuits blanches* Op. 82) or Liszt (*Au bord de la fontaine*, from thirty *Études progressives* Op. 46). His music is facile and pleasant, with a little touch of originality which lifts the best of his music above the

---

[15] See *The Life of Sterndale Bennett*(Cambridge, 1907) by his son, J. R. Sterndale Bennett (p. 40).

common level of the *salon* piece.

Adolf von Henselt (1814–89) studied with Hummel, toured as a piano virtuoso and, in 1838, settled in Russia (some of his music was published only in that country). While there he taught Alexander Serov (1820–71) and Anton Herke, who in turn was a teacher of Mussorgsky, and also Zverov, who taught Scriabin. He is thus a link, like John Field, connecting Western, mainly German, music with a whole series of 'characteristic pieces' by Glinka, Mussorgsky, Balakirev, Tchaikowsky, Rebikov and others.[16] Henselt's pieces tend to have vague titles such as *Frühlingslied* ('Spring Song') or *Wiegenlied* ('Cradle Song'), or, even more generally, *Impromptu* or *Nocturne*. But in 1835 he produced, on the Liszt model, *Douze études caractéristiques*, Op. 2, with titles all in French; some of these, especially the little featherweight *scherzo Si Oiseau j'étais*, certainly deserve to be classed as programme music.

The more brilliant side of Liszt's work was more limited in its direct influence, for there were few, if any, pianist composers with the technique and imagination to carry his style much further. One who took up the challenge was Serge Liapunof (1859–1924), who wrote a set of twelve *Études d'Exécution transcendante*, some of which, for instance *Terek* (this is the river that flows past Tamara's castle) and *Carillon*, are certainly programmatic. Then there is Balakirev's imaginative *Islamey* described as an 'Oriental Fantasy', first performed by Nicholas Rubinstein in 1869 at St Petersburg. This had its origins in a summer holiday spent in the Caucasus in 1862, a region whose exotic folk music was later to inspire Ippolitov-Ivanov's *Caucasian Sketches*. For its time *Islamey* was a remarkably successful evocation of the wild and primitive, with comparatively few concessions to Western musical orthodoxy, but it may be questioned whether it is much more programmatic than, say, the last movement of Mendelssohn's *Italian* symphony.

The piano music of that other great storehouse of nationalist music, Czechoslovakia, is far less interesting than the orchestral music. It is true that the Czech genius has inclined towards illustrative or suggestive music rather than absolute music. Dussek for example, whose battle pieces were discussed in Chapter 3, wrote a number of pianoforte sonatas, and in some of these he is not content to let the music speak for itself but has added titles as in Op. 44, *Les*

---

[16] Some of this music will be considered in Chapter 7.

Adieux de Clementi or Op. 70, *Le Retour à Paris*. The *Eclogues* of Vaclav Jan Tomašek (1775-1850) show the same leanings towards an easy-flowing and undemanding music that we see in the lesser works of Smetana and Dvořák. The former, who was a redoubtable pianist, wrote a quantity of piano music including a concert study, *On the Seashore* (1862) and a set of six pieces entitled *Dreams* (1875). Much of Dvořák's music hovers on the fringe of programme music, but so often shrank from anything more definite in the titles than the non-committal *Silhouettes* (1879) or the *Legends* for orchestra (1881), which Gerald Abraham thinks may have a positive programme behind them. But the six pieces for piano duet of Op. 68 (1884) have a general 'topographical' title *From the Bohemian Woods* (they are slightly later than Smetana's tone-poem *From Bohemia's Woods and Fields*); and the thirteen *Poetic Pictures* Op. 85 (1889), with titles such as *Twilight Way*, *In the Old Castle*, *At the Hero's Grave* or *On the Holy Mount* are clearly programmatic in intent. It is possible to see these works not only as the legacy of Schumann and Liszt, but as owing something to Mussorgsky's *Pictures from an Exhibition* of 1874. The same influence may well be behind Fibich's six studies, *Malirske Studie*, inspired by paintings, as it is certainly behind Janácek's piano cycle *On the Overgrown Path*, to be discussed in Chapter 10.

CHAPTER 7

Late Romantic Programme Music (I)

The symphonic poem in the second half of the nineteenth century can be traced in the main to two sources, Berlioz and Liszt, who through their works, their writings and their travels influenced the whole of Western music whether in Czechoslovakia, Russia, France or Germany.

In Czechoslovakia Bedřich Smetana (1824-84)[1] had fallen under Liszt's spell as early as 1840 when the latter had visited Prague, and some of Smetana's early compositions imitate Liszt's virtuoso style. During a later visit to Prague in 1856 the two met a number of times, when they discussed Wagner and the new music. By this time Smetana had already had some experience as an orchestral composer, notably with a symphony, a *Triumph-Sinfonie*, based on Haydn's Austrian Anthem, for the wedding of the new emperor, Franz Joseph I.

But the political climate in Prague offered little opportunity for a Czech composer. Like much of Europe Bohemia as it was then was only at the beginning of its long struggle for independence. Smetana was later to play an important part in this, but that moment had yet to come, and he was forced to look outside his country for a suitable post. In 1856 he went to Göteborg in Sweden, as conductor of the Harmoniska Sallskapet, a post he held for five years. Whilst there he composed his first symphonic poems, *Richard III, Wallenstein* and *Hakon Jarl*.

Shakespeare was popular, but even so *Richard III* seems an odd

---

[1] The most comprehensive study of Smetana is the biography by Brian Large (London, 1970). On the music of the country in general see the excellent study by Rosa Newmarch, *The Music of Czechoslovakia* (London, 1942), which also touches on the political history of Czechoslovakia.

choice. He had, however, seen the play in Prague;[2] he would be familiar with Mendelssohn's *Midsummer Night's Dream* overture, possibly with Berlioz's *Roméo et Juliette*, and he may also have seen some of Liszt's sketches for *Hamlet* during a visit to Weimar in 1857. The work was first performed, in a version for four hands, at Göteborg on 24 April 1860, but the orchestral version had to wait until January 1862 when it was played at Prague. In a letter to Liszt[3] he outlined the scheme of the work, in one movement, which retains the essentials of the drama. The musical themes, representing Richard and his opponents, undergo some transformation in the Lisztian Manner.[4] *Wallenstein's Camp*, based on Schiller, is more frankly pictorial; its four sections, corresponding to the conventional symphonic movements, portray the rough army camp life, the carousals of the soldiery (*Scherzo*) interrupted by the admonitions of the Friar (*Trio*) and, after a Nocturne, dawn and the regiment marching off. This suggests Berlioz, *Harold in Italy*, as a model rather than Liszt. The third of these early tone-pictures was inspired by a performance of a play by the Danish playwright Oehlenschläger at Göteborg in December 1859. This dealt with the victory of Christianity over paganism—the theme of Liszt's *Hunnenschlacht*. But it was the political element of the play which caught Smetana's imagination, for it deals with the conflict between Hakon Jarl, a Norwegian usurper, and Olaf, the rightful heir but a weakling. There are four main sections—a prologue introducing the characters; the struggle between the two; Olaf's triumph; Jarl's assassination.[5]

Important as these three works are in the history of the *genre* and in Smetana's own development they pale before the magnificent series of tone-poems of the next decade, known collectively as *Ma Vlast* ('My Country').

When Smetana returned to Czechoslovakia in 1861 he found the political situation much eased. The road to political freedom was being cleared, the door to the recognition of an indigenous Czech

---

[2] Large (p. 84) says it was the first of Shakespeare's plays to appear in a complete edition in Czech in 1851.

[3] Dated 24 October, 1858; partially quoted in Large, *op. cit.*

[4] The work is analysed in some detail by Roger Fiske in *Shakespeare in Music*, edited by Phyllis Hartnoll (London, 1964).

[5] See Large, p. 104, and Newmarch, p. 60.

culture was opening. It was Smetana's privilege to be allowed a major share in the musical emancipation of the nation (not, it may be said, without opposition, for he was not the easiest man to work with). He first turned his attention to opera, producing a series of works on nationalistic themes such as *The Brandenburgers in Bohemia*, *Dalibor*, *Libusa* and the work that burst the national boundaries to carry Czech opera all over the world, *The Bartered Bride*, first performed in 1866. The six works constituting *Ma Vlast*, written during the period 1874-79 but possibly conceived slightly earlier, are the climax of his career. Following these he wrote little of importance and indeed his last years were a sad decline into mental illness. The first performance of the complete cycle took place at Prague, under the baton of his friend Adolphe Čech, on 5 November, 1882.

The cycle ranks among the most important orchestral works of the nineteenth century. There are a few *longueurs*, and the occasional moments of bombast or over-protest common to most big works of the period; on the other hand the freshness of ideas, the aptness of the orchestration and the general artistic balance of the whole provide ample compensation. The programme, which we have direct from Smetana, is a blend of legend, history and anecdote. The first, *Vyšehrad*, focusses on the forbidding, gray castle which dominates Prague, symbolizing the tragic history of the Czechs up to the point when their '*risorgimento*' is imminent: 'The harps of the bards begin; a bard sings of the events that have taken place in Vyšehrad — of the glory, splendour, tournaments and battles, and finally of its downfall and ruin'. It is basically in sonata form, with themes manipulated somewhat in the manner of Liszt. The second, *Vltava*, is pastoral and anecdotal, and follows the course of the river Vltava from its birth as the confluence of two tiny streams (most picturesquely depicted by two flutes) to the turbulence of the St John's rapids. As it gathers tributaries it becomes a stately flow through the countryside and past romantic castles. We witness a wedding, and the springing rhythm of the polka fades into the distance as we glide smoothly on in the moonlight (a magical orchestral touch). It comes at last to Prague and the granite Vyšehrad, and the great theme from the first tone-poem rings out proudly. With *Šárka* we are in the realm of legend again. Šárka is a sort of Czech Amazon, revenging herself on the whole race of men for the infidelity of her lover. She has herself bound to a tree; a band of armed men arrive on the scene, determined to punish Šárka and her Amazons; but their leader,

Ctirad, is bewitched by Sárka's beauty and sets her free. Sárka drugs them; when they are all asleep she sounds her horn, her companions who have been hiding near by rush in, and Ctirad and his men are killed. The work is continuous but divisible into five sections, linked by recitative-like transitions. It is the weakest of the six; Ctirad's march is rather obvious in its fanfare-like 'nobility' theme, and the love music not wholly convincing. One can no doubt interpret *Sárka* as symbolizing the spirit of the Czech nation, awaiting only the moment to rise up against their Austrian oppressors.

The cycle was originally intended as a tetralogy, with *From Bohemia's Woods and Fields* as conclusion. This was finished in 1875, and there was quite a gap before he tackled the two remaining works. Though Niecks described this simply as 'A Pastoral Symphony' Smetana himself provided a much more detailed scenario. The opening, *Molto moderato*, is intended to convey the impression of arriving in the country. The change from G minor to G major (bar 46) is meant to picture a simple country girl sauntering through the fields. In the 3/4 section (bar 74, C major, with solo violin prominent) we sense the beauty of nature at noon, the sun directly overhead, while in the forest it is shadowy, with only the occasional shaft of light piercing the foliage. A rising hexachord, in triplets, suggests the twittering of birds, while a broad melody (clarinets and horns in sixths) soars above. The last section returns to G minor for some peasant merry-making—a polka derived from the opening theme. This scheme perhaps represents the townsman's sentimental idealization of country life, and has been echoed in innumerable similar 'poems' by Czechs and Russians; it has rarely if ever been better done.

The last two, *Tabor* and *Blanik*, are much more patriotic and nationalistic in intent. Smetana contrived their scenarios with the help of Palacky's *History of the Czech Nation*.[6] They are really two parts of a single whole, with material, particularly the rugged chorale tune, in common. The action revolves round the fate of Czechoslovakia's great national hero, the religious zealot and reformer John Hus, who in 1415 was burnt as a heretic by order of the Council of Constance. His martyrdom roused the soul of the Czech

---

[6] For a good study in English see R. W. Seton-Watson, *A History of the Czechs and Slovaks* (London, 1943).

nation. The peasant army of revolt found a natural leader in John Ziska, a dour, implacable puritan, who made his headquarters in Mount Tabor. His battle-hymn is a chorale, an unflinching block of music in the Dorian mode; *Tabor* is built entirely round this. The mountain Blanik is a sort of Czech Valhalla. While shepherds pasture their sheep on the brow of the hill the Hussite heroes lie within; when the time is ripe they will rise again, and the fame of Bohemia's land will blaze forth in renewed splendour — a consummation typified in the grandiose conclusion of Blanik when the Hussite chorale is heard in combination with the heroic Vyšehrad theme.

Antonín Dvořák (1841-1904) wrote a number of works for orchestra with more or less programmatic content. They are: Three *Nocturnes* (1872); *Romeo and Juliet* overture (1873 — but apparently never performed); a *Rhapsody* in A minor, which Dvořák later re-named *Symphonic Poem* (1874, unperformed and unpublished in his lifetime); three overtures, a) *In Nature's Realm* Op. 91 (1891); b) *Carnival* Op. 92 (1891); c) *Othello* Op. 93 (1891-92); four symphonic poems, a) *The Water Goblin* Op. 107; b) *The Noon Witch*, Op. 108; c) *The Golden Spinning Wheel* Op. 109 and d) *The Wild Dove* Op. 110 (all 1896). In addition there is *Heroic Song*, a symphonic poem but with no programme (1897) and the *Hussite* overture (1883).

The three overtures Op. 91, 92 and 93 originally had the non-committal titles Nature, Life and Love. He had considered re-naming the first 'Summer Night', or 'In Solitude', and wondered whether he should re-name the third 'Tragic' (perhaps bearing in mind Brahm's *Tragic* overture written in 1880) or 'Eroica'.[7] Op. 91 was dedicated to Cambridge University, which had honoured him with a Doctorate of Philosophy in 1891. The same year Prague similarly honoured him, and *Carnival* Op. 92 was dedicated to that university. Once more we think of Brahms, whose *Academic Festival* overture was due to a similar honour from Breslau University (1880); the two works share a sort of genial breeziness that suggests that Dvořák may have sought to emulate the composer whom he admired and held in affection. In considering this overture, which has

---

[7] See John Claphan, *Antonín Dvořák* (London), 1966) page 113.

remained the most popular of the three with the general public despite the air of disapproval from the pundits,[8] one should bear in mind the original title, 'Life'; the work symbolizes, perhaps, the two sides of man's character, the robust and active, and the contemplative — Schumann's Florestan and Eusebius.

The third overture has a clearer programme than the first two, though some unresolved questions remain. Dr Roger Fiske has suggested with some reason that Dvořák was thinking not so much of Shakespeare's *Othello* as of Verdi's opera, which had been produced in Prague in 1888.[9] The evidence for the programme lies in the autograph score, in which are pencilled references to the plot in 'no less than eleven places'. But aside from the question of just when these notes were written in, this does not get over the fact that the ascription to *Othello* must have come after the original, looser title, 'Love'. Is this yet another instance of a composer, for some rather obscure reason, grafting a programme on to an already existing compositon? His letters, far from clearing up the matter, leave us in completer darkness. For, says Fiske, 'When he sent the score to his publisher, he wrote, "Overture in F sharp minor", "Othello", or "Tragic", or even "Eroica?" Or should I just call it Overture? But to some extent it is programme music'.

The question is further complicated by the fact that all three overtures have a musical theme in common, said to represent Nature. It is an attractive little motif, but it does emphasize the central problem of programme music, for if this represents Nature it is because Dvořák says it does — and for no other reason. Its introduction into the magical middle section of *Carnival* (on solo clarinet, four bars before letter K) has almost the air of a secret code, a private message whose clue is hidden, like the Mendelssohn quotation in the *Romanza* of Elgar's *Enigma Variations*.

Whatever qualms Dvořák may have had over programmes for his three overtures, they had vanished by 1896, when he gave a long and detailed synopsis for each of his four symphonic poems. His source was a collection of Czech legends and folk tales by Karel Erben, first

---

[8] 'All but the middle part is noisy, obvious music' says Alec Robertson *(Dvořák*, Master Musicians Series, p. 148).

[9] *Shakespeare in Music* (ed. Hartnoll) p. 213. Fiske's discussion of the problem is most enlightening

published in 1842 and frequently reprinted. The four chosen by Dvořák are uncommonly ghoulish and macabre; one wonders what inner devil was exorcised by these pieces.

The Water Goblin is a variant of the Russalka or Ondine theme — the supernatural water sprite in love with or wedded to a human.

> We first meet the Water Goblin, the king of the underwater world who holds prisoner the souls of drowned men and women, sitting on a poplar branch in the pale moonlight, making himself a coat of green and shoes of red, for tomorrow is his wedding day. Early next morning a village maid, his chosen victim, goes to the lakeside to wash her clothes, in spite of her mother's forebodings of evil. As she dips the first garment in the water the bridge on which she is standing collapses. She falls in the lake, is drowned, and becomes wedded to the Water Goblin. Bewailing her fate she pours out her sorrows and her passionate desire for home in lullabies to her baby. Her request to be allowed to return to her mother for one day is granted, on two conditions; she must return before vespers, and the Water Goblin will keep the baby as a pledge that she will return. But when the time comes her mother refuses to let her go. A violent storm arises; there is a thud on the doorstep. On opening the door they find the headless body of the baby.

In *The Noon Witch* we have a fretful child scolded by its mother, who threatens it with the Noon Witch; upon which a shrivelled, ghostly figure appears, performs a weird dance, and demands the child. The terror-stricken mother clasps the child in her arms, but the witch approaches. The mother faints, and at noon the witch disappears. When the father comes in from the fields he finds his wife in a swoon and the child suffocated.

The *Golden Spinning Wheel* is even more grisly:

> Out hunting, the king being thirsty calls at a cottage for a drink of water, and at once falls in love with the girl who opens the door to him. He asks her to be his bride, but the girl replies that he must ask her stepmother. The stepmother, wicked as all stepmothers are in fairytales, naturally would prefer the king to marry her own daughter, who as it happens is the image of the stepdaughter. The king commands her to bring the stepdaughter to the palace next day. Mother and daughter take the stepdaughter, Dornicka, through the forest to the palace, but on the way they murder Dornicka and mutilate the body taking the eyes, hands and feet with them to the palace — why is not clear. The king, unsuspecting, marries the daughter, and

goes off to war, leaving his wife diligently spinning. Now a wise magician enters the story. Finding the mutilated body in the wood, he sends his boy three times to the palace, once to exchange a golden spinning wheel for the feet, next a golden distaff for the two hands, and finally a golden spindle for a pair of eyes. Then with the water of life he revivifies Dornicka. When the king returns his wife shows him the magnificent spinning wheel; but no sooner does she begin to use it than it creaks out the secret of the crime. The king seeks his true love, Dornicka, in the forest, finds her and marries her. In Erben's story mother and daughter are torn to pieces by wolves.

The Wild Dove is less macabre. Its plan is as follows: a young widow follows her husband's coffin to the grave, with loud lamentations (*Andante, Marcia funèbre*). A handsome young farmer comes along, invites her to forget her grief and marry him (*Allegro*, afterwards *Andante*). The wedding feast follows (*Molto vivace,* then *Allegretto*). Her conscience is smitten when she hears the cooing of a dove, sitting in a tree overlooking her first husband's grave, for it is revealed that she has poisoned him. Remorse, and expiation by drowning herself (*Andante*). The work ends with a return to the tempo and mood of the original funeral march.

The last symphonic poem, *Heldenlied* ('Hero's Song') has no programme. Otakar Šourek, Dvořák's chief biographer, believed it to be somewhat autobiographical, representing Dvořák's own destiny, but a later critic, Jiří Berkovec, has suggested that Dvořák had in mind a kind of 'spiritual hero'.[10] It is conceivable that Dvořák had Brahms in mind; he had been very much moved by the latter's death on 3 April 1897. The work was first performed under Mahler on 4 December the following year in Vienna, the city that Brahms made his second home.

The question of the impulse driving a composer towards any particular medium or mode of expression is both fascinating and, yet, little explored. That Dvořák after his return from America should turn towards the explicitly programmatic is not surprising in view of the increasingly widespread cultivation of the form and in particular of Strauss's highly successful ventures; it is only the choice of subject that is at all singular. Themes from his native land seemed

---

[10] Clapham, p. 125. This work, incidentally, precedes Strauss's *Ein Heldenleben*.

an obvious choice;[11] but what themes? Smetana had already dealt splendidly with the heroic and patriotic in his operas and his tone-poems, but had ignored the fairy tales and folk legends of ancient Bohemia. Erben's collection had already provided the libretto for Dvořák's cantata *The Spectre's Bride* (1883-84) — a tale with some resemblance to Bürger's *Lenore*. These stories in which horror and cruelty figure so largely mirror to some extent the blood-stained history of the Czech nation, which has had more than its fair share of malicious and vengeful deeds and senseless butchery.

Dvořák's essentially lyrical and discursive style is less of a handicap than one might have expected. His sanguine temperament led him to play down the brutality of the stories, which a later composer might have exploited; consequently we are kept in the land of illusion and make-believe. The orchestration, as always with Dvořák, is sparkling and clear, and with some particularly vivid touches such as in *The Golden Spinning Wheel* when the wheel creaks out the terrible secret. Deft characterization abounds, as for instance the fretful child's theme in *The Noon Witch*, or the trumpet theme which is associated with the self-assured young farmer in *The Wild Dove*. Another long passage which calls for comment in *The Wild Dove* is the wedding music — a *Furiant* in the Lydian mode over a drone bass. In the *Slavonic Dances*, written before he went to America, the dances of his native land are spruced up and made presentable; here Dvořák vouchsafes us a glimpse of what untutored, improvised village music was really like. These five symphonic poems, neglected though they are in our concert life today, are of capital importance in the orchestral music of the nineteenth century.

Dvořák, the first Czech composer to achieve undisputed international standing, was looked up to by young and old. His pupils included Rudolf Karel (1880-1945), Vitézslav Novák (1870-1949), Josef Suk (1874-1935) — Dvořák's son-in-law — and others, who all actively carried on the Czech symphonic poem tradition. Another pupil was Zdenko Fibich (1850-1900),[12] who has the distinction of writing the first symphonic poem deriving inspiration from Czech

---

[11] He had come in for some reproach from the more enthusiastic Czech chauvinists for his 'internationalism', Dvořák standing in relation to the Czech nationalist composers much as Tchaikowsky did to the Five.

[12] See Henri Hantich, *La Musique tchèque* (Paris, 1907), and Rosa Newmarch, *op. cit.* — which has the most extensive account of Fibich's music in English.

history. This was *Zaboj, Slavoj and Ludek*, first played in a four-handed arrangement on 12 December 1873 and first heard in its orchestral form on 25 May 1874, conducted by Čech. It is based on a folk legend, one of many assembled in a famous manuscript, the *Dvůr Králové*. It depicts the struggle between Ludek, whose identifying theme is heard at the outset of the piece, and Zaboj, whose rather melancholy, reflective theme is heard soon after. According to Dr Jiranek (in the preface to the published score) 'it symbolizes the strength and the "dove-like" gentle side of the Czech, slavonic spirit', which finally triumphs, the theme transformed into a polka, the work ending in an 'apotheosis of the Czech homeland'. Dr Jiranek's preface, it must be confessed, is by no means crystal-clear. A later Fibich symphonic poem *Spring* (1881) is in sharp contrast. It has far more individuality than most works with that title, with much imaginative use of the orchestra (its opening clarinet solo, unaccompanied, seems to anticipate Debussy's *L'Après-midi d'un faune*) and some nice impressionistic touches.

After the achievements of Berlioz in the 1830s French instrumental music drifted for many years in the doldrums. The eyes of composers were mainly focussed on the opera house, and instrumental music of all kinds languished until revived under the influence of the École Niedermeyer and its most distinguished pupil, Gabriel Fauré (1845-1924).[13]

One work, however, must be noticed. Félicien David's *Le Désert* has today vanished without trace, but the furore it created when it was first played in 1844 was quite extraordinary. David, who has been previously mentioned in connection with piano music, was the first of France's peripatetic musicians to bring home travelogues. After being a choirboy in a Jesuit college he went on to the Conservatoire, joined the Saint-Simonians, and in 1833 went with other members of the sect to the Near East, to Turkey, Smyrna, Egypt, across the Red Sea, traversed the desert to Beirut and returned to France in 1835.

The work with which he stunned the Parisian audiences and which, more surprisingly perhaps, drew extravagant eulogies not

---

[13] There is as yet no comprehensive study in English of French music and music in France. For the period concerned Martin Cooper's *French Music from the Death of Berlioz to the Death of Fauré* (London, 1951) is useful.

only from competent music journalists like Maurice Bourges[14] but from the great Berlioz, who published a glowing appreciation of the work in the journal *Les Débats*, 15 December, 1844.[15] David described it as 'ode symphonique'; its three parts comprise ten 'scenes' outlining the simplest of scenarios, namely, a caravan approaching across the desert, the night camp at an oasis and the departure next morning. The orchestra is not left to expound this unaided; there is a certain amount of rather simple chorus work and some spoken recitative over sustained chords or single notes. Portions such as the third number, 'La Tempête au Désert' (the chorus sings 'Courbez vos fronts! Le Simoûn, vent de feu, passe comme un fléau de Dieu!') and the eighth, depicting dawn, are frankly descriptive (Berlioz spoke highly of the orchestration, and compared the storm favourably with Beethoven); other movements play on civilized man's romantic hankering after the broad simplicities of nature. 'Ici la vie est un rude combat' sing the chorus in No 2, the 'Marche de la Caravanne'; and in 'Les Rêveries du Soir' they hymn the joys of the open air as opposed to city life. There is quite a touch of atmosphere in No 8, 'Le Lever du Soleil', and the experiment of incorporating some oriental *fioriture* in the 'Chant du Muezzin' is worth noting. The influence of this work in France was probably much greater than we realize today.

The important works of Franck, Saint-Saëns, d'Indy, Duparc and others owe much to the increased opportunities for orchestral performances of high standards under conductors like Pasdeloup, Colonne and Lamoureux. The foundations were laid by François Antoine Habeneck (1781-1849), who established in 1820 the Société des Concerts du Conservatoire, and remained in charge for twenty years. In 1851 Jules Étienne Pasdeloup (1819-87) founded the Société des Jeunes Artistes du Conservatoire, and his programmes included symphonic works by rising young French composers such as Gounod, Lefébure-Wély, Gouvy, Saint-Saëns and others. Later he gave a series of Sunday 'Concerts Populaires'. Édouard Colonne (1838-1910) began as a violinist, in the Opéra orchestra and in the Lamoureux Quartet. At his Concerts du Châtelet he devoted more attention than Pasdeloup had to French composers (he directed the

---

[14] Bourges (1812-81) was from 1839 joint editor of *La Revue Musicale*.
[15] Extracts from this in Niecks; reprinted in *Les Musiciens et la Musique* (Paris, 1903). See Barzun, *Berlioz*, II, p. 384.

first performance of Franck's *les Djinns* at the Châtelet theatre in 1885), but he also championed Wagner, whose *Ride of the Valkyries* he popularized. Charles Lamoureux (1834-99) also began as a violinist, playing in the Société des Concerts du Conservatoire. He founded the Société de la Harmonie Sacrée, modelled on the London Sacred Harmonic Society, performing such works as *Messiah, Judas Maccabaeus,* the *St Matthew Passion* and Massenet's *Eve*. In 1881 he began the Nouveaux Concerts, first of all in the theatre Château d'Eau, afterwards in the Eden theatre and the Cirque des Champs-Elysées.

Another factor of the greatest importance was the formation of the *Société Nationale de Musique française* in 1871, founded by a group of musicians including Saint-Saëns, Romain Bussine, Gabriel Fauré and Edouard Lalo, at a time when France's morale was at a low ebb in consequence of her humiliating defeat at the hands of Prussia in the Franco-Prussian War. As its name implies, it was intended as a rallying ground for French music, but its ventures in the orchestral field were handicapped by lack of funds. Nevertheless its inspiration was real; in 1871 modern French instrumental music was born.

The French have always approached 'absolute' or 'pure' instrumental art rather warily. Music for them is primarily an art of sound, just as painting is an art of colour. The sound is either self-sufficient, with no equivalence in the spoken or written word, or it is not: in which case it must be clearly linked with visual or verbal images. It is not expected to evoke, unaided, states of mind, whether intellectual or emotional. In the matter of programme music, something of the difference between the French attitude and the more mystical approach of the German school of composers is illustrated by comparing Berlioz's *Symphonie fantastique* with Liszt's *Faust* symphony (Liszt in this instance being in the German camp). Berlioz subtitles his work 'Épisode de la vie d'un artiste'; the music tells us little or nothing of the mental state of the 'artiste' who is ostensibly the subject of the work. Liszt on the other hand sets out to probe the inner thoughts of Faust and Margaret. The music seeks to symbolize Faust's world-weariness, his agonies of conscience, his passion for the young girl whom he will betray.[16] The adjective that

---

[16] Compare, too, Berlioz's own treatment of the Faust theme, which began, like his symphony, in episodical fashion, the *Eight Scenes from Faust*.

sums up the French attitude is 'decoratif'. This certainly does not mean 'superficial'; and even if it did, it would not necessarily be pejorative, for 'depth' is not synonymous with 'quality'.

It is true that during the period we are now examining the pellucid clarity on which the French pride themselves was clouded, even muddied, by an admixture of the alien German *penchant* for brooding introspection, typified of course by Wagner. Most French composers found themselves exposed to the infection; of those who succumbed some recovered more quickly than others. Debussy, 'musicien français' as he liked to call himself, indisputably the greatest figure among his compatriots and acknowledged as a seminal force in modern music, was able like all great creative artists to absorb just what he required from this, and other, alien sources. At the other extreme was Fauré, characteristically immune to foreign influence and as French as the poet he set so exquisitely, Verlaine, yet remaining a minor figure by reason of his insularity. To others, of whom d'Indy is typical, Wagnerism proved a danger rather than a release.

The oldest of the group of composers whom we might describe as French nationalists, César Franck (1822-90), was subjected to a complex of cross-currents which he rode only with difficulty. He was, it must be remembered, not French but Belgian by birth. He was a gifted child, indeed a child prodigy; but he was unfortunate enough to have a father whose main object seems to have been to exploit the boy's pianistic gifts, and who dominated César right up to the latter's marriage, in defiance of his tyrannical parent, in 1848. The organ—the instrument so firmly associated in people's minds with Franck—did not figure in his accomplishments until 1840, some three years after he had entered the Paris Conservatoire as a pupil. It is unlikely that the works of J. S. Bach occupied a very prominent place in his instruction, for in fact young Franck's musical background was decidedly ramshackle, as indeed were his own first efforts at composition.[17]

One positive and probably on the whole beneficial influence was that of Liszt, whom Franck met certainly in 1842 if not earlier. Liszt, it is well known, had a warm word of welcome for Franck's early *Trio* Op. 2, dedicated to him, while Franck, for his part, all his life

---

[17]See *César Franck and his Circle* by Laurence Davies (London, 1970).

preserved a high regard for the older composer. In 1885 he wrote:

> Liszt est la plus riche imagination musicale de notre temps. Ses ouvrages sont au piano comme à l'orchestre, une mine de trésors mélodiques et harmoniques; son *Faust* est plus beau de tous ceux qu'on pu écrire . . . [18]

There are certain similarities, in harmonic resource and in melodic outline, between the two, as we can see if we compare the would-be impressive *Maestoso* theme in the first movement of the *Faust* symphony with the grandiloquent and pompous second subject (bar 129 *et seq.*) of the first movement of Franck's symphony. And it is an odd coincidence, if no more, to see the two composers almost contemporaneously writing symphonic poems based on identical material. Franck's *Ce qu'on entend sur la Montagne*, scored for full orchestra (it includes three trombones, ophicleide, timps, cymbals and bass drum; the violins are *divisi* in six parts) was written in 1848 or earlier—ie, it was actually completed *before* Liszt's *Bergsymphonie* though it never got a hearing.[19] Davies says it 'almost looks forward to Debussy's *Nuages*' and praises its 'stereophonic effects in depicting *le chant de la nature* and *le cri humain*'.

It was thirty years before Franck ventured on another work for orchestra alone. It was another symphonic Poem, *Les Éolides* (1876), inspired by some words by the Parnassian poet Leconte de Lisle (1818-94):

> O brises flottantes des cieux,
> Du beau printemps douces haleines,
> Qui, de baisers capricieux,
> Caressez les monts et les plaines,
> Vierges, filles d'Éole, amantes de la paix,
> La nature éternelle à vos chansons s'éveille.

Written for an orchestra that has shed the heavy brass, this short work reveals a Franck full of grace and imagination, handling his instrumental resources with the assurance that seems to come naturally to French composers, mirroring the unsubstantial daughters of Eolus with an enviable lightness of touch.

One wonders how long this work had been simmering in his mind.

---

[18] See Maurice Emmanuel, *César Franck* (Paris, 1930) page 36.
[19] The work is discussed in some detail by Julien Tiersot in 'Les Oeuvres inédites de César Franck', in *La Revue Musicale*, December 1922.

The several disappointments he suffered in the 1850s brought on a crisis and something approaching a breakdown in health. He was apparently making no headway as a composer with either instrumental music or opera (his attempt at the latter, *Le Valet de Ferme*, had been rejected), and through sheer economic necessity he resigned himself to the inevitable and took to the organ loft and the drudgery of teaching. Incentive to proceed with orchestral works was provided by the new *Société nationale* and, no doubt, by the example of Saint-Saëns, whose four symphonic poems date from the 1870s — and conceivably by the stimulus of Augusta Holmès, of whom more later. Wherever the urge sprang from it was powerful enough to drive him along a new creative path, for at the age of fifty-three he suddenly embarked on the series of orchestral and chamber works that more than anything keep his memory green.

The works that concern us are, besides *Les Éolides*, *Le Chasseur Maudit*, *Les Djinns* and *Psyché*. *Le Chasseur Maudit* (1882) is based on a rather obvious poem by the German poet Bürger, *Der Wilde Jäger*, written as long ago as 1778.[20] It tells of the licentious and oppressive Count of the Rhine who, to add to his other crimes, goes hunting on the Sabbath. For this he is himself condemned to be hunted for ever through the flames and terrors of Hell. Franck's work is avowedly pictorial, and very vivid it is. The Sunday morning church bells, the Count's challenging hunting horn, the chase, the hymn floating up from the church service and the frightful *dénouement* as the sacrilegious Count's role changes from hunter to hunted are all there with a realism and a sure orchestral touch that reveal quite another side of the pious Franck. And despite echoes of Wagner's *Ride of the Valkyries* and Berlioz's *Ride to the Abyss* (*La Damnation de Faust* was at that time being promoted by Colonne) the work is stamped with Franck's individuality.

Les Djinns (1884) is another curious and unexpected subject from 'Father' Franck and his organ loft. The source is a poem by Victor Hugo which first appeared in 1829 in *Les Orientales* — is this another rummage in the past? Djinns are evil spirits of Arab mythology; there is no detailed programme as in *Le Chasseur Maudit*, but rather a generalized picture, a struggle between good and evil in the Lisztian manner. The layout is for piano and orchestra, the piano

---

[20] Sir Walter Scott made an excellent English version in 1796.

concertante rather than solo, but its technique deriving from Liszt. The 'exotic' East is cleverly suggested, with languid, syncopated rhythms; the orchestral colouring anticipates Debussy.[21]

Psyché, written in 1887-88, is not only one of Franck's most important works but a landmark in French orchestral music. It is his most ambitious essay in the realm of the symphonic poem. Its three movements are: 1. *Le Sommeil de Psyché* (a slow introductory movement), followed by an *Allegro vivo, Psyché enlevée par les zéphyrs*; 2, also in two sections, *Les Jardins d'Éros* (this includes a chorus, S.A.T.) and an *Andante non troppo, Psyché et Éros*; 3. *Le Châtiment (quasi lento)—souffrances et plaintes de Psyché—Apothéose*. The work is based on the legend that Venus, jealous of Psyche's beauty, sends Eros with orders to slay her. Instead Eros falls prey to Psyche's beauty. For her protection Psyche is wafted by zephyrs to the Garden of Love, where she and Eros enjoy nights of bliss. Eros forbids Psyche to look at him but, as in the Orpheus myth, this prohibition is eventually ignored, and as a result the lovers are parted for ever. In Franck's version after a suitable punishment they are united in the final apotheosis.

D'Indy, to whom the work was dedicated, in his biography of Franck tells us nothing as to the genesis of the work, and insists on regarding it, not simply as an interpretation of the pagan myth, but as part of Franck's 'angelic conception'.[22] The love duet, we might call it, he says, would be difficult to regard otherwise than as an ethereal dialogue between the soul, as the mystical author of 'The Imitation of Christ' conceived it, and a seraph sent from heaven to instruct it in the eternal verities; and later (page 174 ff) he quotes a long panegyric from Gustave Derepas's *César Franck* which takes us still further into a mystic Christian interpretation. It concludes:

> The exceedingly sustained harmony of the strings, the lines traced by the violins, the episodes allotted to the wind, never betray the least sign of sensuous preoccupations, but only express the highest desires of a heart penetrated by the Divine Spirit.

This would be more convincing if we had Franck's own words on the matter. As it is, with all respect to d'Indy, this is nonsense.

---

[21] For further details of *Les Éolides* and *Les Djinns* see Davies *op. cit.* pages 209-213.
[22] Vincent D'Indy, *César Franck*, translated by Rosa Newmarch (London, 1910), page 78 ff.

Franck has for too long been regarded as a sort of French Bruckner, pious, devout, content in his organ loft, a saintly figure unblemished by worldly thoughts. The facts do not bear this out. Taking his work as a whole the secular compositions far outweigh the sacred in number, size and importance. Between *Rebecca*, a biblical scene for soli, chorus and orchestra of 1881, and the *Three Chorales* of 1890 there is nothing whatever that can be related to the church, and his important religious works, the *Béatitudes* and the *Redemption*, were originally conceived long before this, the former in 1869 and the latter in 1871. One is driven to the conclusion that Franck was tied to the organ loft less by conviction than of necessity; our concept of him is still clouded by d'Indy's adoring but biassed and hopelessly inadequate biography of him.

For example, d'Indy barely mentions the colourful Augusta Holmès. She was a composer, and had some lessons from Franck in 1875, when she was twenty-eight and he was fifty-three — a woman composer who made her mark with big compositions (operas and several symphonic poems) a generation or more before Ethel Smyth or Lili Boulanger. There is good reason to suppose that she had a disturbing influence on her master, and in fact Davies, who devotes several pages to her, sees the 'embarrassing ardour' of the *Piano Quintet* of 1879 as inexplicable otherwise than by reference to his feelings for Augusta. Franck, it appears, could no more keep his emotions safely boxed away than the rest of us.

Despite the amount of work already done by Edward Lockspeiser and others as regards Debussy much still remains to be unravelled concerning other composers and their connexions with art and literature. In Franck's case we are handicapped by the dearth of published correspondence. We can, however, trace a link between him and the fashionable Hellenism of the time through his son Georges, who was a teacher and later a lecturer at the University,[23] and who may well have been responsible for the choice of the Greek legend Psyche. Many parallels can be found between music and painting during this period. Maurice Denis (1870-1943), who was a friend of Chausson and who made the lithograph for the cover of the first edition of Debussy's *Blessed Damozel*, painted an *Enlèvement de Psyché* at about the same time Franck composed his *Psyché*. Gustave

---

[23] Davies *op. cit.*, page 213.

Moreau (1826-98), the most important of the Symbolist painters, also betrayed his interest in Greek mythology by a *Hercule et l'Hydre*, c. 1870 (cf. Saint-Saëns *La Jeunesse d'Hercule*, 1877) and a *Phaëton*, c. 1878 (Saint-Saëns *Phaëton*, 1873). D'Indy's *La Forêt enchantée* (1878) reminds us of Puvis de Chavannes's *Le Bois Sacré* of 1884 and *La Forêt enchantée* by Odile Redon, c. 1875. Further research will no doubt establish whether these parallels are due to anything more specific than expressions of the general mood of the times.

Compared with Franck's four master-works, with their rich, evocative harmony and subtle orchestral colouring,[24] the facile and brilliant orchestral works of Camille Saint-Saëns (1835-1921) seem superficial. We have already noticed a tendency for composers to come to programme music comparatively late in life; Saint-Saëns runs true to form here, for he was already well established as a composer of chamber music and symphonies before writing such works as *Omphale's Spinning Wheel* and *Danse Macabre*. The latter (1874) is the only one of his four symphonic poems not based on the fashionable Greek mythology. It began as a song, a setting of a poem by Henri Cazalis; the orchestral score has a dozen lines of this poem attached which are sufficient to indicate the programme, which is a re-working of the old Dance of Death theme. The use of the xylophone to represent the dancing skeletons, which seems obvious enough, was perhaps the cause of its noisy reception when it was first played in 1875. *Le Rouet d'Omphale* (1871) refers to the legend that Omphale, queen of Lydia, had bought Hercules as a slave. The theme, of feminine seductiveness, against which even Hercules is powerless, was already in his mind as the subject of *Samson et Dalila*, a work which was ten years in the making. When *Samson* was at last performed at Weimar in 1877 his thoughts turned again to the other strong man of legend, and he wrote his fourth symphonic poem *La Jeunesse d'Hercule*. This, the least directly pictorial of the four, shows Hercules facing a choice between the primrose path of pleasure and the thorny path of virtue. He chooses the sterner path of sacrifice, with immortality as the only reward. One senses, perhaps, a touch of irony in the choice of subject and its treatment.

---

[24] The time is surely ripe for a re-appraisal of Franck's mature output.

Like so many nineteenth century musicians Saint-Saëns was a compulsive composer. He wrote easily, he was successful; he travelled extensively, and took his inspiration from his surroundings. He put the holiday brochure on the musical map. Works like *Suite algérienne* for orchestra (1880), *Une Nuit à Lisbonne*, also for orchestra (1880), *Rapsodie d'Auvergne*, for piano and orchestra (1884) and the fantasia, *Africa* for the same combination (1891), as well as several for piano solo (*Les Cloches du Soir*, 1889, and *Souvenirs d'Ismailia*, 1895), are the harbingers of a torrent of such compositions, by French and other composers, only a few of which have any strong claims to be considered as programme music—or indeed as music. Often there is at best a suggestion of 'local colour', and of course in the hands of a skilled composer the writing and scoring will be competent, as for instance in Ibert's *Escales*. But all too often what we have is—some pleasant but innocuous music, masquerading under a title that commits an offence under the Misrepresentation of Goods Act.

Two other works from this period deserve more than a passing mention. They are the *Lénore* of Henri Duparc (1848-1933) and *Viviane* by Ernest Chausson (1855-99). *Lenore*, probably the most famous ballad in German literature,[25] had already been the subject of a symphony by Joachim Raff. It is, in essence, a ghost story. Lenore awaits the return of her betrothed from the wars (actually the Seven Years' War of 1756-63). Anxiously peering into the darkness, she perceives a horseman, her Wilhelm. He flings her in the saddle behind him, they ride and ride at breakneck speed. At midnight the horse stops. Transfixed with horror she realizes that her betrothed is no longer flesh and blood, but a skeleton. Duparc's version, composed in 1875, has a few lines in French and German outlining the story. He uses a large orchestra, 3-2-2-4; 4-2-3-1; timps, cymbals, bass drum, two sizes of gongs; strings. The work begins with a slow introduction, with a cello theme that is used as a leit-motif. This leads into a *Più animato*, utilizing some of the opening material combined with more vigorous motifs on the brass. A *Più largamente* closes the work. The whole is well organized, with some imaginative touches in the scoring (e.g., the soft trombone chords near the end of the work).

---

[25] By Gottfried August Bürger (1747-94). The poem, which was like *Der Wilde Jäger* translated by Scott, can be found with a literal prose translation, in *The Penguin Book of German Verse*.

Chausson's *Viviane* was first performed at a *Société nationale* concert on 31 March 1883. The programme, drawn from Arthurian sources, is briefly explained in a *Légende* affixed to the score: Viviane and Merlin in the forest — love scene — trumpet fanfares indicate that King Arthur's messengers are scouring the forest in search of Merlin — Merlin, recalling a sense of duty, attempts to escape from Viviane's embraces, but she charms him to sleep and entwines him with hawthorn branches.

The large orchestra includes two harps, four trumpets (two are off-stage) and 'antique cymbals'. The scoring throughout is delicate and subtle, with many touches (apart from the antique cymbals) that look forward ten years to *L'Après-midi d'un faune*.

Though derived from Arthurian legend[26] the material is obviously linked with Dido/Aeneas, Armide/Roland, Tristan/Isolde, Tannhäuser/Venus and, at least as far as the notion of sleep or dreams goes, Bottom/Titania and Mallarmé's evocative poem. This world of magic has always been a special preserve of French music, and now the improvement of the nineteenth century orchestra (especially in the wind department) and the increased freedom and flexibility of nineteenth century harmony enabled composers to fix its sound-image with a brightness and precision undreamed of by earlier composers. Herein lies the connexion between Impressionist composers and Impressionist painters, for both were rejecting the *ideal* conception of art (the vision filtered and re-structured through the brain) in favour of the *real* appeal direct to the senses. The composer who saw this most clearly was of course Debussy; but the ground had been well and truly prepared by Duparc, Chausson and especially Franck.

As in the other nationalist schools that were emerging during the nineteenth century, the Russians found they could more easily find their own style by cultivating their own folklore and traditions than by pursuing the more classical, absolute music of the sonata or the symphony. This almost inevitably led to programme music, and every one of the dozen or so important Russian composers of the nineteenth century has left examples of the *genre*.

Mikhail Glinka (1804-57) is now remembered almost entirely for his two nationalistic operas, but at least one of his instrumental works

---

[26] Chausson later went on to write a Wagnerian *Roi Arthus*.

does not deserve the neglect into which it has fallen. During his visit to Spain in 1845 he was entranced, as so many Northerners were later, by Spanish popular music, and the outcome of this was a *Souvenir d'une Nuit d'Été à Madrid*; *Fantaisie sur des Thèmes espagnols*, for an orchestra of double woodwind, four horns, two trumpets, one trombone, strings, and a fairly large percussion group which includes triangle, castanets, side drum, bass drum and cymbals. It was written in 1848 in Warsaw, for the Governor's orchestra. Apart from its interest as a very early example of the fantasia, rhapsody or capriccio inspired by Spain and its folk music, it is an engaging work, with many touches that remind us of Chabrier (*España*), Rimsky-Korsakov and Tchaikowsky. The scoring is most attractive, with many unusual and individual touches.

The remarkable story, at once entertaining, puzzling and contradictory, of the group of composers revolving round Mily Balakirev, whose eternal itch for interfering in his comrades' artistic lives was both benevolent and malevolent, is too familiar to require stressing here.[27] Balakirev himself (1837-1910) contributed three works that concern us—the symphonic poems *Russia* and *Tamara* and the overture to *King Lear*. As to the latter there is an interesting letter to Tchaikowsky[28] in which he explains his intentions, with themes that represent Lear, Regan, Goneril, Cordelia, and incidents from the play. *Russia* (1864; revised 1882) was a patriotic gesture; based on Russian themes, it was intended to symbolize three eras in the history of Russia—the pagan period, the period of the Cossack princes, and the modern Russian Empire centred on Moscow. The programmatic content of *Tamara* (1882) is much more specific, being based on a typically decadent romantic poem by Lermontov (1814-41). It is almost a variant of the Loreley legend: Queen Tamara, beautiful, lustful, amoral, in her tower high above, not the Rhine, but the Terek, with her siren voice luring the unsuspecting wayfarer inside. But within the castle is debauchery and death, and dawn sees the young traveller's body being carried away by the swiftly flowing river.[29] The idea of the work began to germinate in

---

[27] One of the best accounts is still *Masters of Russian Music* (London, 1936), by M. D. Calvocoressi and Gerald Abraham.

[28] Quoted in Niecks, page 416 ff. For an analysis of this and other works see Edward Garden, *Balakirev* (London, 1967).

[29] This story of lust and senseless cruelty could be matched by many a true incident of equal ferocity in Lermentov's time; see for example Noel Barber's *Lords of the Golden Horn* (London, 1973).

Balakirev's mind as early as 1862 during a holiday in the Caucasus, when he found himself fascinated by the primitive and exotic sounds of Oriental folk music; in *Tamara* the blend of East and West results in a work of genius. The themes, Tamara's in particular (depicting her loveliness, her passion, her fatal fascination), are full of character, the orchestration is splendid, the pace and rhythmic verve exciting. Moreover, it is not too long. It is put together with great craftsmanship, and remains one of the most satisfactory of all the Russian tone-poems.

The blending of East and West is a characteristic of much Russian music, from Tchaikowsky, Stravinsky and Scriabin to Khachaturian. Another short but excellent example, ante-dating slightly the final version of *Tamara*, is *In the Steppes of Central Asia* by Alexander Borodin (1833-87). This is a most telling picture of the trundling caravan, seen first as in a mirage, gradually approaching, the melancholy and monotonous wail of the oboe typifying the unending journey across the featureless plains, the long procession shambling past to be lost by and by in the burning distance. Like *Tamara* it is a masterpiece.

Of all the group whom Balakirev fussed over, encouraged, cajoled and rebuked the most disturbing, moody and unpredictable was Modest Mussorgsky (1839-81). His disorganized life, cut short by illness and drink, had something in common with that bohemian of the French boulevards, Verlaine (1844-96). Rebels against the establishment, both could transmute dross into purest gold. His only important orchestral contribution to programme music is the short *St. John's Night on the Bare Mountain* (1867) — an essay in diabolism which owes something to Liszt's *Danse Macabre* for piano and orchestra. It is a Witches' Sabbath, and is described by Mussorgsky as follows:

> Witches assemble on the mountain awaiting Satan's arrival. He appears; they form a circle around his throne and glorify him. After some time he gives the signal for the Sabbath to begin.[30]

Mussorgsky apparently wished this programme to be printed whenever the piece was performed. He attached great importance to the work, seeing it as real Russian music as opposed to 'German profundity'.

---

[30] See M. D. Calvocoressi, *Modest Mussorgsky* (London, 1956), page 73.

In his ten *Pictures from an Exhibition* (1874) he made a unique contribution to pianoforte literature. It was occasioned by an exhibition of paintings by his friend Victor Hartmann who had recently died. Here again is no 'profundity', German or otherwise. Each scene, whether that of the two Jews, the children playing, the chickens hatching out or the Great Gate of Kiev, is etched in with economy and a sure touch.

Mussorgsky's music has the rough vigour of poster art, and as such found little favour among those who sought for refinement of taste. Rimsky-Korsakov (1844-1908), for instance, found much of his work crude and amateurish, and seemed unable to realize that this roughness was Mussorgsky's special quality. Rimsky-Korsakov, intellectual, nervous, even neurasthenic, for whom music was not the stuff of realism but an escape, represented the opposite pole of Russia's soul. His masterpiece is the opera *The Golden Cockerel*—brilliant, satirical, other-worldly and slightly dotty. In his instrumental work his taste for the fantastic led him to the tedious *Scheherazade* (1888), based on the Arabian Nights' Entertainments; to *Sadko* (1867, later revised and remodelled as an opera); and to *Antar* (1868). *Sadko* tells of a sort of Russian Jonah, thrown overboard as an appeasement to the ruler of the seas. *Antar*, based on an oriental tale by Senkovsky, tells how Antar, in the desert, rescues a gazelle, who turns out to be the fairy Gul-Nazar. She grants him three pleasures—of power; of vengeance; of love. At the end of the fourth movement after a last passionate embrace she dies in Antar's arms.

Though Petr Ilyich Tchaikowsky (1840-93) achieved more success with absolute music than most of his fellow Russians, like them he seemed happiest when he could link his music with an external programme. This is true even of his symphonies. His first, written in 1866, was entitled 'Winter dreams', with further subtitles to the first two movements, 'Dreams of a Winter Journey' and 'Rugged Country—Cloudland'; the sixth and last also has the title, 'Pathetic', which seems to imply an underlying programme. As to the fourth, written in 1877-78, the composer gave a very detailed synopsis in a letter to Madame von Meck in 1878[31] which, though it must be read

---

[31] Given in Niecks, page 439, and in Herbert Weinstock's *Tchaikowsky* (London, 1946), page 169. Tchaikowsky's correspondence has been published in Russian, but so far only a portion of this and his other literary work (he did some journalism in 1876, reporting on *The Ring* from Bayreuth) is available in English.

with some caution (the symphony was written at the time of his unfortunate marriage, and his mental state at that time was far from stable), throws much light on some aspects of the art of composition. The symphony is dominated by the 'Fate' theme—destiny hanging over our heads, threatening our happiness, seen in the first movement as illusory. A gentler melancholy or nostalgia is reflected in the second movement. In the third are to be found the pleasant sounds that an idle imagination throws up—transitory, of no significance. In the fourth movement Tchaikowsky picks up the Mussorgskyan theme of the common people, whose enjoyment at a fair is unconfined. But Destiny looms; the composer, lonely and sad, finds himself cut off from this rejoicing, and can only experience this pleasure vicariously. This may not be very profound, but it makes a valid framework for the music.

Tchaikowsky's importance as a programme writer rests on the three works, *Romeo and Juliet*, *Francesca da Rimini* and *Manfred*. The themes—the tragedy of innocent love, the guilty love of Paolo and Francesca, the brooding Manfred weighed down with the consciousness of guilt—were ideally suited to his temperament. *Romeo and Juliet* dates from 1869; it was suggested to the composer by Balakirev who in a letter outlined not only the scenario but the form, even suggesting which keys should be used. It is astonishing that this composition, which seems to us so fresh, so full of invention, so apt in its characterization of Friar Laurence, Romeo and especially Juliet, and so graphic in its depiction of the physical clash between the two rival families, should have been so misunderstood at its first performance in 1870.[32]

Francesca da Rimini (1876) was originally intended as an opera; the suggestion of a symphonic fantasia apparently came from his brother Modest. The story, very popular as an opera subject following on Silvio Pellico's dramatization of it in 1818, tells how Francesca, daughter of Polenta, Lord of Ravenna, was given in marriage to Lanciotto, the deformed son of Malatesta, Lord of Rimini. She fell in love with his handsome brother, Paolo; caught in adultery, both were put to death by Lanciotto. Tchaikowsky's interest in the subject was to some extent due to his admiration for Liszt's *Dante* symphony (the whirlwind: ceaselessly tossing

---

[32] Tchaikowsky revised the work in 1871, in which form it was published in May of that year. Ten years later a second, shortened, revision was published.

sinners about, is common to both works), but we also know, since he referred to the matter in a letter to his brother, that he was also inspired by Gustave Doré's edition of Dante, which had been published in 1861. There is also a self-confessed Wagner influence, especially in the gloomy opening; but here and throughout material and colouring are individual Tchaikowsky. The agitated 12/8 (beginning at *Piu mosso, Moderato*, page four of the miniature score), with its nervous chromaticism and syncopations and (later) the cross-rhythm mixtures of 3/4 and 6/8, shows a marked similarity in style to the contemporary fourth symphony. It is interesting to compare the beautiful 'love' theme, first heard on the clarinet, with the corresponding melody in *Romeo and Juliet*. They are rather similar in contour, but the caressing falling sixth in *Romeo* is more prominent; and while in *Romeo* the continuation is a soothing, rocking movement on muted violins, in *Francesca* passion mounts ever higher, in an intensification of the rapture of love.

The circumstances surrounding the composition of *Manfred* are a good illustration of the communal approach to composition that the Russian composers seemed to find congenial. In 1867–68 Berlioz visited Russia, when among other of his works *Harold in Italy* was played, and this inspired Rimsky-Korsakov to write his *Antar*, which similarly employs the idea of a 'motto-theme'. At about the same time Stassof suggested to Balakirev that he should write a work based on Byron's *Manfred*, and drafted a scenario.[33] Balakirev did not rise to the bait, but offered the scenario to Berlioz, who was really too ill to be interested. The same programme was then offered, in 1882, to Tchaikowsky, who initially at any rate was not enthusiastic. But two years later he was in Petersburg for the performance of *Eugen Onegin*, and Balakirev must have returned to the subject and won him over, for he retired to Switzerland with a volume of *Manfred* and began the composition. Perhaps the local colour helped. The work, first performed in 1886, cost the composer much heart searching and trouble, and when it was completed he was in two minds as to its value. At the time of its compositon he was thinking of it as one of his best works; later, in 1888, he professed himself dissatisfied and talked of turning it into a one-movement symphonic poem.

As it stands it is in four big movements — *Lento lugubre*

---

[33] Given in Gerald Abraham's preface to the miniature score of *Manfred*.

—*Moderato con moto—Andante; Vivace con spirito; Andante con moto; Allegro con fuoco.* The first movement deploys material associated with Manfred, brooding in the Alps, and Astarte (Aphrodite). The second movement, headed 'Le Fée des Alpes parait devant Manfred sous l'arc-du-ciel du torrent', sparkles along with motifs rather than themes, with the somewhat 'pointillist' scoring familiar in some of the symphonies. A portion of Manfred's theme appears in the Trio; the movement vanishes, like the waterfall vision, into thin air. The third movement, headed 'Pastorale. Vie simple, libre et paisible des montagnards', 6/8 time, with an oboe melody of Berliozian cast and the sounds of alphorns, recalls many such pastoral movements. The last movement has the longest legend:

> Le palais souterrain d'Arimane. Manfred parait au milieu de la Bachanale. Évocation de l'ombre d'Astarte. Elle lui prédit le terme de ses maux terrestres. Mort de Manfred.

The material, derived from the first movement, is elaborately developed, with scholastic devices such as imitation, diminution and so on. There is something of the fever of the sixth symphony, with some frenetic climaxes. It ends with an *Andante con duolo* (taken from the first movement) for the death of Manfred. The indebtedness to Berlioz is patent.

The appeal of the subject at this particular period in Tchaikowsky's life was understandable. Byron's Manfred is depicted as being in a Faust-like disillusion, but at the same time his conscience is tormented by the gnawing recollections of past crimes, unspecified, whose expiation can come only with death. This can be related to the idea of man's natural sin, but it was clearly relevant to Tchaikowsky's own mental state, his disastrous marriage and his own sense of guilt over his suppressed homosexuality. But *Manfred* also exhibits the loneliness of the creator, the visionary—another theme dear to nineteenth-century thought, which saw the artist as a seer, a prophet, whose mission it was to lead mankind to higher things. From many points of view *Manfred* is Tchaikowsky's most ambitious instrumental work, though modern criticism is not quite so ready as earlier commentators were to hail it as his masterpiece.

Other Russian composers are less important. Both Alexander Dargomyjsky (1813-69) and Anatole Liadof (1855-1914) wrote tone-poems on the subject of Baba Yaga, the witch of Russian legend

LATE ROMANTIC PROGRAMME MUSIC (I)

'whose vehicle was a mortar and whose whip a pestle'. Liadof also contributed two other attractive works, *Kikimora* and the *The Enchanted Lake*. Alexander Glazounov (1865-1936) wrote a number of works with programmatic content, the most notable of which was *Stenka Razin* (1885), based on the exploits of a seventeenth century bandit whose adventures, like those of our own Dick Turpin, were featured in Russian ballads. This is a well constructed work, with some very effective descriptive writing with an exciting ending as the waters of the Volga engulf Stenka Razin's boat. Its material is largely derived from *The Volga Boat Song*. Another Glazounov work to catch our eye is *In Memory of a Hero* Op. 8, for here again is the nineteenth century preoccupation with heroes and hero worship. In this instance the hero is the benevolent man of action, the protector of his people, the champion of the oppressed — an echo of the humanism permeating Russian thought as the result of the writings and examples of such men as Tolstoy (1828-1910), Dostoyevsky (1821-81) or Gogol (1809-52). Alfred Bruneau, who himself wrote an *Overture Hèroique* (1884), was greatly impressed by the work and wrote enthusiastically about it in his *Musiques de Russie*.

CHAPTER 8

Late Romantic Programme Music (II)

The Frenchman Franck and the Swiss Joachim Raff (1822-82) were exact contemporaries. Both were teachers—Franck at the Paris Conservatoire and Raff at Wiesbaden, later at the Frankfurt Conservatory; both were influenced by Liszt. But there the resemblance ends. Raff was prolific (the German music establishment was a greedy consumer), successful, self-assured like his successor, Strauss, and also, like Spohr and Loewe, somewhat complacent. Franck was diffident, retiring, a misfit, but canonized by adoring pupils and biographers. But while Franck's music, or some of it, still lives, Raff's is in the forgotten limbo.[1]

Some of Raff's piano compositions have programmatic titles, such as *Frühlingsboten* ('Spring's message'), *From Switzerland* (c. 1853) or *Les Orientales.* One of his string quartets is labelled *Die Schöne Müllerin,* its six movements *(Der Jüngling; Die Mühle; Die Müllerin; Unruhe; Erklärung; Zum Polterabend)* vaguely indebted to Müller's cycle of poems set by Schubert. But his main contribution to programme music lies in his orchestral works. There are four overtures on Shakespeare themes—*Romeo and Juliet, Macbeth, Othello* and *The Tempest* (a predictable choice), and of his eleven symphonies nine have programmes, or at least titles. These are: 1. *An das Vaterland* (1863); 3. *Im Walde* (1869); 5. *Lenore*; 6. *Gelebt, gestrebt, gelitten, gestritten, gestorben, umworben* ('Lived, strove, suffered, struggled, died, and was glorified') (1876); 7. *Alpensinfonie* (1877); 8. *Frühlingsklänge* (1876); 9. *Im Sommer* (1878); 10. *Zur Herbstzeit* (1879); 11. *Winter* (1876).

Some of the titles are unenterprising. 'The Fatherland', 'The Forest', 'Spring' (the last four symphonies cover the familiar ground of the seasons) have their counterparts in Smetana and are legion

---

[1] Though his *Lenore* symphony has been recorded in recent years.

among the lesser, particularly Czech, composers. No. 5, composed in 1872, perhaps gave a hint to Duparc, whose *Lénore* was only three years later. No. 7 is a pale forerunner of Strauss (1911), and it is not impossible that there is a link between Raff's 'heroic' sixth symphony and Strauss's own *Heldenleben*.

Raff's point of view was set out by himself in the preface to his first symphony, where he echoes some of the high-sounding idealism of his patron and colleague, Liszt,[2] and the most complete working out of his principles is to be found in *Lenore*. This is in three 'Abtheilung' or parts, the first of which, labelled 'Liebesglück' ('happiness in love'), covers the first two movements, an *Allegro* full of upsurging motifs, usually in triplets, expressing rapture (key E major) — quite good pre-Strauss: and an *Andante quasi larghetto*, tenderer and more intimate, in A flat, but with a more agitated section in G sharp minor, a sort of premonition of the impending second part, 'Trennung' ('parting'). This is a stirring march, as Wilhelm goes off to the wars. The last movement is headed 'Reunion in Death' and sub-titled 'Introduction und Ballade (nach G. Bürgers "Lenore")'. This begins solemnly, suggesting a chorale; the music then works up in agitated fashion, with the pounding horse's hooves becoming more and more prominent until the culmination, the ghastly midnight climax when Lenore finds herself in the embrace of her lover's skeleton. The work ends *pianissimo* with the return of the chorale, while the strings ascend seraphically, the first violins divided in three resting on an E major triad high in their top register.

This may be the moment to say something of Raff's relationship with Liszt, whom he first met in 1845. When Liszt forsook the concert platform and went to Weimar Raff followed in 1850, and stayed there until 1856. During these years when Liszt was engaged in the direction of the Ducal theatre and engrossed in the composition of his own tone-poems Raff acted as his amanuesis. It has repeatedly been said that Liszt, having till then concentrated on piano playing and compositions for that instrument, felt insecure with the orchestra and in consequence entrusted Raff with the duty of scoring his symphonic poems. But nobody seems to have wondered where Raff, a younger and far less gifted composer and a less experienced musician, could have acquired *his* knowledge of

---

[2] See Niecks, p. 491.

orchestration. Liszt's acquaintanceship with the great French master of orchestration, Berlioz, and his transcription of the *Symphonie fantastique*, provided at least as effective an apprenticeship in the art of orchestration as anything Raff could have had.

Raff was considered important in his day, but he is essentially a minor composer. He may have had some influence, but the real line of succession in German programme music from Mendelssohn, Weber and Spohr lay not through him or the dozen or more minor composers mentioned in Niecks (they include Julius Rietz, Robert Volkmann,[3] Carl Reinecke, Joseph Joachim, Woldemar Bargiel, Karl Goldmark, Anton Rubinstein, and others) but through Richard Wagner. Wagner was the great colourist, the musical illustrator who could bring to aural life giants and kobolds, birdsong and forest murmurs, the flow of the Rhine, the abode of the gods, crackling flames, heroism and cowardice, honour and duplicity. Wagner's operas are programme music on a grand scale, the orchestra as much a protagonist as the singers on the stage. It was Wagner's orchestral and musical mastery that heralded the greatest exponent of orchestral programme music, Richard Strauss (1864–1949).

Strauss, the son of a hornplayer in the Munich orchestra, sucked in music with his mother's milk. He was precocious, writing his first song at the age of six (his mother had to write in the words); before he attained his majority he had to his credit a string quartet, an overture, two concertos and two symphonies. But as a youth his musical horizon was circumscribed by the conservative outlook of his father, who combined a proper reverence for the classics with an extreme distaste for the 'modernisms' of those upstarts, Liszt and Wagner. Strauss's appointment in September 1885 as assistant to von Bülow at Meiningen came at the very moment when he was ripe for a lunge forward into unknown regions, and at Meiningen he found a mentor, an ardent prophet of the new music, a violinist, a talker and something of a composer, by name Alexander Ritter (1833–96).

It was Ritter, who had known Liszt, who opened Strauss's mind to the potentialities of the 'new music', and the first results of the flexing of his programmatic muscles was a travelogue, *Aus Italien*,

---

[3] Volkmann, who spent some time in Czechoslovakia and ended his career in Budapest, wrote an overture, *Richard III* and a collection of piano pieces entitled *Vysehrad*.

the outcome of a visit to Italy in the spring of 1886. Cast in the traditional four-movement form of the symphony (the movements are headed, 'In the Compagna'; 'In Rome's ruins'; 'the beach at Sorrento'; 'Life in Naples'), it has little overt tone painting beyond the nature music of the third movement,[4] though in the first movement Strauss, like Mendelssohn before him, revels in the beauty of the countryside around Rome.

For his first true tone-poem Strauss went, almost inevitably, to Shakespeare — every composer did! His choice fell on *Macbeth*, perhaps because he saw the complexities of the two main characters as an opportunity and a challenge. The kingly Macbeth, infirm of purpose at the prospect of an ignoble act, Lady Macbeth, her soul twisted by greed and ambition, were surely themes within music's terms of reference. But the problems in the end proved too formidable for the young Strauss to overcome with complete success. Nevertheless the work, already stamped with Strauss's personality, established the pattern of complex and allusive material, displayed in gorgeous tonal array, that was to be his hallmark. The work, begun in 1886 and not performed until 1890, cost him endless trouble and entailed constant revision.

Meanwhile he had come across a subject far more congenial to him — whether, as Del Mar suggests, as a result of falling in love with Pauline von Ahna, his future wife, or as a consequence of the wide reading stimulated by Ritter, Artur Seidl and others of the Munich circle, makes no matter. This was *Don Juan*, in the version by Nikolaus Lenau. This poetic drama, left unfinished at Lenau's death in 1850, is summarized in Del Mar, who also gives an extensive and detailed analysis of Strauss's tone-poem.[5] The three passages from the poem which Strauss quotes at the head of his score give only one aspect — the ideal, Lisztian side — of the composer's intentions — the youthful, ardent Don, pursuing a hedonist philosophy which gradually turns bitter and proves illusory. The score in addition describes episodes from Lenau's poem, some of which, for instance the inviting of the statue to supper and the duel, correspond to scenes in Da Ponte's better known version which was the basis of Mozart's opera. It was in this blend of the ideal and the

---

[4] The work is analysed, along with all the symphonic poems, in Norman Del Mar's comprehensive three-volume biography of the composer.
[5] Vol. I p. 69 ff.

real, the reflective and the active, that Strauss betrayed his mastery and his advance over Liszt. *Don Juan* was a triumph from the first, and has kept its place in the repertory by reason of its verve, the distinction of its material (the ravishing quality of the love music was something new, and was to remain one of his most striking characteristics) and the brilliance of the whole conception.

Almost at the same time he began working on *Tod und Verklärung* ('Death and Transfiguration') (1889, first performed 1890). The scenario was concocted by Strauss himself. We are at the bedside of a dying man, one whose life has been a continued striving towards the highest ideals. His mind goes back to past times, to the innocence of youth, to his ambitions — as he sees it now, only partially realized. As death finally releases the weary body the soul ascends to heaven in transfigured glory.[6] The scenario was worked up by Ritter into a poem — in fact, two poems, a short one, printed in the programme of the first performance, and an expansion of this which prefaces the printed score. It is possible that Strauss discussed the work with Ritter, who himself wrote a symphonic poem, *Sursum Corda* (1894), 'an old man's retrospect of his artist life'.[7]

Del Mar says pertinently 'Strauss succeeded in inverse proportion to the degree of sublimity to which he aspired' — a criticism that applies with even more force to Liszt, who too often mistook aspiration for inspiration. Strauss's musical way of life exposed him to two dangers. On the one hand there was the typical nineteenth century German notion that music not only could, and should, express the sublime, but that it could interpret philosophical ideas. On the other hand his astonishing orchestral virtuosity tempted him to a parade of realism that in its extreme form led to bathos. *Tod und Verklärung* and *Also sprach Zarathustra* must be listened to with the ear of faith, the *Sinfonia domestica* with indulgence. The balance is happily struck in *Don Juan* and *Don Quixote*; the bleating sheep in the latter, ruled out as inadmissible by the eighteenth century Dr Beattie, are nowadays as acceptable as Beethoven's cuckoo and quail.

In *Till Eulenspiegel* Strauss threw philosophy overboard and wrote a piece of direct orchestral pictorialism that is a never-ending

---

[6] See Del Mar Vol. I, p. 76. Del Mar incidentally clears up a number of confusions that have surrounded this work.
[7] Niecks, p. 494.

delight. There is no moralizing or sublimity but simply a straightforward account in music of Till, his adventures and horseplay and happy-go-lucky character, delineated in a profusion of engaging themes worked out with consummate assurance and skill.

Strauss first thought of the subject in terms of the stage. His first opera, *Guntram*, had just been performed with only moderate success, and he was searching for a second libretto. *Till* was in fact no stranger to the stage; Strauss had seen an opera, by Kistler, at Würzburg in 1889. The detailed scenario comes from Strauss himself, but when the work was first performed at Cologne under Wüllner in 1895 he perversely refused to divulge more than a rough outline. He wrote:

> It is impossible for me to furnish a programme to *Eulenspiegel*. Were I to put in words the thoughts which its several incidents suggested to me, they would seldom suffice, and might even give rise to offence . . . By way of helping to a better understanding. it seems sufficient to point out the two Eulenspiegel motifs (they appear at the beginning of the work), which in the most manifold disguises, moods, and situations pervade the whole up to the final catastrophe, when, after he has been condemned to death (a descending major seventh — F to G flat) Till is strung up to the gibbet. For the rest, let them guess at the musical joke which a rogue has offered them.[8]

He later gave Willem Mauke a score with some pencilled annotations, and these notes form the basis of all later analyses.[9]

There was something of Till in Strauss's own make-up. Till was a rogue, a practical joker who was at odds with authority and made a mockery of established beliefs. He seems to have been a real character, but almost certainly many of the pranks attributed to him are later accretions. He was a hobgoblin too, able to escape with seven-leagued boots and hide in mouseholes. But his magic fails him at the end. The pathos of his last strangled cry is unbearable; but, the music says, it is after all only a fairy story, and the final impression after a performance is of the good humour and panache of the work.

It is tempting to read a more conscious autobiographical impulse into *Don Quixote*, the knightly Don representing the idealistic,

---

[8] Niecks, p. 501.
[9] They will be found in Niecks, page 502, but without bar references. Del Mar (Vol. 1 page 126ff) gives them with some of their associated musical themes.

Sancho Panza the more earthy, sides of his character. The work, completed in 1897, is described simply as 'fantastic variations on a theme of knightly character'. There is a long Introduction, twenty-two pages of the miniature score; then follow ten variations, each indicated in the score but with no other clues as to what the music is expressing. Variation 1 sees the two setting out on their travels in search of knightly adventure, with Dulcinea's theme (on the flute) shining as a beacon. They mistake windmills for giants, and the Don is thrown from his horse. In Variation 2 comes the 'celebrated Victorious Conflict with the Host of the Emperor Alifanfaron', where Don Quixote routs a flock of sheep, bleating realistically on muted brass. Then comes a conversation between the Don and his servant. It opens quietly but eloquently, and at the climax (F sharp major) we are given the Don's full statement of the whole theory of knight errantry. In Variation 4 we meet a religious procession carrying an image of the Madonna, petitioning for rain. Don Quixote dashes in to rescue the image, which he imagines is a maiden being abducted, and is knocked senseless. Sancho Panza believing him to be dead, steals off. The fifth variation is Don Quixote's vigil, and in the next he meets Dulcinea, or thinks he does; for Sancho plays a hoax on his master, passing off a peasant girl as the lovely Dulcinea. Both master and servant are the victims of another practical joke in the next variation. They are blindfolded and induced to ride on a wooden horse which, they are told, will whisk them through the air. The orchestra portrays this cinematic effect by flutter-tonguing on the wind, *glissandi* on the harp, and a wind machine. Variation 8 is the 'Famous Adventure of the Enchanted Bark'—a barcarolle, 6/8 time. This also ends in disaster, the boat capsizing and soaking the travellers. Variation 9 is the 'Fight with Two Wizards'—really two Benedictine monks (two bassoons). In the last variation Don Quixote is cured of his madness by the ruse of another friend. The episode as related by Cervantes is curtailed by Strauss, who has only the 'Combat with the Knight of the White Moon', in which the Don is defeated. There is an epilogue depicting Don Quixote's death.

Don Quixote and *Till Eulenspiegel* have strong claims to be considered as Strauss's orchestral masterpieces. Their scale is ample but not inflated, the musical material is distinguished and often of great beauty, and as subjects they lie within music's competence. The next work, *Ein Heldenleben* ('A Hero's Life') raises doubts on all three counts. It is a vast symphonic structure in six movements, which Strauss has labelled: 1. The Hero; 2. The Hero's adversaries (or critics); 3. The Hero's companion (or wife); 4. The Hero's deeds of war; 5. The Hero's works of peace; 6. The Hero's retirement from the world.

The Hero is, of course, Strauss himself: or is it? The numerous self-quotations, listed meticulously in Del Mar, seem reasonably conclusive evidence, and on Strauss's own admission Part 3 was intended to portray his wife. He could be justified in regarding himself as the musical hero of Germany, for with the death of Brahms in 1897 the only German-speaking composer to challenge him was Mahler. But it must be granted that Strauss was not in himself particularly heroic. He was fully conscious of his own talents, but could view himself with detachment, as when he defined himself as 'a first-class second-rate composer'. Also, although like all innovators he suffered from criticism, he was never subjected to such bitterness and stupidity as is portrayed in the second movement. As for the last movement, far from retiring from the world he had hardly begun to enter into his heritage. He was in his late thirties (*Heldenleben* was finished in 1898), and no doubt conscious that he had said farewell to his precocious youth: he was not to know that within a few years he was to be swung up to an even higher peak of fame through his operas, but he must have been aware that his creativity was at its zenith. In fact sections one, two and four would apply much more strongly to Mahler, who *was* cast in a heroic mould, who fought his battles much more savagely, who suffered far more from his opponents on two counts—because of his music, and because he was a Jew. The idealistic Mahler was much more conscious of the Philistinism around him than Strauss (who was a bit of a Philistine himself) ever was.

Strauss has also referred to an earlier symphony in the same key, E flat. But Beethoven's *Eroica* was not autobiographical. His hero was the Man of Action, of Destiny; Strauss's subject was the Hero as Artist; it was a continuation of and a complement to *Don Quixote*.[10] Don Quixote's heroism was in the mind, he battled with shadows and illusions (this was the period when Freud was demonstrating the inner warfare the mind of man wages upon itself); his ideals were

---

[10] We have Strauss's own authority for linking them together: see Del Mar, Vol. I, p. 165.

fantasies, chimeras. In *Heldenleben* we deal, not with visions and nightmares, but with the actualities of life. The Hero's companion is no imaginary Dulcinea, but a flesh and blood wife, virtues and faults intermingled as in the Hero himself. If there is madness it is the divine *afflatus* which is the breath of creation, not the delusions of a mind turned in upon itself.

In the *Sinfonia domestica* the autobiography is still more explicit. The duo had become a trio with the birth of a son on 12 April 1897, and though proud father and happy mother figure prominently, the varying aspects of their characters signalized by an array of themes, it is 'Bubi' who holds the centre of the stage, whether contentedly at play or shrieking his head off. It is scored for an even bigger orchestra than Strauss usually demands, and is on the same Nibelungen scale as *Heldenleben*. Written in 1902-03, and first performed in New York in 1904, it has found few champions, though the composer himself preserved a soft spot for it. It also found an apologist in Romain Rolland, who after hearing it in Paris in 1905 wrote to Strauss that 'elle m'a paru l'oeuvre la plus parfaite que vous ayez écrite depuis *Tod und Verklärung*', but pleads, don't print the programme; simply call it *Sinfonia domestica*.[11] It was followed by only one other orchestral work, the *Alpensinfonie* of 1911-15, topographical like his first, and on the whole of only marginal interest in our present discussion.

With Gustav Mahler (1860-1911) we meet in an acute form that ambivalence towards a literary 'programme' which we have already come across several times. More than most composers he seemed to draw on his own experiences, emotional and otherwise, as the source for his music. His symphonies, immense though they were, were not self-sufficient like those of Beethoven or Brahms but, rather like the novels of Proust's *A la recherche du temps perdu*, seem to group themselves into massive galaxies of music, in a form which Mahler himself perhaps only dimly conceived. The first four for example contain affiliations with each other (emotionally and sometimes thematically), and also embrace other concepts outside the works in question. The first symphony refers to the song-cycle *Lieder eines fahrenden Gesellen;* the last movement of the fourth (it was

---

[11] See the correspondence between Strauss and Rolland, page thirty-four. The work and critical reaction to it are discussed in greater detail in Del Mar, Vol. I, pp. 183-99.

originally planned as the seventh movement in the third) sets words from *Des Knaben Wunderhorn* for soprano solo.

But also, the first three symphonies had programmes of a more or less precise nature, which he subsequently suppressed. When the first symphony was performed in 1889 in Budapest Mahler described it as a 'symphonic poem in two parts' and provided 'an elaborate programme in the manner of Berlioz's *Symphonie fantastique*'.[12] It had five movements; one of these, like the programme, was discarded, its place taken by the third movement inspired by an old painting entitled 'The Hunter's Funeral', in which animals follow the coffin. The programme for the second symphony (1887-94) was given in great detail by Mahler himself in a long letter to his wife in 1901[13] and is a typical mixture of naiveté and the phantasmagoric. The fourth movement for example reads 'The stirring voice of simple faith reaches our ear; I am of God and will go back to God . . .', while the fifth and final movement contains earthquakes, the graves yielding up their dead, and a vision of the glory of God . . . 'an all-powerful feeling of love transfigures us with blissful knowledge and being . . .' In the score of the third symphony (1893-96) the movements are headed: 1. Introduction. Pan awakes. Summer marches in; 2. What the wild flowers tell me; 3. What the animals of the forest tell me; 4. What Man tells me; 5. What the Angels tell me; 6. What Love tells me. This programme is sheer sentimentality which, like the pretentiousness of the second symphony, is redeemed only by Mahler's masterly handling of his musical material.

---

[12] See Redlich, *Bruckner and Mahler* (London, 1955) page 181.
[13] *Gustav Mahler: Memories and Letters* (second edition, London, 1968).

PART III

Programme Music during the Last Hundred Years

CHAPTER 9

The Transition from Romantic to Modern

If it was understandable that the great prestige attached to the works of Strauss, Tchaikowsky and Smetana not only in their respective countries but throughout the western world should have encouraged a flood of enthusiastic imitators, it was equally predictable that the results in the main would be safe and unadventurous. Revolutionary fervour in particular seems to have an especially dampening effect on the creative fire, the Soviet Union after 1917 and Czechoslovakia after 1945 churning out factory-made spring or nature symphonies, or oblations to the brotherhood of man, correctly composed and orchestrated, with never a spark of musical righteousness.

The one Russian composer who during his lifetime seemed the link between the nineteenth century and the new music of the twentieth was Alexander Scriabin (1871-1915). In the early years of this century his harmonic innovations were much discussed, but events have overtaken him, and today there would be few who would wish to compare him as an innovator with Schoenberg, Bartók or his younger compatriot Stravinsky. Nevertheless, his work does show certain pointers to some of the trends of the present century. First, he was engrossed by the sheer *sound* of music. As a pianist he was renowned for the sensuous beauty of his playing, and his piano compositions reflect this. He was a harmonic colourist rather than a linear writer and, from that point of view, close to Debussy. Second, his dabbling in unorthodox systems of religion such as theosophy (a taste he shared with his English admirer Cyril Scott) and his leanings towards an Oriental mysticism[1] reveal him as a precursor of

---

[1] In Scriabin's time the study of Indian and far-Eastern music had hardly begun in Western Europe — but the beginnings were there. Fox-Strangways for example in 1914 wrote a treatise on *The Music of Hindustan*, and the French writer Louis Laloy had already written on Chinese music.

for example Messiaen, who in his *Turangalila* symphony and other works seeks to marry the two cultures, East and West. It is noteworthy, too, that Scriabin unlike the earlier Russian composers had no interest whatever in native Russian folk culture; his art is as 'decadent' as that of Aubrey Beardsley (1872-98).

The works of special interest to us are the three large-scale works *The Divine Poem*, Op. 43 (first performed in Paris, 1905); *The Poem of Ecstasy*, Op. 54 (first performed at Petersburg, 1908); and *Prometheus: A Poem of Fire*, Op. 60 (first performed by Kussevitsky in Moscow, 1911). The first symphony should also be mentioned if only for its last movement which was a setting of a poem by Scriabin himself 'glorifying art as a form of religion'.[2]

The Divine Poem had a programme written for it by Tatiana Schlöser, with whom Scriabin had formed a liaison in about 1902. It runs as follows:

> *The Divine Poem* represents the evolution of the human spirit which, torn from an entire past of beliefs and mysteries which it surmounts and overturns, passes through Pantheism and attains to a joyous and intoxicated affirmation of its liberty and its unity with the universe (the divine 'Ego').
> *Struggles.* The conflict between the man who is the slave of a personal god, supreme master of the world, and the free, powerful man—the man-god. The latter appears to triumph, but it is only the intellect which affirms the divine 'Ego', while the individual will, still too weak, is tempted to sink into Pantheism.
> *Delights.* The man allows himself to be captured by the delights of the sensual world. He is intoxicated and soothed by the voluptuous pleasures into which he plunges. His personality loses itself in nature. It is then that the sense of the sublime arises from the depths of his being and assists him to conquer the passive state of his human 'Ego'.
> *Divine Play.* The spirit finally freed from all the bonds which fasten it to its past of submission to a superior power, the spirit producing the universe by the sole power of its own creative will, conscious of being at one with the Universe, abandons itself to the sublime joy of free activity—the 'Divine Play'.[3]

This makes fascinating reading. It obviously derives from Nietzche

---

[2] Calvocoressi and Abraham, *Masters of Russian Music*, p. 467.
[3] Transcribed from Calvocoressi and Abraham, p. 475.

and his 'super-man'; though high-falutin', it is not unlike some other 'heroic' schemes we have previously come across.

The Poem of Ecstasy is the musical equivalent of a long, rambling poem by Scriabin himself, written in 1904-06 and published in 1906 —or rather of a portion of it, for its second half relates to his fifth piano sonata.[4] This is a practice we have seen, in Liszt and Spohr. But Scriabin did not wish the poem to be published with the music, but did sanction some notes which in part relate the music to the poem, which concerns the spirit's search for ecstasy. As in French Symbolist poetry it would be futile to seek for hard and concrete meaning, and perhaps here we have an instance of music being more exact than words, for at least it is within music's province to bear us away on the wings of ecstasy.[5]

Prometheus was the most ambitious of the three, for not only did Scriabin write for the usual enormous orchestra (in this instance quadruple woodwind, eight horns, five trumpets, piano, organ and wordless chorus), but demanded the collaboration of a 'colour organ'—a 'light keyboard' to 'control the play of visual colour during the performance'. This reminds us of Debussy's ideas concerning the fusion of the senses of sound, colour, even of scent.[6] Needless to say this colour machine proved impracticable, though a complete performance was later achieved in New York. Today this visual assault on our eyes is the commonplace of the dance hall.

---

[4] A translation of this, by Hugh Macdonald, will be found in *Musical Times*, January 1972.

[5] As another illustration of the synchronism of ideas it may be pointed out that at the very moment when Scriabin was struggling to create a new musical language and invoking the assistance of words Schoenberg was engaged in the composition of his Op. 15, the songs for voice and piano to poetry by Stefan George. The portions of George's poetry quoted, in translation, in Austin's *Music in the 20th Century* (page 217) have much the same recondite similes and obscure phraseology of Scriabin in Macdonald's translation. His two monodramas, *Erwartung* and *Die glückliche Hand*, for the latter of which he wrote his own text, exhibit the same involved and complex imagery.

[6] The notion of the possibility of combining sounds, colours and perfumes, curiously enough, goes back some years before Debussy, to the man who was Schumann's inspiration, E. T. A. Hoffmann. Asked by his friend Hitzig if he would improvise for him he replied: Volontiers, mais éteignez ces lumières, ne laissez brûler qu'une ou deux bougies. Dans l'ombre Hoffmann s'était assis au piano: Souvent, disait-il, au moment de m'endormir, je crois trouver une correspondance entre les parfums, les couleurs et les sons. L'odeur des oillets (carnations) rouges agit sur moi avec une puissance magique, je suis plongé dans un rêve, et alors, il me semble entendre au loin les sons graves du cor anglais qui s'enflent et qui expirent.

See Jean Mistler, *Hoffmann le Fantastique* (Paris, 1950), p. 182.

The music, more French in sound than Russian (parts of the *Poème d'Extase* recall Ravel's *Daphnis et Chloe*) is vivid and exciting, full of glorious and grandiloquent sound-gestures, which are welded into coherent forms with the minimum of assistance from classical principles. If they no longer herald the future, they round off an era magnificently.

There were a few composers of Strauss's generation with sufficient individuality to avoid being entirely submerged by the Teutonic waters. One with a lifelong interest in programme music was Jan Sibelius (1865-1957). At first sight there would seem to be little common ground between the rather dour, parsimonious music of the northern composer and the reckless opulence of Strauss, yet it was almost certainly a performance of the latter's *Don Juan* in Berlin in 1890 that turned Sibelius's mind towards the symphonic poem. As with Smetana, Bartók and, with a different emphasis, Debussy and his circle, this was intimately connected with a nationalist movement in Finland.

After a period of study in Germany and Austria Sibelius returned to Finland in 1891 and was immediately caught up in a group of intellectuals, the 'young Finns'. The result was a work on a grand scale for soloists, male chorus and orchestra, *Kullervo*. This, though it is called a 'symphonic poem in five movements', is outside our brief by reason of the forces employed, but is mentioned here because the words were drawn from Finland's great source of myth and legend, the *Kalevala*[7] which was the inspiration of so much of Sibelius's music. The *Kullervo* has never been published, but it was performed on 29 April 1892.[8]

The coterie of musicians, writers and artists to which Sibelius belonged might be compared to the similar group surrounding Debussy in Paris at the same time. The composers were Oskar Merikanto (1868-1924), Robert Kajanus (1856-1933) and Armas Järnefelt (1869-1958), who all wrote works, operatic or symphonic, drawing material from the *Kalevala* (e.g., Järnefelt's *Korsholm* [1894] and Kajanus's *Aino* symphony). The most distinguished of the

---

[7] These legendary stories were first assembled early in the nineteenth century. An English translation of the *Kalevala*, in the tiresome metre of Longfellow's *Hiawatha*, will be found in Everyman's Library Nos. 259 and 260.

[8] For an account of it see Harold E. Johnson, *Sibelius* (London, 1959).

THE TRANSITION FROM ROMANTIC TO MODERN 145

writers was Juhanna Heikki Erkko; the painters included Akseli Gallen-Kallela, who in the 1890s was busy with a series of pictures on episodes from the *Kalevala*, amongst them one entitled 'Lemmenkäinen's Mother'.

The Lemmenkäinen legend furnished the material for Sibelius's first important tone-poems, the four legends, *Lemmenkäinen and the Maiden; Lemmenkäinen in Tuonela; The Swan of Tuonela; The Return of Lemmenkäinen*. (The first of Sibelius's great orchestral works, *En Saga*, is less a symphonic poem than, as Ekman says, 'a romantic tale of chivalry'.)[9] All four were performed on 13 April 1896. With the exception of the well-known *Swan of Tuonela*, all have detailed programmes, furnished by Sibelius himself for the first performance, though it seems that like many composers he later had second thoughts about this and towards the end of his life declared that 'he did not have any specific programmes in mind and that one would do just as well as the other'.[10] In the first piece we hear of Lemmenkainen's prodigious amatory exploits. In the second Lemmenkainen's mother goes to seek him in Tuonela, the Finnish Hades. Learning that he has been killed and cut to pieces, his remains thrown in the river, she reassembles them and magically restores him to life. When she asks him what he most desires his answer is that he would return to the 'charming maids of Pohja'. In the *Swan*, which originated as the prelude to an unfinished opera (the theme likewise drawn from the *Kalevala*), the desolate cor anglais solo merely signifies Lemmenkainen's soul in limbo. The last piece described the rejuvenated hero returning to the scenes of his former triumphs. The whole suite thus symbolizes spring or the renewal of life.

The poor reception of the work, both at rehearsal and at its first performance, is understandable. The whole trend of nineteenth century orchestration had been towards an ever richer orchestral palette. Sibelius, working with the same large orchestra, was producing a new range of colours that seemed cold and unemotional. Even the basic musical material (melody and harmony), which now seems unenterprising compared with what was happening in contemporary Vienna and Paris, sounded odd and unusual in

---

[9] Karl Ekman, *Jean Sibelius; His Life and Personality* (New York, 1938).

[10] Johnson, *op. cit.*, p. 195.

Sibelius's very individual instrumental dress. As it happened, Sibelius was on the threshold of world-wide recognition, by virtue of a piece that became almost embarrassingly popular, *Finlandia*.

The source of this was a series of historical *tableaux* illustrating some of the landmarks of Finland's history, the last of which, following 'Finland in the Thirty Years War' and 'The Great Tribulations', was entitled 'Finland Awakes'. Three numbers were subsequently published as *Scènes Historiques* I (1911); the final *tableau* seemed sufficiently impressive to Sibelius and his friends to be treated as a separate entity, and as such, with the title *Finlandia*, it was published in a piano arrangement in 1900.[11] In this work there is no doubt that Sibelius set out to write patriotic music. The hymn-like character of its main theme and the general impression of heartfelt fervour, which were the causes of its immediate popularity both in and out of Finland, made *Finlandia* the prototype of the 'people's music' of the twentieth century. It displayed a number of characteristic fingerprints of Sibelius's musical style such as melodies of a downright diatonic simplicity, a powerful rhythmic drive, effective use of the brass 'choir' and a resourceful employment of ostinato devices. These can all be observed in his best works, though presented with more subtlety and delicacy.

In *Pohjola's Daughter* (published 1906) he returned to the theme from the *Kalevala* that had been in his mind when attempting an opera, *The Building of the Boat* (1893). The full score contained a paraphrase of Canto VIII in which it is told how the aged hero Väinämöinen attempts to woo the maid of Pohjola as she sits on a rainbow, weaving a fabric of gold. She craftily agreed to yield on the condition that he performs a series of difficult feats to prove the power of his magic. The final one is to construct a boat from the splinters of her spindle and launch it without touching it. The old man's magic fails him at the crucial moment. He wounds himself with his axe and gives up in despair to seek a magic cure that will staunch the flow of blood.[12]

---

[11] For further details, and some interesting information as to the political significance of these *tableaux* and the personalities mentioned in the final *tableau*, which included representations of 'the first folk school and the first locomotive', see Johnson *op. cit.*, pp. 22ff and 86ff.

[12] Quoted from Johnson *op. cit.*, page 114. The account in *Sibelius; a Symposium* (London, 1947) is very similar. Oddly enough, Johnson later (p. 194) says 'Other tone-poems such as *En Saga*, *Pohjola's Daughter* and *Night Ride and Sunrise* appear to

The work, besides containing descriptive touches such as the whir of the spinning wheel, was a good deal nearer to contemporary ideals in its exploitation of tone-colour. Sibelius was at the time much preoccupied by this aspect, as we see when we look at the oriental colouring in his incidental music to *Belshazzar's Feast*, the suite from which *(Oriental Procession; Solitude; Night Music; Khadra's Dance)*, written in 1906, must be regarded, like so much of his incidental music, as being at least on the fringe of true programme music. This colouristic trend can be seen also in the work commissioned for America in 1914, *The Oceanides*, a work for very large orchestra employing devices such as muted brass, *divisi* strings, tremolo, etc, etc, that inevitably invite comparisons with Debussy's *La Mer*.

The last major piece of programme music, and virtually his last composition, was *Tapiola* Op. 112, written in 1925 and first performed in New York, 26 December 1926. This is not action-music but mood-music — an attempt to translate into musical terms the quatrain Sibelius affixed to the score:

> Widespread they stand, the Northland's dusky forests,
> Ancient, mysterious, brooding savage dreams;
> And within them dwells the forest's mighty God[13]
> And wood-sprites in the gloom weave magic secrets.

The atmosphere conveyed in this remarkable work is quite extraordinary. This is not the German forest of *Hänsel und Gretel* with its homely fairy-tale witch, and it is far removed from the cosiness of Bax's *November Woods* (1917). It is a landscape numb and unfeeling — nature not hostile to life, but merely indifferent. Sibelius's themes have always tended to the enigmatic or elliptic; here they are stunted like the tundra of the Arctic wastes. Forbidding and uncompromising, it stands out as one of Sibelius's grandest works.

Other contemporaries of Strauss include Edward Elgar (1857-1943), Frederick Delius (1862-1934), Carl Nielsen (1865-1931). and lesser figures like William Wallace (1860-1940), Granville Bantock

---

have no programmes other than their titles'. Cecil Gray on the other hand (in *Sibelius*, London 1931) says *'Pohjola's Daughter* belongs more definitely to the category of programme music than any of Sibelius's other works'.

[13] ie, Tapio.

(1868-1946) and Hamish MacCunn (1868-1916). Of these Elgar is nearest to Strauss in his methods of composition, his large-scale orchestral works, written with uncommon assurance and apparent ease, having the same amplitude of gesture, richness and wealth of themes, a comparable harmonic resource and a similar leaning towards verbosity. The overtures *Froissart* (1890) and *In the South* (1904) have little that is programmatic bar their titles, but *Cockaigne* (1901) is a more explicit picture of London life with its Salvation Army band, its lovers and its general air of breezy *bonhomie*. Clearer portraits are drawn in the *Enigma Variations* (1899) — fourteen variations on an original theme, 'dedicated to my friends pictured therein'. In this novel scheme[14] the composer has enshrined in some of his most exquisite music the foibles and endearing traits of a few of his immediate circle, whether the impetuosity of 'Troyte', 'Dorabella's' attractive hesitancy of speech, 'G.R.S.' at the organ (or his dog in the river), the affectionate personality of his wife, 'C.A.E.', or his own bluff nature. The musical picture of the hum of a great liner's engines in No. XIII, *Romanza*, is one of the great classics of twentieth century onomatopoeia in music, less virtuosic than Honegger's later *Pacific 231*, but far more poetic.

But the most detailed of all his programme music, and for which he himself provided an elaborate scenario, is *Falstaff* (1913).[15] Apart from the unimportant *Polonia* written in the early days (1915) of the First World War for a concert in aid of the Polish Relief Fund, and the charming *Nursery Suite* (1931), this was his last essay in programme music. It was called a 'Symphonic Study', and in it he sought to portray Falstaff's character, just as Strauss had grappled with Don Quixote, and it is important to note his own comment on Falstaff, that he was 'a knight, a gentlemen and a soldier'. His aim was to draw Falstaff in the round, to see him not in his decay but in his prime, to glance back to his boyhood, to lay him reverently in his grave. Thus, while the purely imitative is not lacking (Strauss, pastmaster in such feats, must have admired the snores), the music discloses aspects of Falstaff's character and incidents of his life with

---

[14] Precedents for some aspects can be found in Schumann's *Carnaval* and Mussorgsky's *Pictures from an Exhibition;* the variation form was anticipated by Strauss's *Don Quixote*.
[15] Printed in *Musical Times*, September 1913. See also Tovey, *Essays in Musical Analysis*, Vol. IV (London 1936).

the musical decorum of an earlier style.

Delius, a composer of very different stamp, wrote little that could be classed as absolute music. His original cast of mind and independence of thought enabled him to absorb only what was necessary for his own development from the prevailing Wagnerism, and though he was brought up in the Teutonic musical tradition and had his first successes in Germany the piece that is probably his best-known work, *On Hearing the First Cuckoo in Spring* (1912) is without a trace of Teutonic heaviness. This gently swaying, drowsy music, enveloping as in a heat haze a blur of half-heard melodies and the cuckoo's call, as yet not too insistent, is as accurate a musical picture of a balmy spring day as one could wish for. The countryside, it should be said, is as much French as English, for the work reflects the soft landscape round Grez-sur-Loing as much as Delius's native Yorkshire.

This and the other works for small orchestra with which it is often paired, *Summer Night on the River* (1914) and *In a Summer Garden* (1908), are perhaps only just within the confines of programme music, and no doubt all the more successful for that. They are small in scale and so do not pose problems in construction. Delius, like Debussy, was impatient with the traditional symphonic methods, which depend among other qualities on taut and incisive rhythms, deriving from the march and the dance. A notable but as yet little studied feature of music during the past hundred years has been the attitude towards rhythm, which since the time of *Tristan* has been losing its ascendancy. 'In the beginning was Rhythm' wrote von Bülow; but composers seem to have been striving to free themselves from this motor impulse, groping towards a wider conception of rhythm than one based on the fact that we have two legs and a heart that pulses regularly. This can be seen as part of a wider movement towards an a-thematic, 'abstract' musical art, comparable to some aspects of abstract visual art. Themes and motifs (the composer's 'images') have lost their position of absolute supremacy, a change in musical thinking due in part at least to Debussy and Delius.

Delius lived in Paris for about six years, from 1890–96. Like Debussy he numbered writers and artists among his friends (Strindberg and Gauguin; his composer acquaintances included Florent Schmitt and Ravel), but their circles seem never to have intersected. His stay there left sufficient impression on him to produce his first really important orchestral work, *Paris, the Song of a Great City. Nocturne for Orchestra* (1899), first performed at Elberfeld in 1901. The word 'nocturne' is significant. We recall Debussy's *Nocturnes*, of about the same period, and their indebtedness to Whistler, but whether Delius had any knowledge of these works is at present only conjecture. The contrast between this fine work and Elgar's more pictorial study of another great city is a measure of the differing temperaments of the two composers.

Three of Carl Nielsen's symphonies are programmatic to a greater or lesser extent. Like so many composers, he professed to dislike programmes, but he gave a fairly detailed one to the second, *The Four Temperaments*.[16] The inspiration goes back to a picture he had seen in a pub in Zealand depicting the four temperaments, *The Choleric, The Phlegmatic, The Melancholic, The Sanguine*. These are the titles of the four movements, in which Nielsen seeks to exemplify these ideas in music. The third symphony, *Sinfonia espansiva*, and the fourth, *The Inextinguishable*, are programmatic in a much more general way, the first concerned with the idea of growth or expansion, (of music, of art, of his own personality), the second with the idea of the *élan vital* behind art and life, a renewing and invigorating force that is irresistible. These symphonies, full of drive and power, are less well known than they deserve to be.

Of the lesser composers William Wallace interests us because he was the first composer of the 'English renaissance' to write a symphonic poem, *The Passing of Beatrice* (1892), and because he was one of the few British composers to betray an interest in the philosophy of music. He read a paper on *Programme Music* to the Musical Association, 1898-99[17] and followed this up with other examples, of which *Villon* (1909) is perhaps the best. Hamish MacCunn's *Land of the Mountain and Flood* (1887) retains its freshness better than much of the music of the period, and far better than most of Bantock's enormous output.

Gifted with a riotous fancy, immense energy, boundless ambition but little true originality, Bantock poured out works conceived, in true late nineteenth century fashion, on a grandiose scale. He planned, for example, twenty-four symphonic poems on Southey's *Kehama*; fourteen were actually written, two only were published.

---

[16] See Robert Simpson, *Carl Nielsen, Symphonist* (London, 1952) p. 42.

[17] His interesting definition of programme music was 'Music which attempts to excite a mental image by means of an auditory impression'.

THE TRANSITION FROM ROMANTIC TO MODERN 151

They were *The Funeral*, and *Jaga-Naut*—'highly pictorial' says Anderton[18] 'and shows the lofty car swaying as it ploughs its course through the crowd of devotees who throw themselves in its way and are crushed, while a band of Yogis dance in honour of the god'. Their dance, in 5/4 time, looks forward to Holst's *Hymn of Jesus* and *The Planets*. His two works with the greatest following were *The Pierrot of the Minute* (1908) and *Fifine at the Fair*. The former is based on a poem by Ernest Dowson: The Pierrot falls asleep in the Parc du Petit Trianon, under a statue of Cupid. He dreams he is visited by a Moon-maiden who warns him of the 'fatal kisses of the moon'. Dawn comes, when she must leave him; but the dream has in fact lasted only a minute. *Fifine* is based on Browning. She is a rope-dancer; she, and the Fair where she dances, stand for the gaudy, transient things of life. Her beauty turns the head of a visitor to the Fair, who leaves his wife, Elvire, for her. In Browning's epilogue man and wife are united in death; in Bantock the husband tires of Fifine and returns to Elvire.

Conditions in England up to the outbreak of the First World War in 1914 were not ideal, but there was a wider orchestral fare than is often supposed. The ground had been prepared by the Crystal Palace concerts under Manns and, later, the Promenade concerts. Native conductors like Wood and Beecham were busier with novelties than we realize. Nor was orchestral playing confined to London. In Manchester the Hallé under Richter was enhancing its reputation, and a provincial orchestra, that of Liverpool, which could tackle *Ein Heldenleben* must have been competent. The New Brighton Orchestra which Bantock conducted 1897–1900 included modern, difficult works in their repertory, including some of Bantock's own. The way was becoming slightly easier for younger composers such as Gustav Holst (1874–1934), Ralph Vaughan Williams (1872–1958) and Cyril Scott (1879–1970).

Holst's outstanding achievement in the domain of programme music is his orchestral suite, *The Planets*. The notion of a suite derived from the astrological attributes of the seven planets was as novel as the execution was bold. There is no specific programme apart from the sub-headings—Mars, the Bringer of War; Uranus, the Magician, and so on. The very large orchestra includes a considerable array of percussion (seven players) and, in 'Neptune,

---

[18] H. Orsmond Anderton, *Granville Bantock* (London, 1915).

the Mystic', a hidden six-part choir of female voices. The percussion includes glockenspiel, bells, xylophone and celesta which, in conjunction with the harps, conjure up a sort of mysterious clarity, a non-atmospheric music of interplanetary space. Of his other programme works the most notable is the bleak *Egdon Heath*, first performed at Cheltenham in 1928.

Cyril Scott was a composer whose distinct originality was uncontrolled by either intellectual rigour or the discipline of concentrated study; he brought to music the advantages and drawbacks associated with a sophisticated, intelligent, supersensitive dilettante. His music was diversified by excursions into theosophy and Yoga, both of which he wrote about. He published several volumes of piano music, with evocative titles such as *The Garden of Soul-Sympathy; The Twilight of the Year* (from his suite, *Poems*); The *Egypt* suite consists of: *In the Temple of Memphis; By the Waters of the Nile; Egyptian Boat Song; Funeral March of the great Ramases; Song of the Spirits of the Nile*.

This is mood music, into which one can read what one wants. Eaglefield Hull in his monograph of 1918 certainly overpraised him, but Cecil Gray's dismissal of him as 'imitation Debussy' is too slick and obvious. Scott, with Delius and Bax, and to a lesser extent Bantock, form a mini-school of English composers who, as we can see now, were instinctively picking their way between the German establishment (Brahms or Wagner) and folk whimsy.

The best programme works of Arnold Bax (1879-1953) such as *The Garden of Fand* (1916) and *Tintagel* (1917) have a grandeur and sweep, a richness of imagination and a command of the orchestra which places them among the programme masterpieces of this century. Of *Tintagel* the composer said:

> It is intended to evoke a tone-picture of the castle-crowned cliff of Tintagel, and more particularly the wide distances of the Atlantic as seen from the cliffs . . . In the middle section it may be imagined that with the increasing tumult of the sea arise memories of the historical and legendary association of the place, especially those connected with King Arthur, King Mark and Tristan and Iseult.

Indebted as it is to Wagner, Debussy and the Ravel of *Daphnis et Chloe*, Bax's own individuality nevertheless shines through.

Several works of Vaughan Williams deserve consideration. The first two are complementary—the 'London' symphony, evocative rather than descriptive, though we do hear the chimes of Big Ben, the *Pastoral*, following Beethoven in allowing music to draw our attention to the tranquillity of the countryside and the spiritual refreshment this engenders. Other symphonies such as the fourth in F minor, a violent and disturbing work seemingly reflecting the evil threatened by a re-arming Germany (it was written in 1935) and the sixth (1947), the last movement of which sounds like a musical impression of the desolation in the wake of the holocaust of the hydrogen bomb, seem to have clear programmatic intent, but the matter is complicated by the composer's refusal to endorse these interpretations. Concerning the seventh symphony (1953) there is no doubt at all. Subtitled 'Antartica', its material was drawn from the music Vaughan Williams had previously composed for the film, *Scott of the Antarctic* (1949). Its five movements, 'Prelude'; 'Scherzo'; 'Landscape'; 'Intermezzo'; 'Epilogue', are headed by superscriptions, from Shelley's *Prometheus Unbound*; from Psalm 104 ('There go the ships, and there is that Leviathan whom thou hast made to take his pastime therein'); from Coleridge (a description of an Alpine glacier, from *Hymn before Sunrise in the Vale of Chamouni*); from John Donne; and lastly, an extract from Captain Scott's journal. These all help to make clear the symbolic intention of the whole work, man's confrontation with inhospitable nature, his spiritual triumph but physical defeat. Withal it is, as Frank Howes says of the third movement,[19] 'Tone painting on the grandest possible scale'.

Vaughan Williams made his early reputation as a vocal writer, and in cantatas like *Toward the Unknown Region* the orchestral writing aspired to nothing more than competence. But from the *London* symphony onwards he began to emerge as an orchestrator with his own special flavour, and in *Sinfonia Antartica* orchestral colour becomes a major ingredient of his art. The big forces he demanded included some of the more exotic percussion instruments such as celesta, glockenspiel, vibraphone and bells. This interest in colour *per se* (the seeds of which were already present in his friend Holst's *Planets*, as we have already noted) was to be pushed further in symphonies eight and nine. The preoccupation with sheer sound,

---

[19] In *The Music of Vaughan Williams* (London, 1954) p. 75. Howe's book should be consulted for its exposition of the relation between the symphony and the music for the film.

which is one of the most significant developments in music in the second half of the present century, goes hand in hand with the decline in the importance of the theme or motif, which has already been remarked. The inclination towards an 'abstract' music dispensing with themes was probably latent in Vaughan Williams from the first, and it was, paradoxically, intensified by his interest in English folksong, in which crisp rhythmic definition is often lacking. Two very characteristic pieces of programme music which are the quintessence of his style are *Flos Campi* and the romance, *The Lark Ascending*, both of which show his care for orchestral sound (though using small forces) and his habit of writing a sort of 'generalized' music from which themes can be extracted only with difficulty.

Flos Campi dates from 1925, a period when to judge by some of the works such as the piano concerto and the masterly *Sancta Civitas* (1924), with which it has something in common, the composer was undergoing some kind of crisis. The somewhat exotic scoring consists of single wind, strings, harp, celesta, triangle, cymbals, drums and tabor, plus solo viola and a wordless chorus. The composer offered a little elucidation in some notes he wrote for a Royal Philharmonic Society concert in 1927. 'Flos Campi' is the Vulgate equivalent of 'Rose of Sharon'—'ego Flos Campi, et Lillium Convallium' 'I am the Rose of Sharon, and the Lily of the Valleys'. The six movements have quotations from *The Song of Songs*, in Latin, translated as follows:

1. As the lily among thorns, so is my love among the daughters . . . Stay me with flagons, comfort me with apples: for I am sick of love (ie, I faint from longing).
2. For lo, the winter is past, the rain is over and gone, the flowers appear on the earth, the time of singing birds is come, and the voice of the turtle is heard in our land.
3. I sought him whom my soul loveth, but I found him not . . . I charge you, O daughters of Jerusalem, if ye find my beloved, that you tell him I am sick of love . . . Whither is my beloved gone, O thou fairest among women? Whither is thy beloved turned aside? that we may seek him with thee.
4. Behold his bed, which is Solomon's, three score valiant men are about it . . . They all hold swords, being expert in war.
5. Return, return, O Shulamite. Return, return, that we may look upon thee . . . How beautiful are thy feet with shoes, O Prince's daughter.
6. Set a seal upon my heart.

Howes, discussing the works at some length, remarks on the sensuous beauty of sound, and observes that:

THE TRANSITION FROM ROMANTIC TO MODERN

the actual stuff of the music is a progress from a keyless, rhythmless, arabesque-like melody signifying desire and longing for the beloved, to a diatonic, rhythmic, almost marchlike, theme, worked contrapuntally in canon and imitation expressive of fulfilment.[20]

The work nonplussed its first hearers, and left even Holst puzzled, for all his own flirting with the Orient.

The Lark Ascending was much earlier (1914, though not performed until 1921). The programmatic intent is crystal clear; there is no mistaking the lark's trillings and twitterings; and to make doubly sure the composer prefaced the score with some lines of George Meredith beginning:

> He rises and begins to round,
> He drops the silver chain of sound,
> Of many links without a break,
> In chirrup, whistle, slur and shake.

It is as open and uninhibited a musical display of sublimated bird song as has ever been written.

In Czechoslovakia the vein of programme music continued to be worked by composers such as Vitězslav Novák (1870-1949), Josef Suk (1874-1935), Leoš Janáček (1854-1928) and Josef Bohuslav Foerster (1859-1951).

The oldest of this group, Janáček, is the most esteemed today, largely by reason of his operas. His dates are deceptive, for he was a slow developer, an individualist who had to work out his own salvation as a composer by grubbing away at the roots of his Moravian heritage. His best works in all media were written comparatively late in life, after his fiftieth birthday, and he speaks a more modern, idiosyncratic language than his younger confrères do. He wrote little 'pure' music; even his essays in that sometimes rather austere medium, the string quartet, owe their existence to external stimuli. The first, written in 1923, was inspired by Tolstoy's *Kreutzer Sonata*. He said of it 'I had in mind an unhappy, tortured, beaten woman, beaten to death as Tolstoy described her'.[21] Out of this Janáček distilled some of his most poignant music. His passionate concern for all humanity led him to the greatest sympathy for all victims of

---

[20] *Op. cit.*, p. 143ff.

[21] *Janáček: Letters and Reminiscences*, collected by Bohumír Štědroň, translated by Geraldine Thomsen (Prague, 1955) p. 171.

tyranny, and political events in his own country and in Russia roused strong emotions which found their outlet in the rhapsody *Taras Bulba* (1915-16), based on Gogol's legend of the Cossack leader, burned at the stake after having beaten his own son to death for having betrayed his country, and *The Ballad of Blaník* (1920), which retreads some of the ground of Smetana's *Ma Vlast*. The piano cycles *On the Overgrown Path* (1901-08) and *In the Mist* (1912) are mood pictures, with titles such as 'Our Evenings', 'They chattered like Swallows' or 'So unutterably anxious'.

Listening to Janáček's music one recalls with astonishment that he was only a few years Dvořák's junior. Compared to his language, which is as individual as Sibelius's very different musical speech, Fibich, Novák and Suk write a variety of the common Teutonic language interlarded with Czech words and phrases, but they somehow manage to preserve a characteristic Czech quality, with its undercurrent of melancholy and wistfulness. They write for large orchestras, their music is effective in a somewhat cinematic way, but leaves no very lasting impression on the listener. One might cite as typical Novák's *Eternal Longing* (1905) or his *In the Tatras* (1907). The former illustrates a poem by Hans Andersen:

> A flock of swans are flying in the moonlight over the sea. One, weaker than the rest, brings up in the rear, and drops exhausted into the sea. A violent wind springs up. The swan, summoning all its strength makes a last desperate effort to follow the main flock, now far ahead towards the rising sun.

This is a typical nineteenth century parable, the blind, instinctive effort of the lone swan (represented as in Sibelius's *Swan of Tuonela* by the cor anglais) symbolizing man's indomitable spirit, eternally aching for the unattainable. There are some beautiful impressionistic touches, and the whole is worked out with considerable mastery. *In the Tatras* is a mountain study (Novák was a keen mountaineer) with a brilliantly effective storm which yields to a peaceful evening, the sunset glow on the mountain peaks well illustrated. In both works the orchestra is handled with real assurance and insight.

Almost the whole of Suk's instrumental output has a programmatic basis. At the head stands the symphony *Asrael*, born of the intense grief over the death of his wife, who was Dvořák's daughter, in 1905. Another work that scored a success in its day was *Zrani* ('Maturity', 1913-18). The titles of Foerster's works (*Ma*

Jeunesse, 1900; *A Legend of Happiness*, 1905; *Springtime and Desire*, 1912) show that preference for 'nature' or 'aspiration' subjects common to Czech composers, but he also wrote a more anecdotal work, *Cyrano de Bergerac* (1905), based on Rostand's play.

Most of this well constructed, beautifully scored music has inevitably become neglected, edged out of our concert programmes by more controversial if not more vital works. But the best of it, whether for orchestra or piano, is too good to be lost for ever. It has a place in the European gallery of music, as an expression of the Slav temperament at a crucial moment in their history.

In Italy orchestral music began to assume importance from about 1870, as a consequence of the increased attention being given to instrumental music in the big centres Rome, Florence, Milan and Turin. The first important piece of orchestral programme music would seem to be a *Sinfonia descrittiva, Leonora* (1883) by Antonio Smareglia (1854-1929). The new Italian school of instrumental composition came to fuller fruition with three composers, Ildebrando Pizzetti (1880-1968), Ottorino Respighi (1879-1936) and Gian Francesco Malipiero (1882-1973). The latter's long list of symphonic poems, with titles such as *Sinfonia del Mare* (1906-cf. Debussy, *La Mer*, 1905), *Sinfonia del Silenzio e della Morte* (1910) and *Symphonic Fragments, San Francisco d'Assisi* (1921) have on the whole made little impact. The same is true of Pizzetti, but Resphigi made a welcome contribution with his unpretentious but charming *Fountains of Rome* (1917), *Pines of Rome* (1924) and *The Birds* (1927). The same year saw the production of his *Vetrate di Chiesa* ('Church Windows'—cf. Karg-Elert's *Cathedral Windows* for organ, 1924) and in the following year he wrote a series of three pieces based on pictures by Botticelli—*La Primavera, L'Adorazione dei Magi, La Nascita di Venere*. His most ambitious, but most inflated and therefore least successful, was a big *Feste Romane, Poema sinfonico per orchestra* (1929). Other Italian composers who might be mentioned are Vincenzo Davico (*La Principessa lontana*, 1911; *Impressioni romane*, 1913); Vittorio Gnecchi (1876-1954) *(Poema erotico*, 1948); Riccardo Pick-Mangiagalli (1882-1949) (*Sortilegi*, for piano and orchestra, 1917) and Francesco Santoliquido (1883-1971) (*Crepuscole sul Mare*, c. 1909).

Alfredo Casella (1883-1947) was more cosmopolitan in tastes and outlook. He spent some time in Paris, and absorbed something of the impressionism of the times, as can be seen in his *A Notte alta*, for piano and orchestra (1917). In the preface to the score (published by Ricordi, 1923) Casella begins with the customary disclaimer, that it is not 'programme music', yet goes on to say that it was inspired by actual experiences, some of which are recalled in the music, and adds a long and pretentious scenario, the gist of which is the contrast between the human love of man for woman and the 'deep, enigmatic indifference of nature' to these human emotions. His case is very similar to another cosmopolitan Italian, Ferruccio Busoni (1866–1924), whose many compositions, programmatic and otherwise, have compelled admiration without winning affection.

CHAPTER 10

French Programme Music from 1870

A complete survey of French programme music over the last hundred years would entail the examination of the work of about one hundred composers. It would involve us in side excursions into the theatre (opera, incidental music, ballet, film), and to be really comprehensive it would mean examining the many orchestral compositions which, like Berlioz's *Romeo and Juliet*, engage the support of the human voice in one way or another. It is possible in this short survey to look at a few only of the more important works.

The pre-eminence of Claude Debussy (1862-1918) has tended to overshadow his forbears and contemporaries, somewhat unfairly, the historian may feel. Among the host of other composers with something individual to say are: Emmanuel Chabrier (1812-94), very much admired by Debussy (*Marche joyeuse*, 1880; *España*, 1883; *Pièces pittoresques pour le Piano*, 1881, and several others); Charles-Valentin Alkan (1813-88), whose many piano pieces include some which are programmatic;[1] Déodat de Séverac (1873-1921), with a number of charming suites for piano; Gabriel Grovlez (1879-1944), whose fanciful *Almanach aux Images* illustrates in a most delightful way some poems by 'Tristan Klingsor' (a pseudonym which pointedly testifies to 'le Wagnerisme' of the time); and Erik Satie (1866-1925), under-rated in his time, over-rated today, a musical cartoonist who like Chabrier and indeed to some extent Debussy himself had an acute sense of the ridiculous and enjoyed pricking the bubble of pomposity. Paul Dukas (1865-1935) has won a little niche for himself in the history of programme music by his entertaining *jeu d'esprit*, *L'Apprenti Sorcier* (1897), which illustrates graphically and amusingly Goethe's account of the apprentice wizard who by magic persuades his broomsticks to carry water for him but cannot

---

[1] A selection is recorded on ORYX 1803.

remember the spell that will reverse the process. There is also Gabriel Fauré (1845-1924), whose elegant *Masques et Bergamasques* suite, his incidental music to *Pelléas et Mélisande* and his *Dolly* (for piano duet) are in the orbit of programme music in its widest sense.

A composer with a long list of ambitious symphonic poems to his credit who appeared of supreme importance to his generation, but who now seems relegated to the status of an Important Historical Figure, is Vincent d'Indy (1851-1931).[2] He was of the establishment, being a pupil of Franck, and director of the conservatory which he founded in conjunction with Charles Bordes and Alexandre Guilmant in 1894, the *Schola Cantorum*; he might be compared with Stanford or Parry. His earliest programme works, for example the overture *Piccolomini* (1874, subsequently incorporated in the large-scale trilogy, *Wallenstein*) and *La Forêt enchantée* (1878) antedate those of his master, Franck; his latest, for instance his third symphony *De Bello gallico* (1919) and *Tableaux de Voyages* (1926) were written after Debussy's death. His best works were those which, like the *Symphonie sur un thème montagnard* ('Symphonie cévenole', 1886) or *Jour d'Été à la montagne* (1905) owed nothing to literature or philosophy but were nature-inspired. The former, for piano and orchestra (the piano playing a concertante role as in Franck's *Les Djinns*) kept his memory alive for some years after his death.

Debussy was surprisingly slow in finding himself. He was over thirty when he wrote his first important orchestral work, *L'Après-midi d'un faune*, and even stranger is the fact that his revolutionary piano works date from his forties, beginning with *Estampes* in 1903 and ending with the two books of *Préludes* between 1910 and 1913.

Though the documentation on him is still far from complete we know much about his artistic ideas, his methods of approach to music and his attitude to nature and the visual arts.[3] Much of this in-

---

[2] He has continued to have champions after his death, not only among his compatriots, for example Paul Landormy, in *La Musique française après Debussy* (Paris, 1943) but in Norman Demuth's biography, *Vincent d'Indy* (London, 1951). He is also discussed sympathetically in Martin Cooper, *French Music from the Death of Berlioz to the Death of Fauré* (London, 1951).

[3] The essential book for the study of Debussy is Edward Lockspeiser, *Debussy; His Life and Mind* (London, 1962 and 1965), two volumes. See also Oscar Thompson, *Debussy, Man and Artist* (New York, 1940) and Léon Vallas, *Claude Debussy, His Life and Works,* translated by Maire and Grace O'Brien (London, 1933).

formation comes from the composer himself. He spoke of his desire to create a music independent of themes and motifs—a species of 'abstract' music such as has already been mentioned. Of his *Nocturnes* for orchestra (*Nuages, Fêtes, Sirènes*) he disclaimed any association with the nocturne as a musical form, but linked the term with 'various impressions and the special effects of light that the word suggests',[4] and spoke of them as an experiment in the combinations that can be achieved with one colour—'what a study in gray would be in painting'. This brings to mind Whistler's *Nocturnes*, which Debussy had seen when he met Whistler in Paris in 1887. Referring specifically to *Nuages* he said he intended this piece to represent:

> the unchanging aspect of the sky, with the slow and melancholy passing of the clouds dissolving in a gray vagueness tinged with white.[5]

He made pertinent and perspicacious observations on Impressionism. Thus, referring to the composition of his orchestral pieces called, significantly, *Images* (1906-12), he remarked that he was
> trying to achieve something *different*—an effect of *reality* —what some imbeciles call *impressionism*, a term that is utterly misapplied, especially by the critics; for they do not hesitate to use it in connexion with Turner, the finest creator of mysterious effects in the whole world of art.[6]

And after the composition of *La Mer* (1905) he pointed out the superiority of music over painting, wherein the play of light can be shown only in a static manner, as in Monet's various versions of Rouen Cathedral; whereas in the continuous, fluid art of music all these effects of light can be combined.

Evidence also comes from other sources. Music in France has never been isolated as it has tended to be in England, and the interrelationship between all the arts has constantly been the concern of literary and art critics. One of them, Lucien Favre, was already in 1900 talking about painting as a sort of music of colours without movement, and a couple of years later Camille Mauclair could write

> The Landscapes of Claude Monet are in fact symphonies of luminous waves, and the music of Debussy, based not on a succession of themes but on the relative values of sounds in

---

[4] Thompson, p. 11.
[5] Thompson, p. 319.
[6] Quoted from Vallas, p. 196; see also Lockspeiser, Vol. II, p. 22.

themselves bears a remarkable resemblance to these pictures. It is Impressionism consisting of sonorous patches.[7]

Debussy's debt to landscape and the visual world is obvious from the large number of his compositions with titles like *Reflets dans l'eau, Jardins sous la pluie, Clair de lune, Snow is dancing* (a snow scene from his *Children's Corner Suite* which recalls the snow scenes beloved of the impressionist painters), *Le Vent dans la Plaine, Brouillards, La Mer*. And the technique used is that of the impressionist painters. Just as for them the 'image' is less important in itself than as a reflector of light and colour, and subservient to the total effect which is as precise a recapturing of the evanescent moment as the painter can achieve, so in Debussy the musical 'images' — melody, harmony, rhythm — have lost their classical clarity and identity, to become merged in the work as a whole.

Debussy as a programme writer stands at the opposite pole to Strauss. He seeks not to depict, but to evoke. In one of his greatest masterpieces, *L'Île joyeuse* (1904), inspired by a contemplation of Watteau's *L'Embarquement pour l'Île de Cythère*, the music picks up all the allusions lying behind the static experience of the picture, illustrating not simply the embarcation for the enchanted island of love (or the return from it, as some modern historians have it), but, in the ambiguous manner which is music's special prerogative, describing for us the physical bustle and excitement of departure and the rolling movement as the ship gets under weigh (the work is a *Barcarole*, owing something to Chopin), and giving us more than a glimpse of the pagan pleasures that await us. In one of the most specific of his piano works, *La Cathédrale engloutie*,[8] the wonderfully descriptive writing depicting the ocean's depths and the dim vision of the outline of the cathedral, only half seen through the mist, also stimulates our imagination to recall past generations of monks and congregations at prayer. This shadowy world of Debussy, with its twilight, darkness, mist, distance, the haze of summer or the fogs of winter, by blurring outlines and by changing or removing

---

[7] Lockspeiser, Vol. II, p. 18.
[8] The legend of church, cathedral or city sunk beneath the waves, in this instance stemming from Britanny, is by no means uncommon. Wilhelm Müller, the poet of Schubert's *Schöne Müllerin* and *Winterreise*, was responsible for one such poem, *Vineta*, of which Brahms in about 1860 did a masterly setting for six-voice mixed choir, unaccompanied.

entirely familiar landmarks or points of reference, can transport us out of the everyday world of confident reality into another realm of mystery, make-believe and fairyland, to the very edge of the unknown and infinite. This is far removed from the Strauss of either graphic realism or sublimity.

There are no heroes in Debussy. Indeed, one suspects that his ultimate dissatisfaction with Wagner was more ideological than musical; he had no patience with men like gods and gods like men. Musically he could no more claim immunity from Wagner's influence than any of his generation. A close study of *L'Après-midi d'un faune*, that marvellous transubstantiation of Mallarmé's Hellenist poem, reveals a sort of essence of Wagner, a harmony purged of grossness, a refined sensuality — qualities which Mallarmé, who was close to Debussy and who had some insight into music, appreciated.

Debussy's largest and grandest orchestral work, his finest in this medium and one of the masterpieces of the twentieth century, is *La Mer*, subtitled 'Three symphonic sketches'— *De l'aube à midi sur la mer; Jeux de vagues; Dialogue du vent et de la mer*. It was written in 1903-05.[9]

The sea in all its moods had always fascinated Debussy. He once told Messager that he had been destined for the life of a sailor, and only by chance was led away from it. What kind of a sailor would he have made, one wonders? But he was no fair weather navigator, for it is recorded that he was once at sea in a wild storm off the coast of Britanny, and enjoyed it hugely. Some of these impressions are embodied in the second and third movements of *La Mer*, and are also enshrined, pictorially, on the cover of the score which, on Debussy's insistence, carried a copy of Hokusai's celebrated print *Deep-sea wave off Kanagawa*.

Maurice Ravel (1875-1937) has been so often coupled with Debussy, as the two outstanding French composers of their time, that critics have been at pains to stress their differences. A comparison of two pieces, Debussy's *Reflets dans l'eau* and Ravel's rather earlier (1901) *Jeux d'eau*, brings out startlingly the dissimilarities of approach.

---

[9] It was completed at, of all places, Eastbourne — 'a little English seaside place, silly as these places sometimes are — too many draughts and too much music.' Thompson, *op. cit.*, p. 157.

Debussy, the passionate, intense observer, is entranced by the distorted images seen through the ripples on the surface, so his music is correspondingly indistinct, the harmonies blurred at the edges. Ravel is fascinated by the water itself, by its movement, whether languidly lapping over the fountain's basin, or thrown up in corruscating jets catching the brilliance of the sunlight. Compared with Debussy's inward brooding Ravel is an externalist, an illustrator. He himself said:

> Inspired by the noise of water, and the musical sounds which fountains of water, cascades and streams make, it is founded on two themes, in sonata form, always without subjecting itself to a classical tonal scheme.[10]

His reference to 'themes' is revealing; his instinct was much less towards Debussy's themelessness. His images are sharp, his melodies, extended or fragmentary, clear-cut, his harmonies rarely dissolve into the sensual wash of colour characteristic of Debussy. When in 1908 he followed Debussy in constructing a large paraphrase of a poem, *Gaspard de la nuit*, both choice of poem and treatment were significantly different. The author of the three fragments *(Ondine, Le Gibet* and *Scarbo)*, Aloysius Bertrand (1807-41) relates in his preface 'that he once asked a stranger to tell him what were the laws of a literary aesthetic, whereupon the stranger, Gaspard de la Nuit *(alias* Satan), gave him in reply the manuscript of these poems in prose'.[11] Each poem deals with some aspect of the supernatural. *Ondine* tells of the water-sprite who wished to marry a mortal, but in this instance is disappointed. Ravel's music mirrors the text in an uncanny way, from the first spatter of water on the windowpane to the disappearance of the disconsolate Ondine in a shower of spray. In *Le Gibet* we are transfixed by the monotonous passing bell and the creaking of the gibbet as its macabre burden sways in the wind; *Scarbo*, a scherzo, conjures up the nightmare fantasies, the shadowy distortions, the unexplained noises, the 'things that go bump in the night', that can assail an over-heated imagination in a dimly lit bedchamber.

---

[10] From his own Autobiographical Sketch, quoted in Norman Demuth, *Ravel* (London, 1947).
[11] Quoted from Rollo Myers, *Ravel: Life and Works* (London, 1960) p. 162. Myers prints the poems with a translation.

Ma Mère l'Oye (1908) also has its counterpart in Debussy, whose *Children's Corner Suite* happens to date from about the same time; and once again Ravel's is the more tangible music. As with *Gaspard de la Nuit* a knowledge of the programme is necessary for a full understanding of these dainty miniatures. In No 2, for instance, *Petit Poucet*, the aimlessly wandering melody is the perfect representation of the puzzled Hop-o'-my-Thumb searching for the crumbs he had dropped, by which he hoped to retrace his steps, but which had been eaten by birds whom we hear twittering excitedly in the branches above him; and when in No 3 the Empress of the Pagodas takes her bath she is saluted by a Liliputian orchestra of theorbos made of nutshells, and viols made from almond shells, and little tinkling bells. Originally written for piano duet, it was subsequently adapted as a ballet and orchestrated with Ravel's usual ingenuity and felicity.

Although he is recognized as one of the outstanding masters of the orchestra it is curious that only one work, the *Rapsodie espagnole* of 1917, was originally conceived for that medium.

During the nineteenth century Spain, which behind its Pyrenean bastion had seemed almost as remote as the Balkans, was gradually drawn into the circle of Western Europe. In 1843 George Borrow's *The Bible in Spain* brought the country's customs and manners to English readers, and a few years later Prosper Mérimée turned his knowledge of Spain to good account in his low-life novel, *Carmen*. A Franco-Spanish musical *entente* began in earnest in 1875 with Bizet's opera based on Mérimée. Lalo's *Symphonie espagnole* for violin and orchestra (dedicated to the Spanish violinist Sarasate) also dates from 1875, and from then on works with a Spanish flavour such as Chabrier's *España* or Rimsky-Korsakov's *Capriccio espagnole* began to appear more frequently. In the meantime Spain herself was enjoying a musical renaissance, headed by the scholar Felipe Pedrell (1841-1922), who in 1881 contributed a symphonic poem, *Marcha de la Coronacion a Mistral*. He was followed by Isaac Albeniz (1860-1909), whose collection of twelve 'Impressions' entitled *Iberia* was published between 1906 and 1909; Enrique Granados (1867-1916), whose best known work is the programme suite of six pieces for piano, *Goyescas* (published 1912-14), inspired by pictures by Goya and subsequently adapted as an opera; and Manuel de Falla (1876-1946) whose *Nights in the Gardens of Spain* (1921) follows Franck's *Les Djinns* in employing a 'concertante' piano with orchestra in a work which distills the essence of the soft air and velvety atmosphere of the Spanish evening.[12]

In this collection of travel brochures Debussy's *Iberia* (the second of his *Images* for orchestra) and Ravel's *Rapsodie* fit comfortably, and are as convincingly 'Spanish' as anything by the native masters; and we must add to this group Ravel's delightful *Alborada del Gracioso* (No . 4 of *Miroirs*, written in 1905 for piano and subsequently scored for orchestra) and Debussy's *Soirée dans Grenade* (No. 2 of *Estampes* for piano, 1903), and *La Puerta del Vino*, from the second set of piano preludes.

The comparison between Debussy's *Iberia* and Ravel's *Rapsodie espagnole* is particularly interesting. The three pieces which constitute *Images* (1908-12), viz., *Gigues, Iberia* and *Ronde de Printemps* were intended by Debussy to typify the English, Spanish and Italian nationalities. The intrusion of a distorted version of *The Keel Row* in *Gigues* is explained by the fact that a poem, *Streets*, written by Verlaine when he was living in Soho, was set to this tune by Charles Bordes.[13] The short, melancholy poem, a recollection of a poor lover's hopes and disappointments, has as refrain an ironic 'dansons la gigue!'[14] The *Ronde de Printemps* was a tribute to Italy *via* a French translation of some verses by Poliziano, whose *Orfeo* began a chain of dramas and pastorals leading to Monteverdi and Gluck. The poem, in praise of May, the month of rejuvenation when lovers dance and sing, inspired Debussy to write a rustic May-day festival, a gentler and more bucolic *Rite of Spring*. The Spanish interlude, in three sections, *Par les Rues et par les Chemins, Les Parfums de la Nuit* and *Le Matin d'un Jour de Fête*, has us strolling through the streets, enjoying the sweet-scented evening before retiring to bed, to awaken next morning at dawn to face the tasks of the day and prepare for the evening's festivities. Ravel goes over much the same ground. His first movement, *Prélude à la Nuit*, is as sensuous as anything he ever wrote, more evocative even than Debussy's *Les Parfums de la Nuit;* two characteristic Spanish dances, *Malagueña* and *Habanera* (an orchestration of his two-piano work of 1895), follow, and then comes the *Feria* in which the hard, surface

---

[12] See Gilbert Chase, *The Music of Spain* (New York, 1941, 1959).
[13] See Lockspeiser, Vol. II, p. 31ff, where Verlaine's verses are printed.
[14] The title was originally *Gigues tristes*.

glitter of Spanish gaiety is conveyed in a movement of exceptional virtuosity.

By 1914 Debussy was a sick man. His later works are outside the scope of this study. By then Ravel, too, had done practically all his best work, and as far as programme music goes there was only the *Tombeau de Couperin* to come (1917). This, another of his many works first conceived in terms of the piano and later orchestrated, is a return to the practice of Denis Gaultier and others; this elegy is programmatic only in as much as it reincarnates Couperin's elegance and fastidiousness in twentieth century terms — an undertaking for which Ravel was ideally suited.

Though Debussy and Ravel dominated the French scene, there were among their contemporaries and successors a large number who played important supporting roles. Each of these could claim our attention in the field of programme music, for Cooper's remark that 'the pictorial element, varying from the most naive to the most sophisticated has been a permanent feature of French music' is as true today as ever.

If we look at the composers discussed in Jean Roy's *Musique française*[15] — Erik Satie, Charles Koechlin, Albert Roussel, Florent Schmitt, Edgard Varèse, Georges Migot, Arthur Honegger, Darius Milhaud, Francis Poulenc, Maurice Jaubert, Henri Sauguet, André Jolivet, Daniel Lesur, Olivier Messiaen, Maurice Ohana, Henri Dutilleux, Serge Nigg, Maurice Jarre, Pierre Boulez, Jacques Bondon — we are struck by their prodigality and their versatility. They can, it seems, turn their hand to anything, be it opera, ballet, incidental music, songs, piano pieces, chamber music, orchestral music — and film music. Migot, for instance, who barely qualifies for mention in Cooper or in William Austin's comprehensive *Music in the 20th Century*, has written six stage works, fourteen cantatas or oratorios, twenty orchestral scores, forty-two works for various chamber combinations, pieces for piano and organ, songs, music for the church, and four films. Honegger's long list of works follow the same pattern, but with more emphasis on incidental and film music (no fewer than thirty-three films between 1923 and 1951). The same remarks apply to Milhaud, with an even longer list of compositions.

---

[15] Paris, 1962. This contains a fair cross-section of the French composers active, 1910-62. Other useful works are, besides Cooper's book, René Dumesnil's *La Musique en France entre les deux Guerres, 1919-39* (Paris, 1946) and Paul Landormy's *La Musique française après Debussy* (Paris, 1943).

Sauguet too has written much for film, and also for radio and television. Their range of interests are wide and varied. Migot for instance was a painter as well as composer; others, for example Koechlin, Schmitt, Honegger and Messiaen, produced textbooks and have continued the French tradition of lively criticism of their own and other people's compositions.

Charles Koechlin (1867-1950), with at least eight symphonic poems to his credit on a wide variety of subjects (he must be the only composer to write a symphony — *The Seven Stars*, 1933 — inspired by the personalities and acting of Hollywood screen stars), which are unpublished, unknown and inaccessible,[16] must remain something of a question mark until more of his music is available for study. French commentators who know his work pay tribute to his sincerity and high ideals, and certainly one work which is available on records whets the appetite for more. This is *Les Bandar-Log* Op. 176 (1939-40; first performed in Brussels, 1946). The source of this is Kipling's *Jungle Book*, which has attracted a number of French composers, and which Koechlin had turned to at least as early as 1925 when he wrote a symphonic poem based on it, *Le Cours de Printemps*. *Les Bandar-Log* is a monkey-scherzo, and he has left some notes as to his intentions. Monkeys are vain, inquisitive, imitative, but not creative; so the score not only parodies modern techniques and composers such as serialism, Debussy, Stravinsky and Boulez, but makes fun of the older 'academic' music of Bach's time (a fugal section on the French folksong, *J'ai du mon tabac)*. He writes for a large orchestra with a big percussion section which includes gongs, celesta, glockenspiel and other tuned percussion. After a slow, mysterious opening the music drifts into a fantastic section in which the chattering monkeys are realistically but musically portrayed. The whole is brilliant, exciting, evocative, and of marked originality, and a remarkable contribution to twentieth century programme music, all the more welcome for not being overlaid with ideology or moralizing.

Albert Roussel (1869-1937)[17] has written several large-scale works for orchestra, one of which, *Le Poème de la Forêt*, has the seasons as

---

[16] For some details of Koechlin's connexions with film see *Proceedings of the Royal Musical Association*, Vol. 98 (1971-72); Robert Orledge, 'Charles Koechlin and the Early Sound Film, 1933-38'.

[17] For information on Roussel see the important monograph, *Albert Roussel*, by Basil Deane (London, 1961).

its subject. It is a series of four nature frescoes (*Forêt d'Hiver; Renouveau; Soir d'été; Faunes et Dryades*) comparable in scope and scale with Debussy's seascape, *La Mer* (almost exactly contemporary). For his *Évocations* Op. 15 (1910-11) Roussel, like several modern composers, went for inspiration to India. Its movements are: *Les Dieux dans l'ombre des Cavernes; La Villa Rose; Aux Bords du Fleuve sacré*.[18] Florent Schmitt (1870-1958) is another composer with a long list of programme works which are only rare visitors to our concert halls. They include a symphonic poem based on Poe, *Le Palais hanté* (1904), six *Épisodes symphoniques d'après Shakespeare, Antoine et Cléopâtre* (1920) and six *Épisodes symphoniques d'après Flaubert, Salammbô* (1925). The former suite was based on incidental music, the latter was extracted from a film score. Another work with a rather enigmatic title, *Suite sans esprit de Suite*, was published in 1938. Its five movements (*Majeza, Charmilles, Pécorée de Calabre, Thrène* and *Bronx*) all represent different aspects of the dance, and are accompanied by some heavily scented prose, for instance *Thrène*: 'Sur la dalle de marbre, une jonché de lys . . . Les Cyprès frissonent contre le ciel d'azur . . . Elle dort . . .' or *Bronx*: 'Dans les verres scintillent les boissons multicolores: des couples sombres, les mâles aux mâchoires simiesques enlaçant leurs compagnes aux cheveux crépus . . . Le jazz nostalgique déchire l'air lourd d'alcool et du fumée.'

Arthur Honegger (1892-1955) — Swiss, but a member of the Parisian group known as 'les Six' — followed his successful *Pacific 231*[19] with a musical interpretation of the football field, *Rugby* (1928), while his contemporary Darius Milhaud (1892-1974) has written several 'musical posters' — *Le Carnaval d'Aix* (1926), *Le Carnaval à la Nouvelle-Orleans* (1949) and an interesting work for piano, *Le Candélabre à sept Branches* (1952).

---

[18] This and other works are discussed in Deane, *op. cit.*
[19] See below, Chapter 12.

CHAPTER 11

Programme Music in America

Writing in 1905 Niecks had to confess to considerable ignorance of trans-Atlantic music, and concentrated mainly on Edward MacDowell (1861-1908), who is now as under-rated as he was formerly over-rated. Since then American music has burgeoned, with a profusion and variety that defies summary and daunts the cataloguer.

In the nineteenth century the United States drew its musical nourishment from Europe, as it could hardly fail to do. Most of the music written, derivative and rootless, understandably lies buried on library shelves, politely acknowledged in histories of music, its bones occasionally disinterred by some devoted scholar. William Henry Fry,[1] who has a little niche in the history of American opera (*Leonora*, 1845), and who fought valiantly for American music, was early in the field with four programme symphonies — *Childe Harold; A Day in the Country; The Breaking Heart; Santa Claus* — a nice range of subjects, one would think. John Knowles Paine (1839-1906), whom Austin calls 'the first academically respectable composer' (he was the first holder of a chair in music in an American University, at Harvard in 1875), studied in Europe, mainly in Berlin (the German influence was long to continue in New England). By the time he, Arthur Foote (1853-1937) and Silas Gamaliel Pratt (1846-1916) had arrived at maturity orchestral concerts especially in New York and Boston were becoming sufficiently frequent to provide platforms for native composers. Paine's *Spring* symphony was given in New York in 1880, while Foote had a 'topographical' overture, *In the Mountains*, performed at Boston in 1887, and a 'prologue', *Francesca da Rimini*, in 1892. His *Four Characteristic Pieces after Omar Khayyám* (1912),

---

[1] For details of Fry's interesting and varied career see Gilbert Chase, *America's Music* (New York, 1966). His symphonies were performed in America by Jullien, who in 1853 and 1854 was touring America with a large orchestra from England.

each prefaced by a quotation from the Rubaíyat, is pleasant salon music, sensitively scored; but of course by then much programme music of an advanced kind had gone under the bridge. Daniel Gregory Mason's output includes a symphony, *The Prodigal Son*, which was performed at the Crystal Palace in 1885. Other works are: *Paul Revere's Ride: A Lincoln Symphony* and *A Tragedy of the Deep* (on the sinking of the Titanic).

While much of this is dead wood, the music of Louis Moreau Gottschalk (1829-69) has sufficient vitality and originality to interest us today. Born in New Orleans, he spent a few years in Europe, studying in Paris with Charles Halle[2] and touring as a concert pianist before returning to the States in about 1852. His works include a symphony, *La Nuit des Tropiques,* and a quantity of piano music with titles like *Danse Ossianique* (1854), *Illusions perdues* (1864) and *Chanson nègre* (1850?). *Danse Ossianique* sounds promising, but turns out to be only a *Schottische*. *Le Banjo: Caprice américan* (sic) is more to the point with its banjo-like strumming and its 'cake-walk' rhythm, for Gottschalk was the first American composer to refuse to be over-awed by the solemnity of 'respectable' pseudo-European music and to turn for inspiration to his native land. Fascinated by Negro and Creole melodies and rhythms, he took the first step towards the emancipation of American music, although his influence at the time was probably very little.[3]

So far we have been considering native composers, but America shares with France the knack of absorbing foreign musicians into the community. The first of these immigrants with whom we are concerned was Charles Martin Loeffler (1861-1935). Born in Mulhausen, Alsace, he was a violinist, studying under Joachim and others. He played for a while in Pasdeloup's orchestra in Paris, then emigrated to America and settled in Boston, introducing a little Gallic lightness to that Teutonic musical stronghold. He seems indeed to have brought to prim and proper Boston[4] a taste for French Symbolist poetry and a penchant for unusual orchestral colour, for the first version of his symphonic poem *Le Mort de*

---

[2] Charles (later Sir Charles) Halle left Paris for London and, later, Manchester in 1848.
[3] For further information regarding Gottschalk see Chase, *America's Music*, Chapter 15.
[4] See Chase, *op. cit.*, Chapter 18, 'The Boston Classicists'.

Tintagiles (1897), based on Maeterlinck's play of 1894, included two *viole d'amore* in the orchestra. His literary leanings are further exemplified in *Les Veillées de l'Ukraine* (1891), inspired by Gogol (part of his childhood had been spent in Russia); his symphonic rhapsody, *La Villanelle du Diable,* for orchestra and organ (1905), after a poem by the symbolist poet Maurice Rollinat, and *La Bonne Chanson* (1901), related to Verlaine's cycle of poems. A Pagan Poem, originally for piano and chamber orchestra, subsequently scored for full orchestra (1907) was based on Virgil's eighth *Eclogue*.[5]

Edward MacDowell (1861-1908) was born in New York, of mixed Scottish and Irish descent. After some early instruction, mainly piano, he moved to Europe in 1876 to continue his studies. Interestingly, his first objective was Paris, where he was for a short time at the Conservatoire; a fellow pupil was Debussy. But the teaching and the ambience did not suit him and he moved to Germany, first to Stuttgart, then to Frankfurt, where Raff was the director of the Conservatory. Through Raff he met Liszt, at that time at Weimar; it was Raff, too, who encouraged him to persevere with composition. He and his wife (they were married in 1884 at Waterford, Connecticut) lived in Germany for several years, moving back to the States in 1888, first to Boston, then to New York.

Interested in literature and the visual arts, himself a capable draughtsman (Gilman's biography of him contains a lively sketch of Liszt, drawn in 1883), it was natural that his taste in composition should lean towards the descriptive—or at least, the allusive. This is seen in his piano music, a large portion of which consists of short pieces with fanciful titles, grouped into collections or suites, and similar in intent to the very numerous salon pieces of, say, Smetana or Fibich. If some of these, for instance the *Woodland Sketches* Op. 51 (1896), are as ingenuous as a faded Victorian photograph, nevertheless the charm of his best work is undeniable. Occasionally, as in some of the *Sea Pieces* Op. 55 (1898) this is combined with a considerable feeling for atmosphere. No. 2 ('From a wandering iceberg') or No. 7 ('Nautilus') stand midway between Grieg's *Lyric Pieces* and Debussy's *Préludes*, which came some years later, 1910-13. Indeed, if one compares MacDowell's work with Debussy's

---

[5] Loeffler has been rather neglected by scholars apart from Carl Engel's excellent study in *Music Quarterly* for 1925.

Petite Suite for piano duet of 1891, MacDowell's achievement is seen in better perspective.

The influence of the Raff/Liszt school can also be remarked in the very early piano suites Op. 10 and Op. 14 (both 1883) in that literary mottoes, from Virgil, Dante and Byron are attached to some of the pieces. Those called *Moon Pictures* Op. 21 (1886) were inspired by Hans Andersen, and Op. 28 (1887) is labelled *Six Idylls after Goethe*. Qualifying titles were also applied to bigger and more ambitious works such as the piano sonatas.

In 1884 during a visit to London he was moved by a performance of *Hamlet*, played by Irving and Ellen Terry, to write his first symphonic poems for orchestra, *Hamlet* and *Ophelia* Op. 22 (1885; the works were dedicated to these two players). Then, like so many of our own countrymen (Tennyson, William Morris and, later, the composer Rutland Boughton), he succumbed to the fascination of the Arthurian legends and wrote a third symphonic poem, *Lancelot and Elaine* Op. 25 (1888). The same Arthurian fever lies behind his *Sonata Eroica* Op. 50 (1896). He wrote:

> While not exactly programme music I had in mind the Arthurian legend when writing this work. The first movement typifies the coming of Arthur. The Scherzo was suggested by a picture by Doré showing a knight in the woods surrounded by elves. The third movement was suggested by my idea of Guinevere. That following represents the passing of Arthur.

In his fourth, *Keltic*, sonata Op. 59 (1901) he attempted to evoke the Celtic legends of Deidre, Cuchullin, Fergus, Queen Maeve, and other aspects of the Cycle of the Red Branch Knights.[6]

MacDowell was the most gifted of the numerous group of American composers working at that time. His younger colleagues Converse, Farwell, Hadley and Carpenter had greater challenges to face, for some of the great series of Strauss tone-poems were by now appearing in American concert life. These not only were explicit in their pictorialism in a way that MacDowell (or Raff or Liszt) had not aspired to, but they displayed an orchestral resource that outdistanced their rivals. Of the music of these American composers Austin aptly says that it 'measures up very well to that of a Glazounov

---

[6] Particulars of the Red Branch order of chivalry and of Deirdre, Cuchullin and other figures of Ireland's legendary history will be found in some detail in T. W. Rolleston, *Myths and Legends of the Celtic Race* (London, 1911).

or Respighi or Franz Schmidt: occasional revivals mix patriotic piety with real pleasure'. But revivals in England are not even occasional; we can find little enough time for our own forgotten band. The music Austin was thinking of might have included Frederick Shepherd Converse's (1871-1940) *The Festival of Pan* (1902) or his *Mystic Trumpeter* (after Whitman, 1907); or perhaps, as a *jeu d'esprit*, and jumping a generation, *Flivver ten million* (1927: the movements are, 'Dawn in Detroit'; 'The Birth of the Hero'; 'May night by the roadside'; 'The Joyriders'; 'The Collision'). The long list of compositions by Henry Kimball Hadley (1871-1937) includes an overture, *Hector and Andromache* (1897); a tone-poem, *Salome* (published in 1906, at the height of the European Salome fever), and symphonies with titles implying programmatic content or intent—No. 1. *Youth and Life* (1897); No. 2. *The Four Seasons* (1901); No. 4. *North, South, East and West* (1911), and No. 5. *Connecticut Tercentenary*. Arthur Farwell (1872-1951) was an unusual personality whose keen and enquiring mind led him into criticism, publishing and folklore as well as composition. Taking a hint from Dvořák and MacDowell, who had written an *Indian Suite* Op. 48 (1897), he interested himself in the music of the native Indians and wrote a number of works based on Indian tunes and legend—*The Domain of Hurakan* Op. 15 (1902), *Impressions of the Wa-Wan Ceremony* Op. 21 (1906) and *Owasco Memories* Op. 8 (1907).

Another writer of some individuality was a pupil of MacDowell, Henry F. Gilbert (1868-1928), whose 1918 orchestral score, *The Dance in Place Congo*, deserves to be remembered. Writing of this he says it was his ambition to compose something more specifically *American* than his colleagues were doing. The inspiration was an article by George W. Cable in the *Century Magazine*, February 1886, entitled 'The Dance in Place Congo' 'in which are described the wild and qausi-barbaric revels of the slaves on late Sunday afternoons in the outskirts of New Orleans'. The article was illustrated with fragments of song and dance melodies which Gilbert has incorporated in his score. This is a sizeable work of 100 pages, using a large orchestra. The gloomy introduction gradually merges into a wild dance; a quieter middle section intervenes, the dance is renewed, and the piece finishes *maestoso*. The tunes have the catchiness of Gottschalk, and the work stands midway between him and later composers such as Gershwin and Bernstein.

This was the period when American composers were exerting themselves most strongly to cut the European apron strings. While some composers such as Foote and Rubin Goldmark (1872-1936; he was the son of Karl Goldmark) still sought inspiration in the accepted 'poetic' subject matter of the old world (Foote's *Omar Khayyám* or Goldmark's *Samson*, 1916), others turned to the domestic front or, following a line that had been suggested in Europe by such a composer as Erik Satie, abandoned the high-minded and heroic in favour of, not so much the 'non-heroic' (Debussy had explored that field) as the 'anti-heroic'. Converse's *Flivver ten million*, already mentioned, followed this line; so did a somewhat earlier work, *Adventures in a perambulator* (1914), by John Alden Carpenter (1876-1951). This is in six sections: 'En Voiture' (*Larghetto*); 'The Policeman' (*Animato, ma non troppo*); 'The Hurdy-Gurdy' (*Più animato*); 'The Lake' (*Largo* — the most poetic of the six); 'Dogs' (*moderato*); 'Dreams' (*Larghetto*). It is a mixture of the onomatopoeic (the perambulator wheels, the policeman's tread) and the cosily sentimental, as illustrated by Carpenter's own programme. The orchestra used is large, and includes an array of percussion — timpani, a xylophone, a celesta, a piano and a harp.

It is only comparatively recently that Carpenter's contemporary, Charles Ives (1874-1954), has come to be taken seriously. Ives, a New Englander, was a loner, an individualistic experimenter who went out of his way to resist any influence from his fellow composers. We have seen his prototype over and over again in the Hollywood film — the self-reliant, self-made American, bluff, homespun, down to earth, a grass roots citizen for whom simplicity and sincerity are the touchstones by which mankind and its achievements are to be judged. In his own words, if there is to be a distinction between 'substance' and 'manner' he rates the former above the latter. His literary idols were Whitman and Emerson, rather than Poe. Emerson's value, he wrote, is higher than Poe's because 'substance' is higher than 'manner' — because 'substance' leans towards optimism, and 'manner' towards pessimism. This ideal, this faith in the ultimate goodness of man, brackets him not only with Whitman, who belonged to a much earlier generation (1819-92), but with his exact contemporary Vaughan Williams. Like Vaughan Williams, and like Bartók, Ives found his chief inspiration in the music on his own doorstep. The music of everyday life, whether that of a village hop, a square dance, a brass band or a circus, was the catalyst. This brings to mind Chabrier: but there is a vital distinction. Chabrier's optimism is direct and uncomplicated, but Ives could never entirely rid himself of the cloudy philosophy of the New England transcendentalists.

His second piano sonata, *Concord, Mass., 1840-1860*, composed in 1909-15 and revised 1940-47, seeks to sketch those writers and idealists based on Concord, the little community some miles west of Boston, Mass.—Emerson, Thoreau, the Alcotts; and Ives put forward his ideas in the substantial *Essays before a Sonata*.[7] In this he explicitly states his intention 'to present one person's impression of the spirit of transcendentalism associated with Concord of over half a century ago'. This is done by 'impressionistic pictures of Emerson and Thoreau, a sketch of the Alcotts, and a Scherzo supposed to reflect a lighter quality which is often found in the fantastic side of Hawthorne'. The first movement, 'Emerson', is designed as a sort of commentary on Emerson's writings and philosophy.

> We see him standing on a summit, at the door of the infinite where many men do not dare to climb, peering into the mysteries of life, contemplating the eternities, hurling back whatever he discovers there.

The second movement (Scherzo) has to do with that 'frosty morning in Berkshire', 'the old hymn tune', or 'the seven vagabonds of Circe's palace, or something else in the Wonderbook'.[8] The third movement refers to the 'Orchard House', the Alcott's Concord home—a recollection of the Scottish songs and hymns sung in the evening, old Scottish airs, and Beethoven's fifth, played on an old spinet. Of the last movement, 'Thoreau', Ives wrote a long commentary[9] which seeks to summarize Thoreau's musings over *Walden*. It ends:

> Is it a transcendental tune of Concord? 'Tis an evening when the 'whole body is one sense' . . . and before ending his day he looks out over the clear, crystalline water of the pond and catches a glimpse of the shadow-thought he saw in the morning's mist and haze—he knows that by his final submission, he possesses the 'Freedom of the Night'. He goes up the 'pleasant hillside of

---

[7] Published, with the sonata, in 1919. See Chase, *op. cit.*, p. 418. Chase devotes a complete chapter to Ives.
[8] The Wonderbook was an adaptation of Greek myths for children, by Hawthorne, published in 1852.
[9] Printed in Chase, p. 422ff.

pines, hickories' and moonlight, to his cabin 'with a strange liberty in Nature, a part of herself.'

'Substance' or 'manner'? Ives seems to be caught in the thickets of his own philosophy; but in any case to ask music to clarify such idealism as is expressed by Emerson and Thoreau (who in *Walden*, 1854, had already come to see that the complexities of civilization were threatening man's spiritual existence) is to put too great a strain on it. Yet perhaps the impulse to construct such a monumental work as the *Concord* sonata is no more confused than Strauss's compulsion some ten years earlier to try to embody Nietzschean philosophy in music.

The simplicity referred to above applies to intent rather than means. Ives discovered for himself, and jumbled together in his compositions, new techniques such as polytonality, note-clusters, rhythms of conflicting complexity, microtones, jazz effects, etc., and these were then fitted together like the parts of a motor car, to produce a complicated machine that performs a fairly simple function. The music is elaborate, but the programmatic intentions simple and obvious, even banal. In the symphony entitled, *Holidays* (1904-13), the holidays are: 'Washington's Birthday'; 'Decoration Day'; 'Fourth of July'; 'Thanksgiving'. The *Orchestral set No. 2* (1912-15) comprises: 'An Elegy for our Forefathers'; 'The Rock-strewn Hills Join in the People's Outdoor Meeting'; 'From Hanover Square North at the end of a Tragic Day'. Examples could be multiplied.

If Ives does not speak a private language, yet his music does call for some specialized, even local, knowledge. It is not only, in Austin's words, that his music must be studied 'along with his trenchant, choppy prose . . . without the prose, unfortunately, much of the music fails to make any clear effect'. This charge can be levelled against all programme music—and Ives was essentially a programmatic writer. It is rather, to quote Austin again, that 'To guess what Ives is getting at in his sonatas and symphonies, it is essential to recognize the tunes he quoted, especially from popular church music, but also from dance music and military band music'.[10] The same point can be made concerning Tchaikowsky's *1812 Overture*, or Beethoven's *Battle Symphony*, or Berlioz's *Symphonie fantastique*.

---

[10] Austin, *op. cit.*, p. 51.

In the latter, for instance, the effect of the *Dies irae* quotation on a non-Catholic and secular audience would be quite different from that produced on a Catholic listener brought up in familiarity with the tune.

Part of Ives's appeal to the present generation is undoubtedly extra-musical. Not only is there much to admire in his sincerity and his single-minded pursuit of his own artistic ideals, but his work was achieved in the face of the 'establishment'—musical and otherwise. He was a sort of musical Grandma Moses; like her he sought inspiration in the homely doings of village or small town life. He saw America's pioneers through a romantic haze, but it was a democratic romanticism—the deification of *Homo vulgaris*, the Common Man, which is the religion of the twentieth century.

Though Ives had little influence on his contemporaries and seemed to be ploughing a lonely furrow it is now apparent that his younger colleagues were often motivated by similar ideals. Carl Ruggles (1876-1971), like Ives a 'loner', wrote an orchestral work, *Men and Mountains* (1921-24; revised 1936), which carries a quotation from Blake, 'Great things are done when men and mountains meet'. Douglas Moore (1893-1961) contributed to 'Musical Americana' (Chase's phrase) with *The Pageant of P. T. Barnum* (1924), an orchestral suite in five movements; *Moby Dick* (1928), deriving from Melville's novel; and an *Overture on an American Tune* (1931) based on Sinclair Lewis's *Babbitt*. William Grant Still (b. 1893), with Negro and Indian blood in his veins, has written works which strive towards the emancipation of these oppressed minorities—*Darker America* (1924); *From the Black Belt*, for chamber orchestra (1931) and *In Memoriam; The Coloured Soldiers who died for Democracy* (1944). Roy Harris (b. 1898) comes not from the Eastern seaboard but from the far mid-West, Oklahoma, and even from the far West, since his family moved to California in his youth. Of his first symphony (1933) he writes: 'In the first movement I have tried to capture the mood of adventure and physical exuberance; in the second, of the pathos which seems to underlie all human existence; in the third, the will to power and action'. In the symphonies written during the second World War Harris harnesses music to the war effort. The sixth for instance, based on the Gettysburg Address and dedicated 'to the armed forces of our nation', has the four movements entitled 'Awakening'; 'Conflict'; 'Dedication'; 'Affirmation'. One is inevitably tempted to compare these works with the products of the Soviet Union, to be considered in the next chapter.

Another far West composer was Arthur Shepherd (1880-1958). His first symphony called *Horizons: Four Western Pieces for symphony orchestra* (1927) takes us on a Cook's Tour of the West. Its movements are 'Westward'; 'The Lone Prairie'; 'The Old Chisholm Trail'; 'Canyons'. The most famous, or notorious, of these topographical suites is probably the *Grand Canyon Suite* of Ferde Grofe (1892-1972), written in 1932. He followed this with an *Aviation Suite* (1946); a *Death Valley Suite* (1957) and a *World's Fair Suite* (1964). A not unfair comparison to these would be the *London Suite* of Eric Coates (1886-1958). Aaron Copland (b. 1900) with his *El Salon Mexico* (1936) and Virgil Thomson (b. 1896) with his *Three Landscapes* ('The Seine at night'; 'Wheatfield at noon'; 'Sea Piece with Birds') (1947-52) offer more refined versions of the topographical suite. Like Ives, Thomson found himself much influenced by literature, but the influences were more international and eclectic, even esoteric—Cocteau, James Joyce, Ezra Pound, Gertrude Stein, in place of Emerson and Walt Whitman.

A composer whom it will be convenient to treat here is the Swiss Jew Ernest Bloch (1880-1959), who emigrated to the United States in 1917. His large output, covering most of the forms, and largely programmatic (exceptions are the powerful piano Quintet and the masterly violin Concerto), includes one blazing masterpiece, *Schelomo*, one near miss, *Israel*, and one disaster, *America*.

His first orchestral work was significantly entitled *Sinfonia orientale* (1894). Its three movements are: 1. *Introduction, Prayer*; 2. *Allegro, Caravan in the Desert; Intermezzo, Oases*; 3. *Adagio, Funeral Ceremonies*. It was based on Hebrew melodies, sung to him by his father. Another symphonic poem, *Vivre-Aimer*, was performed under the composer's direction at Geneva in 1901. A more ambitious work dates from the same year, though not performed until 1908. It was a four-movement symphony, with subtitles: 1. 'Destiny; doubt, hope, conflict'; 2. 'Of happiness, of faith'; 3. 'Struggle; the battle of life and (in the Trio), refuge in the simplicity of rustic life'; 4. 'La Volontà' (a fugue-like movement); the triumph of man through reason and intelligence'. The links with Strauss, by whom Bloch was almost inevitably influenced, are obvious. It also gives us Bloch's ethical creed. Aware of man's folly and stupidity, he refused to countenance the idea of man's inherent wickedness. He believed in the perfectibility of man—a byproduct of nineteenth century Darwinism and the idea of progress, social, ethical, economic, which today to many people looks sadly illusory.

Two 'Calendar' pieces (*Hiver, Printemps*) of 1904 enhanced his growing reputation. Work on his great Shakespeare opera, *Macbeth*, occupied him from 1909 (two *entr'actes* which can be played detached from the opera certainly deserve to be catalogued as programme music). Then in 1910 he began an immense *Hebrew Cycle*, to consist of: *Three Psalms; Schelomo; Israel*, which was not finished until 1916.[11]

In *Schelomo* Bloch follows Strauss's *Don Quixote* in employing a solo cello as the incarnation of Schelomo (Solomon). The orchestra is also on a Straussian scale, with triple woodwind, full brass and a wealth of percussion. He called it 'A Hebrew Rhapsody for Violoncello solo and Full Orchestra'. It was inspired by the Book of Ecclesiastes, and his first conception involved words. But Bloch knew no Hebrew, which he felt was the only possible language for the work. However, in 1915 Bloch met the cellist Barjansky, and showed him the manuscripts of the *Poemi Ebraici* and *Israel*. Barjansky was excited by the music, and Bloch, equally excited by Barjansky's playing, conceived the idea of casting the cello as the voice part. There seems originally to have been no very clear programmatic intention, but in connexion with a performance of the work in Rome early in 1933 Bloch set about 'psycho-analysing' his score and produced a long programme, which he emphasized (as so many composers have done) was written *after* the music. The following summary incorporates most of the important ideas.[12]

The cello is the incarnation of Solomon, and the orchestra represents the world around him. But sometimes the orchestra seems to reflect his thoughts, which the solo instrument articulates. The Introduction, *Lento moderato (a bene placito, quasi cadenza)*, containing the germs of most of the essential motifs of the work, is a lament on the vanity of things, and expresses a pessimistic philosophy. With a new motif in the violas (p. 6 of Schirmer's Study Score) the mood changes, though still gloomy and pessimistic. Soon

---

[11] The most extensive and intensive study of Bloch so far is by the Italian Mary Chiesa Tibaldi, *Ernest Bloch* (Turin, 1933), to which I am indebted for much of the biographical information concerning him.

[12] See Tibaldi for a fuller discussion.

the rhythm of a languid dance is heard (p. 10), as Solomon's concubines endeavour to banish his gloomy thoughts. They succeed for a time, flattering him: is not Solomon king, all-powerful? But revulsion follows. He is overcome by the contrast between his terrestial pomp, expressed by a brilliant orchestral 'cadenza' (p. 31ff), and the recognition of his own lost opportunities. A theme is heard, first on the bassoon (p. 34), one that Bloch's father used to sing; and a vision arises, of a better world, where peace, love and justice reign. But this is seen to be an illusion, and the work ends quietly with a sense of the vanity of mortal life, in a mood of despair, emptiness and nothingness.

Israel, originally entitled *Feste Ebraiche*, was planned in several sections, each to express a state of soul. This was subsequently modified, and the second plan envisaged two parts, of which only the first was completed. The second part was to have included a chorus expressing Bloch's philosophical creed. The work as it stands consists of an introduction and two movements, one inspired by the feast of Yom Kippur, the second by the festival Succoth. Though Bloch left no detailed synopsis Tibaldi suggests that the second movement is linked with the feminine in the Bible—the Song of Songs, Rebecca at the Well, etc. It is scored for a very large orchestra including a choir of female voices and a bass solo. These have very little to do, coming in only at the end to sing 'Adonai, O Elohin! Hear my prayer. Thou art my refuge. I am steadfast, O my Elohin!'. After the slow introduction (*Adagio molto*) the main movement begins *Allegro agitato*, but with many fluctuations of pace. The work displays the same nervous, ecstatic quality as *Schelomo*; like that work the texture exploits *ostinati*, and deploys brilliant brass figuration allied to broad slabs of melody, with fourths and fifths very prominent. As in *Schelomo*, and as in another large 'topographical' work, *Helvetia* (1912), the orchestral sound is very individual to Bloch.

In 1917, after an earlier visit to the United States, where his work was gaining an increased hearing, he left his native Switzerland and took up permanent residence, first in New York, then in Cleveland, Ohio, as head of the Cleveland Institute of Music. He continued to write programmatic works, as for example the piano pieces called *Sea Poems* (1922-23), inspired by Walt Whitman, the Suite for viola and orchestra (1918-19) subtitled 'Sumatra', and the two pieces for string quartet entitled *In the Mountains (Haute Savoie)*: 1. Dusk; 2. Rustic dance. Then in 1926 he undertook the largest, most grandiloquent and most misguided of all his programme works.

The score, published in 1928, is headed: *America. An epic Rhapsody in three parts for orchestra.* 'This symphony has been written in love for this country; In reverence to its Past—In faith in its Future'. It is dedicated to those two patron saints of America who have inspired so much American music, Abraham Lincoln and Walt Whitman. A sort of article of faith follows:

> The ideals of America are imperishable. They embody the future Credo of all mankind: a Union, in common purpose and under willingly accepted guidance, of widely diversified races, ultimately to become one race, strong and great. But, as Walt Whitman has said; 'To hold men together by paper and seal or by compulsion is of no account. That only holds men together which aggregates all in a living principle, as the hold of the limbs of the body or the fibres of plants'.

The composer goes on to say that though the work has no programme (a statement belied by the score itself), he has been inspired by this ideal.

The large score contains triple woodwind, brass, organ, four timps, tambourine, tambourine *basque*, two bass drums, cymbals, gong, triangle, wood box, Indian drum, campanella (glockenspiel), campana (in D), two anvils, one steel plate, one motor horn (ad lib!) in D flat, celesta, two harps, strings and—for the culminating Anthem—chorus. The score is bespattered with explanatory references and quotations from Whitman. They were not intended to be printed in a programme but, says the composer, 'may stimulate the performers and facilitate their task in making clearer to them the intentions of the composer'.

There are three movements, headed as follows: I. 1620. The soil—The Indian—(England)—The Mayflower—The Landing of the Pilgrims. II. 1861-65 (ie, the American Civil War). Hours of Joy, Hours of Sorrow. III. The Present—The Future. This movement has some gloomily prophetic moments, eg, Turmoil of the present time—Materialistic 'prosperity'—Speed—Noise—Man slave of the machines (the Russian composer Mossolov's *Factory*, in praise of machines, was contemporary, 1928)—America's call of Distress—The inevitable Collapse. But in 1926 an incurable optimist such as Bloch was not ready to face the possibility of the complete and total collapse of civilization such as threatens us today, so, with The Mastery of Man over the Machines, his environment and—himself, we move on to the culminating Anthem.

The work is a hotch-potch of naïveté and sophistication. The naïveté resides partly in the use of themes, as when in the first movement he utilizes Indian pueblo songs (taken from collections of Indian music by Francis Dinsmore, Dorothy Scarborough and others) to suggest primitive life on the American continent before the arrival of the Pilgrim Fathers, who are characterized by folksongs, real or pseudo, from England. The second movement mingles 'John Brown's Body', 'Tramp, tramp, tramp, the boys are marching', 'The Old Folks at Home', 'Dixie' and a Creole folksong. In the third movement Negro folksongs such as 'I went to the hop joint' and 'The Coon-can game' jostle with factory and motor noises. The sophistication lies in the variegated resources of harmony, rhythm and orchestral colour open to the twentieth century composer. The Anthem is a broad, simple diatonic melody, a sort of 'Unison song for massed singing' such as Women's Institute choirs sang in the 1930s — and maybe still do.

The symphony had numerous performances in America and was usually well received. This must be taken in its context. It was the time of the birth of the League of Nations and the hopeful spirit of the period post-World War I, before the terrible depression of the late 1920s and the 1930s. Bloch is a neglected composer today, but if he is to be rehabilitated it must be on the strength of his chamber music, his violin concerto, his smaller programme pieces and — his masterpiece — *Schelomo*.

CHAPTER 12

Conclusion

Bloch's *America* represents the last dying embers of the fires of late nineteenth century romanticism. It was a dinosaur, a cumbersome, inelegant creature ill adapted to the times. It preached the brotherhood of man in a language that was outmoded. The younger generation, no less idealistic, even more aware than their forefathers of the spiritual enigma of humanity, either discarded music as a means of improvement and turned towards a neutral, 'absolute' music wherein the sounds themselves are sufficient, or meant to be; or, if they intended their music to be didactic or uplifting, the instrumental sound was given definition by enlisting the more precise aid of words. Benjamin Britten, for instance, who is the reverse of an absolute composer, writes a *Spring* symphony or a *War Requiem* wherein the evocative power of music is given a specific direction by the poetry and all the verbal and spiritual images it conveys.

It might be thought odd, even paradoxical, that at a time when musical composition has been 'liberated' from almost every restriction, when melody, harmony, rhythm, form and colour are technical matters open to any interpretation the composer likes to put on them, and when the sound palette has become almost immeasurably enlarged by electronic means, composers should choose this very moment to abandon almost any attempt at realistic portrayal. Yet on second thoughts there is no paradox. Part of the charm of illustrative, imitative music is that it *is* imitative. The intrusion of a real cuckoo in the *Pastoral* symphony would detract from its artistry rather than enhance it. Honegger's brilliant *Pacific 231* (1924) was successful because it drew a realistic picture of a great steam locomotive gathering speed, using nothing but the resources of the normal symphony orchestra.[1] It is understandable that once com-

---

[1] In these days of electric and diesel locomotives it is perhaps necessary to point out that steam locomotives were classified by their wheel arrangement. The 'Pacific' class

posers have the means to reproduce accurately any sound from real life they should lose interest in this aspect and seek other difficulties to conquer.[2]

Not that composers have entirely abandoned the descriptive, or at least the suggestive, title; indeed the need for some verbalization in instrumental music seems as great as ever. The titles, however, are often laconic or cryptic, with words like 'Structures' replacing the old fashioned 'Nocturne' or 'Aquarelle'. Sometimes they attempt to be too specific, as when Penderecki (b. 1933) writes a *Threnody for the victims of Hiroshima* (1961).

If the concert hall from the 1930s onwards seem to be less favourable to the genre of programme music one reason is that descriptive music has been siphoned off into the sound-film. This is a continuation of the traditional outlets for composers in the related fields of ballet and incidental music. The composer invited to supply music for a film need have no qualms of conscience over writing realistic music, and indeed if his music does not suggest atmosphere, depict galloping horses or give graphic illustrations of storms and battles it will not have made its proper contribution. True, much of this music is distinctly ephemeral. It is as cardboard as its accompanying stage props, and collapses ignominiously in the glare of the concert hall, and re-runs of old films even show up much of the music not only as pasteboard and tinsel, but as fundamentally unnecessary. Nevertheless the sound-film from the 1930s onwards was a musical education for both composers and audiences, opening our ears to the possibilities of new techniques such as abstract, antithematic, atonal and serial writing and breaking down barriers between classical, jazz and pop far more effectively than the conventional concert could do.

By its very nature film-music is unsuited to the concert hall. When it is not *Gebrauchmusik*—journalese, blown out with a factitious portentousness—it is scrappy and disjointed; or it labours a secondrate 'theme' with the maddening insistence of the cuckoo in May. It is only rarely, as with Walton's *Death of Falstaff*, that a morsel can be extracted without a laborious re-working (Vaughan Williams's

---

of locomotives had a leading bogie of two axles, three pairs of driving wheels, and a trailing axle—hence 2.3.1. In England we counted wheels not axles, so that if Honegger had been an Englishman his title would have been 'Pacific 462'.

[2] There is a parallel in the theatre, where the modern designer is apt to find anything approaching Wagner's Bayreuth realism intolerable.

Sinfonia Antartica, mentioned previously, is one such wholesale reworking). But every now and then the discipline of writing music aimed at a universal audience, whether through the medium of the film or the musical, has stood a composer in good stead. Leonard Bernstein's second symphony, subtitled 'The Age of Anxiety' (after W. H. Auden) (1949), mingles traditional and modern serious music with jazz in a manner typical of the composer and of many American writers. It is programmatic ('The Seven Ages; The Seven Stages; The Dirge; The Masque; The Epilogue'); but though it is post-war and written with our modern doubts and difficulties in mind these are kept within a *musical* discussion. Like most good programme music of the past it can be listened to for its own sake. Bernstein uses a large orchestra, with a *concertante* piano part and the customary array of percussion.

Another composer with a foot in both camps was George Gershwin (1898-1937), born in Brooklyn of Russian parents. In 1928 he joined the ranks of those composers (Delius, Vaughan Williams, Elgar, John Ireland, Suk) who have written studies of a single city, when his *An American in Paris* was first performed in Carnegie Hall on 13 December. For this performance Deems Taylor wrote a programme note (published in the full score, 1930) which is entertaining in itself, but too long to quote here. The work makes no pretensions to profundity, but is a sort of foil to Delius's *Paris*. Written in the period when so many American composers were gravitating to Paris to sit at the feet of the Parisian Gamaliel, Nadia Boulanger, it gives a good-tempered, even frivolous, picture of the visitor's self-confident saunter through a city of taxi cabs, girls and dance-halls where the Blues and the Charleston had arrived. The contrast between this light-hearted homage to the gay city of the American's imagination and Bloch's contemporary musical sacrifice to America could hardly be more pronounced.

So much of this epigonic music, whether German, Italian, Spanish, Scandinavian or whatever, illustrates the eternal dilemma in which the writer of programme music finds himself. If on the one hand he attempts the purely illustrative or descriptive—the topographical study, the travelogue, the anecdote—the besetting risk is banality. Often the mere statement of the aims is enough to prejudice the work. Moreover, the dividing line between what is acceptable and what is not seems to be drawn on no very sure aesthetic principles.

For most people I suppose Ketelbey's *In a Monastery Garden* is 'out', while Ibert's *Petit âne blanc* is 'in'. But what is the criterion? How do we judge whether or not to accept, say, Abram Chasins' *Rush Hour in Hongkong,* or Malcolm Williamson's *Travel Diaries?* If on the other hand we choose more spiritual, elevated, themes, we run into risks that are just as great. We reach for the sublime; but who shall measure sublimity?

Programme music in its heyday in the nineteenth century was positive, optimistic, anthropocentric. Man's spirit was indomitable — unquenchable, in the words of Nielsen's fourth symphony. Apart from the pantheism of Debussy mother nature was seen almost entirely as a framework for man, providing support, inspiration and challenge; man himself, as artist, poet, thinker, dreamer or man of action, was enshrined in monumental Faust or Dante symphonies, Heldenlebens, eroica sonatas and symphonies, epics, as imposing and permanent as the Albert Memorial. The New World, land of opportunity, eagerly embraced these beliefs, finding ample inspiration in the humanistic ideals of Abraham Lincoln and the evocative but misty language of Walt Whitman; while at the opposite extreme from 'free enterprise' composers in socialist countries, in a new dispensation, found themselves more or less willing servants of the state religion, vestal virgins tending the fire on an altar dedicated to official optimism.

If it is difficult to arrive at an objective assessment of the value of music in our own country, where the cultural background is familiar and taken for granted, it becomes almost impossible when faced with works written in quite different situations and designed for quite other purposes. This is true to some extent even of the USSR's greatest living composer, Dmitri Shostakovich (b. 1906),[3] who carried the programme symphony into the twentieth century with his second (1927), dedicated to the October revolution; his third (1929), entitled 'The first of May'; his *Leningrad* symphony, written under the stimulus of the siege of Leningrad during 1941 and first per-

---

[3] For an important discussion on Soviet music generally see the chapter by Boris Schwartz, 'Soviet Music since the Second World War', in *Contemporary Music in Europe*, edited by Paul Henry Láng and Nathan Broder (London, New York, 1965). Of their programme music he says: 'Many of the symphonic poems with programmatic content now being composed in the USSR fill the needs of the Soviet concert repertory, but they will hardly penetrate beyond the borders'. See also Boris Schwartz, *Music and Musical Life in Soviet Russia, 1917-1970*' (London, 1972).

formed by Toscanini in New York in 1942; his eleventh, (1957), inspired by the abortive 1905 revolution, and the twelfth (1961), dealing with the events of the decisive year 1917.

These are works in the nineteenth century tradition—basically tonal, heroic in gesture and ample in length. The eleventh begins with an *Adagio*, 'Palace Square'—calm, with subterranean rumblings of discontent. The second movement is headed '9th January', and is a vivid re-enactment of the massacres perpetrated on that day. The third is a lament, 'Eternal Memory'; the fourth, entitled 'Alarm', calls for eternal vigilance, but ends calmly and serenely. The twelfth symphony, dedicated to the memory of Lenin, is also in four movements—'Revolutionary Petrograd'; 'Razliv'; 'Aurora'; 'Dawn of Humanity'. This goes over some of the same ground as No. 11 but with less conviction. Needless to say both are well written and effectively scored, but contain little that is memorable.

Works by lesser composers such as Maximilian Steinberg's *Turk-Sib* symphony (1935), commemorating the opening of the Turkestan-Siberian railway, or Rheinhold Glière's *Zapovit* (1939-41) offer less interest. The latter, preceded by some conventional lines by Taras Shevelienko entitled 'Testament' on the familiar theme of 'the evil blood of tyrants' the flow of which 'your freedom shall sanctify', is effective in an oldfashioned, Glazounovish way—in fact, like *Stenka Razin* it employs the *Volga Boat Song* as one of its themes.

One important minority group remains to be discussed—the stained glass music of the Church. The term is not at all meant to be pejorative; it is simply a convenient tag for identification. For the *milieu* in which music is heard is important. Just as no firm opinion on opera can be arrived at outside the opera house, so liturgical music demands its proper surroundings for its true assessment. The great Gothic cathedrals and churches of France are the repository of this tradition; in these monumental temples the solemn, opulent and penetrating sounds of Cavaillé-Coll's organs, transformed by the building's turbulent reverberations into something rich and strange, combined with the suffused light, prismatic colours and the aroma of incense to approach the ideal combination of sounds, sights and smells of which Debussy dreamed.

This is the stage—the mystical arena, one might call it—of the

French and Belgian organist-composers Franck, Alexandre Guilmant (1837-1911), Charles-Marie Widor (1845-1937), Louis Vierne (1870-1937), Charles Tournemire (1870-1939), Marcel Dupré (1886-1971) and Paul de Maleingreau (1887-1956), to name a few of the most outstanding. All were skilled in improvization, and all made significant contributions in the field of programme music for liturgical use, as Frescobaldi, Froberger and Bach had previously done.

This religious fervour is seen in a most exalted form in the magnificently imaginative *Passion Symphonie* of Marcel Dupré, which had its origins in a recital at Philadelphia on 8 December 1922. The composer, given the customary themes on which to extemporize, chose four plainsong tunes and wove elaborate 'choral preludes' around these. The extemporized music remained running in his head after the recital, he made notes, and a year or two later worked the music up into a four-movement symphony which was first performed by the composer in Westminster Cathedral on 9 October 1924. The four movements are: 1. *Le Monde dans l'attente du Sauveur*; 2. *Nativité*; 3. *Crucifixion*; 4. *Résurrection* — a scheme which corresponds to the most important events in the Church's year, Advent, Christmas, Good Friday and Easter Day. The programmatic intent of the work is especially apparent in the second movement, a *berceuse*, and the third, where the physical action of nailing Christ to the Cross and the subsequent erection of the Cross are movingly and agonizingly depicted. The symphony as a whole is one of the masterpieces of organ literature.

The music of this school, normally the preserve of a comparatively narrow circle of initiates, has been brought to the attention of a wider audience by the activities of Olivier Messiaen (b. 1908).[4] An organist with a consummate technique, an inspired improvisor, teacher, writer and composer, Messiaen is one of the outstanding figures of the twentieth century. His output has been large, and it will be possible here to touch on only a few aspects of his work.

---

[4] There is a fairly extensive bibliography on Messiaen. See especially Claude Samuel, *Entretiens avec Olivier Messiaen* (Paris, 1967) and Oliver Messiaen, *Techniques de mon langage musicale*, 2 volumes, (Paris, 1944); translated into English as *The Technique of My Musical Language* (Paris, 1950).

In much of his music the tendencies towards abstract or motif-less music and a slack or non-existent motor-rhythm can be observed. With this goes the typical twentieth century preoccupation with sound *per se*. *Le Banquet céleste*, for instance, written originally in 1926, is headed by a quotation from St John's Gospel: 'Celui qui mange ma chair et boit ma sang demeur en moi et moi en lui'. It consists of twentyfive bars of almost static music, exploiting sonority rather than themes (though some are recognizable). It is marked *Très lent, extatique*, with an added direction at the opening, *lointain, mystérieux*. Beginning *pianissimo*, it grows in sound to a *forte*, then declines to a long held *pianissimo* chord of C sharp minor. Much of the registration is precisely indicated; but how does one interpret the pedal part in bar twenty-three—three notes, *staccato, 'irisé, poétique'? Apparition de l'Église éternelle* (1934), sixty-five bars, *Très lent*, is built on the same simple plan, a *crescendo* from *pp* to *fff* and back again, the first four bars behaving somewhat as a small rondo theme. A feature of the writing is dissonant chords dissolving into concords of bare fourths and fifths, with a complete chord in the *fff* section standing out all the more gloriously. A much bigger and more varied work is *Les Corps glorieux—sept visions brèves de la vie des ressuscités* (1939). The seven visions, each with quotations from the Scriptures attached, are: 1. *Subtilité des Corps glorieux* (a single melodic line, no time signature); 2. *Les eaux de la grâce (Rêveur, bien modére)* (no key or time signature, RH in persistent semiquavers, LH in chords, highly dissonant with RH and pedals, which move in an *ostinato*, Stravinsky-like pattern); 3. *L'Ange aux parfums* (a complex and varied movement in five sections); 4. *Combat de la mort et de la vie* (two parts, the first, after two bars introductory monody, *plus vif, agité et tumultueux, ff*, with note clusters in both hands; the second half, marked *Extrêmement lent, tendre, serein (dans la Paix ensoleillée du Divin Amour)* (based on the opening monody or its derivatives, ending *pp*); 5. *Force et agilité du corps glorieux* (headed *vif*, this is another monody, both hands in octaves); 6. *Joie et clarté des corps glorieux* (chords and monody, a sort of birdsong); 7. *Le mystère de la Sainte Trinité* (a trio, *très lent, lointain*, with no time or key signature, ending on a bare fifth). The five portions of the *Messe de la Pentecôte* (1950) have similar headings: 1. *Entrée (Les langues de feu)*; 2. *Offertoire (Les choses visibles et invisibles)*; 3. *Consécration (Le don da Sagesse)*; 4. *Communion (Les oiseaux et les sources)*; 5. *Sortie (Le vent de l'Esprit)*.

Words, whether from the Holy Scriptures or from other sources, have a sort of incantory appeal for him. This is seen not only in his religious music as above or in such a work as *Couleurs de la cité céléste (Les visions de l'amen)* but in titles such as *Quatuor pour le fin de temps* (written in 1940 when he was a prisoner of war). To submit to their appeal is to meet Messiaen halfway; but as regards his religious music a further *rapprochement* is necessary. Intensely religious himself, he regards this music as the servant of religious mysticism. It is an aid to the devout worshipper who, sheltered from the garish outside world by thick cathedral walls, a harmonious glow filtering through the windows,[5] could comtemplate the eternal mysteries. to the evocative murmur of a 'Méditation', or allow himself to be immersed in the realizations of the might and majesty of God, symbolized by the full power of the organ, issuing mysteriously from the shadows and enveloping him on all sides. We have Messiaen's sanction for this interpretation, for in connexion with the first performance of his composition *Et expecto resurrectionem mortuorum* on 7 May 1965 in the Sainte Chapel, Paris, he wrote:

> Dans cette merveilleuse eglise édifiée par ordre de Saint Louis, roi de France — où fut déposée le Couronne d'épines — où les bleus, les rouges, les ors, les violets, résonnent dans chaque vitrail avec la musique. Ce fut pour l'oeuvre un cadre idéal, tant pour le mariage des complexes sonores avec l'eblouissement des couleurs, que par les résonances croisées dues à l'encerclement des vitraux. Il était onze heures du matin, et le soleil aussi jouait son rôle, transportant ça et là de nouvelles taches de couleurs avec le rebondissement des sons.

There is another side to Messiaen, and that is his preoccupation, one might say his obsession, with birdsong. He has written about this at length and with authority, for he has pursued his bird studies with the zeal of the professional ornithologist. The calls of European, American, Asiatic and tropical birds are as familiar to him as the melodies of the Catholic liturgy, though what the eighteenth century 'imitation of nature' philosophers would make of his birdsong canvases such as *Oiseaux exotiques* (1955) or the *Catalogue*

---

[5] Cf. Kakg-Elert's op. 106, entitled Cathedral Windows.

d'Oiseaux (1959) it would be hard to say. His attitude is quite the reverse of that of earlier composers, who subjected birdsong to manmade musical disciplines, inviting us to contemplate the untrammelled, careless raptures through a double symbolism: trills on the flute or cadenzas on the violin suggesting birdsong which in turn suggests the unfettered freedom of man's soul. Messiaen on the contrary attempts a true 'imitation of nature'—an impersonal reconstruction of the sounds of the wild, recorded as objectively as possible. Far from conceiving birdsong as raw material for a musical construction controlled by man's intellect he sees it as 'the true forgotten face of music'. This is hardly 'absolute' music; but if it is programme music it is Hamlet without the Prince of Denmark— programme music that lacks a programme.

Messiaen is perhaps a suitable figure with which to bring this study to an end. He is a typical twentieth century composer, in that he combines a Debussian delight in the sheer sound-impact of music with a highly sophisticated theory of the technique of musical composition. Neither of these qualities lends itself ideally to the composition of programme music. The essence of programme music is that the sounds should be significant: they should convey some meaning beyond the sounds themselves. Complexity likewise should have an assignable meaning. There is no theoretical objection to complexity any more than there is to simplicity; but in programme music complexity should be a means to an end, not the end itself. Whatever the merits of Bach's *Art of Fugue,* it is not programme music. There is in truth in all programme music, even the most elaborate, a certain directness of approach, something of innocence or naïveté— the quality that most modern composers would least wish to be accused of. The path followed by all programme composers from Kuhnau to Sibelius has become confused and difficult, not because their techniques are outmoded, but because they adopted an unselfconscious attitude towards their art which today's composers find uncomfortable.

APPENDIX

Programme music from 1800 to the present day. The list is a representative selection and does not pretend to be exhaustive. Works are for orchestra unless otherwise stated.

AKIMENKO, Feodor (1876-1945). Russian. *Lyric poem* Op . 20, 1903; *Ange,* 1925; *Sonate fantastique,* for piano Op. 44

ALAIN, Jehan (1911-40), French. *Litanies,* for organ, 1937

ALBENIZ, Isaac (1860-1909), Spanish. *Iberia,* for piano, 1906-09

d'ALBERT, Eugen (1864-1932), Scottish, of Fr. descent. *Aschenputtel* (originally for piano), 1924.

ALFVÉN, Hugo (1872-1960), Swedish. *En Skärgardssägen,* 1921

ALKAN, Charles-Valentin (1813-88), French. Piano music, much of it programmatic

ALLENDE, Pedro Umberto (b. 1885), Chilean. *Escenas campesinas chilenas,* 1916; *La Voz de las Calles,* 1920

ALWYN, William (b. 1905), English. *The Magic Island,* 1953; *Lyra angelica,* 1954

AMBROS, Vladimir (1891-1956), Czech. *Symphony of Nature,* 1944; *Piccadilly,* for wind quintet, *c. 1935*

ANTOINE, Georges (1892-1918), Belgian. *Veillée d'Armes,* 1918

APIVOR, Denis (b. 1916), Welsh. *Overtones* (based on pictures by Paul Klee) 1962

ARNELL, Richard (b. 1917), English. *Landscapes and Figures,* 1961; *Lord Byron,* 1952

ARNOLD, Malcolm (b. 1921), English. Overture, *Tam O'Shanter,* 1943

AURIC, Georges (b. 1899), French. *Chandelles romaines*

AXMAN, Emil (1877-1949), Czech. *Spring* symph., 1928; *Patriotic* symph., 1942; *Sorrow and Hope,* 1919-20; *Light,* 1921-22

BAINES, William (1899-1922), English. Piano music, *Silver points; Paradise Gardens; Twilight pieces,* etc.

BAINTON, Edgar (1880-1956), English. *Pompilia,* 1903

BAIRD, Tadeusz (b. 1928), Polish. *Colas Breugnon,* for fl. and strs., 1951; *Overture giocosa,* 1952

BALAKIREV, Mily (1837-1910), Russian. *Tamara*, 1882; *Russia*, 1884; *Islamey*, for piano, 1869

BANTOCK, Granville (1868-1946), English. *Jaga-naut*, 1900; *The Witch of Atlas*, 1902; *Pierrot of the Minute*, 1908; *Dante and Beatrice*, 1911; *Fifine at the Fair*, 1912

BARLOW, Samuel L. (b. 1892), American. *Alba*, 1927; *Babar*, 1936

BARRAUD, Henry (b. 1900), French. *Poème*, 1934; *Rapsodie cartésienne*, 1962; *Rapsodie dionysienne*, 1963

BARTÓK, Bela (1881-1945), Hungarian. *Kossuth*, 1903

BAX, Arnold (1883-1953), English. *The Garden of Fand*, 1916; *November Woods*, 1917; *Tintagel*, 1917; *The Happy Forest*, 1922; *The Tale the Pinetrees knew*, 1931

BEDFORD, David (b. 1937); *The Garden of Love*, for instrumental ensemble, 1970

BEETHOVEN, Ludwig van (1770-1827), German. *Pastoral* symphony, 1807-08; *Die Schlacht bei Vittoria*, 1813; *Rondo a capriccio, rage over a lost penny*, 1823

BELL, William H. (1873-1946), English. *The Pardoner's Tale*, 1900; *Two tone-pictures from Mother Carey*, 1902

BENNETT, Robert Russell (b. 1894), American. *Paysage*, 1928; *Abraham Lincoln* symphony, 1929

BENNETT, William Sterndale (1816-75), English. Overtures, *The Naiads*, 1836; *The Wood-nymphs*, 1838; *Paradise and the Peri*, 1862; *Ajax*, 1872; *Three Musical Sketches* for piano, 1835; *The Maid of Orleans*, piano sonata 1869-73

BERLIOZ, Hector (1803-69), French. *Symphonie fantastique*, 1830; *Harold en Italie*, 1834; *Roméo et Juliette*, 1839; *Monodrame lyrique, Lélio, ou le Retour à la vie*, 1831

BERNERS, Lord (Gerald Tyrwhitt), (1883-1950), English. *Fragments psychologiques* (hatred; laughter; a sigh); three *funeral marches* (for a statesman; a canary; a rich aunt) for piano

BERNSTEIN, Leonard (b. 1918), American. Symphony No. 1, *Jeremiah*, 1942; symphony No. 2, *The Age of Anxiety*, 1949

BIRTWISTLE, Harrison (b. 1934), English. *An Imaginary Landscape*, 1971; *The Triumph of Time*, 1972

BLACHER, Boris (1903-75), German. *Hamlet*, 1940

BLISS, Arthur (1891-1975). English. *A Colour symphony*, 1922; *Hymn to Apollo*, 1926

BLOCH, Ernest (1880-1959), Swiss. *Schelomo*, 1916; *Israel*, 1916; *Printemps-Hiver*, 1918; *America*, 1927; *Helvetia*, 1929; *Voice in the Wilderness*, 1936; *In the Mountains*, 1925, and *Paysages*, 1923, for str. quartet; *Baal Shem*, for vln and orchestra, 1940; etc.

APPENDIX

BLOCKX, Jan (1851-1912), Belgian. Overture, *Rubens;* triptych *(All Soul's Day; Christmas Eve; Easter)*, 1906

BORGSTRÖM, Hjalmar (1864-1925), Norwegian. *Hamlet* (piano and orchestra), 1903; *Jesus in Gethsemane*, 1904; *John Gabriel Borkman*, 1905

BORODIN, Alexander (1833-87), Russian. *In the Steppes of Central Asia*, 1880

BOUGHTON, Rutland (1878-1960), English. *Into the everlasting* (based on Walt Whitman), 1903

BOULEZ, Pierre (b. 1925), French. *Improvisations sur Mallarmé*

BOURGAULT-DUCOUDRAY, Louis (1840-1910), French. *L'Interrement d'Ophélie*, 1877; *Le Carnaval d'Athènes*, 1884

BOWEN, York (1884-1951), English. *The Lament of Tasso*, 1903

BRÉVILLE, Pierre de (1861-1949), French. *Stamboul*, 1897; *Sans Pardon des Châtiments*, 1930; Suite for piano, *À la manière de . . .* , 1890

BRIDGE, Frank (1879-1940), English. *Isabella*, 1907; *Dance poem*, 1913; *Summer*, 1914; *The Sea*, 1923

BRONSART, Hans von (1830-1913), German. *Manfred*, 1901; fantasia for piano, *Melusina* (based on pictures by Moritz von Schwind)

BRUCH, Max (1838-1920), German. *Scottish Fantasia; Kol Nidrei*, for cello and orch.

BRUNEAU, Alfred (1857-1934), French. *La Belle au Bois dormant*, 1884; *Ouverture Héroique*, 1884

BRUSSELMANS, Michel (1886-1960), Belgian. *Scènes breugheliennes* 1911; *Kermesse flamande*, 1912; *Helen de Sparte*, 1914

BUSH, Alan (b. 1900), English. Symphony, *Byron*, 1962

BUSONI, Ferruccio (1866-1924), Italian. *Berceuse élégiaque*, 1909; *Rondo Arlechinesco*, 1915; *Indianisches Tagebuch*, 1915

BÜSSER, Henri (1872-1973), French. *A la Villa Medicis*, suite symphonique, 1895; *Hercule au Jardin des Hespérides*, 1900

BUTTERWORTH, George (1885-1916), English. *A Shropshire Lad*, 1912; *The Banks of green Willow*, 1913

CADMAN, Charles Wakefield (1881-1946), American. *The Rubaiyat of Omar Khayyám*, 1922; *Thunderbird Suite*, 1914; *Oriental Rhapsody*, 1917; etc.

CAMPO Y ZABALETA, Conrado del (1879-1953), Spanish. *Passages de Granada; Poema para los Caidos*

CARPENTER, John Alden (1876-1951), American. *Adventures in a Perambulator*, 1914; *Skyscrapers*, 1926; *The Birthday of the Infanta*, 1932

CASADESUS, Francis (1870-1954), French. *Quasimodo*, 1905; *La Vision d'Olivier Métra*, 1932
CASELLA, Alfredo (1881-1947), Italian. *Notte di Maggio*, 1914; *A Notte alta*, 1917; *Italia*, 1909; *Elegia eroica*, 1916
CASTELNUOVO-TEDESCO, Mario (1895-1968), Italian. *Sonata zoologica*, for piano, 1960; *Cipressi*, 1940
CATALANI, Alfredo (1854-93), Italian. *Ero e Leandro*, 1885
CHABRIER, Emmanuel (1814-94), French. *Marche joyeuse*, 1880; *España*, 1883; *Souvenirs de Munich*, 1886; *Suite pastorale*, 1896; *Pièces Pittoresques* for piano (later scored by Ravel) 1881
CHADWICK, George Whitfield (1854-1931), American. Three overtures (*Thalia*, 1883; *Melpomene*, 1887; *Euterpe*, 1906); *Aphrodite*, 1913
CHAMPAGNE, Claude (1891-1965), Canadian. *Hercule et Omphale*, 1926; *Symphonie gaspésienne*, 1945
CHARPENTIER, Gustave (1860-1956), French. *Impressions d'Italie*, 1890
CHAUSSON, Ernest (1855-99), French. *Viviane*, 1882
CHLUBNA, Osvald (1893-1971), Czech. *Distance and Dreams*, 1916; *Before I became silent*, 1918; three-part cycle, *Nature and Man*, 1949-53; Six-part cycle, *This is the Land of Mine*, 1956-62
CIKKER, Ján (b. 1911), Czech. *The Enduring Summer*, 1941; *The Battle*, 1932; *Morning*, 1946
CLEMENTI, Muzio (1752-1832), Italian. Sonata for piano, *Didone abbandonata*, c. 1820
COATES, Eric (1886-1958), English. *London Suite*, 1933; *The Three Bears*, 1926; etc.
CONSTANT, Marius (b. 1925), Rumanian. Three Essays, *Turner (Rain, Steam and Speed; a Self-portrait; Windsor)*, 1962
CONVERSE, Frederick Shepherd (1871-1940), American. *Festival of Pan*, 1900; *Endymion's Narrative*, 1903; *The Mystic Trumpeter*, 1907; *Ormazd*, 1912; *Flivver ten million*, 1927; *California*, 1928
COPLAND, Aaron (b. 1900), American. *El Salon Mexico*, 1936; *A Lincoln Portrait*, for speaker and orch., 1942; *Music for a Great City*, 1964; *Inscape*, 1967
COURVOISIER, Walter (1875-1931), Swiss. *Olimpischer Frühling*, 1905
COWELL, Henry (1892-1965), American. *Persian Set*, 1957; *Ongaku*, 1957; *Madras* Symphony, 1957-58

DARGOMIJSHY, Alexander (1812-69), Russian. *Baba-Yaga*, 1857
DAVICO, Vincenzo (1889-1969), Italian. *La Principessa lontana*, 1911; *Polifemo*, 1910; *Impressioni romane*, 1913; *Poeme erotico*, 1913

DAVID, Félicien (1810-76), French. Symphonic odes, *Le Désert*, 1844; *Christophe Colomb*, 1847; *Mélodies orientales*, for piano, 1829-30

DEBUSSY, Claude Achille (1862-1918), French. *Printemps*, 1887; *Prélude à l'Après-midi d'un faune*, 1892-94; *Nocturnes*, 1893-99; *La Mer*, 1903-05; *Images*, 1906-12; for piano, *Estampes*, 1903; *L'Isle joyeuse*, 1904; *Images* (first series) 1905; (second series) 1907; *Children's Corner* suite, 1906-08; *Préludes* I ,1912; *Préludes* II, 1910-13

DELIUS, Frederick (1863-1934), English. *Paris*, 1899; *Brigg Fair*, 1907; *In a Summer Garden*, 1908; *On hearing the first Cuckoo in Spring*, 1912; *North Country Sketches*, 1913-14; *Eventyr*, 1917; *Summer Night on the River*, 1912; *A song before Sunrise*, 1918

DELVINCOURT, Claude (1886-1954), French. *Typhon*, 1919; *L'Offrande à Siva*, 1927; *Pamir*, 1935

DUKAS, Paul (1865-1935), French. Overtures, *King Lear*, 1888; *Polyeucte*, 1892; *L'Apprenti Sorcier*, 1897

DUPARC, Henri (1848-1933), French. *Lénore*, 1875

DUPRÉ, Marcel (1886-1971), French. *Suite bretonne; Le Chemin de la Croix*, 1931-32; *Symphonie Passion* 1923; *Le Tombeau de Titelouze*, 1942-43; all for organ

DUPUIS, Sylvain (1856-1931), Belgian. *Macbeth*, c. 1913

DUTILLEUX, Henri (b. 1916), French. *Metaboles*, 1965

DVOŘÁK, Antonin (1841-1904), Czech. *The Water Goblin*, 1896; *The Noon Witch*, 1896; *The Golden Spinning Wheel*, 1896; *The Wild Dove*, 1899; *Heroic Song*, 1899; Three overtures, *In Nature's Realm; Carnival*, 1891; *Othello*, 1892. For Piano: *Silhouettes*, 1879; *Poetic Pictures*, 1889; *From the Bohemian Woods* (piano duet), 1884

EICHHEIM, Henry (1870-1942), American. *Oriental Impressions*, 1921; *Burma*, 1927; *Java*, 1929; *Japanese Nocturne*, 1930; *Korean Sketch*, 1934 (all for piano)

EINEM, Gottfried (b. 1918), German. *Philadelphia* Symph., 1960

ELGAR, Edward (1857-1934), English. *Froissart*, 1890; *Variations on an Original Theme*, 1899; *Cockaigne*, 1901; *Dream Children*, 1902; *In the South*, 1904; *Wand of Youth* Suite I, 1907; II, 1908; *Falstaff*, 1913; *Polonia*, 1915; *Nursery Suite*, 1931

ERTEL, J. Paul (1865-1933), Czech. *Maria Stuart*, 1896; *Der Mensch*, 1905; *Hero and Leander*, 1909

ESPLÁ, Oscar (b. 1886), Spanish. *Ciclopes de Ifach*, 1916; *El Ambito de la Danza*, 1924; *Las Cumbras*, 1924; *La Nochebuena del Diabolo*, 1921; *Don Quixote velando las Armas*, 1925

FALLA, Manuel de (1876-1946), Spanish. *Nights in the Gardens of Spain*, 1921

FARRAR, Ernest Bristow (1885-1918), English. *The Forsaken Merman*

FARWELL, Arthur (1872-1952), American. *The Gods of the Mountain*, 1927; *Rudolf Gott* symphony, 1934; for piano *The Domain of Hurakon*, 1902; *Impressions of the Wa—Wan Ceremony; Owasco Memories*, 1907

FAURÉ, Gabriel (1845-1924), French. *Masques et Bergamasques*, 1920; Suite, *Dolly*, for piano duet, 1893-96

FERROUD, Pierre-Octave (1900-36), French. *Foules;* suite for piano, *Types (le vieux Beau; La Bourgeoise de quality; Le Business-man)*

FIBICH, Zdeněk (1850-1900), Czech. Overture, *The Jew of Prague* 1871; *Othello*, 1873; *Zaboj, Slavoj and Ludek*, 1873; Overture, *A Night at Karlstein*, 1886; *Toman and the Wood-nymph*, 1875; *Spring*, 1881

FIELD, John (1782-1837), Irish. Piano concerto, *L'Incendi par l'Orage*, 1817

FIŠER, Luboš (b. 1935), Czech. *Fifteen pages after Dürer's Apocalypse*, 1967

FITELBERG, Grzegorz (1879-1953), Polish. *The Song of the Falcon* (from Gorky), 1906; *Protesilaus and Laodamia; In der Meerestiefe*, 1914

FOERSTER, Josef Bohuslav (1859-1951), Czech. *My Youth*, 1900; *Cyrano de Bergerac*, 1905; *A Legend of Happiness*, 1909; *The Enigma*, 1909; *Springtime and Desire*, 1912. Also symph. No. 2, *In Memoriam sororis Mariae*, 1892-1931; No. 4, *Easter Eve*, 1905; Piano Trio, *A Lament for his son*, 1921

FOOTE, Arthur William (1853-1937), American. Overture, *In the Mountains*, 1887; *Francesca da Rimini*, 1893; *Four Character Pieces after Omar Khayyám*, 1912

FRANCHETTI, Alberto (1860-1942), Italian. *Loreley; Nella selva nera*

FRANCK, César (1822-90), Belgian. *Ce qu'on entend sur la Montagne*, 1848; *Les Éolides*, 1876; *Le Chasseur maudit*, 1882; *Les Djinns*, 1884; *Psyché*, 1888

FRY, William Henry (1815-64), American. *Childe Harold; A Day in the Country; The Breaking Heart; Santa Claus*

GADE, Niels W. (1817-1890), Danish. Overtures, *Ossian*, 1841; *In the Highlands; Hamlet; Michaelangelo*; Five pieces for orch., *A Summerday in the Country*

GAUBERT, Phillipe (1879-1941), French. *Fresques*, 1921; *Chant de la Mer*, 1929; *Au Pays basque*, 1930; *Inscriptions pour les Portes de la Ville* (after a poem by Régnier), 1934

GERMAN, Edward 1862-1936), English. *Hamlet*, 1897

GERSHWIN, George (1898-1937), American. *An American in Paris*, 1928

GILBERT, Henry Franklin Belknap (1868-1928), American. Symph. prologue, *Riders to the Sea*, for small orch., 1904; *Negro Rhapsody*, 1913; *Dance in Place Congo*, 1918; for Piano, *The Island of the Fay*, 1903; *Two Verlaine Moods*, 1903

GILLIS, Don (b. 1912), American. *An American Symphony*, 1939-40; *A Lincoln Legend*, 1942; *Prairie Poem*, 1943; *The Alamo*, 1944; *Portrait of a Frontier Town*, 1947

GILSON, Paul (1865-1942), Belgian. *La Mer*, 1892

GLAZOUNOV, Alexander (1865-1936), Russian. *Stenka Razin*, 1885; *The Forest*, 1887; *The Sea*, 1889; *Spring*, 1891

GLIÈRE, Reinhold (1875-1956), Russian. *The Sirens*, 1908; *Zaporojzi* (on a picture by Repin), 1921; *Zapovit*, 1941; Overture, *The Friendship of Peoples*, 1947; *24 Pièces caractéristiques pour la jeunesse* (for piano), 1908

GLINKA, Mikhail (1804-57), Russian. *Une Nuit à Madrid*, 1848

GNECCHI Vittorio (1876-1954), Italian. *Poema erotico (Notte nel campo di Holopherne)*, 1948

GNESSI, Michael Fabianovich (1883-1957), Russian. Symphonic Dithyramb, *Vrubel*, 1911; *Symphonic Movement, 1905-17* (written for tenth Anniversary of the October revolution), 1927

GODARD, Benjamin (1849-95), French. *Suite gothique*, 1883; *Kermesse*, 1880; *Symphonie orientale*, 1884. For piano, *Une Fête au Village; Lanterne magique; Scènes poétiques* (four hands), 1907

GOLDMARK, Karl (1830-1915), German. Overture, *Sakuntala*, 1865; *Penthesilea*, 1879; Overtures, *Im Frühling*, 1889; *In Italien*, 1904

GOLDMARK, Rubin (1872-1936), American. Overture, *Hiawatha*, 1896; *Samson*, 1913; *Gettysburg Requiem*, 1919

GOOSSENS, Eugène (1893-1960), English. *The Eternal Rhythm*, 1922

GOUNOD, Charles (1818-93), French. *Funeral March for a marionette*

GOTTSCHALK, Louis Moreau (1829-69), American. *The night of the Tropics*, c. 1856; *Cuban Country Scenes*, c. 1856; for piano, *Midnight in Seville*, 1850; *Le Bananier (Chanson nègre); The Banjo (Fantaisie grotesque); The Dying Poet;* etc.

GRAENER, Paul, (1872-1944), German. *Aus dem Reiche des Pan, Musik am Abend* (three pieces)

GRANADOS CAMPINA, Enrique (1867-1916), Spanish. *La Nit del Mort; Dante*, 1915. For piano, *Goyescas*, 1911; *Escenas poéticas; Libro de Horas*; etc., etc

GRIEG, Edvard Hagerup (1843-1907), Norwegian. Overture, *In Autumn*, 1866. For piano see the ten sets of *Lyric Pieces*, 1867-1901; *Six Poetic Tone-Pictures*, 1863; *Moods*, 1905

GRIFFES, Charles Tomlinson (1884-1920), American. *The Pleasure Dome of Kubla Khan*, 1916; *Poem for fl. and orch.*, 1918. For piano, *The Lake at Evening*, 1910; *The Night Winds*, 1911; *The Vale of Dreams*, 1912; *The White Peacock*, 1915

GROFÉ, Ferde (1892-1972), American. *Symphony in Steel; Hollywood; Grand Canyon Suite*, 1932; *Aviation Suite* (for piano), 1946; *Death Valley Suite*, 1957; *World's Fair Suite*, 1964

GROVLEZ, Gabriel (1879-1944), French. *La Vengeance des Fleurs; Le Reposoir des Amants; Ariane à Naxos*. For Piano, *L'Almanach aux Images; Au Jardin de l'Enfance*, 1917

GUIRAUD, Ernest (1837-92), French. *Chasse fantastique*, 1900

GURIDI, Jesús (1886-1961), Spanish. *Égloga; Leyende Vasca; Una Aventura de Don Quixote; Sinfonia Pirenaica*, 1945; Fantasia for piano and orchestra, *Homenaje a Walt Disney*, 1956

HÁBA, Alois (b. 1893), Czech. *The Way of Life*, 1934

HADLEY, Henry Kimball (1871-1937), American. Four symphonies, *Youth and Life; The Four Seasons*, 1902; *North, East, South and West*, 1911; *Connecticut Tercentenary; Salome*, 1906; Overture, *Othello*, 1921

HAHN, Reynaldo (1874-1947), French. *Études latines*, 1922

HAKKÉN, Johan Andréas (1846-1925), Swedish. *A Summer Saga; In the Autumn; Toteninsel; Sphärenklänge*

HAMERIK, Asger (1843-1923), Danish. *Nordic Suite*; five symphonies *Poetic; Tragic; Majestic; Lyric; Serious; Opera ohne Worte*, 1880

HANSON, Howard (b. 1896), American. *Before the Dawn*, 1920; *Exultation*, 1920; *Nordic* symphony; *Lux Eterna* (for vla. and orch.), 1923; *Pan and the Priest*, 1926; *Summer Seascapes*, 1959

HARRIS, Roy (b. 1898), American. Sixth symphony (based on the Gettysburg Address), 1944

HARTY, Hamilton (1880-1941), Irish. *The Children of Lir*, 1939

HAUSEGGER, Siegmund von (1872-1948), German. *Barbarossa*, 1900; *Dionysische Phantasia*, 1902; *Wieland der Schmied*, 1904; *Natursymphonie* (with concluding chorus), 1911

HAYDN, Joseph (1732-1809), Austrian. Symphony, *Le Soir*, 1761; *The Seven Words of our Saviour on the Cross*, 1785; arr. for str. quartet, 1787

HELLER, Stephen (1814-88), Hungarian. Piano pieces, *Promenades d'un Solitaire* and *Rêveries du Promeneur* (the titles borrowed from Rousseau); *Nuits blanches; Dans les Bois; Voyage autour de ma chambre*

HENSELT, Adolf von (1814-39), German. Piano studies, especially Op. 2 and Op. 5

HILL, Edward Burlinghame (1872-1960), American. *Launcelot and Guinevre*, 1915; *Pan and the Star*, 1914; *The Fall of the House of Usher*, 1920; *Jack Frost in Midsummer*, 1908

HILLEMACHER, Lucien (1860-1909) and Paul (1852-1933), French. *Loreley*, 1882

HINDEMITH, Paul (1895-1963), German. *Morgenmusik*, 1922; *Der Schwanendreher*, 1935; Symphony, *Harmonie der Welt*, 1951; *Nobilissima Visione*, 1938

HODDINOTT, Alun (b. 1929), Welsh. *Music for orchestra* (based on James Joyce), 1970

HOLBROOK, Joseph (1878-1958), English. *The Raven* (based on Poe), 1900; *Queen Mab*, 1904; *Ulalume*, 1904; *Masque of the Red Death* (Poe)

HOLST, Gustav (1874-1934), English. *Indra*, 1903; *Beni Mora*, 1910; *The Planets*, 1915; *Egdon Heath*, 1928

HOLMBOE, Vagn (b. 1909), Danish. *Sinfonia rustica; Sinfonia sacra*, 1941

HOLMÈS, Augusta (1847-94), Irish. Symphonies, *Orlando furioso; Lutèce; les Argonauts*; symph. poems, *Irlande; Pologne*

HOLOUBEK, Ladislav (b. 1913), Czech. Str. quartet, *Hatred and Love*, 1936

HONEGGER, Arthur (1892-1955), Swiss. *Pacific 231*, 1923; *Rugby*, 1928; Symphonies, *Liturgique*, 1945-46; *Deliciae basilienses*, 1946; *Di tre Re*, 1951

HOWELL, Dorothy (b. 1898), English. *Lamia* (based on Keats), 1919

HOWELLS, Herbert (b. 1892), English. *Puck's Minuet*, 1918; *Merry Eve*, 1918; *Procession*, 1922; *Pastoral Rhapsody*, 1923. For organ, *Psalm Preludes*, 1920; *Saraband for the Morning of Easter*, 1953

HUBER, Hans (1852-1921), Swiss. Symphonies, *Boecklin*, 1901; *Heroic* (based partly on Holbein's *Dance of Death*), 1902; *The Fiddler of Gmund*, 1906

HUË, Georges (1858-1948), French. *Rübezahl*, 1883; *Résurrection*, 1893; *Jeunesse*, 1893

HUMMEL, Johann Nepomuk (1778-1837), Czech. For piano, *Oberons Zauberhorn*, c. 1830; *Rondolette Russe—Le Contemplazione*, c. 1823

IBERT, Jacques (1890-1962), French. *Escales*, 1922; *Féerique*, 1924; *Le Chevalier errant*, 1952; *Bacchanale*, 1958; *Bostoniana*, 1964. For piano, *Histoires*, 1943; *Noël en Picardie*, 1946

INDY, Vincent d' (1851-1931), French. *Wallenstein*, 1874 and 1880; *La Forêt enchantée*, 1878; *Medée*, 1898; *Jour d'Été à la*

Montagne, 1905; *La Légende de St. Christophe*, 1917; *Poème des Rivages*, 1922; *Diptique méditerranéen*, 1926; *Symphonie Brevis de Bello Gallico*, 1919

INGHELBRECHT, D. E. (1880-1965), French. *Automne*, 1905; *Pour le jour de la première neige au vieux Japon*, 1908, For piano, *The Nursery*

IRELAND, John (1879-1962), English. *The Forgotten Rite*, 1913; *Mai-Dun*, 1921; Overtures, *London*, 1936; *Satyricon*, 1946. Piano music, *Decorations*, 1913; *London Pieces*, 1919; *Sarnia*, 1940-42

IPPOLITOF-IVANOF, Mikhail (1859-1935), Russian. *Caucasian Sketches*, 1895; *Mzyri* (after Lermontov), 1929; *Turkish Fragments* (on Azerbaijan themes), c. 1930; *On the Steppes of Turkmenistan*, 1930; *Uzbek Pictures*, c. 1930

IVES, Charles Edward (1874-1954), American. Symphony, *Holidays*, 1904-13; *Central park in the Dark*, 1898-1907; *Orchestral Set No. 2*, 1912-15; *The Unanswered Question*, for trumpet, four flutes and string quartet, 1908; for piano, the *Concord* sonata, begun 1909

JANÁCEK, Leos (1854-1928), Czech. *Danube*, 1915-16; *Taras Bulba*, 1918; *Ballad of Blaník*, 1920; *Mládí* (Youth), for wind sextet, 1925. For piano, *Up the Overgrown Path*, 1908; *In the Mists*, 1912; String quartets, *Kreutzer Sonata*, 1923; *Intimate Letters*, 1928

JARNEFELT, Edvard Armas (1869-1958), Finnish. *Korsholm*, 1894

JENSEN, Adolf (1837-79), German. *Erotikon*, for piano, 1872

JEREMIÁŠ, Otakar (1892-1962), Czech. Overture, *Spring*, 1912

JOACHIM, Joseph (1831-1907), Hungarian. Overtures, *Hamlet*; *Demetrius* (Hermann Grimm); *Henry IV*; *To a Comedy of Gozzi*; *To the Memory of Kleist*

JOIO, Norman Dello (b. 1913), American. *American Landscape*, 1944; *The Triumph of Saint Joan*, 1951

JOLIVET, André (b. 1905), French. *Pysché*, 1950

JONGEN, Joseph (1873-1953), Belgian. *Lalla-Rookh*, 1903; *Impressions d'Ardennes*, 1913; *Tableaux pittoresques*, 1922. For organ, *Symphonie de Noël*; *Symphonie de la Passion*; *Sonata eroica*, 1949

KABALÁČ, Miloslav (b. 1908), Czech. *The Mystery of Time*, 1953-57; *Reflections*, 1963-64

KAJANUS, Robert (1856-1933), Finnish. *Aino* symphony, 1885; *Kullervo, funeral march*, 1881

KAREL, Rudolf (1880-1945), Slovak. Symphonies, *Renaissance*,

1910-11, and *Spring*, 1935-38; *The Ideals*, 1906-09; *The Demon*, 1918-20; *Revolutionary Overture*, 1938-41

KARG-ELERT, Sigfrid (1877-1933), German. For organ, *Cathedral Windows*, 1923; *Seven Pastels of Lake Constance*, 1923; *Harmonies du Soir*, 1934

KARLOWICZ, Mieczyslaw (1876-1909), Polish. *Returning Waves*, 1904; *Three Eternal Songs*, 1907; *A Lithuanian Rhapsody, Stanislaw and Anna Oswiecimowie*, 1908

KIESSIG, Georg (1874-1949), German. *Ahasuerus*, 1914; *My Fatherland*, 1915; *A Dance of Death*, 1916

KLOSE, Friedrich (1862-1942), Swiss. *Jeanne d'Arc*, 1882; *König Elf*, 1884; *Das Leben ein Traum* (for reciter and orchestra), 1899

KODÁLY, Zoltán (1882-1967), Hungarian. *Summer Evening*, 1906; *Háry János*, 1927

KOECHLIN, Charles (1867-1950), French. *Les Vendanges*, 1896-1906; *Vers la Plage lointaine* 1898-1909; *En Mer, la Nuit, La Nuit de Walpurgis classique* (after Verlaine), 1901-07; *The Seven Stars Symphony*, 1933; *Les Bandar-Log*, 1939-40

KOLAR, Victor (1888-1957), American. *Hiawatha*, 1908; *A Fairy Tale*, 1913; *Americana*, 1914

KOVAŘOVIC, Karel (1862-1920), Czech. *Persefona*; Melodramas, *The Orphan; The Golden Spinning Wheel*

KŘIČKA, Jaroslav (1882-1961), Czech. Symphony, *Spring*, 1905-06; *Faith*, 1907; Overture, *A Blue Bird* (Maeterlinck), 1911

LAMBERT, Constant (1909-51), English. *Rondo burlesca, King Pest* (from *Summer's Last Will and Testament*)

LANGLAIS, Jean (b. 1907), French. *Essai sur l'Evangèle de Noël*, for organ and orchestra, 1938

LEKEU, Guillaume (1870-94), Belgian. *Hamlet and Ophelia*, 1889-90

LESUR, Daniel (b. 1908), French. *Andrea del Sarto*, 1949; for organ, *Scène de la Passion*, 1931; *la Vie intérieure*, 1932; *In Paradisium*, 1933

LIADOV, Anatoly Konstantinovich (1855-1914), Russian. *Baba-Yaga*, 1905; *The Enchanted Lake*, 1909; *Kikimora*, 1910

LINDBERG, Oskar Fredrik (1887-1955), Swedish. *Three Pictures from Dalarne*, 1908; *Wilderness*, 1912. *Flor and Blanchflor*, 1913

LISZT, Ferencz (1811-86), Hungarian. *Ce qu'on entend sur la Montagne*, 1848-49, 1850, 1854; *Tasso, Lamento e Trionfo*, 1849-54; *Les Préludes*, 1848-54; *Orpheus*, 1853-54; *Prometheus*, 1850, 1859; *Mazeppa*, 1851, 1854; *Festklänge*, 1853; *Héroide funèbre*, 1848-50, 1854; *Hungaria*, 1854; *Hunnenschlacht*, 1857; *Die Ideale*, 1857; *Hamlet*, 1858. Symphonies, *Faust*, 1854; *Dante*,

1855-56. Piano music, *Album d'un voyageur*, 1835-36; *Années de Pèlerinage* I, 1848-54; II, 1849; III, 1877; *Harmonies poétiques et religieuses*, 1847-52; *Légendes*, 1863; *Weihnachtsbaum* (The Christmas Tree), 1874-76; *Seven Hungarian Historical Portraits*, 1885

LOEFFLER, Charles Martin (1861-1935), American, b. Alsace. *Les Veillées de l'Ukraine*, 1891; *La Mort de Tintagiles*, 1897; *La Bonne Chanson*, 1901; *La Villanelle du Diable*, 1905; *A Pagan Poem*, 1907

LUTOSLAWSKI, Witold (b. 1913), Polish. *Music funèbre*, for string orchestra (in memory of Béla Bartók), 1958

MACCUNN, Hamish (1868-1916), Scottish. *Land of the Mountain and Flood*, 1887

MACDOWELL, Edward (1861-1908), American. *Hamlet, Ophelia*, 1885; *Lancelot and Elaine*, 1888; *Lamia*, 1908; *Indian* Suite, 1897. Piano sonatas, *Tragica*, 1893; *Eroica*, 1894; *Norse*, 1898; *Keltic*, 1901; much miscellaneous piano music

MAHLER, Gustav (1860-1911), Austrian. Symphonies, one, 1884-88; two, 1887-94; three, 1893-96

MALEINGREAU, Paul de (1887-1956), Belgian. For organ, *Symphonie de Noël*, 1920; *Symph. de l'Agneau mystique*, 1926; *Symph. de la Passion*, 1934; *Suite Mariale*, 1940; *Diptych for All Saints*, 1952

MALIPIERO, Gian Francesco (1882-1973), Italian. *Sinfonia del Mare*, 1906; *Sinf. del Silenzio e della Morte*, 1910; *San Francisco d'Assisi*, 1921; and others

MARIOTTE, Antoine (1875-1944), French. For piano, *Impressions urbains*, 1921

MARKEVICH, Igor (b. 1912), Russian. *Le nouvel Age*, 1938; *Icare*, 1952

MARTIN, Frank (1890-1974), Swiss. Pavane, *Couleur du Temps*, 1953; *Les quatre Éléments*, 1963

MARTINŮ, Bohuslav (1890-1959), Czech. *Vanishing midnight*, 1922; *La Bagarre* (inspired by Lindbergh's arrival at Le Bourget after his Transatlantic flight), 1928. *Memorial to Lidice*, 1943. *La Revue de Cuisine* (for vln., cello, clt., fag., tpt., and piano), 1928

MARX, Joseph (1882-1964), Austrian. *Herbstsymphonie*, 1922; *Castelli Romani*, 1930

MASCAGNI, Pietro (1863-1945), Italian. *Symphonic impressions*, 1923

MASON, Daniel Gregory (1873-1953), American. Overture, *Chanticleer*, 1928; *A Lincoln symphony*, 1936

MASSENET, Jules (1842-1912), French. *Scènes dramatiques* (inspired by *The Tempest, Othello, Romeo and Juliet, Macbeth*), 1874

MCEWEN, John Blackwood (1868-1948), Scottish. *A Winter Poem*, 1926

MENDELSSOHN-BARTHOLDY, Felix (1809-47), German. Overtures, *A Midsummer Night's Dream*, 1826; *The Hebrides (Fingal's Cave)*, 1830; *Calm Sea and Prosperous Voyage*, 1828; *Melusina*, 1833; Symphonies, *Italian*, 1833; *Scotch*, 1842; *Reformation*, 1830

MESSIAEN, Olivier (b. 1908), French. (A selection only.) *L'Ascension* (originally for organ), 1933; *Couleurs de la Cité céleste*, 1966; *Chronochromie*, 1966. For organ, *Le Banquet céleste*, 1928; *Apparition de l'Église éternelle*, 1934; *Les Corps glorieux*, 1939. *Oiseaux exotiques* (for piano and instrumental ensemble), 1956

MIASKOVSKY, Nikolai (1881-1950), Russian. *The Silence*, 1909-11; *Alastor*, 1912-13; also three 'war' symphonies, 22, 23 and 24, 1942-43

MIGOT, Georges (b. 1891), French. *Les Agrestides*, 1920; *La Jungle* (for org. and orch.). 1932

MILHAUD, Darius (1892-1974), French. *Le Carnaval d'Aix*, 1926; *Le Carnaval à la Nouvelle-Orléans*, 1949; Overture, *Mediterranéene*, 1953; *The Globetrotter Suite*, 1961. For piano, *Le Candélabre à sept branches*, 1952

MOORE, Douglas (b. 1895), American. *The Pageant of P. T. Barnum*, 1926; *Moby Dick*, 1928; *A Symphony of Autumn*, 1930

MOSCHELES, Ignaz (1794-1870), Czech. Much piano music, including *Twelve Characteristic Studies*, c. 1836; *Domestic Life: Twelve Characteristic Duets*, 1867

MOSSOLOV, Aleksander Vasil'evich (b. 1900). *Fonderie d'Acier*, 1928

MUSSORGSKY, Modest (1839-81), Russian. *Night on the Bare Mountain*, 1867

NIELSEN, Carl (1865-1931), Danish. Overture, *Helios*, 1903; *Saga-Dram*, 1908; *Pan and Syrinx*, 1918. Symphonies, No. 2, *The Four Temperaments*, 1904; No. 3, *Espansiva*, 1911; No. 4, *The Inextinguishable*, 1916

NIGG, Serge (b. 1924), French. *Timour*, 1944; *Pour un poète captif*, 1950; *Le combat des Amazones*, 1958

NOSKOWSKI, Zymunt (1846-1909), Polish. Symph. No. 2, *From Spring to Spring*, 1903; *Tatra Lake; The Steppe*, 1896

NOVÁK, Vitězslav (1870-1949), Czech. *Eternal Longing*, 1903; *Toman and the Wood-nymph*, 1904-07; *Lady Godiva*, 1907; *In the Tatras*, 1910; *Herbstsymphonie*, 1931-34; *De Profundis* (for org. and orch.), 1941

OREFICE, Giacomo (1865-1922), Italian. For Piano, *Crepuscoli*, 1904; *Quadri di Boecklin*, 1905; *Preludi del Mare*, 1913

ORNSTEIN, Leo (b. 1895), American, Russian-born. *The Fog*, 1915; Two piano pieces, *Danse sauvage*, 1915; and *Impression de la Tamise*, 1920

PAINE, John Knowles (1839-1906), American. *The Tempest*, 1877; a *Spring* symphony, 1880; *Island Fantasy*, 1882; *Poseidon and Aphrodite*, 1906

PALMGREN, Selim (1878-1951), Finnish. Two piano concertos, No. 2, *The River*, and No. 4, *Metamorphoses*, 1931

PANUFNIK, Andrzej (b. 1914), Polish. *Sinfonia rustica*, 1950

PEDRELL, Felipe (1841-1922), Spanish. *Marcha de la Coronacion a Mistral*, 1881

PENDERECKI, Krystof (b. 1933), Polish. *Threnody for the victims of Hiroshima*, 1960

PICK-MANGIAGALLI, Riccardo (1882-1949), Italian. *Sortilegi*, (for pfte. and orch.), 1917; *Quattro poemi*, 1923-25

PIERNÉ, Gabriel (1863-1937), French. *Paysages franciscains*, 1920; *Les Cathédrales* (for org. and orch.). For piano, *Album pour mes petits amis*, 1888; *Impressions de Music-Hall*, 1927

PIERSON, Henry Hugo (1815-73), English. *Macbeth*; overtures, *As you like it; Romeo and Juliet; Julius Caesar*

PIJPER, Wilhelm (1894-1947): Dutch. *Six Epigrams*, 1933

PIZZETTI, Ildebrando (1880-1968), Italian. *Tre Preludi sinfonici per l'Edipo re di Sofocle*, 1904; *Concerto dell' Estate*, 1928

POULENC, Francis (1899-1963), French. *L'Embarquement pour Cythère* (for two pianos, from the film score, *Le Voyage en Amèrique*), 1951; *Promenades*, for piano, 1921

PRATT, Silas Gamaliel (1846-1916), American. *Paul Revere's Ride*; A *Lincoln* symphony; *The Battle of Manila; A Tragedy of the Deep* (on the sinking of the *Titanic*)

PROKOVIEF, Serge (1891-1953), Russian. *Träume*, 1910; *Scythian Suite*, 1914; *Egyptian Nights*, 1934; *Russian Overture*, 1936; *The Year 1941*, 1941; *Ode on the end of the war*, 1945; For piano, *Visions fugitives*, 1915-17

RACHMANINOV, Serge (1873-1943), Russian. *The Rock*, 1893; *The Isle of the Dead* (after Boecklin), 1909

RAFF, Joachim (1822-82), Swiss. Symphonies, *An das Vaterland*, 1861; *Im Walde*, 1869; *Lenore*, 1872; *In den Alpen*, 1875; *Frühlingsklänge*, 1876; *Im Sommer*, 1878; *Zur Herbstzeit*, 1879; *Der Winter*, 1876; Overtures, *Romeo and Juliet; Othello; Macbeth; The Tempest*

APPENDIX

RANGSTRÖM, Ture (1884-1947), Swedish. *Dithyramb*, 1909; *A Midsummer piece*, 1910; *An Autumn song*, 1911; *The Sea sings*, 1913

RAVEL, Maurice (1875-1937), French. *Rapsodie espagnole*, 1907; For piano, *Pavane pour une Infante défunte*, 1899; *Jeux d'eau*, 1901; *Miroirs*, 1905; *Gaspard de la nuit*, 1908; *Ma Mère l'Oye* (piano duet), 1908; *Le Tombeau de Couperin*, 1917

REGER, Max (1873-1916), German. Four *Tone-poems after Boecklin*, 1913

RESPIGHI, Ottorino (1879-1936), Italian. *The Fountains of Rome*, 1917; *The Pines of Rome*, 1924; *Brazilian Impressions*, 1927; *The Birds*, 1927; *Church Windows*, 1927; *Feste Romane*, 1929

REZNIČEK, Emil Nicolaus von (1860-1945), Austrian. *Peter Schlehmil; The Conqueror*

RIMSKY-KORSAKOV, Nikolai (1844-1908), Russian. *Sadko*, 1867; *Antar*, 1868; *Capriccio espagnol*, 1887; *Scheherazade*, 1888

RITTER, Alexander (1833-96), German. *Sursum Corda*, 1894; *Eine Sturm und Drang Phantasie*, 1894; *Kaiser Rudolfs Ritt zum Grabe*, 1895

RIVIER, Jean (b. 1896), French. *Le Voyage d'Urien* (after Gide), 1933; *Paysage pour Jeanne d'Arc à Domrémy*, 1936

ROGER-DUCASSE, (1875-1954), French. *Au Jardin de Marguerite*, 1905; *Le joli jeu du Furet*, 1912; *Nocturne de Printemps*, 1919

ROPARTZ, Guy (1864-1955), French. *La Cloche des Morts*, 1902; *À Marie endormie*, 1912; *La Chasse du Prince Arthur*, 1912

ROREM, Ned (b. 1923), American. *Lions*, 1963

ROSENTHAL, Manuel (b. 1904), French. *Jeanne d'Arc*, 1936

ROSSELLINI, Renzo (b. 1908), Italian. *Stampa della vecchia Roma*, 1961

ROUSSEL, Albert (1869-1937), French. *La Poème de la Forêt*, 1904-06; *Evocations*, 1910; *Pour une Fête de Printemps*, 1920

ROZYCKI, Ludomir (1884-1953), Polish. *Anhelli*, 1909; *King Cophetua*, 1910; *Mona Lisa*, 1911; *Stanczyk*, 1934

RUGGLES, Carl (1876-1971), *The Sun-Treader*, 1927-32; *Men and Mountains*, 1921-24 (rev. 1936)

SAINT-SAËNS, Camille (1835-1921), French. *Le Rouet d'Omphale*, 1872; *Phaëton*, 1875; *Danse macabre*, 1875; *La Jeunesse d'Hercule*, 1877; *Suite algérienne*, 1880

SANTOLIQUIDO, Francesco (1883-1971), Italian. *La Mort de Tintagiles; Crepuscolo sul mare*, 1910; *Il profumo delle oasi sahariane*, 1915

SATIE, Erik (1866-1925), French. *Descriptions automatiques*, 1913;

Embryons desséchés, 1913; *Enfantines*, 1913, etc., etc. All for piano

SCHMITT, Florent (1870-1958), French. *Musique foraines*, 1902; *Le Palais hanté*, 1904; *Reflets d'Allemagne*, 1906; *Crépuscules* 1913; *Mirages*, 1925

SCHOEK, Othmar (1886-1957), Swiss. *Penthesilea*, 1927; *Sommernacht* (Pastorale, after Keller), 1956

SCHOENBERG, Arnold (1874-1951), Austrian. *Verklärte Nacht* (for str. sextet), 1899; *Pelleas und Melisande*, 1902-03

SCHUMANN, Robert (1810-56), German. Piano music, especially *Papillons; Carnaval; Scenes from Childhood; Album for the Young; Waldscenen*

SCHUMANN, William (b. 1910), American. *George Washington Bridge*, for concert band, c. 1968

SCHURMANN, Gerard (b. 1928), American. *Six Studies of Francis Bacon* (the painter), 1970

SCOTT, Cyril (1879-1970), English. *Pelleas and Melisande*, c. 1900; *Rhapsody*, 1904; Overture, *Princess Maleine*, 1907

SCRIABIN, Alexander Nicolaevich (1871-1915), Russian. *The Divine Poem*, 1905; *Poem of Ecstacy*, 1908; *Prometheus*, 1910

SEARLE, Humphrey (b. 1915), English. *Zodiac Variations*, 1970

SÉVERAC, Déodat de (1873-1921), French. For piano, *Le Chant de la Terre*, 1903; Suite, *En Languedoc*, 1905; *Baigneuses au Soleil*, 1908; *Cerdana*, 1910; *En Vacances*, 1930

SHOSTAKOVICH, Dmitri (b. 1906), Russian. Symphonies, No. 7 *Leningrad*, 1941-42; No. 11, *Year 1905*, 1957; No. 12, *Lenin (Year 1917)*, 1961

SIBELIUS, Jan (1865-1957), Finnish. *Lemminkäinen* suite, 1895; *Finlandia*, 1899; *The Dryad*, 1910; *Pohjola's Daughter*, 1906; *Night Ride and Sunrise*, 1907; *The Bard*, 1913; *The Oceanides*, 1914; *Tapiola*, 1926

SMAREGLIA, Antonio (1854-1929), Italian. *Leonora*, 1877

SMETANA, Bedřich (1824-84), Czech. *Richard III*, 1858; *Wallenstein's Camp*, 1858; *Hakon Jarl*, 1861; *Ma Vlast*, 1874-79. Piano music, *Dreams*, 1875

SOMERS, Harry (b. 1925), Canadian. *Picasso* suite

SOWERBY, Leo (1895-1968), American. *Prairie* (based on Carl Sandburg's poem), 1929; Suite for piano, *Florida*, 1939; *Poem* (for vln. or vla. and org.), 1942

SPOHR, Louis (1784-1859), German. Symphonies, *Die Weihe der Töne*, 1832; *Irdisches und Göttliches im Menschenleben* (The earthly and heavenly in human life), 1841; *Die Jahreszeiten* (The Seasons), 1850

APPENDIX

STANFORD, Charles Villiers (1852-1924), Irish. Symphonies, *Elegiac*, 1882; *Irish*, 1887; *L'Allegro ed il Pensieroso*, 1895

STEIBELT, Daniel (1765-1823), German. Piano concerto, *L'Orage précédé d'un Rondeau pastorale*, 1798; several 'battle' sonatas and symphonies

STEINBERG, Maximilian (1883-1946), Russian. Fourth symphony, *Turk-Sib*, 1935

STILL, William Grant (b. 1893), American. *Darker America*, 1924; *From the black belt*, 1926; *Afro-American symphony*, 1931

STOCKHAUSEN, Karlheinz (b. 1928), German. *Ylem*, 1973

STRAUSS, Richard (1864-1949), German. *Aus Italien*, 1886; *Don Juan*, 1887-88; *Macbeth*, 1887-90; *Tod und Verklärung*, 1888-89; *Till Eulenspiegel*, 1894-95; *Also Sprach Zarathustra*, 1894-95; *Don Quixote*, 1897; *Sinfonia Domestica*, 1902-03; *Eine Alpensinfonie*, 1911-15

STRAVINSKY, Igor (1882-1971), Russian. *The Song of the Nightingale*, 1917

SUCHON, Eugen (b. 1908), Czech. *King Svätopluk*, 1934-35; *Poème macabre*, for vln. and piano, 1963

SUK, Josef (1874-1935), Czech. *Asrael*, 1907; *Printemps*, 1906; *Prague*, 1910; *Zrani* (Maturity), 1913-18

SZYMANOWSKI, Karol (1882-1937), Polish. *Penthesilea* (with obbligato vocal part), 1909; *Myths*, for vln. and piano, 1915-16; *Masques*, for piano, 1919; *Metope*, for piano, 1922

TCHAIKOWSKY, Petr Ilyich (1840-93), Russian. *Romeo and Juliet*, 1869, 1870 and 1880; *The Tempest*, 1873; *Francesca da Rimini*, 1876; *Manfred*, 1885; *Hamlet*, 1888. Symphonies, No. 1, 1866; No. 4., 1877

TCHEREPNIN, Nicolas (1873-1945), Russian. *La Princesse Lointaine*, 1899; *Macbeth*, 1901; *Le Royaume enchanté*

TOMAŠEK, Vaclav Jan (1774-1850), Czech. *Ten Eclogues*, 1810; *Dithyrambs*, 1823; both for piano

TOMASI, Henri (1901-71), French, of Corsican parentage. *Cyrnos* (inspired by Corsica), 1929

TOMMASINI, Vincenzo (b. 1880), Italian. *Poema erotico*, 1909; Diptych, *Chiari di Luna*, 1914

TOURNEMIRE, Charles (1870-1939), French. For organ, *Triptyque*, c. 1930; *L'Orgue mystique*, 1928-36

TURINA, Joaquin (1882-1949), Spanish. *La Procesión del Rocio*, 1913; *Evangelio de Navidad*, 1915; *Sinfonia sevillana*, 1920. For piano, *Album de viage*, 1916; *Jardins d'Andalousie*, 1921; *Le Cirque*, 1931

VAUGHAN WILLIAMS, Ralph (1872-1958). *A London Symphony*, 1910; *The Lark Ascending* (for vln. and small orch.), 1914; *Flos Campi* (for vla. and small orch.), 1926; *Sinfonia Antartica*, 1953

VALEN, Fartein (1887-1952), Swedish. *Sonetto di Michelangelo*, 1932; *Le Cimetière marin*, 1934; *La Isla de las Calmas*, 1934

VALLERAND, Jean (b. 1915), Canadian. *Le Diable dans le Beffroi*, 1942

VASSILENKO, Sergei (1872-1956), Russian. *The Garden of Death*, 1908; *Turkumenian Pictures*, 1931; *The Soviet East*, 1932

VIERNE, Louis (1870-1937), French. *Les Djinns*, 1925; *Naiades*, for organ

VILLA-LOBOS, Heitor (1887-1959), Brazilian. *Uirapúrú*, 1917; *Amazonas*, 1929; *Caixinha de boas festas*, 1952; *El Trompo* (the Top), for wind band, 1944; *Erosion: The Origin of the Amazon River*, 1950; *La Famille du Bébé*, eight pieces for piano, 1932

WAGENAAR, Johan (1862-1941), Dutch. *Frithjofs Meerfahrt*, 1886; *Cyrano de Bergerac*, 1905; *Saul and David*, 1906; *The Philosophic Princess* (based on Gozzi), 1932

WAGNER, Richard (1813-83), German. A *Faust* overture, 1832

WALLACE, William (1860-1940), Scottish. *The Passing of Beatrice*, 1892; *Anvil or Hammer* (based on Goethe), 1896; *Sister Helen* (based on Rossetti), 1899; *Pelleas and Melisande*, 1903; *William Wallace, A.D. 1305-1905*, 1905; *Villon*, 1909

WALTON, William (b. 1902), *Portsmouth Point*, 1925

WEBER, Carl Maria von (1786-1826), German. *Aufförderung zum Tanze*, for piano, 1819; *Konzertstück*, for piano and orch, 1821

WEINBERGER, Jaromir (1896-1967), Czech. *Don Quixote*, c. 1924; A *Lincoln* symphony, 1941

WIDOR, Charles-Marie (1845-1937), French. *La Nuit de Walpurgis*, 1880; *Ouverture espagnole*, 1898; For organ, *Symph. gothique*, 1895; *Symph. romane*, 1900; *Sinfonia sacra*, for org. and orch., 1908

WILLIAMSON, Malcolm (b. 1931), Australian. For organ, *Fons Amoris*, c. 1956; *Resurgence du Feu Pasqual*, 1960; *Vision of Christ-Phoenix*, 1962; *Travel Diaries*, for piano, 1962

WILSON, Thomas ( ), Scottish. *Touchstone* (based on *As you like it*), 1967

WOLF, Hugo (1860-1903), Austrian. *Penthesilea*, 1883-85

ZANELLA, Amilcare (1873-1949), Italian. *Faith*, 1906

BIBLIOGRAPHY

This is a selection only. It is confined to books, mainly in English, except in Section (B), where some of the important specialist literature is listed.

(A) DICTIONARIES, HISTORIES AND GENERAL WORKS OF REFERENCE

Grove's Dictionary of Music (5th Edition). London, 1954.
Die Musik in Geschichte und Gegenwart. Kassel, 1949-68.

Austin, William. *Music in the 20th Century*. London, 1966
Eaglefield-Hull, A. *A Dictionary of Modern Music and Musicians*. London, 1924.
Lang, Paul Henry and Broder, Nathan. *Contemporary Music in Europe*. London, 1965
Strunk, Oliver. *Source Readings in Music History*. New York, 1950
Stuckenschmidt, H. *Twentieth Century Composers 2: Germany and Central Europe*. London, 1970
Thompson, Oscar. *The International Cyclopedia of Music and Musicians*. New York, 1964

CZECHOSLOVAKIA
Gardavský, Ceněk. *Contemporary Czechoslovak Composers*. Prague, 1965.
Hantich, Henri. *La Musique tchèque*. Paris, 1907
Newmarch, Rosa. *The Music of Czechoslovakia*. London, 1942

FRANCE
Cooper, Martin. *French Music from the Death of Berlioz to the Death of Fauré*. London, 1951
Cortot, Alfred. *La Musique française de Piano*. Paris, 1930-44
Dumesnil, René. *La Musique en France entre les deux Guerres, 1919-1939*. Paris, 1946
Landormy, Paul. *La Musique française après Debussy*. Paris, 1943
Roy, Jean. *Musique française*. Paris, 1962

GREAT BRITAIN
Walker, Ernest. *A History of Music in England* (revised Westrup). London, 1952.
Young, Percy. *A History of British Music*. London, 1967

LATIN AMERICA
Slonimsky, Nicholas. *Music in Latin America*. New York, 1945

RUSSIA and SOVIET UNION
Calvocoressi, M. D. and Abraham, Gerald. *Masters of Russian Music*. London, 1936
Schwarz, Boris. *Music and Musical Life in Soviet Russia, 1917-1970*. London, 1972

SCANDINAVIA
Horton, John. *Scandinavian Music: A short Survey*. London, 1963

SPAIN
Chase, Gilbert. *The Music of Spain*. New York, 1959
Gorina, Manuel Valls. *la Música española después de Manuel de Falla*. Madrid, 1962

UNITED STATES
Chase, Gilbert. *America's Music*. New York, 1966

(B) PROGRAMME MUSIC

Bienenfeld, Elsa. *Über ein bestimmtes Problem der Programmusik*, in 'Zeitschrift der Internationalen Musikgesellschaft', Jahrgang VIII, Heft 5, 1907
Calvocoressi, M. D. *Esquisse d'une esthetique de la Musique à Programme*, in 'Sammelbände der Internationalen Musikgesellschaft' IX, 1907-08.
Cooke, Deryck. *The Language of Music*. London, 1959
Hartnoll, Phyllis (editor). *Shakespeare in Music*. London, 1964
Heuss, A. *Leopold Mozart als Programmusiker*, in 'Neue Zeitschrift für Musik', LXXIX, 1912
Hohenemser, R. *Über der programmusik*, in 'Sammelbände der Internationalen Musikgesellschaft' I, 1899-1900
Klatte, W. *Zur Geschichte des Program-Musik*, in 'Die Music VII', 1905
Klauwell, Otto. *Geschichte der programmusik*. Leipzig, 1910
La Laurencie, Lionel de. *Le Goût musical en France*. Paris, 1905
Lanier, Sidney. *Music and Poetry*. New York, 1909
Marx, Adolf Bernard. *Über Malerei in der Tonkunst*. Berlin, 1828

BIBLIOGRAPHY

Niecks, Frederick. *Programme Music in the last Four Centuries.* London, 1906
Oliver, Alfred Richard. *The Encyclopedists as Critics of Music.* New York, 1949
Sandberger, Adolf. *Ausgewählte Aufätze zur Musikgeschichte*, Vol. II. Munich, 1924
Schering, Arnold. See under Beethoven
Tappert, Wilhelm. *Über Programmusik*, in 'Neue Zeitschrift für Musik', 1968
Tovey, Donald. *Essays in Musical Analysis* Vol. IV. London, 1936

(C) INDIVIDUAL COMPOSERS

BALAKIREV, Milly
Garden, Edward. *Balakirev: A critical study of his life and music.* London, 1967

BEETHOVEN, Ludwig van
Grove, Sir George. *Beethoven and his Nine Symphonies.* London, 1898
Nettl, Paul. *Beethoven Encyclopedia.* London, 1957
Schering, Arnold. *Beethoven in neuer Deutung.* Berlin, 1934
— *Beethoven und die Dichtung.* Berlin, 1936

BERLIOZ
Berlioz, Hector. *Lettres intimes.* Paris, 1882
— *Memoirs*, tr. David Cairns. London, 1969
Barzun, Jacques. *Berlioz and the Romantic Century.* Two Volumes. London, 1951

BLOCH
Tibaldi, Mary Chiesa. *Ernest Bloch.* Turin, 1933

COUPERIN
Mellers, Wilfrid. *François Couperin and the French Classical Tradition.* London, 1950

DEBUSSY
Laloy, Louis. *Claude Debussy.* Paris, 1909
Lockspeiser, Edward. *Debussy: His Life and Mind.* Two volumes. London, 1962, 1965
Schmitz, E. Robert. *The piano works of Claude Debussy.* New York, 1950 and 1967
Thompson, Oscar. *Debussy, Man and Artist.* New York, 1940
Vallas, Léon. *Claude Debussy: His Life and Works.* London, 1933

DELIUS
Hutchings, Arthur. *Delius.* London, 1948

DVOŘÁK
Clapham, John. *Antonín Dvořák*. London, 1966

FRANCK
Davies, Laurence. *César Franck and his Circle*. London, 1970
d'Indy, Vincent. *César Franck*. Translated by Rosa Newmarch. London, 1910

GRIEG
Abraham, Gerald. (editor.) *Grieg: A Symposium*. London, 1948

D'INDY
Demuth, Norman. *Vincent d'Indy, 1851-1931: Champion of Classicism*. London, 1951

LISZT
Raabe, Peter. *Franz Liszt: Leben und Schaffen*. Two volumes. Stuttgart, 1968
Walker, Alan. (editor). *Franz Liszt: The Man and his Music*. London, 1970

MACDOWELL
Gilman, Lawrence. *Edward MacDowell: A Study*. New York, 1931

MAHLER
Mahler, Alma. *Gustav Mahler: Memories and Letters*. Enlarged and revised edition, edited by Donald Mitchell, translated by Basil Creighton. London, 1968
Mitchell, Donald. *Gustav Mahler: The Early Years*. London, 1958
Redlich, H. F. *Bruckner and Mahler*. London, 1955

MENDELSSOHN
Jacob, Heinrich Eduard. *Felix Mendelssohn and his times*. London, 1959
Kaufman, Schima. *Mendelssohn, 'a second Elijah'*. New York, 1934

MUSSORGSKY
Calvocoressi, M. D. *Modest Mussorgsky*. London, 1956

RAVEL
Demuth, Norman. *Ravel*. London, 1947
Myers, Rollo H. *Ravel: Life and Works*. London, 1960

SCHUMANN
Abraham, Gerald (editor). *Schumann: A Symposium*. London, 1952
Brion, Marcel. *Schumann and the Romantic Age*. Translated by Geoffrey Sainsbury. London, 1956

Niecks, Frederick. *Robert Schumann: A Supplementary and Corrective Biography.* London, 1925.
Pleasants, Henry. *The Musical World of Robert Schumann.* London, 1965
Schumann, Robert. *Early Letters of Robert Schumann.* Translated by May Herbert. London, 1888
—*Music and Musicians.* Translated by Fanny Raymond Ritter. Two volumes. London, 1880 and 1888
Walker, Alan (editor). *Robert Schumann: The Man and His Music.* London, 1972

SIBELIUS

Abraham, Gerald (editor). *Sibelius: A Symposium.* London, 1947
Johnson, Harold E. *Sibelius.* London, 1960

SMETANA

Large, Brian. *Smetana.* London, 1970

STRAUSS

Del Mar, Norman. *Richard Strauss: A critical commentary on his life and works.* Three volumes. London, 1962, 1969, 1973

TCHAIKOWSKY

Garden, Edward. *Tchaikowsky.* London, 1973
Weinstock, Herbert. *Tchaikowsky.* London, 1946

VAUGHAN WILLIAMS

Howes, Frank. *The Music of Ralph Vaughan Williams.* London, 1954
Kennedy, Michael. *The Works of Vaughan Williams.* London, 1964

WEBER

Warrack, John. *Carl Maria von Weber.* London, 1968

Index

A

Abraham, Gerald, 65n., 89n., 100, 121n., 125n., 142n.
Agoult, Comtesse d', 79n., 93
Ahna, Pauline von, 131
Albeniz, Isaac, 165
Alcotts, The, 176
Alembert, Jean d', 18
Alkan, Charles-Valentin, 159
Andersen, Hans, 156
Anderton, H. Orsmond, 151, 173
Anglebert, Jean-Henri d', 41
Aristotle, 18
Auden, Wystan Hugh, 186
Austin, William, 143n., 167, 170, 173, 174, 177
Autran, Joseph, 81

B

Bach, Johann Christian, 32
Bach, Johann Jakob, 36
Bach, Johann Sebastian, 25, 32-3, 34, 35, 36, 37, 39, 46, 47, 48, 76, 113, 168, 189, 192
Balakirev, Mily, 99, 121-2, 124
  Tamara, 121-2
Banister, John, 31
Bantock, Granville, 147, 150-1, 152
Barber, Noel, 122n.
Bargiel, Woldemar, 130
Barjansky, 180
Bartók, Béla, 141, 144, 175
Barzun, Jacques, 71n., 72, 73, 73n., 111n.
Batteux, Charles, 18-19, 22
Bax, Arnold, 147, 152
Beardsley, Aubrey, 142
Beattie, James, 18, 21-2, 132
Beecham, Sir Thomas, 151
Beethoven, Ludwig van, 25, 27, 28, 29, 30, 32, 40, 44, 46, 47, 48, 50, 57, 63, 64, 66, 71, 73, 77, 86, 95, 135, 136, 176
  Pastoral symphony, 21, 25, 46, 47, 48-52, 72, 78, 93, 132, 184
  Schlacht bei Vittoria, 52, 56-7, 177
Benedict, Julius, 62
Bennett, William Sterndale, 97-8
Berkovec, Jiří, 108
Berlioz, Hector, 23, 24, 32, 47, 62, 66n., 67, 68, 69, 70, 71, 73, 74, 77, 84n., 93, 95, 101, 110, 111, 112n., 115, 125, 126, 130
  Harold en Italie, 66, 67, 68, 71-2, 102, 125
  Roméo et Juliette, 11, 68, 73-4, 112, 130, 137, 177-8
  Symphonie fantastique, 68-71, 74, 112, 130, 137, 177-8
Bernstein, Leonard, 174, 186
Bertrand, Aloysius, 164
Bezozzi brothers, 23
Biber, Heinrich, 33-4
Bienenfeld, Elsa, 53n.
Blake, William, 178
Bloch, Ernest, 11, 179-83
  America, 179, 182-3, 186
  Israel, 179, 181
  Schelomo, 179, 180-1, 183, 184
Boccaccio, Giovanni, 46
Boccherini, Luigi, 47
Boehm, Georg, 33
Bonaparte, Jerome, 56
Bondon, Jacques, 167
Bonington, Richard, 65
Bordes, Charles, 160, 166
Borodin, Alexander, 122
Borrow, George, 165
Botticelli, Sandro, 157
Boucher, François, 39
Boughton, Rutland, 173
Boulanger, Lili, 171
Boulanger, Nadia, 186
Boulez, Pierre, 167, 168
Bourges, Maurice, 111
Brahms, Johannes, 105, 108, 135, 136, 152, 162n.
Brewer, E. Cobham, 65
Bridault, Theodore, 55
Brion, Marcel, 87, 91
Britten, Benjamin, 11, 184
Broder, Nathan, 187n.
Bronsart, Hans von, 79
Brossart, Sebastien de, 24
Brown, Dr, 20, 22
Browning, Robert, 151
Bruckner, Anton, 117
Bruneau, Alfred, 10, 127
Bukofzer, Manfred, 22, 41, 41n.

INDEX

Bull, John, 31
Bülow, Hans von, 130, 149
Bürger, Gottfried August, 10, 109, 115, 119n., 129
Burney, Charles, 23, 44, 53
Busoni, Ferruccio, 158
Bussine, Romain, 112
Butler, Thomas Hamly, 55
Buxtehude, Dietrich, 31, 33
Byrd, William, 30-1
Byron, George, Lord, 72, 80, 82, 125, 126, 173

C

Cable, George W., 174
Calvocoressi, Michael D., 122n., 142n.
Campra, André, 47
Carlyle, Thomas, 80n.
Carpani, Giuseppe, 40
Carpenter, John Alden, 173, 175
Casella, Alfredo, 157-8
Cazalis, Henri, 118
Čech, Adolphe, 103, 110
Chabanon, Guy de, 22
Chabrier, Emmanuel, 121, 159, 165, 176
Chambonnières, J. Champion de, 31, 40
Charles I, 31
Charles V (Emperor), 67
Charpentier, Marc-Antoine, 24-5
Chase, Gilbert, 166n., 170n., 171n., 176n., 178
Chasins, Abram, 187
Chausson, Ernest, 117, 119, 120
Chavannes, Puvis de 118
Chopin, Frédéric, 26, 51, 62, 86, 89, 95, 162
Clapham, John, 105n., 108n.
Coates, Eric, 179
Cocteau, Jean, 179
Coleridge, Samuel Taylor, 153
Colonne, Édouard, 111, 115
Converse, Frederick Shepherd, 173, 174, 175
Cooke, Deryck, 16, 22
Cooper, Martin, 110n., 160n., 167
Copland, Aaron, 179
Corder, Frederick, 9
Corelli, Arcangelo, 19, 32, 34, 43
 Christmas Concerto, 19, 39, 47
Cornelius, Peter (artist), 96
Cornelius, Peter (composer), 79, 82, 96
Couperin, Charles, 41
Couperin, François, 19, 34, 41-3, 47, 90, 167
Couperin, Louis, 40

Cowell, Henry, 49
Crussard, Claude, 24n.
Cucuel, Georges, 23n.

D

Daguerre, Louis-Jacques, 84n.
Dale, Joseph, 55
Dante (Alighieri) 84, 94, 125, 173
Da Ponte, Lorenzo, 131
Daquin, Louis, 47
Dargomyjsky, Alexander, 126
Daval, Pierre, 41n., 42
Davico, Vincenzo, 157
David, Félicien, 93n., 110-1
 Le Désert, 11
Davies, Laurence, 113n., 114, 117
Davison, James William, 52
Deane, Basil, 168n., 169n.
Debussy, Claude Achille, 10, 16, 39, 92, 94, 96, 97, 113, 117, 120, 141, 143, 144, 149, 152, 159, 160ff, 164, 165, 166, 167, 168, 172, 175, 188, 192
 L'Après-midi d'un faune, 110, 120, 160, 163
 La Cathédrale engloutie, 162
 Estampes, 160
 Iberia, 166
 Images, 161, 166
 La Mer, 157, 163, 169
 Nocturnes, 150, 161
 Nuages, 114, 161
 Préludes, 160, 172
Delacroix, Eugène, 70, 70n., 93n.
De la Laurencie, Lionel, 10
Delius, Frederick, 147, 149-50, 152, 186
Del Mar, Norman, 131, 131n., 132, 132n., 135, 136n.
Demuth, Norman, 160n., 164n.
Denis, Maurice, 117
Delmas, Marc, 11
De Quincey, Thomas, 70
Derepas, Gustave, 116
De Séverac, Déodat, 159
Devienne, 55
Diderot, Denis, 18
Dinsmore, Francis, 183
Dittersdorf, Karl Ditters von, 44
Donizetti, Gaetano, 72n.
Donne, John, 153
Doré, Gustave, 125, 173
Dorn, Heinrich, 91
Dostoyevsky, Feodor, 12
Dowson, Ernest, 151
Draeseke, Felix, 10

Dubos, Abbé, 18
Dukas, Paul, 159
Dumesnil, René, 167n.
Duparc, Henri, 111, 119, 120, 129
Dupré, Marcel, 189
Dussek, Jan Ladislav, 53, 54–5, 61, 99
Dutilleux, Henri, 167
Dvořák, Antonín, 93n., 100, 105ff, 156, 174
   Carnival Overture, 105
   Golden Spinning Wheel, 105, 107-8, 109
   In Nature's Realm, 109
   The Noon Witch, 105, 107, 109
   Othello, 105, 106
   The Water Goblin, 105, 107
   The Wild Dove, 105, 108, 109

E

Eichendorff, Joseph von, 92
Ekman, Karl, 145n.
Elgar, Edward, 10, 147ff, 186
   Cockaigne Overture, 148, 150
   Enigma Variations, 106, 148
   Falstaff, 148
Ella, John, 52
Emmanuel, Maurice, 114n.
Engel, Carl, 9, 172n.
Emerson, Ralph Waldo, 175, 176, 177, 179
Erben, Karel, 106, 109
Erkko, Juhanna Heikki, 145
Esterházy, Prince, 39

F

Falla, Manuel de, 165
Farina, Carlo, 33
Farnaby, Giles, 29
Farwell, Arthur, 173, 174
Fauré, Gabriel, 10, 92, 110, 112, 113, 160
Favre, Lucien, 161
Fellowes, Edmund Horace, 30n.
Fénelon, François, 43
Ferguson, Howard, 34n.
Ferrand, Humbert, 68, 69, 72
Fiamengo, Fr., 46
Fibich, Zdeněk, 100, 109-10, 156, 172
Field, John, 51, 52, 86, 99
Finck, Henry T., 97n.
Fiske, Roger, 102n., 106
Flaubert, Gustave, 169
Foerster, Joseph Bohuslav, 155, 157
Foote, Arthur; 170, 175

Fox-Strangways, Arthur Henry, 141
Franck, César, 85, 97, 111, 113ff, 120, 128, 160, 189
   Le Chasseur maudit, 115
   Les Djinns, 112, 115, 160, 165
   Les Éolides, 114, 115
   Psyché, 115, 116-17
Franck, Georges, 117
Franz Josef I (Emperor), 101
Frescobaldi, Girolamo, 33, 36, 47, 189
Freud, Sigmund, 135
Friedrich, Carl, 79
Froberger, Johann Jakob, 33, 34, 35, 36, 189
Fry, William Henry, 170
Fuller Maitland, John A., 30n.

G

Gabrieli, Andrea, 30
Gade, Niels W., 97, 98
Gallen-Kallela, Akseli, 145
Garden, Edward, 121n.
Gauguin, Paul, 149
Gaultier, Denis, 41, 167
Geibel, Emanuel, 66n.
Geminiani, Francesco, 44
Genelli, Buonaventura, 84n.
George, Stefan, 143n.
Géricault, Jean Louis, 70
Gershwin, George, 174, 186
Gertler, Wolfgang, 89n.
Gilbert, Henry F., 174
Gilman, Lawrence, 172
Glazounov, Alexander, 127, 173
Glière, Reinhold, 188
Glinka, Mikhail, 99, 120, 121
Gluck, Christopher Willibald, 19, 47, 79, 166
Gnecchi, Vittorio, 157
Goethe, Johann Wolfgang, 27, 28, 64, 68, 69, 80, 159, 173
Gogol, Nikolai, 127, 156, 172
Goldmark, Karl, 10, 130, 175
Goldmark, Rubin, 175
Gossec, François Joseph, 38, 47
Gottschalk, Louis Moreau, 171, 174
Gounod, Charles, 111
Grace, Harvey, 33
Granados, Enrique, 165
Gray, Cecil, 147n., 152
Grieg, Edvard, 97, 172
Griesinger, Georg August, 40
Grillparzer, Franz, 65
Grofé, Ferde, 179

INDEX

Grove, George, 28, 57
Grovlez, Gabriel, 159
Guarini, Giovanni Battista, 46
Guilmant, Alexandre, 160, 189
Guinguené, M., 24

H

Habeneck, François Antoine, 68, 111
Hadley, Henry Kimball, 173, 174
Hahn, Arthur, 81n., 84n.
Halle, Charles, 171
Handel, Georg Frederick, 19, 21, 32, 35, 36, 39, 47, 48, 50
Hantich, Henri, 109n.
Harris, Roy, 178
Hartmann, Victor, 123
Hawthorne, Nathaniel, 176
Haydn, Joseph, 18, 19, 32, 34, 37, 40, 56, 101
Hayter, Alethea, 70n.
Hebbel, Christian Friedrich, 92
Heller, Stephen, 92, 98
Henselt, Adolphe, 92, 99
Herder, Johann Friedrich, 80, 81n.
Herke, Anton, 99
Hoffmann, Ernest Theodor Wilhelm, 27, 90, 91, 91n., 143n.
Hokusai, Katsushika, 163
Holmès, Augusta, 115, 117
Holst, Gustav, 151
  Egdon Heath, 152
  The Planets, 151-2, 153
Homer, 27, 28
Honegger, Arthur, 148, 167, 168, 169, 184
Howes, Frank, 153, 154
Hugo, Victor, 70, 78, 82, 115
Hull, A. Eaglefield, 152
Hummel, Johann Nepomuk, 98
Hus, John, 104

I

Ibert, Jacques, 119, 187
Indy, Vincent d', 111, 113, 116, 117, 118, 160
Ingres, Jean Auguste Dominique, 70n.
Ippolitov-Ivanov, Mikhail, 99
Ireland, John, 186
Irving, Henry, 173
Ives, Charles, 175-8, 179

J

Jacob, Heinrich Eduard, 40, 63n., 65n.
Jadin, Louis, 55

Janáček, Leoš, 100, 155-6
Jannequin, Clément, 30
Järnefelt, Armas, 144
Jarre, Maurice, 167
Jaubert, Maurice, 167
Jean-Aubrey, Georges, 70n.
Joachim, Joseph, 130, 171
Johnson, Harold E., 144n., 145n., 146n., 147n.
Johnson, Samuel, 65
Jolivet, André, 167
Joyce, James Augustine, 179
Jullien, Louis, 51n.

K

Kajanus, Robert, 144
Karel, Rudolf, 109
Karg-Elert, Sigfrid, 97, 157, 191n.
Kastner, Georges, 29
Kauer, 56
Kaufman, Schima, 63n.
Kaulbach, Wilhelm von, 82
Keble, John, 96
Kelterborn, Louis, 11
Kentner, Louis 94n.
Kerll, Johann Caspar, 47
Ketèlbey, Albert, 187
Khachaturian, Aram, 122
Kipling, Rudyard, 168
Klauwell, Otto, 10, 35, 38n.
Kleist, Heinrich Wilhelm von, 10
Klingsor', 'Tristan, 159
Kloffer, M., 53
Knecht, Justin Heinrich, 49-50
Koch, Anton, 79
Koechlin, Charles, 167, 168
Kotzwara, Franz, 53, 55
Krebs, Carl, 44n.
Kreutzer, Conradin, 65
Kuhnau, Johann, 31, 32, 34-6, 40, 192
Kussevitsky, Sergei, 142

L

Lacépède, Comte de, 20-1, 22-3, 180
Lalo, Édouard, 112, 165
Laloy, Louis, 17
Lamartine, Alphonse-Marie-Louis, 79n., 93
Lammenais, Félicité Robert de, 79n., 93
Lamoureux, Charles, 111, 112
Landormy, Paul, 160n., 167n.
Láng, Paul Henry, 22, 187n.
Lanier, Sidney, 16, 17
Large, Brian, 101n., 102n.

Le Bègue, Nicholas, 40
Leconte de Lisle, Charles, 114
Lenau, Nikolaus, 131
Lenz, Wilhelm von, 28
Lermentov, Mikhail, 121, 121n.
Lesur, Daniel, 167
Lewis, Sinclair, 178
Liadov, Anatole, 126-7
Liapunof, Sergei, 99
Lichtenstein, Hinrich, 60
Lincoln, Abraham, 182, 187
Liszt, Ferencz, 19, 20, 21, 29, 41, 77ff, 92ff, 97, 98, 99, 100, 101, 102, 103, 113, 114, 166, 122, 129, 130, 131, 132, 143, 172
  Année de pèlerinage, 94-5, 98
  Dante symphony, 83, 84-5, 124
  Faust Symphony, 83-4, 112, 114
  Symphonic poems:
  Cequ'on entend sur la montagne, 77-9, 114
  Hunnenschlacht, 82-3
  Mazeppa, 82, 92
  Orpheus, 79-80
  Les Préludes, 81-2
  Prometheus, 81
  Tasso, 80-1
Lockspeiser, Edward, 117, 160n., 161
Loeffler, Charles Martin, 171
Loewe, Carl, 64, 128
Longfellow, Henry Wadsworth, 80n., 144n.
Lorenzo, Giovanni, 46
Louis, XIV, 40, 43
Louis XV, 43
Loutherbourg, Philippe de, 79n.
Lully, Jean Baptiste, 23, 32, 39, 41, 43, 46, 47
Luther, Martin, 67

M

MacCunn, Hamish, 148, 150
MacDonald, Hugh, 145n.
MacDowell, Edward, 92, 170, 172-3, 174
Mackenzie, Alexander C., 9
Maelzel, Johann Nepomuk, 56, 57
Maeterlinck, Maurice, 10, 172
Mahler, Gustav, 76, 108, 135, 136-7
Maleingreau, Paul de, 189
Malipiero, Gian Francesco, 157
Mallarmé, Stéphane, 120, 163
Manfredini, 47
Manns, August, 151

Martin, Thomas, 70
Marx, Adolph Bernhard, 9, 27, 28, 64n.
Mary Stuart (Mary, Queen of Scots), 72, 72n.
Marzin (Morzin), Count Wenceslao, 37
Mason, Daniel Gregory, 171
Massenet, Jules, 112
Matheson, Johann, 35, 36
Mauclair, Camille, 161
Mauke, Willem, 133
Meck, Madame von, 123
Melancthon, 67
Mellers, Wilfred, 42n.
Melville, Herman, 178
Mendelssohn, Fanny, 64n., 65
Mendelssohn, Felix, 26, 63-8, 76, 77, 84n., 95, 97, 130, 131
  Scotch Symphony, 66-7
  Fingal's Cave Overture, 65, 66
  Italian Symphony, 26, 67, 99
  Melusina Overture, 65-6
  Midsummer Night's Dream Overture, 26, 63-4, 102
  Reformation Symphony, 67-8
Mercer, Frank, 52n.
Merikanto, Oskar, 144
Mérimée, Prosper, 72, 165
Mersenne, Father, 23
Messager, André, 163
Messiaen, Olivier, 16, 97, 141, 167, 168, 189-92
Meyerbeer, Giacomo, 70
Michelangelo (Buonarotti), 94
Migot, Georges, 167, 168
Milhaud, Darius, 167, 169
Mistler, Jean, 143n.
Moke, Marie, 69, 70, 71
Monet, Claude, 161
Monteverdi, Claudio, 32, 46, 166
Moore, Douglas, 178
Moreau, Gustave, 118
Morris, William, 173
Morsin, Count, 39
Moscheles, Ignaz, 89
Mossolov, Alexander, 182
Mouton, 41
Mozart, Leopold, 38
Mozart, Wolfgang Amadeus, 18, 25, 32, 34, 48, 56, 131
Müller, Wilhelm, 128, 162n.
Munday, John, 30
Musset, Alfred de, 70
Mussorgsky, Modest, 99, 122-3, 124
  Night on the Bare Mountain, 122

INDEX

Pictures at an Exhibition, 100, 123, 148n.
Myers, Rollo, 164n.
Mysliweczek, Josef, 38

N

Nerval, Gérhard de, 68
Nettl, Paul, 56n.
Neubauer, F. C., 55
Newman, Ernest, 18n., 69
Newman, Cardinal John Henry, 96
Newman, William S., 35
Newmarch, Rosa, 101n., 109n., 116n.
Niecks, Frederick, 9, 10, 15, 19, 34, 41n., 51, 52, 54, 69n., 73, 89n., 90n., 97, 104, 111n., 121n., 124n., 129n., 130, 132n., 133n., 170
Nielsen, Carl, 147, 150, 187
Nietzsche, Friedrich Wilhelm, 142, 177
Nigg, Serge, 167
Novák, Vitezslav, 79, 109, 155, 156
Novello, Clara, 90

O

Oehlenschläger, Adam Gottlob, 102
Ohana, Maurice, 167
Ohl, John F., 36n.
Oliver, A. H., 18n.
Oulibichev, Alexander von, 28
Overbeck, Friedrich, 96
Ovid, 44

P

Pachelbel, Johann, 33, 47
Padovana, Annibale, 30
Paganini, Niccolo, 71, 72, 73, 93
Paine, John Knowles, 170
Palacký, František, 104
Parrish, Carl, 36n.
Pasdeloup, Jules Étienne, 111, 171
Pasquini, Bernardo, 47
Pedrell, Felipe, 165
Pellico, Silvio, 124
Penderecki, Krzysztof, 185
Petrarch (Petrarca Francesco), 94
Pforr, Franz, 96
Pichl, Wenzel, 38
Pick-Mangiagalli, Riccardo, 157
Picquet, L., 47n.
Pizzetti, Ildebrando, 157
Poe, Edgar Allan, 70, 169, 175
Poliziano, Angelo, 166
Polko, Elise, 66n.
Poulenc, Francis, 167

Pound, Ezra, 179
Pratt, Silas Gamaliel, 170
Prokofiev, Sergei, 76
Proust, Marcel, 136
Prunières, Henry, 23
Purcell, Henry, 32, 36
Pusey, Edward Bouverie, 96

R

Raff, Joachim, 79, 82, 128-30, 172
Raimondi, Ignazio, 43-4, 53
Rameau, Jean-Philippe, 19, 24, 25, 32, 42
Raphael (Rafaello Sanzio), 94
Ravel, Maurice, 21, 76, 94, 96, 144, 149, 152, 163ff
  Gaspard de la nuit, 164, 165
  Ma Mère l'Oye, 165
  Rapsodie espagnol, 165, 166
Rebikov, Vladimir, 99
Redlich, Hans F., 137n.
Redon, Odilon, 118
Reger, Max, 97
Reicha, Anton, 93n.
Reichardt, 9
Reinecke, Carl, 130
Reitz, Robert, 34n.
Rellstab, Ludwig, 91
Respighi, Ottorino, 157, 174
Richter, Hans, 151
Richter, Jean Paul, 85
Rietz, Julius, 130
Rimsky-Korsakov, Nikolai, 121, 123, 125, 165
Ritter, Alexander, 130, 131, 132
Robertson, Alec, 106n.
Rochlitz, Johann Friedrich, 28, 62
Rolland, Romain, 136
Rolleston, T. W., 173n.
Rollinat, Maurice, 172
Rosetti, Franz Anton, 44
Rossini, Gioacchino, 30, 94n.
Rostand, Edmond, 157
Rousseau, Jean-Jacques, 18, 39
Roussel, Albert, 167, 168-9
Roy, Jean, 167
Rubinstein, Anton, 130
Rubinstein, Nicholas, 99
Ruggles, Carl, 178
Runge, Philip, 91

S

Saint-Cricq, Caroline de, 79n., 93
Saint-Saëns, Camille, 111, 112, 115, 118-19

Danse Macabre, 118
Jeunesse d'Hercule, La, 118
Phaëton, 118
Rouet d'Omphale, 118
Sammartini, Giovanni Battista, 32
Sampieri, N., 55
Samuel, Claude, 189n.
Sandberger, Adolf, 46, 46n.
Santoliquido, Francesco, 157
Sarasate, Pablo, 165
Satie, Erik, 159, 167, 175
Sauguet, Henri, 167, 168
Sayn-Wittgenstein, Princess, 80n., 81, 82, 93
Scarborough, Dorothy, 183
Scarlatti, Domenico, 47
Schadow, Friedrich Wilhelm, 66
Schering, Arnold, 27-8, 40
Schiller, Johann Friedrich, 27, 28, 79n., 98, 102
Schindler, Anton Felix, 27
Schirmer, Johann Wilhelm, 66
Schlöser, Tatiana, 142
Schmidt, Franz, 174
Schmitt, Florent, 149, 167, 168, 169
Schoeck, Othmar, 10
Schoenberg, Arnold, 10, 97, 141, 143n.
Schubert, Franz Peter, 11, 21, 29, 50, 64, 78, 86, 92, 93, 94, 128, 162n.
Schulz, Johann Abraham Peter, 18
Schumann, Clara, 90, 91
Schumann, Robert Alexander, 26, 28, 74, 86ff, 93, 95, 96, 98, 100, 143n.
  Carnaval, 86, 89-90, 148n.
  Davidsbündlertänze, 86
  Fantasiestücke, 86
  Kinderscenen, 86, 91
  Kreisleriana, 86, 90
  Papillons, 86, 87-9
  Waldscenen, 86, 92
Schwartz, Boris, 187n.
Schweitzer, Albert, 33
Schwind, Moritz von, 78
Scott, Captain, 153
Scott, Cyril, 141, 151, 152
Scott, Sir Walter, 115n., 119n.
Scriabin, Alexander, 99, 141ff
  Divine Poem, 142-3
  Poem of Ecstasy, 142
  Prometheus, 142, 143
Searle, Humphrey, 81n., 83n.
Senancour, Étienne de, 94
Senkovsky, 123
Serov, Alexander, 99

Seton-Watson, R. W., 104n.
Shakespeare, William, 27, 28, 63, 68, 73, 101, 106, 128, 131, 173, 180
Shaw, George Bernard, 81n.
Shedlock, John South, 34n.
Shelley, Mary Wollstonecraft, 70
Shelley, Percy Bysshe, 153
Shepherd, Arthur, 179
Shostakovich, Dmitri, 187-8
Sibelius, Jan, 10, 149ff, 156, 192
  Finlandia, 146
  Four Legends, 145
  Pohjohla's Daughter, 146
  Tapiola, 147
Simpson, Robert, 150n.
Sitwell, Sacheverell, 81n.
Smareglia, Antonio, 157
Smart, Sir George, 57
Smetana, Bedrich, 21, 92, 93n., 100, 101ff, 109, 128, 141, 144, 172
  From Bohemia's Woods and Fields, 100, 104
  Hakon Jarl, 101
  Ma Vlast, 103-5, 156
  Richard III, 101-2
  Vltava, 21, 94, 103
  Wallenstein, 101, 102
Smithson, Harriet, 68, 69, 71, 73
Smyth, Ethel, 117
Šourek, Otakar, 108
Southey, Robert, 150
Spitta, Philipp, 35
Spohr, Louis, 74, 76, 77, 78, 128, 130, 143
  Historical Symphony, 76
  Die Weihe der Töne, 74-6, 78
Squire, William Barclay, 30n.
Stamitz, Johann, 38
Stassov, Vladimir, 125
Steibelt, Daniel, 50, 53, 54, 55, 61
Stein, Gertrude, 179
Steinberg, Maximilian, 188
Still, William Grant, 178
Strauss, Johann, 62
Strauss, Richard, 108n., 128, 129, 130ff, 141, 144, 148, 162, 163, 177, 179
  Alpine Symphonie, 79, 136
  Also sprach Zarathustra, 132
  Aus Italien, 130-1
  Don Juan, 131-2, 133-4, 144
  Don Quixote, 132, 135, 148
  Ein Heldenleben, 108n., 129, 134-6
  Macbeth, 131

INDEX

Sinfonia domestica, 132, 136
Till Eulenspiegel, 132-3
Tod und Verklärung, 132, 136
Stravinsky, Igor, 76, 122, 141, 168, 190
Strindberg, August, 149
Strunk, Oliver, 18n.
Suk, Josef, 109, 155, 156, 186
Sulzer, Johann Georg, 18
Szymanowski, Karol, 11

T

Taylor, Joseph Deems, 186
Tchaikowsky, Modest, 124
Tchaikowsky, Petr Ilyich, 52, 76, 92, 97, 99, 109n., 121, 122, 123ff, 141, 177
 Francesca da Rimini, 124-5
 Manfred, 124, 125-6
 Romeo and Juliet, 124, 125
 Symphony No. 4, 11, 123-4
Tennyson, Alfred, Lord, 81n., 97n.
Terry, Ellen, 173
Thompson, Oscar, 160n., 161, 163n.
Thomson, Virgil, 179
Thoreau, Henry David, 176, 177
Tibaldi, Mary Chiesa, 180n., 181
Tiersot, Julien, 114n.
Tolstoy, Count Leo, 127, 155
Tomasek, Vaclav Jan, 93n., 100
Tomkins, Thomas, 31
Torelli, Giuseppe, 46
Tournemire, Charles, 189
Tovey, Donald, 9, 76, 148n.
Tregian, Francis, 30n.
Tunder, Franz, 33
Turner, Joseph Mallord William, 65, 161

U

Uccellini, Marco, 33
Urhan, Chrétien, 71

V

Vallas, Léon, 160n., 161n.
Varèse, Edgard, 167
Vaughan Williams, Ralph, 10, 151, 152ff, 175, 185, 186
 Flos Campi, 154-5
 The Lark Ascending, 154, 155
Verdi, Giuseppe, 106
Verlaine, Paul, 39, 113, 122, 166, 172
Vierne, Louis, 189
Virgil, 46, 173
Vivaldi, Antonio, 19, 30, 32, 34, 36-7, 39, 40
 Quattro Stagioni, 32, 33, 35, 37, 44

Tempesta di Mare, La, 39
Vogler, Georg Joseph, 48, 49, 50, 61, 95
Volkmann, Robert, 130

W

Wagner, Richard, 28, 65, 66, 77, 78, 81, 83, 84n., 96, 97, 101, 112, 113, 115, 125, 130, 149, 152, 163
Waldmüller, Georg, 78
Walker, Alan, 81n., 83n., 84n., 97n.
Wallace, William, 10, 147, 150
Walther, Johann Georg, 47
Walton, William, 185
Wanhal, Johann Baptist, 55
Warrack, John, 61n.
Watteau, Jean-Antoine, 39, 162
Weber, Carl Maria von, 48, 61, 63, 64, 95, 130
 Aufforderung zum Tanze, 61-2
 Concertstück, 61-3
Weber, Caroline, 62
Weinstock, Herbert, 124n.
Wellington, first Duke of, 56
Werner, Gregorius Josef, 38, 39
Werrecore, Hermann, 30
Whistler, James Abbot McNeill, 150, 161
Whitman, Walt, 174, 175, 181, 182, 187
Widor, Charles Marie, 189
Williamson, Malcolm, 187
Wolf, Hugo, 10
Wood, Henry J., 151
Wranitsky, Paul, 38
Wüllner, Franz, 133

Z

Ziska, John, 105
Zverov, 99